HERETIC

MIGUEL CONNER

ÆON BYTE PRESS

Heretic © 2012 by Miguel Conner

ISBN 9780615569604

Aeon Byte Press
Chicago, IL 60622
www.thegodabovegod.com

Cover art by Melinda MacCullen
Copy edited by Frank Bertrand

For my daughter Evangeline, who revealed to me that all dreamers and artists make up constellations lighting the dark cosmos of mere being.

HERETIC

MIGUEL CONNER

If a person were to try stripping the disguises from actors while they play a scene upon the stage, showing to the audience their real looks and the faces they were born with, would not such a one spoil the whole play? And would not the spectators think he deserved to be driven out of the theater with brickbats, as a drunken disturber? Now what else is the whole life of mortals but a sort of comedy, in which the various actors, disguised by various costumes and masks, walk on and play each one his part, until the manager waves them off the stage? Moreover, this manager frequently bids the same actor to go back in a different costume, so that he who has but lately played the king in scarlet now acts the flunkey in patched clothes. Thus, all things are presented by shadows.

-Erasmus, The Praise of Folly-

I, Death, come, and yet I remain not, for life eternal exists in the All; only an obstacle, I in the pathway, quick to be conquered by the infinite light. Awaken, O flame that burns ever inward, flame forth and conquer the veil of the night.

-The Emerald Tablets of Thoth-

I was born in between the ages, between the ice of a mortal civilization and the fire of wild gods and their bracken lust, in a time when time stopped briefly because of a war that never was a war but more like a feverish coup. As the planet screamed in rage when the sky boiled and the cities melted and the mountains shuddered, I screamed into a changed dusk in some military shelter many feet underneath the hot ground. By the time I had slithered out from my mother's swollen womb, the landscape choked in ash and elemental radiation. A new era had just begun for an old world, and the new victors rose quickly from their own shelters and machinations as if crawling out from a terrible dream. And it was a terrible dream, for these victors, plotting creatures who despised the light of day and disobeyed the laws of nature and logic, enslaved my kind with impunity. Taking a seat at the top of evolution, they branded us with names like Warm Ones, animals, food. We were now part of their barren playground of sleek, lonely cities sprouting from the wastes they had envisioned for so long. They ruled the world. I made sure they never enjoyed it.

My name is Byron Solsbury. I have been born many times since.

The first time, as I said, was after the beginning of what the old Warm Ones called the twenty first century and the dawn of the victor's rule, separated by my birth and the Holocaust, the nuclear plague which changed history and imagination forever. It also destroyed billions of life forms, made them into ash and memory, still luckier than those who survived. The survivors like my family and the others quickly realized and accepted that the rules had changed forever. It was the victors' rules now. More than that, it was Her rules only, the one who truly orchestrated this, who created these grim creatures in order to punish creation. And I was also to be condemned to this new set of rules which made us into food, into prey for the victors and not much else. Their rules and their world, a dark world of ruin and decay. A carnival for nihilistic desires.

Her world.

In this world I endured with my kind, trapped in one of their city-states, corralled, bred for the purpose to feed Her off-

spring, to satisfy their craving for destruction, which is all that it was really.

My memories are still not totally mine, pieces of emotional debris floating in a lagoon of sparks. They will probably never be fully mine, just as She took them away from me as She took my identity, and as She took the identity of the planet.

I do have a few recollections here and there: My family, my fight as a revolutionary in the city, built upon the carcass of a former metropolis, failure and success. Our rulers called it Utopia; we called it Hell. Before that there isn't much. I recall my father whom I briefly met underneath the city of Xanadu in a dream. He was a heroic yet jaded figure, a true warrior who tried hard to smile while raising me in a time gone delirious. Sometimes I can picture my mother as well. She was so different from him. As he was large and glaring, she was small and quiet, a teacher who had never risen to her aspiration of being a story-teller because of shyness. She gave me a certain sensitivity and a good eye. I've wondered on occasion if those were really gifts, and whether those qualities have landed me in scandal a few thousand times. Then again, my father's volcanic temperament didn't exactly save me each specific time.

Between the two, they were a balance growing up as a Warm One. Residing in dilapidated projects with thousands of others, we thrived in fear and hope. Every cycle of the months seemed the same: silly holidays and entertainment created to pass that dreaded time, always so afraid when the day ended and we had to face what was on the other side of the horizon—the night, them, the hunting...the terror. My youth was spent cowering in locked cellars with the mold and the darkness and the women who read us stories, rocked us to the uncertainty of sleep, while the men fought upstairs against our new rulers.

And we still called them by their old names.

Vampires.

I know that once in a while one entered the cellars and took some of the women or children. I can still hear the screaming and tearing of a boy that was a friend of mine. I'll never remember his name, or the growling laughter when they entered our hiding places. It's all an uncomfortable blur, which was what the day also brought. During those periods, we played and learned and attempted to forget the night or a missing friend, while the adults tried and tried to find ways to combat these monsters. They could never reached this goal, too preoccupied with finding ways to feed the masses; trying not to succumb to despair; or simply staring at the sky and knowing it was their rulers who protected us from the deadly climate with their Ozone Processors; and even fed us from the other side of the bridge-less river.

There was nothing we could do, but my father never believed it. I grew up to believe that too, even after he and my mother fell to their claws, even as I reared my own family and moved to the edge of their hunting grounds. I plotted intensely for years and never fell to despair. I had balance, I had a different type of hunger, I would never relent. I devised a plan when I rose to leadership of a covert movement that employed sabotaging tactics that stunted their growth into technology and stable infrastructure. In the end, I destroyed their portion of the city on the other side of the river and ultimately mine, placing bombs in many of their reactors and plants. I wanted this nightmare to end, one way or another. I wanted them to crawl back into their terrible dream. I thought some of us would survive.

None of us did.

She, the ruler of our rulers, made a visit to our side of Utopia. She slew thousands of my kind without effort in minutes. Then She found me amid the smoldering ruins with my cowering family. I did the only thing a warrior should have done. I killed my mate and my daughter before She imparted her vicious judgment. Facing her without fear, Byron Solsbury was cursed for his bravery. She cursed me and sent me into another existence, taking me with her to another city far away, a city of teal domes and trains and tighter rules for the rulers and their chattel. I was born a second time with a second nightmare, baptized with something called the Dark Instinct, part of herself and her lust for destruction. She made me into one of them, a vampire, without any prior knowledge of my mortal past, a creature that thirsted for those with warmth and the thing called life, that existed forever despising the light of day and disobeying the laws of nature and logic.

Her name was Lilith, The Queen of Darkness.

In Xanadu I become part of her court. From Byron Sols-bury I turned to Lord Byron, Head of the Ravens, who oversaw Her discipline and aided in creating a tight farm system for the Warm Ones. We were never vampires there but Stargazers, gods hoping to see the stars and a naked Luna one of these nights, which only meant we had come full circle as the victors, trying to prove to nature and time that we deserved to be at the top of evo-lution, the world itself. I made sure that this vision was enforced and did well but not well enough. Revolutionaries and their pas-sions never truly perish. In retrospect, I knew that part of me still struggled subliminally with my reality, wanted to see beyond the cloudy haze that was Lilith's vision.

Eventually I did, mostly because I met Medea. Almost a century after being demoted for rash behavior, a reflex of my soul fighting its curse and the dream of the activist, I was asked to solve a nefarious crime in one of the Farms, where we tightly bred and slaughtered the Warm Ones. Having little choice, I took this task and uncovered much more. I uncovered a new faith, the Blood Of Circles, born from ancient religions that had fought my kind for millennia, that could shatter Lilith's yolk and somehow chose me as its savior. I discovered the Killer of Giants, a plague that devoured both Warm One and Stargazer, kept secretly inside the bodies of their leaders and passed from generation to genera-tion in that specific Farm until the moment was well seasoned for revolt. I discovered that I had been a Warm One and so had every Stargazer except for Lilith, Our Mistress, The MoonQueen, as she was called in Xanadu. I discovered that we had no place in evolu-tion because evolution was about life and its fumbling towards salvation, not the blind eradication of it.

Most of all, I discovered that I hated Medea and could never let her go. I did let her go temporarily, though, when The Queen of Darkness kidnapped and took the Warm One to her abode in the center of the City of Domes. Lilith almost destroyed Medea. but I granted her the anathema to mortality that is the Dark Instinct because I couldn't let her go. The MoonQueen, in turn, pretty much destroyed me, swatting me down and giving me a funeral in the sand miles away. There I was discovered by Prox-os Commodore, who I had ironically betrayed as a Warm One in

Utopia. In a cavern with his meek possessions and lonely hobbies, this person nursed me back to my former glory, except I was like him, a Heretic, an outcast in a numb world with no place in Stargazer society. Proxos had once been an Elder, part of the seven that governed the Stargazer cities—now he was my companion. I learned more about myself, my lost memories, and Lilith. Eventually I decided I needed a mouthful of vengeance.

*I received my feast when I returned. It's a sordid tale I'd rather not repeat, but Medea, who was paradoxically turned into an Elder, aided me when I imparted the truth of our origins **back** to her. With the Killer of Giants (the only malady that could destroy a Stargazer and one with which Media could infect anyone), the faith-magic she had once possessed as the Shaman of the Circle, and a little help from a mad Elder named Balkros, I savored my revenge and shattered the City of Domes. I finished the revolution I started as a Warm One. I even faced The Queen of Darkness and showed her that the faith-magic and the Killer of Giants could still shift the balance to a cunning opponent. I vanquished her being. Vengeance never tasted better after stewing for over a century and a half.*

Two cities I finished. Other Stargazer cities had fallen to natural and unnatural cataclysms, and thus Lilith's terrible fantasy was over. The Stargazer age was done. Almost, though. The revolution wasn't quite finished. Vengeance wasn't sated. The nightmare still blinked.

The Egg, it was also called.

That was the last Stargazer metropolis. New Atlantis. We sojourned there to find the cure for the Killer of Giants, a ravaging malady from a Mad God which Medea possessed both as a Warm One and a Stargazer, sent there by the Elder Balkros in order to get us out of his new territory. But all three of us knew deep inside we ultimately went to end it all, to finish a brief but unholy rule by creatures that should have never been, beings that were a reflex to Lilith's wrath at being rejected by The Mad God in a time before time had gained any weight.

I never could have fathomed what I was to meet in this place, vast horrors and dreams that were one and the same, distorted wonders that betrayed reality, beings older, perhaps might-

ier than The Queen of Darkness herself, and beautiful, untamed things forgotten in history's arrogance. Most of all, I would meet myself, my true self.

I don't know if that was my final undoing. All I know is that New Atlantis was the end of me, the beginning of another me as well. In that city I would become Byron, and that was my greatest tragedy, my final doom. I would lose everything and gain an identity. Lilith once told me it was the journey not the destination that mattered. I never thought it was all a painful circle.

Time...mirrors...just a reflection...I know...your face...Mon Cheri...time...I know your face...

It was always you. It was always me.

But to understand my story you would have to understand the other stories, the other actors that contributed to my end. So many stories, so many characters, so many tragedies it could create oceans from tears.

We should start from the beginning of our quest. A painful circle. The journey, my friends. The journey...

Time...mirrors...a reflection...

It was always you. I was born in between ages, I was born a second time between life's frontiers. I have been cursed, I have failed several times, I have ingested victory so sweet it made me mock the skies. I have been born a Liberator of Warm One prophecy, a revolutionary for the armies of despair, an enforcer of evil, an artist, a comedian, an outcast in a world of outcasts. The only way to figure out the rest is to take another step, go a little further, see where the road leads.

In the end, I'm not much different from all the rest, Warm One or Stargazer, god or material being. I'm trying to find out who I am without forgetting who I was, and just wondering, hoping about what I'll be.

The road is ending and these are our stories. Look a little closer, yes, start from two beginnings which are also two ends, then start the story of that painful circle. There I am, in chains, broken and destroyed, ready to meet Him. There I am...

What I'll be.

My name is Byron Solsbury.

INTRODUCTION

I: AD 29

Lucius Cornelius met her at the edge of the city. The sky was a swimming gray, eclipsing slowly with the peril of storm. The air was heavy and stale. The wind welled between the huts and rustic buildings in lapping cold. There seemed to be very few people around, for they had all probably gone to the celebration at the mound of skulls. Nothing out of the ordinary. Too out of the ordinary.

Except for the fact that he had risen during the day. He existed without harm in the late afternoon below the ceiling of clouds and the silence of a place called Jerusalem.

She waited for him around the corner of a house. Lucius could smell fresh slaughter inside by her hand, a whole family and a small meal to her wrath. He had not fed yet, too fascinated with the shock of being able to wander before dusk. It was amazing. More amazing than her at the moment, who stood hidden by heavy robes of darkest canvas, slouched to hide a towering height, only her shining eyes visible.

"You are unaffected as well, Whore of Babylon?" A smile broke from his feral, handsome features as he tipped his helmet at her. "How can this be? Have you changed the rules? Does the daylight finally hold pleasure for you?"

He could sense her sacred smile, so gorgeous it could melt the soul like idle wax.

"Never, sweet Lucius," she responded. "But we presently have no choice. We can wander because it is the changing of an age; the breath of my enemy is so strong that all the rules are bent for a small spell."

Lucius glanced upward after removing his bronze helmet. "It has been a long time. Two, three hundred years since you took away any chance of me ever seeing the day again. Ah, and it is a cloudy day, by Mars!"

"Yes, it is," she said. "Do you regret what I did to you, sweetest of sweetest?"

He laughed with confidence, exposing fangs larger than most of his kind. Thoughts of his travels across the world, the civilizations, the experiences, the gods and heroes encountered tumbled through his mind like the clouds passing in the horizon. From the smoky shores of Gaul all the way to India, from the tip of Africa all the way to kingdom of druids in the icelands. Lucius had seen so much, and enjoyed it. Unlike the other brethren of Her, he savored his state and immortality, thrived with his hunger and dominant attitude. Mortal or not, he was a warrior, and adventurer, a dreamer who made dreams into imposing substance.

"Of course not," he said with a bow. "I can only give you my gratitude. But you did not summon me here for that or to wonder why I can almost see a naked sky away from the night."

She lowered her head slightly. "I think you know why I summoned you, Dearest Lucius."

"I have heard stories on the way to Galilee," he said. "Silly stories about a certain Jewish prophet. Do you believe them?"

"Yes," she hissed, narrowing eyes that seemed to be made of mellifluous gems. "They are true. He is the one, Lucius. He is the progeny of my enemy, the one who banished me. He is the closet link to him and his dream."

"The Greek philosophers talk about all mortals being his progeny, or having a spark of him like I have an ink drop of your God-soul."

Her fangs glowed through the hood in dark jade hue. "The Greek philosophers spent too much time thinking and play acting, like all mortals, and look where it got them! This is His true avatar, ushering the shift of the wheel of the stars."

Lucius shook his head, glancing down at his sandaled feet. Dust flittered on the ground, welted by random tears of rain.

"And we need to take action," he said. Why did she bother with this deity? There were so many others, battling for creation and its spoils. He was the greatest, the true one? Never!

"We must, sweetest. The progeny's passing will begin a final and grim age, when mankind will spread and The Unimaginable will wilt, fade away with all the creatures of wonder along with the Maya, the tender, the female aspect of creation. You do not understand, for you cannot see what I see, know what I have known when I first came into this aspect of the universe."

"Then why do you not take action?" he asked, never afraid of any question, any comment, any action. Not even to her. "I am a gnat compared to you, Whore of Babylon."

She lowered her head again. "Perhaps I am afraid, Lucius. Afraid to be so close to him again. I need you."

"To do what?"

Her gaze was solid yet piercing, urgent yet cunning.

"To impede his passing, for when he passes he truly gains power, truly brings about a loophole in the wheel of the stars. To do this, you must go to him and grant him my God-Soul, which I have granted to all of my offspring, sever his bond to my enemy, corrupt his mortality so much he will be partly ours forever."

He pursed his lips slightly. "That is all? This could be dangerous."

"Of course, but I will protect you as long as you follow me. Will you do it?"

Never afraid of anything.

"I will," he said loudly. "That is all I have to do?"

"Yes," she said. "You know how to create, how to pass the God-Soul. Go to him and do that, nothing else, do you hear? Stop this age from washing us away. You are my favorite and always will be my favorite, Dearest Lucius. You will succeed. I will succeed." He donned his helmet and bowed to his mistress. He pivoted on his heel and marched towards the small hill they called Golgotha. Lucius wasn't worried about the few mortals encountered. The ones called Jews never met his glowing stare or commented on his sallow skin, for he was garbed in the common military uniform of a captain, hand always close to his *gladius*, the stabbing sword, in warning. Although Lucius was not born a Roman, he had taken that identity from a famous general in Africa, even learning Latin in order to facilitate his movement through the burgeoning empire. The few Roman soldiers on the way saluted him while he lowered his helmet over his features.

Lucius worried a bit when he neared the mound of skulls. The earth began to shudder under his feet, the wind turned to smashing pillows against his body. Mortals rushed by him in fear, clouds cackled with lightning. He could almost feel the world trembling, the horizon blurring, for something was warning him.

He does not want you near, he heard the Whore's voice. *He does not want you near his progeny.*

Lucius kept his pace, undaunted by the elements and terror around him. He reached the open area where three criminals were crucified. All the spectators and soldier that might have been here were now seeking shelter from the pelting rain.

He focused on the middle one, knowing immediately it was him. His existence was thinning away but there was some in him yet. Why had he allowed this? After all, this was a common punishment by this empire. The Romans publicly crucified their conquered people in order to make sure no one transgressed against them or broke the law a second time. It was worse for these odd Jews, who saw their race perish naked, which was very shameful to their beliefs, and unburied, which guaranteed eternal damnation. Many crucified lived for days, some fortunate ones asphyxiated quickly, but most bled to death or succumbed to dehydration. The Romans were known to feed the ones they wanted to suffer or just slay the ones who lived for more than a day or two.

He would not survive much longer, Lucius thought, seeing a beaten, cut body, filthy with mud and crowned with a thorny reef over his head. This was the progeny of the enemy of his mistress, The Mad God? This prophet did not seem like much, he mused, condemned and abandoned by all he knew at the moment. But he had heard of stories of his powers, his words, his attitude towards the downtrodden and needy. He had heard much traveling to Jerusalem, and for some reason, even with the tempest around them, felt a certain pity for this creature who was being slain for some mystical, unknown reason-- a victim of destiny.

"And you will change the ages?" he asked the unmoving body in the center cross. "And you will melt away the wonders of The Unimaginable? Why would you do such a thing?"

There was no answer, except for the wind and the thunder and the shouts of fear from those hiding under carts a few feet away. But Lucius stood strong and stable.

"But your words are different," he said. "You bring hope, I hear. You bring a gentleness never experienced in this savage world. Are you a pawn like my mistress was? Cast out after fulfilling your role? Or are you just another charlatan, and the Whore is misguided one more time?"

No answer. The weather was calming, all of a sudden. He could feel the last touches of life leaving the progeny. Curiosity rose inside Lucius. He wondered then who was the pawn between the two of them. But he wasn't afraid.

"Perhaps I should find out." He took a step forward as the body jolted in dying spasms. Craning his head forward, he opened his mouth as blood dripped from many places.

NO! He heard her voice, shrill and full of terror. *NO, SWEETEST! NOT THAT!*

Lucius did not listen, sticking out his tongue to catch the liquid. For some reason he had not felt hunger for this person. It did not matter. He wanted to find out the power of the progeny.

YOU DO NOT UNDERSTAND!!!

Droplets of blood touched his tongue. He closed his mouth, swallowed, and suddenly his eyes were wide as he beheld infinity.

I: AD 2239

It was a place so different from the rest of the structure. There was no lighting and there were no mirrors. Mirrors were set everywhere else, in every corridor, in every chamber, in every crevasse and compartment. Mirrors and light. There was no privacy in this place. Privacy was for the weak, for those who had something to hide. Privacy was against the Forgotten.

The darkness existed here for more interesting matters besides philosophical bondage. Stretching before and straddling a long alley were metal pens. In these pens resided beings that had never truly seen naked light. They scuttled around curiously, hunched and barely able to contain their feeble weight upon sinewy arms and legs. Their thin, ropy bodies were lathered in their own excrements and slivers of synthetic straw. They could not see the elevator door opening because they had no functioning pupils;

they could not smell the two figures that departed the mirrored interior because they had no real odor. But their keen ears instantly detected their watery movement. Primordial instincts granted them the hope that it was feeding time. That's all that mattered to them in the grayness of their existence—feeding time. In turn, the two beings could clearly see them, pale lanky things bred here since birth, untouched by the genetic wizardry performed on the ones above in the Kingdom of Mirrors. In The Egg. No, these creatures were natural except for their own nature. As they could not see, they could not truly think, gather light into structure. All they knew was being fed and obeying a few minor bodily urges. They were very unlike the ones the population had heard existed in another city. They were not like the altered armies and servants above. They were pathetic and they were a delicacy. They were called GR27's by the population, but a few called them Veals.

If these creatures had eyes they would have seen that the two figures were very distinct from the others. One was elegantly tall, royally thin, draped in long silken robes from a bygone era. His face was majestic, long and daintily noble, with beautiful features that pushed perfection. He had long and pale flaxen hair that almost shone like curdling fog. But it was his eyes that were his true triumph of beauty and intelligence, seasoned with eternal innocence and so much brightness. Like those of his kind, they changed color with mood, yet they were much larger with almost oval pupils. Tonight they were a crystal orange.

The other, slumped and hopping right behind him, was much shorter. His clothing was a crude, burlap robe, torn in several places. A hood concealed a face he was used to hiding for thousands of years but it could not hide large round eyes that palpitated with neon green. This one grunted with each step, a sound that could have been mistaken for throttling laughter.

The Veals could not have seen this and could not care. In every pen, they huddled close to the cell doors, crafting their own grunting. Perhaps it was feeding time, they hoped. Perhaps these two would throw morsels through the bars, fill their small, aching stomachs. Many couldn't help but urinate on themselves, while others jumped up and down as if to vault past the barbed wire over the pens.

"We really have other matters to address," the slumped one said with a gritty voice, which made some of the Veals moan even louder. "The Pharisees are waiting for your counsel, Marcion. You lingered in *Moratoria* for three nights."

The other kept his pace until stopping at the center of the area. By now many of the creatures were slamming into the bars and metal doors, perhaps mad that they had not drank the scent of meat they enjoyed, meat that was from the same creatures they were.

"For that reason I require nourishment, Prince Poppykettle," the one called Marcion said lightly, his vision darting from side to side.

"Of course," Poppykettle mumbled from large cracked lips that were always matted in filmy, thick saliva. "But you know that the other Pharisees might be somewhat interested in your results. The occurrence at Xanadu has worsened. We are curious. You are The Good Neighbor."

Marcion smiled slightly, and the agitated denizens of the pens could have never known that their conversation meant little but symbolism. There was no privacy here. The population of The Egg was listening to every word they spoke and they could see what they saw. The population felt the hunger of Marcion and the sadness of his smile. But the population needed his gift, his visions, which they could not enter or see or use because he was the last of his kind. He was unique, beyond anything that existed centuries before and after the Holocaust. But they needed to converse like they needed rituals in this perfect city, for it was a symbolism of reality, and more than that, it was entertaining.

"I understand, Poppykettle," he said, his liquid voice soothing the Veals slightly. If desired, his voice could easily control their soft minds. "But I needed a delicacy before we all meet. Do you understand as well?"

"I do understand as well, Good Neighbor." He lowered his odd-shaped head and also began feeling hunger. It seemed like the hunger never ended. It was always there, as if it was their true ruler besides their Prince. "But are you aware that we have lost total communication with Xanadu? We're still receiving those odd transmissions that started six nights ago but that is all."

"I am aware." He scanned every Veal in the area. The population wondered which one he would choose. The Veals just thought it was feeding time. They were right.

"Are you furthermore aware that reconnaissance photographs show less destruction, less movement. It seems the Warm Ones are being driven back to their Farms, as if they're being herded again. It also seems the Stargazers are also coagulating, as if by leadership. Yet there is still no movement from the remnants of the Tower and Her abode?"

"Yes, Poppykettle."

"Then what it is?" he asked, knowing the population was split between his explanation of the catastrophe to the city of Xanadu and which one he would choose. "What happened in that explosion nights ago that shattered the main dome? What happened in Xanadu? Where is The Queen of Darkness?"

Marcion narrowed his eyes and took a few paces towards one of the doors. Poppykettle was shaking behind him, foamy liquid coming from his flat nostrils. The population wondered. The animals wondered as well. It was feeding time.

"You remember her prophecy, Prince Poppykettle?" Marcion asked, placing his hands on one of the pen-doors. "Do you remember what she told us when we were brought to this city, this county of her empire?"

"Yes, Good Neighbor," Poppykettle said between nervous giggles. "We all think of it night after night...her words sing to us through *Moratoria* and the din of our starvation."

His fingers flexed with a cracking sound while he spoke, wrenching the Veals into a frenzy. The sound was like bones breaking. It had to be feeding time! If they only knew how excited the population was. If they could only have seen what Marcion saw when he briefly turned his head towards the end of the pens.

Marcion spoke the prophecy anyway, because they needed to hear it again, from his lips.

"If a knight should come, a champion of eternity, errant on a darkening quest, knocking on your gates, then you should let him in..."

"Yes, yes," Poppykettle closed his eyes, but light still seeped from underneath puffy lids. "I remember..."

"And if he bests the Warden and drinks in generations with the Centurion, then he must be stripped of his sword, his shield, and armor..."

"Yes, Yes!" The population also joined in.

"And brought naked like a newborn into the gray dusk, into the awakening of our Prince."

"Yes, Yes!" said Poppykettle, jumping up and down, his movement similar to the other Veals. "But what does that have to do with Xanadu? What does that have to do with The Queen of Darkness?"

And none except the Good Neighbor saw an image of somebody laying at the end of the corridor, bound to a cross and thinking about being born between ages. None saw the image fade away suddenly, leaving only whispers of eternal sadness, of potential freedom.

Marcion opened the door. An animal scuttled towards him with its stringy body on all fours, face hopeful, hungry. The sound of the door meant they brought a lot of food. Pale and blind, it didn't understand time or thought, just nourishment. It was feeding time. It stopped right in front of the Pharisee. It wasn't even fifteen yet. The perfect age for a Veal.

And it was the perfect time to share his visions with the population.

"It has nothing to do with her, Prince Poppykettle, good citizens of New Atlantis, because she has departed our universe."

"No!" he said this time with the population.

No, no, no! Yes!

"Yes, Poppykettle," Marcion said, grinning to show fangs that marked his own hunger and what he truly was, even though he had never been a Warm One. "The Queen of Darkness is no more."

"Good Neighbor." Poppykettle took a step in surprised retreat. "That...that cannot be--"

Marcion entered the small space. "Yes, it can. I have searched the winds and the sighs of creation, and she is nowhere to be found."

"Then how can we exist? Without the Dark Instinct, we would crumble into dust."

"So it would seem," Marcion said casually. "But nothing is ever as it seems after the Holocaust. Something to look into, unless we're a fading dream from empty husks."

"It cannot be! What happened to her?"

Yes, Yes!

The Veal moved its head to touch the outstretched hand of Marcion. The fanged smile grew, as his soft fingers caressed the animal's face. The Veal smiled back.

"I do not know that, as yet either, Prince Poppykettle. I will have to search more. But I know of one thing—we shall have many visitors coming to our gates for sanctuary. Thus, we might have a knight, a champion of eternity among them." His fingers prodded into the Veal's clumpy hair, suddenly tugging so hard the animal yelped. The creature could not fight the arm that brought it towards the mouth of the Good Neighbor. "And thus, we might finally realize the prophecy and have our freedom, finally have our time."

It was feeding time.

The rest of the Veals knew that too, but it wasn't their feeding time. They cowered towards the back when they heard a pitiful scream, not knowing that the other figure ran excitedly towards the elevator weeping crimson tears of bursting joy, knowing not to turn his head for it was not allowed to observe the Good Neighbor when feeding. The scream quickly turned into a ripping sound. The population groaned in pleasure, also having to shut out the tasty vision.

Yes, yes, yes...freedom!

Chapter 1

"What's the population, Prox?"

There it was: their destination, the final part of their crusade, a turned bowl of solid mercury in the middle of a large, barren valley.

"I'm not sure. But I believe it was designed to hold a fraction of the population of Xanadu. I'd be surprised if there were a thousand Stargazers behind its walls."

"You've never been there?"

There it was, marred by a haze of dirty colors swirling around it, thanks to chaotic currents slithering in and out of the towering mountains.

"No," his companion said, shaking his head. "It was still in its Alpha stages when I was one of the rulers of Utopia. As a Heretic, I never traveled this far south and never heard much about it."

He took a step closer to the ledge. The hot wind bit his handsome face, as he had removed his helmet. This face was frozen in the age context of late thirties, noble and vicious at the same time, with strong yet sardonic eyes, accentuated by milky long hair and pointed ears, a mark of his alleged status in evolution.

There it was, he told himself yet another time, his sight grappling the gigantic dome that became so apparent as the mountains dissipated to give a sweeping view of the flat lowland. The Rocky Mountains, Proxos called them, stating more than once that gentle parks with a bragging nature once filled these vales that broke the mammoth range. Now there was only wasteland and that one dome, metallic and featureless from where he stood, so different from the city they'd just left that owned many domes. A city that was no more. A city he'd helped destroy.

"I hear they are ruled by a group called the Pharisees," he said, glancing up briefly to meet the nighttime sky, a whirlpool of creamy colors, always temperamental. *Luna* could be barely noticed behind the angry haze, a foggy ball of fake light.

"That is correct, Mr. Solsbury."

"I also hear that they are more advanced than any of the other city-states. That they use genetics and advanced robotics to completely alter and dominate their Warm One stock."

His companion snorted. "More advanced is a relative term. But yes, New Atlantis was more isolated than the other cities despite its nearness to our capital. It's less than five hundred miles away. At the same time, like the others, it was its own social experiment, allowed to flourish at a specific rate, an attempt by....The MoonQueen to find the most utilitarian results. That is what I've heard."

He turned to the figure standing a few steps backward. There was a hollowness in his voice that was disturbing. He should know the plain looking Stargazer by now. As a Warm One, his companion had falsely forged an alliance with him when he was an Elder and later betrayed him. As a Stargazer, his own existence had been saved by his companion while lying in a sandy tomb after The MoonQueen had defeated him. For years they had been Heretics together, the worse punishment set by MoonQueen and The Elders, expelled into the nuclear wilderness until the urge for vindication had brought him back to Xanadu.

His companion's name was Proxos Commodore. He was many thousands of years in age and had served most of his existence as an Elder, a direct servant to The Queen of Darkness. His betrayal had sent Proxos into excommunication and eventually into their friendship.

Several paces down the rocky slope, another friend was also acting oddly, to his senses. All she did, and all it seemed she had done since they had left Proxos' cavernous headquarters on the other side of the mountains six nights ago, was stare at him. She still stared at him quietly, only her eyes visible through the helmet that, along with their insulated suits, aided their godly bodies against the heat that perhaps might injure their hard skins. Two titanium supercoolers storing their food were held under each arm. Proxos had been kind to empty all the Warm One juice from his stock for their voyage to the remaining Stargazer city. The other city lay several hundred miles behind their backs, probably still churning by the destruction imparted by their claws.

That thought still bothered him slightly, but her sight made it better. Much better.

Her name was Medea. Her small stature was balanced by her amazing valor and zeal; her always sober face and large eyes were balanced by a fierce soul. She had once been the spiritual leader of the Warm Ones in one of the farms in Xanadu. She had opened his eyes to the lies of The Elders, The MoonQueen, and himself. She had been cursed to starving immortality by his own hand after they had started a revolution against Xanadu, in which she was mortally wounded by The Queen of Darkness. In The MoonQueen's and Proxos' coveted game of chess, Her next move had been to make Medea an Elder, a leader of Xanadu. In time, he simply did to Medea what she had done to him when they next met as adversaries: open her eyes to the reality of the seething mirage the Stargazer civilization was. She then aided him in finishing this revolution which he had started even before, in the city of Utopia. She was so lovely to him, and all she did was stare at him for fourteen nights. It took six nights to clip a rigorous landscape, flying when the climate allowed, marching through ravines and melted dales, passing the carbonized remnants of ancient Warm One villages, crossing betraying ledges and rocky terrain. They might have arrived sooner, but eight nights were spent nursing his body to respectability from the fight with The Queen of Darkness and preparing for the journey.

All he could do himself was take out a cigarette and again stare at the silvery dome. He couldn't blame his two allies. After all they had gone through, changing lifetimes, allegiances, played and re-played in a nefarious game that had eventually exploded in The MoonQueen's face, there was still so much more to do.

At this point, there was a nuclear missile pointed at the dome that was called New Atlantis. As Medea and he ravaged Xanadu using different methods, Proxos, sold on his drive to end the malefic reign of his present kind, had gone to one of the many forgotten missile silos of the extinct Warm One empire and started the countdown on the missile. He aimed it at New Atlantis for the end of the last Stargazer city.

At this point, Medea still possessed the Killer of Giants, an ancient sickness that was lethal to Stargazers. It was this malady she had spread throughout Xanadu that had weakened the ranks of the Stargazers. One of The Elders, a mad genius named Balkros, had been working on the cure for this terminal illness to benefit The MoonQueen, since she had contracted it by feeding on Medea's warm blood. Byron found Medea before she died and made her a vampire. Balkros told them he had sent the records of the cure to New Atlantis. He had done this simply to get them out of Xanadu, claiming he now ruled in a different state of being: half-Stargazer, half-computer system. They had no choice but to comply and leave The Elder in the fuming ruins.

At this point, they had sixteen nights to find out if Balkros spoke the truth. Sixteen nights and fury would shatter that one, perfect dome rising from yet another desert. Medea still seemed healthy enough, except for her staring. Proxos' tones bothered him, but they had sixteen nights to enter and leave a place they knew very little about. The past—how they had arrived—seemed so complicated at the moment. At the same time, their goals were very simple.

It was his last quest, he hoped. The last quest of Byron Solsbury. To end it all, he had once told Medea in Xanadu when she was an Elder and her wounded memory was still arriving like a screeching train. He had destroyed Utopia and Xanadu. Now it was New Atlantis and the hope that he would save Medea from her deadly illness and exist as a Heretic forever with his friends. It was that or nothing.

"I guess you do know as much as I do," Byron said, eyes shining with laughter. "A small population and no worry about Warm One defiance. What a concept, eh?"

He nodded. "It seems like the most practical way, doesn't it?"

Byron nodded with him. His eyes weren't laughing anymore.

"I suppose. But it's still nothing more than part of the lie we all experienced. It's still nothing more than a puppet government controlled by the members of the Rose and Lilith."

"Once controlled, Byron."

"You think so, Proxos? Yes, I did destroy Lilith with my own hands, but we're still here. The Dark Instinct is still granting us this..." He grimaced. "Existence. I'm still wondering how this can be."

"Don't," Proxos said, rolling his eyes. "Xanadu is no more. The Warm Ones, which you and I once were before Lilith cursed us, are free. Xanadu was the capital, and you know New Atlantis is next. Then there will be no more Stargazer civilization. What else matters but the final goal?"

"One thing I learned about Lilith is that she plays for keeps, and ultimate destruction is her favorite game. Legacy is something she really cared about, unless it brought her more pawns to manipulate."

"She also gambled too much, Mr. Solsbury, as she became more isolated these many centuries. Daring the Killer of Giants was easily her worse decision, besides letting you live more than once."

Byron didn't answer, taking a heavy drag from his smoke. Sixteen nights. They had plenty of time, but Byron felt all of sudden as if he needed to hurry. It was a sense of bitter and irrational urgency.

"We better get going," he said after tossing the cigarette over the ledge. "*Moratoria* will be in about an hour, but I think we can make it."

"Barely," Proxos said. "It's farther than you think. This is an immense desert, much larger than the valley Xanadu was nestled in to our north. Besides, getting there doesn't mean that we'll have immediate entrance. I believe that the outer part is covered by some sort of magnetized steel, which even our divine strength might not break. We must plan a better strategy to enter The Egg."

"The Egg?" Byron narrowed his slanting eyes, thinking of an odd dream he had just nights ago in Xanadu. A circular object, large and shiny, floating over waters towards a destination that was unknown but scared him. He shuddered, allowing a slight anger to replace that image. "Magnetized steel? I thought you knew so little."

Proxos shrugged. "That is little, Mr. Solsbury. The name is something I've heard a few times. A nickname does not clandestine intelligence make. The magnetized steel is a theory, if this place were to survive in the open for the last sixty years."

Visions of tornado storms, radioactive gales, mutant erosion, and other semi-natural horrors this side of The Holocaust, when the Stargazers destroyed the world with nuclear spite, forced Byron for once to agree with Proxos Commodore.

"Why do they call it The Egg?"

"I don't know. Like I said, its creation was after I lost my position as an Elder. Thanks to you, Mr. Solsbury."

He half-smiled. The other ex-Elder that was Medea nodded briefly. Even thirty feet away and through the moaning sirocco, Byron knew she heard every drop of the conversation.

"I guess we should wait until tomorrow," he said to both of his companions. "If you think that a secret entrance might be out of the plan."

"What plan? You never have a plan, and if you do you rarely tell me, Mr. Solsbury. In any case, I know of shelter nearby."

"One of your many hideouts, Prox?"

He finally decided to don his head protection.

"One of *our* hideouts."

"Ours?"

He started for one of the trails behind Medea. The heaving wind had already informed them that flight might not be desirable at the moment.

"You'll see. Don't try getting any more information out of me."

"I won't." Byron followed him, still concerned about his behavior. His concern relocated to Medea when he stopped in front of her. It struck him then that she just hadn't been staring at him for the last few nights. It was more like a glare, so pretty in features he'd known when they held living Juice and color, when she had been simultaneously his enemy and greatest ally. Now the features were devoid of color and always would be. Those features reminded him of something that was still good in him, that could understand love, at the same time always reminding him that they were still but corpses existing in The Queen of Darkness' dark fantasies, not the next step in evolution.

He offered Medea to carry the cases. He felt slightly nervous at her look, which did not falter. Byron wanted her words. As usual, Medea would give them to him in the most direct of ways.

"Back in the caverns," she said, "I felt you that first night when we arrived, Byron."

He nodded, knowing that because he had created her, no, cursed her with the Dark Instinct, they were spiritually connected in odd, mystic ways. He then attempted a rather bad, nonchalant smile.

"You wanted to see *Sol*, Byron. You almost stood at the entrance during dawn. You almost didn't make it to *Moratoria*."

The bad, nonchalant smile faded. He wanted another cigarette.

"And a cigarette, Byron? What a terrible excuse."

"I don't make excuses, Medea."

"That's not the point," she hissed. "Why did you do it?"

He sighed, hearing Proxos already calling for them a hundred feet away.

"Medea, I wasn't...trying to end things. I...wouldn't leave you..."

"That's not the point either," she said. "But I know why you did it. Because it's always you, Byron. Like everything, you have to take things to the limit. And then you have to test that limit just because it's there. You see, it's not good or justice that drives you most of the time, but a burning curiosity that feeds on itself, that wants to experience everything at any or anyone's cost. You have to take things to the limit, see how far you can go. Like Xanadu. Like the games you played with me at the Farm when I was a Warm One."

He raised a hand. Growing nails betrayed his agitation at her words.

"Now hold on, Medea. I don't play games—"

"We all do, but with you it's so much more intense. Whether it's *Sol* or The Queen of Darkness or where we're going, you'll play those games. But when does it stop, Byron? How far is too far?"

"I don't understand," Byron said softly. "Don't you agree with me, Medea? Have you changed your mind? Do you regret the ruin, the thousands of Stargazer and Warm Ones we destroyed back there?"

"I agree with you, Byron," Medea said firmly. She was so pretty to him. "And I believe in what we're doing now. More than that, I believe in *you*."

"So what's the problem?" he asked, halfway up a slope of irritation.

"There is no problem," she said. "But, again, how far is too far, Byron? And how many others will you take with you, burn up in your testing of the limit?"

She turned and quickly disappeared down the narrow pathway. Byron stood there for a minute, trying to muster a quick argument about how he hadn't faced *Sol* that dawn and how he could only be rationalizing the right thing.

But he knew that the only right thing was the fact that she was right.

How far was too far?

At this point, they had sixteen nights.

"There's only one way to know," Byron Solsbury whispered and kicked a loose stone by his side, realizing that the sense of urgency was nothing more than excitement and curiosity.

He decided to save that cigarette urging him to smoke it and followed his companions.

2

They had been commanded to a certain place. From underneath rubble, in holes dug in the underground tunnels beneath the city, inside the torsos of trains that once flowed through the veins of the metropolis, they rose and heard his voice. His voice told them that he had repelled their destroyers, that he had slowed the swarm of destruction. His voice, sounding from speakers and splintered television sets, also told them where to meet him. They obeyed, disoriented and demoralized, knowing that any leadership, any authority was better than what they'd suffered the past nights. As they made their way in flight or in mist form or by foot, they witnessed the totality of the destruction. Factories and buildings still smoked, charred walkways and bridges knitting the various sections barely held on to their intended forms, large holes and craters exposed them to the outside world they had thought would never threaten them. The radioactive climate entered, burning away the fake vegetation, melting the glass that had once been so prominent here. Worse, the domes that had once shielded them were all but gone, shattered or cracked to reveal more of the outside hatred. The main dome, where their leaders and The MoonQueen had presided over them no longer existed, now but a giant mess of wreckage that covered a mile in diameter. What had happened? How had it happened so quickly?

They had no time to ask. Many hobbled, healing slowly from their battles against the Warm Ones or those that had gone insane through the ordeal. Some felt that something was wrong with their bodies, that they were rotting from the inside by something that even the Dark Instinct could not defeat. A few had heard rumors of a traitorous Elder that had poisoned the juice supply with a mighty ailment concocted by a Warm One religious sect. Even less had heard that Byron Solsbury, ex-Lord of the Ravens and Warm One befriender, had caused their plight. But how could that be? He had been destroyed by The MoonQueen herself after triggering the war in the North West Farm? Some said the Heretic had returned a second time, but was quickly caught in one of the tunnels and reduced to ashes by the Ravens. Nobody survived Her wrath! But what had happened to Her, Our Mistress, The Queen of Darkness?

It didn't matter. They just wanted leadership. Once there had been engineers, artists, soldiers called Ravens, scientists, and guild members that made sure Xanadu thrived like the jewel that it was underneath the emerald domes. Now they were all equal, in tatters and battered, wondering if those destroyed by the Warm Ones weren't the lucky ones. There were no signs of any other Elders or The MoonQueen. There was only *his* voice, which urged them to come to him if they wanted safety. If they wanted food. Hunger drove them more than the sense of finding stability. Juice was scarce, as if it had vanished from all the tanks and plumbing areas. The Warm Ones were free now, their Farms their kingdom from where they could raid them when *Sol* rose with its venom. Nothing worked anymore, it seemed, especially their sacred cupula, chambers underneath the city, where they had once thought was the safest place in the cosmos. The Warm Ones had gained access and the population had to find other, cruder shelter.

Once over thirty thousand Stargazers had enjoyed this place, from the train tunnels that moved cargo, to the ice rinks and bars and places of menial work. Now it appeared, as they all joined in the meeting place, that they were but in the hundreds. How had it happened? How had She allowed it?

None dared to look at one another as they sauntered into one of the auditoriums. They were hungry, they could smell something wrong with some of them, they didn't believe in one another anymore. They were all alone, obeying the voice. They were so hungry.

All they could do was sit in the many chairs of a place that once showed old documentaries, news shows, or Stargazer movies. Now it was blank, until the last one sat down and the lights palpitated to dimness. A face appeared on the screen. A familiar face that gave many hope but some dread as they knew this person.

His name was Master Balkros. An Elder. The mightiest Elder, it was rumored by a few brave ones. It was his face but it wasn't. It was digitized to the point his features were cartoonish. His grin had always been large, glaring—now it was huge and burlesque.

"Welcome, good citizens of former Xanadu," his voice said with an electronic echo. "Welcome to our city now, our playground. We are Balkros, the newest god in a void of mad gods!"

Many eyes blinked. Many heads shook. So much hunger. What was going on here?

A few stood up, not wanting to hear this lunacy. The image was talking about a marriage of Stargazer and machine, the newest step in evolution, the true step. They headed for the exit, wondering why they had come at all.

They stopped and those sitting down flinched in their seats. Mouths opened, exposing fangs that had not tasted juice in a while. So much hunger.

Balkros' face was no longer there. Instead, the screen revealed the inside of large tanks that held abundant amounts of juice. It shifted and the spectators growled in despair. So much hunger. It flashed to chambers where Warm Ones were contained, soldiers that had been sent out from the Farms to destroy them, now trapped and banging on shut doors.

"You'll never find them," Balkros image said as it appeared in sickly gray. "We are the city and the city is us. There is no Xanadu, Our Mistress has abandoned you. There is only Balkros."

His name exploded on the screen in a bright flash. Former scientists and engineers whispered the name 'Matrix', the computer system that ran Xanadu, designed by Balkros. Where was the Elder? Obviously somewhere else controlling situations.

"And you are in we," he sneered, the image restraining laughter. "And you have two choices. We." The endless juice and trapped Warm Ones briefly materialized again. "Or yourselves." The screen suddenly went blank.

The spectators groaned in unison. Hands grabbed on to chairs and twisted metal. Feet slammed into the cement floor and fractured it. The groaning rose. So much hunger. The groaning turned into pleading tones. His face re-appeared.

"Good!" Balkros said. "Good. You will all obey us, yes? There is much work to do. All is not done yet."

The groaning stopped, although a few stood up and shouted questions at the screen. The image seemed to hear them. It couldn't be. He had to be somewhere else.

"First things first," the image rasped with crackles. "We are the city but the city isn't enough, pets. There is more and I must be more. There is another place and this place belongs to Balkros. We are a god, the true god of Stargazers."

Thousands raised their hands in supplication to him. What did he want? They were hungry. When would feeding time be?

The image's eyes narrowed, turned to a somber crimson.

"First things first," he repeated in a softer, humming tone. "A quest for a king, a quest for a god. The medium is the message, we must be the medium. You will be fed but to exist in me we ask a boon, a command. Take a present you will, take a present I should have given to a friend of ours. But you will do. The medium is the message, yes? A quest for a god. A present for The

Forgotten. Balkros. Only Balkros matters."

They couldn't help but glance at one another. He wasn't right! What was he stammering about? What quest?

"But first," he roared so loud the walls of the auditorium shook. "FIRST KNEEL DOWN TO YOUR GOD! KNEEL DOWN TO BALKROS! BALKROS. BALKROS. BALKROS."

And they did, with so much hunger, many with pulverized knees or no real legs, a few lowering their heads forward in tired, desperate resignation. They had little choice. Deep in their tortured souls they knew he spoke of one thing being true. Whether he was a god or this was his city didn't matter. The only thing that mattered besides their hunger was one thing they all finally realized—Xanadu was no longer.

Chapter 2

Black Gomez was having a bad week. He'd sifted through weeks like this one before, cataclysmic nights that seemed to turn the universe upside down. They had to happen eventually in his elevated status, but it appeared this one was the worst of all. This one had shattered a slow yet steady rise to power jealously overseen for a long time. Six hundred years, at least, he mused. Luck had always aided him as much as an opportunistic penchant. Both opportunity and luck had vanished. He was homeless, without a leader and no structure. Even the silver rose pin marking him as one of the leaders of the world seemed dull attached to grimy robes that once impressed many a Stargazer during balls or parties. No such events would ever grace his homeland, and his only hope was dissecting the mountains quickly before starvation or the weather betrayed them.

"Hurry, fools!" he screamed at his attendants, who just a few nights ago had been working in his offices, controlling all media and news distribution in Xanadu. Now they served him in his hurried journey towards New Atlantis, knowing that his status was their only hope besides the quick trip.

None of the nine dared a glance at his gangly form, busily digging upon the hard surface of a small, graveled ravine. They weren't moving any quicker, though, wan skins almost collapsing against their cheekbones, eyes sinking with every hour. They had found a few Rukas a night ago, large rodents that shared the world with the Stargazers, but their foul juice had rapidly evacuated their godlike forms. Rukas, Gomez thought while pinning eyes shut. How did it come to this?

This quandary was much worse than when he ruled New Tenochtitlan, which he had named in reverence of another city The Elder oversaw. It was a different city, though, a herd of massive pyramids connected by underground tunnels to Rice City, which straddled the cliffs of the western coast. He had ruled both of them so well for a few decades. Sixty years ago, when a typhoon and an earthquake had simultaneously smashed the cities

built to withstand one or the other but not both, Gomez had escaped as well. Oh, it was horrible to miss New Tenochtitlan, a
tight place of finely crafted corridors and jade statues in the form
of animals he enjoyed. He still yearned for the pre-Colombian
fountains and chambers, the gilded walls and imitation marble
piazzas. Even better were the squadrons of tanks that came in an
out every night, collecting raw materials, slowly scoping the land
for expansion. He still wished he could have truly used the ad-
vantages of the submarine pens in Rice City, a coarser metropolis
that like Utopia was fashioned from remnants of a city called San
Diego. In those nights, the submarines had been just beginning to
dispatch Stargazer sailors deep underneath the ocean in exploration of fuel, more materials, and eventually other lands that might
be less touched by the nails of The Holocaust. Balkros had even
begun sending potential plans to create an underwater metropolis
in the old Pacific Oceans. As the mayor of both places, Gomez
had imagined that the bases below the waves would do nothing
but increase their hold on the world. But New Tenochtitlan and
Rice City had been decimated, the poor submarines with their
population lost at sea, and he had survived to return to serve Our
Mistress. That had been bad, but this seemed worse.

"Hurry," he repeated with gritted teeth. "We have less than
an hour, do you hear? Besides *Sol*, Goddess knows what horrors
might lurk in these places while we are in *Moratoria*."

It struck the Elder then that it would help if he joined in
the process of creating descent cupulae for their rest. The stone
was hard and a few already labored with broken fingers. But their
cupola, tombs as they were once called, had to be deep for con-
cealment as well as protection. Whether he helped didn't matter.
Although his long hair was clotted with dirt, his fringed and laced
outfit was grated, and his makeup had melted away miles ago,
they needed his stature and lofty orders to reach to New Atlantis.
They were less than a night away. Good. Then he might get his
answers on how this week had happened.

Six hundred years to come to this. It couldn't be, By The
MoonQueen.

After all, it had started with Her. Once Rigoberto Gomez
had been a Warm One, as had most Stargazers, although most

post-Holocaust ones thought they were a different species created by The Queen of Darkness. He had been a lusty voyager in an age of exploration, in a time of handsome galleys braving wide oceans. Conquistadores, they were called, sheathed in smooth armor, armed with thin swords, and handsome pointed beards. He had been serving another queen in those young nights, using her wealth to prospect a new world. As a Warm One, Gomez thought he could have never experienced such delights. There were hot jungles and chilly mountains, cities of gold and polished limestone divided by canals and high pyramids, half naked people with coppery skins and feathered hats and jade jewelry who had never heard of a wheel or a horse or the concept of zero. What odd people, intelligent but humorless, whose warriors surrendered whenever one took out any of their leaders. That's how they had conquered an empire that was larger than their small forces arriving from their ships. How easy it had been to battle these people, who didn't even fight to the death but for submission. Submission in order to later be sacrificed to *Sol* by having one's heart torn out and eaten atop one of the pyramids. Eventually, they slew their king, throwing him off a balcony while held hostage. They had taken flight from the angry population, many of his men drowning as they fell into the canals, unwilling to release their heavy bags of loot. Then the Conquistadores returned from the coast with reinforcements and destroyed the city. The population was enslaved, the women raped in order to terminate their race, the men often hung upside down until the juice gorged their heads to death, the precious materials ravaged. So quickly this city once built on a swamp vanished, replaced by a place called New Spain. The wealth was amazing and there were many little boys to enjoy. Their excuse to convert all to their religion and the ships traveling every night back to their homeland plump with precious goods blanketed their actions for years.

It was a nice period, but not good enough. Lust is so hard to sate once it is tended to maturity. Many of his comrades eventually returned to the old country ready to retire in newly bought villas or spend their gold in the southern beaches; some, like Hernan, took political positions in the newly formed cities and counties. But not Rigoberto Gomez. If this was easy, Gomez told many, imagine if it got a little difficult. Imagine the wealth. From the enslaved population in the central parts of this kingdom rumors were rampart about even richer cities. Rumors of cities like El Dorado floated over his hungry eyes. He envisioned these places corpulent with endless gems and gold and silver and ancient sorcery that could turn a man into a god. Cities older than time with little defenses against his lust and the lust of his men.

Thus, Black Gomez, as he'd been nicknamed by many of the silly priests throughout his stay, took a group of soldiers farther to the south, into the deep jungles and past steep mountains to enter even deeper jungles. They searched for a place called the Citadel of Jaguars that they heard more and more about with each village of natives, the true capital of the few empires in this continent, especially for those who worshipped *Luna* more than *Sol*.

Things became difficult, so much more difficult. Gomez had a bad week when he arrived to the final jungles, after years of exploration. Errant maps, horrible maladies that turned some of his men's innards into black pus, invisible stalkers that prospered in the thickets, and other horrors more than maimed his morale. The hundred men, able soldiers who also wanted to retire back to Spain, soon became thirty. Then came more of those primitive people, but these had no qualm about murdering. The savages used poisoned darts and nets to halve his troops again. Quicksand and more unknown sickness and soon it was only Gomez, delirious and starving, rushing through the jungle like a madman who had just seen *el infierno*, who was getting ready to go there.

And just like that, Gomez arrived at the City of Jaguars one evening, almost unable to walk, his tongue so thick with thirst he could barely speak. It was greater than the other cities, greater than New Spain, carved from glowing malachite and encrusted with jewels larger than fists. It shone under the light of *Luna* like a dream. Rigoberto Gomez stood before it, but he was not alone. He wandered into the center and there She was, sitting on a throne of bones surrounded by the remnants of eaten babies and an army of creatures that were half human and half feline. She introduced herself with another name. Kilya, goddess of *Luna*, enemy of *Viracocha*, lord of creation and *Sol*. She was more gorgeous than anything he'd ever seen, the color of brass and the face of a heavenly seraph. Feathers barely covered her flawless body that towered over him.

All Gomez could do was weep. She smiled at him and told him that this place was forbidden to mortals. There was only one judgment. He would stay here forever. He fell on his knees, begging for his freedom, for a chance to sail the Atlantic and see Gibraltar one more time.

She asked him to give her one reason why he shouldn't serve her in this place that was as beautiful as Heaven but no better than Hell?

"Because I am a coward at heart," he answered. "And I would not serve you well, Lady."

She smiled and a cloud of bats miles high appeared over them. The feline creatures advanced towards him.

A coward has no heart, Kilya told him with the voice of a tender wind, *and I can use one without a heart. Kukulkan has returned, I see, and like any progeny of The Mad God, he brings doom. The ages have changed one more time, once again destroying the wonder of The Unimaginable because of Viracocha. It is time I returned to the lands of Ovid and began my final retribution.*

The rest was worse than *el infierno*. They brought Gomez before her, peeled him of his clothes, and tore his limbs away. She bit him with powerful fangs that snapped his neck before his blood had been drained. He was devoured by blackness, by a cold pain so deep it swallowed his memory for a long time. When he opened his eyes an eternity later, Gomez knew he was different, knew that several nights had passed. He rose from the ground with newly grown appendages. He was different. The city seemed different. Everything seemed different. He asked one of the creatures where She was. He felt so afraid now with his new power, which begged him to hunt like the beasts of the jungles.

The creature told him that She had left, saying that an age had ended by his presence, that maybe it was time to return to the old world now that the Burning Time was ending and begin the fight one more time. The creature seemed very sad. It added that She promised she would avenge what this new age would bring to this continent, which was the same with all the other lands and eras.

And what could Black Gomez do? He was different, touched with a new existence that defied reason. At the same time, he was a being of the twilight, who consumed his former kind and could never be sated. All he knew was that he had to find the goddess, find out what she wanted and desired, what she wanted to inflict on the world. What else could he do? He knew She was much more powerful than he, or than anything probably on this earth. Demon or not, this deity was responsible for his immortality.

And he wasn't a coward, Gomez would prove to her. He was just rash when he said that. He was useful as he'd always been to rulers.

It would be two hundred and twenty years later that he would finally find Kilya. Gomez had survived many lands and civilizations, devoured so many races, changed identities, and even met many of his kind in search for purpose other than the eternal supper. He was almost not surprised when he found Her in Portugal sometime in 1755, in the court of King Joseph, in a form in which he would never have expected her to be.

"Will you join me?" Kilya asked him, her face painted like a clown, a crowd from the other side of the curtain clapping eagerly.

"I am not a coward," he said, pushing back his cloak to show the regal attire he had always worn in either aspect.

"We will go very far," she said. "And that will not be far enough."

"I..." He started and saw something in her inviolate eyes that terrified him more than anything. "I will join you."

"Good," she said. "The show must go on."

And it did. Even after they fled, a group of wild priests chasing them out of Lisbon with their faith-magic. The city was oddly destroyed the next evening by an earthquake. It was then that Gomez joined her with the others like Proxos and Tsing-Tao for the next four hundred years, loosely planning and executing the Holocaust. It had begun with the circus; it had ended with fire from the sky. At first, he did not understand the goddess' plan, but it became so apparent through her odd moods and identities, like her self-banishment to ice, when she became the White Witch again. Kilya had planned it all along, it seemed, perhaps before his arrival to the City of Jaguars. He never tried to understand her will, only wanting to finally capitalize his lust, forget his hunger for the greater picture. He could have the world, the universe, if he followed her icy hem. What had happened? How had the *hijo de puta*, Byron, mucked things up so easily? It *had* to be another one of Her tricks. Only in New Atlantis, a place he had never visited, would he find out.

"Hurry," he said and it came out like a sigh. He wasn't a coward. He was an explorer of ages indescribable to mortals and their little goals. A Conquistador, always.

One of the Stargazers suddenly looked at him and pointed upwards.

"Master Gomez," she said. "Look at that!"

Black Gomez, the Conquistador, followed the finger and couldn't help feel very, very afraid. It was smoke, but more than that by the sentient movement pulsing away, it had to be one of the forms that his kind took.

2

"Amazing isn't it?" Proxos said, and Byron wondered if he spoke of the objects before them or the fact he'd started a decent fire (one of his habits he never forgot before being cursed thousands of years ago in a place he called Greece).

It was amazing, they had to agree with reverent silence. Medea and Byron had not stopped gazing around the large cavern they had been lead to in a crease of one of the mountains. Its ceiling easily stretched two hundred feet. The wind could be heard complaining not too far away, here at the base of the chain.

"How long has this been here?" Medea asked, touching Byron's sight again in a sort of sick wonderment of this place.

"Since before the Holocaust," Proxos said, kneeling before the fire. "There were many like these in any place a Stargazer was to begin a metropolis. Oklahoma for Utopia, near Norad and

Fema for Xanadu, California—"

"So it was all perfectly mapped out," Byron said, absorbing the endless stock that stretched to the other side of this place.

"It had to be," Proxos said. "We stockpiled as well as we could all over the continent. We were to destroy all of these stores after each city was built, erase any vestige that we might have 'borrowed' from The Warm Ones. I suppose the denizens of New Atlantis became lazy or simply forgot."

"No," Medea said shaking her head. "Look at the dunes that cover much of it. Little sand gets in here from the long tunnel past the tightly-fit boulder. All of this has not been used in a very long time."

She was right, Byron agreed with a nod. Dirt sloped from many of the odd vehicles strewn around the area, objects that looked like trains, many with large cranes or monstrous shovels protruding. It was amazing, all the shapes and sizes. Beyond them, also many shapes and sizes, tanks and containers filled the cavern, as well as tons of raw materials—fiber glass frames, copper wiring, aluminum beams, bags of dusty cement, and so much else. Stacks of computers and mainframes, and all sort of miscellaneous paraphernalia added to the fact this place was for one purpose: To create...to create from the destruction of something else. The cavern stretched to almost half a mile and there was barely enough room for the three.

It struck Byron that the Stargazer insurgents who began the Holocaust had simply stored just enough for their cities, the five ones that graced this planet. As he'd heard in stories, this was a small fraction of what the Warm Ones once possessed in their many empires. They had cities a thousand times the size of Xanadu, overflowing with puking factories and plants that could sustain millions of his former species. They ruled the world and also abused it for a long time, covering it slowly, tainting what the Stargazers had blotted out. It seemed neither was that different, even though one owned the Dark Instinct and the other...the other was just human.

"That is odd," Proxos said, pretending that by holding his hands to the fire it might warm them. They would never be warm again. "You make a good point. But this is the only place on this side of the mountain range. They would have had to use most of this to build The Egg."

"It looks like they didn't," Byron said. "But they sure couldn't have transported all that material to make a city from another part."

Proxos shrugged. "Unless I have missed another one through my wanderings. But I do recall the exact location of each stockpile before the Holocaust. All The Elders knew of them very well. There is nothing else near here."

"Are you sure, Prox?"

He blinked, as if recalling something. For the first time since Byron had known the ex-Elder, his companion in the wilderness when he was also banished from Xanadu after falling to Lilith, Byron caught a look of slight fear and confusion in his face.

"Are you sure, Prox?" he asked again. "Something built that city."

Proxos blinked, shook his head, and stood up.

"I probably did miss something else," he said quickly. "We must eat soon."

As he turned his back and walked to one of the supercooler cases, Byron looked at Medea. He knew her expression mirrored his. Proxos was hiding something. Something big, serious perhaps, since Proxos never had a problem hiding things if it added to his love of surprising people. The ex-Elder's tone was similar to the one in his headquarters when Byron was his guest after his defeat to Lilith; when he posited to him one night that nuclear winter should have ended decades ago.

They didn't say a word, though, once again turning their attention to the museum of another time, relics that abetted this age.

"So," Byron said loudly and casually after lighting a cigarette. "This is one of the ways you made the transition. You stole from the Warm Ones and hid the loot in hidden areas all over the land where the nuclear fallout wouldn't be as severe."

"We didn't steal," Proxos said, opening one of the cases and removing several containers. The fire was actually useful to heat the frozen juice in increments. "We had ways, Mr. Solsbury.

We had Balkros and we had Lilith."

"Lilith?" he echoed, and could feel Medea cringe to his side at that name. "Was she also a high standing member of this Warm One kingdom?"

"No," Proxos scoffed. "She had other ways to make material possession her own. By the way, there is a lot of flammable material here. An ember from your silly habit could detain our mission very easily."

"Point taken," he said, taking another drag. "So all you had to do was wait here during the Holocaust and wake up to a hard night of work, uh?"

Proxos smiled fastidiously, putting one of the containers over the flames.

"We've already gone through this, Mr. Solsbury. We didn't hide here, but in other areas. We planned it well, you see. Many of the Stargazers were ordered in areas where they wouldn't survive, to trim our ranks afterwards, since we didn't know really how many Warm Ones we could snare in these outposts away from Utopia."

"And that way," Byron interjected with a wry smile. "You could create new and ignorant ones from these Warm Ones."

"Disgusting," Medea said, clenching her jaw.

"Of course," Proxos said thoughtfully. "It all worked out fine...until you came along."

"Did you see any of the Holocaust?" Byron asked suddenly, thinking of a pup being born in between ages.

"No," he said. "We all went to *Moratoria* early that eve, except for Lilith. She wanted to witness what she'd wrought."

"Disgusting," Medea repeated, but Byron thought she braved a small smile. Why was everyone acting weird, he mused, reminding himself a second time it was what they had gone through and the mission. But he hadn't changed. He was still just Byron.

"And don't ask me anymore, Mr. Solsbury," the ex-Elder said. "I don't like to talk about her. I feel as if she can hear me sometimes."

"Nonsense," Byron said, gently wrapping his arms around Medea. "That is over with, and we've got plenty ahead. How are you?"

Medea smiled at him. Byron was glad that at least she didn't glare at him anymore.

"Fine," she said. "I feel fine right now, Byron. The Killer is dormant for now. And how are you?"

"Dead," he answered. "Only moving because of you, of what you are to me."

"Aren't you forgetting about the stars," Proxos said casually, not bothering to waste a glance at them.

"No," Byron whispered, thinking about that night when a tornado storm opened the toxic clouds like a bursting scar and showed the harmony the universe had, what this fleck of it where they stood should and could have been. "That is exactly what I'm thinking, Prox. Stars..."

Medea started to giggle, but Byron's kiss cut her off. He held her tighter. She hugged him back with her small arms. There was still something odd about her, but again he had to remind himself of their reality. Individuals reacted differently, and it usually took a few revolutions and cataclysms to rattle Byron Solsbury, unlike most.

Byron kissed her harder. Her lips were still cold but he sought the warmth of potential, of symbolism. He wanted more, feeling lonely with his two closest friends in this cavern. Medea understood, nodded and motioned for a place somewhere behind a row of tanks similar to the one used to leave Xanadu.

"Proxos," he said, touching her cheek with the back of his hand. Cold. Just symbolism, though. "We'll be right back. Don't eat all—"

Medea suddenly escaped his grasp and stood rigidly. Before Byron could rationalize her behavior to individual reaction, she was speaking rapidly.

"Did you hear that, Byron?"

"Hear what?"

"Somebody is close by!" she exclaimed. "Not somebody but many."

Byron craned his head, pretending that if he had a functioning heart it might be beating harder at the moment. So much ahead, he mused, listening to what was to be distant and complaining words.

3

All was going as planned.

Their servants were leaving the wreckage of Xanadu after being nicely fed. *They* knew the fools would not return until realizing the quest, the quest that would take their godly being one step further. One more step. *Their* servants flew and walked over the gritty terrain, heading towards the southern mountains and the shiny thing that lay in another valley. The Stargazers were full of energy, understanding that more nourishment than what currently bubbled in their bodies and in small provisions wouldn't repeat until they returned with the results. *They* didn't care if the servants returned. If they did, it wouldn't matter. The crusading Stargazers were as doomed as the Warm Ones driven back with high-pitched sounds that cracked eardrums and hypnotic lights that drove their little minds mad. The Stargazers thought a new leader would take them in if they served him, The Warm Ones thought that this was just another footfall in their revolution, that they could return to their farms and arm themselves more with man-power and those silly idols that no longer affected *them*. They were all fools and they were all doomed, sooner or later. How wonderful, electronic thoughts told *them*, all neat and swaddled and moving at nine million megahertz through the computerized web that was *their* being.

Once *their* thoughts had been an adventure, though. Ideas and images crackled like lightning in *their* head constantly, bursting with such joy and genius *they* had trouble grasping them. It had always been that way ever since the angels had given *them* immortality. The angels, *they* smiled in a hundred screens across the city, through binary transmissions and chip sparks. The angels had tried to unlock so much in them. As a Warm One, *they* had been so timid and meek, despite *their* stature and importance to the empire they served. As a Stargazer, *they* fed fear and wonder to the population, using all that *they* had learned to bring the society together. The thoughts always cracked, the memories always came and went. But it had all been so wrong, for none of *their* prior identities were balance, were harmony, were duality, complete and tamed duality

Now *they* were more. Now *they* had fused the Dark Instinct into the Matrix, baiting it to believe that his persona was in one of his computers. They had simply willed it to happen, and his bodily destruction at the hands of the Warm Ones had finished the process, convincing the God-Soul—who only wanted to exist in any aspect in order to end, to destroy forever—to enter the Matrix, dominate it. Technology and the ancient magic that was the Dark Instinct were now one, with Balkros' persona ruling over both. *They*—Balkros, computer, and God-Soul—knew it might never have work, but what choice did *they* have. Destiny in the evolution of cosmic transcendence had made it work. As a Stargazer, *they* had been prostrate to the demanding bitch-queen, as a Warm One *they* had been prostrate to his mate. Both had been domineering, frustrating, and *their* material forms had somehow enjoyed it to the point of lunacy.

There was more, though, as a million charges like neurons coursed across the Matrix, which connected everything electronic in Xanadu, and tried to tether memories from *their* aspects. There had been more, though. There had been a rage, an anger, that had overlapped one existence into the one as an Elder. That rage had truly created the lightning in his brain, had made him enjoy the destruction of humanity as much as he enjoyed the destruction of Xanadu. That rage propelled him to where *they* were now, drove them, gave them a sense of humor. How had it happened, Balkros asked and the Dark Instinct roared and a thousand circuits searched the databases. The answer came to *them*, shivering in images created from the data *they* had fed the Matrix throughout many years.

The angels had visited *them* as a Warm One. Despair. It had been a woman. No, not his mate, not the queen-bitch.

It had been her...the angels.

Remember...

It had been her.

Everything was going as planned, *they* thought again, yet

part of *their* being retreated to a place so real and unsafe they, no, *he* could almost taste the rage again.

Remember...

In the beginning...

4

Proxos was still crouching before the fire when they returned. He had been contemplating the same issue since they had left the remains of Xanadu. To end it all. How simple. Lilith had destroyed the world and its offspring, leaving the undead to rule it. Now it was time to finish what they had done, what Byron had done. To end it all and start from the beginning.

Or at least spend the rest of eternity in his hideout playing chess with Medea and Byron, a true poetic justice for any mercurial cabal of heroes.

But it wasn't so simple. It never had been truly simple, ever since The Queen of Darkness, Hecate as she had been called in Leros millennia ago, had christened him with the God-Soul. Where they went definitely wasn't simple. It was very complicated. And very dangerous.

When he saw Byron's face in Xanadu after the fall of Lilith, more determined even than the night he witnessed the naked constellations as a Heretic and vowed to battle The MoonQueen to the end, the ex-Elder knew convincing otherwise would not materialize. That was Byron—stubborn like the planetary revolutions and brighter than their solar lords. Proxos had little choice but to subscribe to his mission. After all, while Byron recruited a brainwashed Medea in Xanadu and spread the idols of the Blood of Circles and the Killer of Giants, he, Proxos, had traveled to a silo and pointed a missile at New Atlantis. Very simple. But Byron wanted to go behind those walls and help the ailing Medea. Byron and Medea had a bond, more than the fact that his friend had given her the Dark Instinct. A bond he couldn't understand, but envied. When they gazed into each other's eyes, it seemed these two sometimes conflicted, intense individuals somehow could taste a yielding harmony, a sense of totality. How could he convince him (or her) that this phase of their campaign wasn't a good idea?

How could he convince his comrades that once they entered New Atlantis they would never leave, one way or another, because no one ever left The Egg. No one. Ever.

"So what did we find?" Proxos asked, turning his sight back to the fire, knowing tonight wouldn't be a good night. Tomorrow. Before it was too late. "Some old Heretics that still wander the mountains where Rukas or other vermin are abundant. Perhaps some hopeful fugitives from Xanadu trying to do what we are?"

"Not exactly," Byron said, flexing his jaw as if in hunger. "We found an old friend of mine, ready to go into *Moratoria*."

"They almost spotted us," Medea said, eyeing Byron. "Since Byron almost leaped at them. We turned into mist form before, though."

"I might as well have," he said rigidly. "We have to stop them."

Medea shook her head. "We might as well do it the next evening when we are well fed and before they rise from *Moratoria*. I told you it will be easier if we surprise them as they rise since they outnumber us."

"It's ten of them," Byron spat. "Easy odds."

"If you don't mind," Proxos said, standing up, "Just for once not excluding me from your semi-silent conversations. Who did you see?"

Byron smiled, and there was a hunger there.

"Like I said, Prox. An old friend of mine."

Proxos nodded once. "Can I assume sarcasm somewhere, Mr. Solsbury?"

"A lot of it," he said, raising a fist. "And hope, the same one you had when you defeated Shibboleth in the desert. It's Black Gomez."

"The Elder," Proxos said. "He was mayor of New Tenochtitlan after I was banished."

"Right," Medea said. "But he returned after the Cataclysm of Tears to join the members of the Rose."

Proxos nodded again. "And Mr. Solsbury and the Elder are no admirers of one another."

"Never have been," Byron agreed. "But I wish this was just personal, Prox. It's obvious he's trying to get into New Atlantis. We can't allow that."

Proxos almost nodded a third time, swallowed by the reasons and the fact again they were going to New Atlantis. The trio had agreed that breaking into New Atlantis wasn't the best way. And why should they? Medea had offered before arriving to these caverns while they brain stormed a course of action. After all, an Elder traveled with them. New Atlantis couldn't possibly know about Medea's betrayal since it occurred so quickly, and The Elders would have never allowed this information out. The best way to gain entrance was to demand sanctuary from the Pharisees by Medea and her two assistants from the Stargazer capital. Then it would be rather easy to pry access to their computer banks and find the cure for the Killer of Giants just before the warhead struck. Sixteen nights.

But another Elder also wanted sanctuary to the remaining city of the world. The only one besides Medea who had survived.

"Perhaps it is better to stop them now?" Proxos commented, knowing that he needed to tell them tomorrow as soon as possible. "After all, we need all of our energy and wits to cross twenty miles and beg our way in."

"Medea's right," Byron said. "They're going into *Moratoria*. It will be an easier task if we strike right as they rise next evening. Besides that, I'm famished. The Dark Instinct is already starting to nag me."

Proxos gave his third and final nod. He couldn't understand, but knew that because Byron had spent over a year fixing his ruined body in the sand after losing to The Queen of Darkness during the Warm One revolution, The God-Soul was more active in him—it had usurped part of his personality, as it did everything in order to fulfill its wrecking essence. But he needed to speak to him, to them. Tomorrow.

"I understand, Mr. Solsbury. Do we have to destroy them all, Mr. Solsbury?"

Byron shrugged. "We'll take it one Stargazer at a time."

"Don't let your passion take hold of you, Byron," Medea warned.

He smiled. The hunger was still there. Proxos knew it wouldn't be good time now. It would have to be tomorrow. No one ever left New Atlantis. More like no real Stargazer ever left The Egg.

"Don't worry," he said plainly, eyes burning with that hunger now. "It's not passion at all. It'll just be pleasure."Perhaps he should tell them now...

"Fine," Proxos said with resignation, moving away from the fire to the readied food in sealed cups. "Let us eat. Tomorrow then."

5

The Pharisees all turned their heads towards Marcion. He stood before the many screens, which were connected to the satellites that The MoonQueen had forbidden them to use. They used them now. They saw as much as they could through the murk that was the atmosphere. They had seen Xanadu and exiting Stargazers and Warm Ones, afraid and lost. They had seen the destruction and much of what was left in the world.

But they needed what was reflected in the eyes of the seer, Marcion, the last of his kind, who had never been a Warm One and never had even been mortal like them. None present in the city had ever been like those Stargazers in the other cities, and few had ever been ordinary in their past aspects. He was perhaps the greatest, the most amazing, the one with a sight that only The Queen of Darkness or the Prince of Shadows might have matched. They needed the Good Neighbor's sight.

He blinked once. His tone was serious. Yet he smiled, wide and healthy, perhaps for the first time in centuries since Lilith had destroyed his kind in a dimension underneath the Hollow Hills.

"Tomorrow," he said. "Me thinks we will have the first visitors. Perhaps one will come knocking on our gates; perhaps we might have a knight among them."

Chapter 3

It was an odd dream. An odd silly dream. She'd had many in the past, both as a Warm One and Stargazer. Many angered her with tingling longing when she awoke in either aspect. As a Warm One, she once dreamt about rising from bed to a land where no monsters existed, where the Den of Thieves, as the territory outside the Farms was known, no longer marred their daily rigors, and neither did the septic climate. When she truly awoke it fueled her outrage at fate, made her want to urge the Shaman of the Circle to speed the revolution that had been planned for generations. "Dreams are nothing," he told her, already feeble from the Killer of Giants that had to be secretly passed from Shaman to Shaman by sexual congress. "They are insecurities becoming secure. They are hopes like melting clouds. Don't worry about them. Worry about meditation and the hell surrounding us."

Medea Seth Durgo didn't listen to him. She heard her dream. She wanted that world where there were no monsters. As a monster, she was succeeding. This dream was very different, though. It had less weight but somehow made her apprehensive of *Moratoria*. Byron had once told her the whole mess had started with a dream about *Sol*. It didn't seem like anything but nothing is the beginning of something. Nothing is everything if you look very hard. He still didn't know if it had been *Sol* or some beyonder deity at the other side of the night which had called upon him to become the Liberator of humanity.

There was no *Sol* in this dream. Medea was in a crowd. A crowd of Warm Ones, wearing clothing that had never been seen after the Holocaust. They clapped and cheered and clucked away upon rising benches. A pinstriped tent of black and silver covered their heads. Medea didn't know if in the dream she was Stargazer or Warm One since she never glanced at herself. She watched what made the crowd so delighted.

People flew from in the air, back and forth, perching and clinging to swinging ropes. Others danced around the floor, somersaulting at will, gamboling with the polish of raw delight. The costumes were myriad, some of frilled pastels, some perhaps tight-fitting and garnished with bright hues like a work of art; others still pranced around in outlandish threads, puffed and laced, wearing caricature masks of animals or smiling faces. Those without masks had their faces painted in all sorts of designs conforming the outfit or current dance. It all made a hypnotic blend, seasoned by flowing, repetitive music from musicians to-wards the back. There was an orderly chaos here, perfected by artistic zeal, repetitive yet daring, darling even, shifting slightly as performers came and left, just as the music slightly quivered to other moods. Behind the creative pageant, beyond the musicians who were also in costumes, large cages stood at the back of the tent, revealing amazing creatures of all shapes and sizes, which also moved and growled with the pulse of the show.

Medea could have sat there for eternity, absorbed in the spectacle, but suddenly the crowd stood up. Someone shouted something in a flowing language she couldn't understand. The lights dimmed suddenly. There was no source of the illumination. The dancers and jumpers shunted to the edges of the production that lacked a real stage.

And as always, as in every silly, odd dream, she came out from the folds of a part of the tent, captured by a beam of velvety light. Her clothes were an outflow of more of that silver and black. Her face was painted with exaggerated features—elongated lips, dark eyes, bone-white cheeks, forehead and chin. Yet Medea couldn't deny her beauty, her starry movement. The music, which had been fast and merry at the time, veered to moodier tones, as if in anticipation.

She was going to dance. That is why the crowd was here, Medea knew, coming every night as they did in every city in this world that wasn't her world. She was going to dance, this most beautiful of females, this most consummate of performers. Medea had never reached this far, watching this person glide to the mid-dle of the area.

She was going to dance...

Medea jolted as something shattered the visions. The sand covering her burst away from her flaying body, caught by eyes that snapped open quickly. She was in the large cave. Byron stood before her, still wiping grime from his own clothes.

"Are you okay?" he asked. "Didn't mean to startle you. We need to get on the move if the element of surprise is going to be exploited."

"I'm fine," she said, swallowing hard. Reality made itself harsher in her perfect vision. "Just didn't hear you."

"That's odd." He slightly tilted his head. "You amazingly heard Black Gomez before we did. Yet you didn't hear me."

She sat up with a frown. Medea didn't like his tone while teetering between *Moratoria's* satiny respite and the harsh consciousness she faced ever since being born. She had almost danced, though. The female was so beautiful, the spectacle was so harmonious like a sliver of sound peace.

"Byron, you and your questions. Maybe it's because I stay cautious for queer things, while you just simply slam into any situation without care."

"That's not entirely true."

"That's not entirely false."

He chuckled, and she was glad he relaxed. It was odd that he hadn't perceived her dream. After all, connected by the Dark Instinct, many times sharing emotions, brief thoughts, or even sensations, Medea sometimes could see into his dreams. She had seen the one about the silvery object ripping through the sky. She had felt Byron speak to his father in a frontier of existence. But he had not mentioned anything about this dream born on their last night in Xanadu. It was very strange, but she didn't want to talk about it for some reason. Even with him.

"Oh, Medea," he said. "I hate you so much sometimes."

She stood up and smiled back at him.

"And I hate you, Byron."

"We'll never be apart?" he asked, rather timidly. "We'll always be with one another."

Something inside her, like a voice down a corridor leading to *Moratoria* made her spine tense, made her jaw clench for a second.

"We'll always be together, one way or another."

"Even if I take it to the limit?" he asked with a grin. "Even if I slam into any situation?"

Medea sighed and kissed him.

"Better wake up Proxos, Liberator. We must feed quickly and be on our way."

His eyes narrowed, perhaps in disappointment, but he turned towards where Proxos had been buried. Medea sighed again, this time in relief. Not even him. What was wrong with her? Byron, never one to suffocate any opinion floating before his whim, had said during their trek to this cavern that the quest was making them act peculiarly. Except for him, he then added. Perhaps that was it, she reflected. It was just what they had done, what they were doing.

She shook her head and walked towards one of the super-cooler containers. Her other comrade replaced Byron in her waking thoughts. He spent thousands of years cursed and destroyed several billion existences, she thought. How does Proxos deal with it? Passing the remnants of the fire, now ashes, the answer trickled down to her head like water coming from a small hole in the wall. She nodded at herself. Dreams were for Byron and his destiny; Medea was one who kept her feet on the ground. There was balance between them, just as there was with him and Proxos.

Yes, she thought, knowing how Proxos had done it. Keep it simple, keep the things that mean something to you, and you might just be fine. Just might be.

2

A Stargazer was allowed to exit *Moratoria* as soon as *Sol* relinquished its javelins. The Dark Instinct allowed perhaps an hour of more respite before it urged the body to rise and feed. That was rare even, and only did it allow longer periods when the body needed sober healing and regeneration.

Byron hoped that this party would test the limit of resting. That was probable, since they were not as prepared as the trio in crossing hundreds of treacherous miles. Their skins the prior evening had looked burnt, lacerated, their expressions lost if not slightly despondent. A few might even house the Killer of Giants, imparted by Medea to the population through her body and the plumbing system she had once been in charge of as an Elder.

His hopes quickly surged when they arrived to the top of the small gorge. Unmoving mounds remained intact at the bottom. The weather around them seemed cooler then, as the low, tumbling clouds were probably shedding some precipitation high up in the mountains.

"Perfect," Proxos whispered. "Shall we strike?"

"Strike?" I mouthed. "Which one belongs to Black Gomez?"

"It doesn't matter. We should take care of them all, like you advised."

"I didn't advise that, Prox."

He looked at Byron oddly.

"So are you changing your mind? What are you going to do? Even some vendetta and convince the others to follow the Liberator?"

"He's right," Medea said. "We must be practical."

"If we want to be practical," Proxos said. "Then we can quickly return to the cavern and bring out a vat of acid. It should take no time."

"I don't know." He shook his head. "Maybe we—"

"Mr. Solsbury," Proxos hissed. "They're already dead, remember? We're already dead. We don't belong. We don't belong anywhere, because this whole planet was constructed to allow the balanced flow of life and death, creation and destruction...not both at the same time."

Byron didn't answer, still staring at the mounds that were nothing but graves. So much destruction, he thought, ever since he was born between the ages. And from the beginning he himself had never truly belonged anywhere.

"Furthermore, your mission is to destroy all Stargazers, is it not?"

"Just their society, Proxos" Medea added. "Just what...She wove."

Proxos groaned lightly, but Byron was grinning. The mounds were beginning to stir, pebbles rolling off the top, cracks appearing as their skins palpitated. They had more than likely heard the trio's usual bickering.

"You're severely wrong again," he said in a normal tone, falling over the ledge. "I just wanted to make it a fair battle, Prox."

By the time he had landed before the mounds, they had ceased to be mounds. Stargazer after Stargazer jolted from their *Moratoria*, appearing worse than the night before. Their looks emitted shock at first at seeing them in their suits. Byron waited until their leader rose, the last one, before he took off his helmet. Byron thought that look on his face was almost worth this little risk, this little distraction to their mission.

"Byron!" Black Gomez shouted, his own shock burning away against a swelling indignation. Like the others, his face was caked in dirt, his fringed, fake satin clothing was more torn; yet he still held on to that foppish quality he was famous for in the Stargazer cities.

"Master Gomez," Byron greeted, enjoying the startled expressions on the others' faces, who also recognized him as the greatest evil the society had ever encountered.

The Elder's wide eyes shifted to his companions, who had also taken off their head protection. Byron was slightly disappointed.

"Medea!" Black Gomez shouted. "I cannot believe it!"

The attendants glanced at one another, some probably not knowing that she had also been a traitor.

"No!" he shouted even louder. "Proxos Commodore! You still exist!"

"Greetings, Master," he said. "It has been a long time."

All of the Elder's minions seemed dumbfounded, most knowing that he had allegedly perished when Utopia fell at Byron's hand over a century and a half ago.

"By The MoonQueen," Black Gomez said unevenly, taking a step backward. "This horrible reality only gets worse."

"There is no MoonQueen," Byron stated, and many in the group growled. "And you're not going anywhere."

"How dare you say that?" he snapped. "How dare you insult Our Mistress after what you've done? After what you *all* have done!"

"Where is she?" Byron asked evilly. "I, the villain of villains is standing right here, and you're still not going anywhere."

It was his turn to shake his head, adding a disbelieving, nervous smile to features that usually were frothed in makeup, not residue from the ground.

"She is in New Atlantis, *maldito*," The Elder explained. "She is there waiting for us."

"That's interesting," Byron countered. "Why did she allow the destruction of our capital, eh?"

"You cannot question her motives!" Black Gomez roared. "That is why she allowed it. We were too soft, too impetuous, and you are the focus, the symbol of this, Byron. That is why we must destroy you now."

"You lie, Master Gomez," Medea said. "And you know it."

He didn't miss a beat, like all Elders using his mouth at all times to advance his motives.

"All I know is that three of the greatest threats to Our Mistress stand before us. Three vile beings that will make all of you heroes in the glory of New Atlantis. The choice is obvious, blessed be Our Mistress."

Byron almost wanted to applaud his quick thinking. Yet the Stargazers, hungry and losing their morale with each flutter of the whipping breeze, glanced at each other, as if hoping for one of them to strike first, or at least speak. Byron almost wished they had brought the acid, instead of dealing with this duel of pasts and wits. Almost, he reminded himself a second time.

"Strike, fools!" bellowed Black Gomez, still retreating. "Strike quickly and at once, for they are not here to parley. They are here to do what they did in Xanadu: exterminate our kind for the glory of animals."

That reasoning and the word 'animal' caused their motivation to flow. They all looked at each other again with a sense of urgent fear. Fangs were exposed from tattered lips and cut gums, claws grew from twisted fingers. They advanced towards the three, slowly gaining in confidence.

Two lunged at Byron from the group. He quickly grabbed

each by the head and slammed them together. He instantly felt a certain remorse when their skulls joined and imploded against one another. They were weaker than he thought, perhaps going for a night or so with little to no Juice. The Dark Instinct within them was failing, perhaps less supportive of their present conditions.

Byron allowed the next one to strike him, since he used his fists instead of claw. After the second blow to his face, Byron jammed his hand into the Stargazer's mouth. Cheeks ripping, jaw disjoining, throat giving way along with tongue, Byron used his own claws to rapidly scoop out part of his opponent's brain. By then, the others were in full battle. A certain fighting lust had gripped his being, the same lust he owned when fighting alongside Warm Ones in a canyon years ago, just realizing that Stargazers were created from the corpses of humans and not the frosty womb of Lilith, the same one he had when battling a close friend centuries ago in another Farm. Byron was a warrior and the moment had possessed him. He had no true adversaries anymore, but battle is what he longed for in eternity.

"Byron!" Medea's voice said behind him, beyond the din of breaking of bones. "Look...Black Gomez."

His head turned towards the obvious move of the Elder. Black Gomez had quickly left the melee, grabbing one of the suitcases from the pile. He had taken to flight, ready to leave the gorge.

"Shit!" Byron shouted angrily. "Gomez, don't think you're—"

Something hard slapped his face. He felt his neck reaching maximum tension, could feel certain bones chip. His head coiled back to its former position, while eyes blinked and tried to wrestle with swirling colors.

One of the Stargazers, a smarter one, had grabbed a long boulder and introduced it to his features. If she had been at full strength, the fifty-pound object would have been ten times the force in weight. She was also filled with battle lust, almost glad the blow had not incapacitated him. She lifted the rock again. Byron had things to do.

He was faster, much faster, and even at full strength she would never have beaten Byron Solsbury. His fist struck the stone, shattered it, and continued towards her face. She catapulted backwards and smacked into the high walls of the gorge. Byron doubted if she was finished, but he had things to do.

And that was to stop Black Gomez from reaching New Atlantis.

3

In the beginning...
Remember...
Data: AD 2014
...he had been powerful, he had been respected. He was a war leader, a bright thinker who fully understood the implications of the wily matrimony of technology and warfare. It was a great empire, respected by few, feared by all, although every other kingdom owed it so much.

Data: United States of America. North America. Washington DC

He was a member of an elite circle of warlords that stood separate yet below the leader of this kingdom. He had access to every secret inside a building with eight sides, amazed technicians and politicians with his mind, and was always at the forefront of tuning their vast webwork of computer systems that lubricated their weapon facilities. It had almost been a juxtaposition of worlds that made him who he was. Since his male creator had always been a warrior and so had many of his family, that was the path chosen for him. Since his female parent had come from a family of intellectuals, he used a keen mind to aid in this journey. He had never been strong, barely being able to join the army's physical standards but making up for it with his thought process. It was a duality in him, and it worked oddly in a section of the kingdom in which the war leaders weren't known for their sharpness, only their passion for carnage and the coolness on how to do it. Yet his skill had aided his country in their last war when technology was fully used instead of hand-to-hand combat.

Data: Eugene Balkros, Four Star General, prime consult-

ant to Norad and The NSA. Hero of the Gulf Wars.

He was so respected and so admired in his duality. People bowed their heads to him, people asked him for advice. The leader of the kingdom often called him and so did many others from different departments. He understood nuclear fission as well as he understood complex computer idioms. What he lacked in body he made up in mind. The duality. He was Balkros, respected and admired.

Except when he returned to his abode. There she was, waiting for him, so fat and so clammy. Never happy. She always seemed too angry and large. He wanted to make her happy, part of his success, but his uniform and accomplishment made little sense to this person. Only smoking and card-playing seemed something she fully understood. Every time he walked into their dwelling, his mate seemed to always be waiting for him.

Data: Dorothy Ferdig Balkros. Married in AD 2006.

"Eugene!" she always shouted at first. "Where have you been?"

He would place the hat under his arm and run thin fingers through thick hair. He had meetings. The security of the nation was important. One never knew when an adversary might unravel the webs of information that controlled their armies, their weapons.

"I don't care," she would usually say. On this particular evening she added. "I've been having neck spasms all day. Couldn't get anything done."

She was always sick. She smoked and drank too much. She rarely left the house. He had always tried hard to make her happy.

Data: Hypochondriac.

He was sorry. He was always so sorry when it came to her, it seemed.

"That's great," the mate spat. "Anyway, Gina hasn't taken a bath yet. Her teacher says she might be dyslexic. Don't have time to go to her school and have her take tests. I'm not having the maid do it, either. Are you going to give her a bath? Tonight's *Shore to Shore* has a guest who is convinced the true apocalypse will a zombie one, created by a virus, and I want to listen to it at eight. Where have you been?"

He was always sorry. He left his mate and walked up the stairs into a room they used for relaxation. His offspring was sitting in front of the television, her homework strewn before it. She was thin and almost sickly like him, but possessed a similar inner stamina. She was so beautiful and she wasn't his mate.

Data: Gina Balkros. Born June 18, 2007.

"Hey Daddy," the little girl said. "What are you doing?"

He smiled and felt so glad to see her, felt like some part of his home could be perfect like the life outside. The duality. He was respected.

"Just got home from work, doll," he said. "Your mommy said you haven't taken a bath yet."

Her small face crinkled for a moment. "No, but I did my school work."

"You mean your homework?"

"It's school work, Daddy."

He tilted his head. "That's what they call it these days, uh? Anyway, why don't we go take a bath. Or can you take one by yourself now?"

"No!" she giggled, immediately pulling off her clothes. His mate would scream at them if they were left there. He picked the pink clothes from the carpet and tossed them in a basket while following her down the hallway. She made him so happy, this little creature. She made it worth returning to his abode. He wanted to see her grow and enjoy her existence as he had.

Yet, as Balkros watched her nude body enter the bathroom and turn on the water, he felt a certain dread he couldn't understand, a dread that tightened his living chest.

He was respected, except for here. She made him so happy.

And his offspring made him excited in a way that shouldn't have been.

Data: In the beginning. The beginning of the end.

4

"No!" Proxos shouted, finishing off his adversary by ripping both arms off. "He's escaping. He's going towards The Egg."

Medea had just used fangs to shred a Stargazer's face, who had grappled her to the ground. She moved her head down and up upon the creature until most of his midsection was exposed. The Stargazer rolled over and began thrashing in pain and defeat. Medea stood up, tossed away some of her adversary's intestines to the side and quickly looked around. They had easily won, and she had successfully warned Byron. She had done that once in the battle of the canyon, although her pause had caused other Stargazer soldiers, Ravens, to kidnap and take her to be fatally wounded by The MoonQueen.

"Byron will get to him," she said, wiping innards from her chest. "But we must follow him."

"No," Proxos repeated, jumping to her side. "You don't understand. If they get there...it will be too late."

She eyed him seriously.

"Proxos, we realize that you might have been hiding something recently, but now is not the time."

He placed each hand at the side of his head. "When is the time, Medea? He mustn't get there."

She allowed gravity to dissolve and headed for the direction of the desert, saying, "Then let's stop him first."

"Stop!" Proxos shouted. "You mustn't."

Medea had no time for his eccentricity. He wasn't keeping it simple, and that was not a good sign. Simple meant following Byron, aiding him before the despicable Elder reached New Atlantis. Keep it simple.

5

Black Gomez was already two hundred feet away and without his suitcase when Byron appeared into the open desert. New Atlantis beckoned him. He was very fast, Byron thought with surprise, understanding that he was probably one of the older Stargazers. As one carved through time, one's powers many times increased as the God-Soul deepened into that respective sliver of material reality. Except for Byron, who had been given a generous dose by Lilith.

The caustic wind, tinged with radioactive heat and scalding sand pebbles, made vision hard, flight less than perfect and as close to the ground as they could. After many minutes, Byron's sight only focused on one thing, and it wasn't his prey.

New Atlantis swelled quickly before him. Less than five miles away, he could see that the dome was many times larger than any dome in Xanadu. It was at least a thousand feet in altitude. The closer Byron got, the more he was amazed at seeing no blemishes on the perfectly smooth surface. Black Gomez was also getting closer. He hadn't gained very much. The Elder glanced back at him, and Byron did the same to his companions, which were a good four hundred feet away from him. The food, their helmets, the memory of the cavern were all left behind. It was only the battering wind, his prey, and the place they called The Egg. And *Luna*, once a symbol of their leader, their status, stared at them in its always splotchy form behind gurgling clouds.

The wind shifted, no, almost twisted before him. Tufts of smashing air made their path into a zigzag. Byron strained harder, knowing that the chaotic gusts could quickly alter his path to a dangerous conclusion. Unlike the other desert in another valley where Lilith had deposited him, this land was hard and featureless by a more open area that had allowed the climate to compact it with its anger.

It was suddenly less than a mile, and Byron still hadn't closed in enough with Black Gomez. Flying was getting harder by the second. Byron screamed at him, trying to get his attention, knowing that their mission to save Medea would be in immediate peril if Gomez arrived to the last remaining Stargazer city. In between flying and screaming, Byron cursed himself for not handling the Elder first, or at least not following Proxos' plan with the damn acid.

Black Gomez glanced back at second time or perhaps third time. He was nearly upon the city. This time he allowed a nasty smile. A gloating smile.

The shifting wind shifted yet one more time. He wobbled dangerously, pushing against the wrong swirling tide. The herd of seconds taken to gloat had been a mistake often done by opponents with the advantage. His body plunged downward and kissed the ground. Dust rose from the impact and his body tumbled from the cloud. Byron used all his will to increase speed a little more. He closed in quickly, the lust returning, urging him to forget the structure.

The Elder rose to his feet after his rolling ended. He appeared too stunned to regain flight, perhaps too afraid. He started running. He glanced back a few times, not seeing Byron come over his right shoulder.

He screamed in joy as his body slapped the Elder's. Byron's arms wrapped his waist to make sure there would be no further escape. They collapsed on the ground and skidded a few more feet, bouncing against the metallic base of New Atlantis.

"Byron!" he shouted a second time as they ricocheted backward, but now his fangs were trying to find the source of his discomfort. Byron wouldn't allow his adversary's body to pivot. He pinned him down on the ground and squeezed hard. Black Gomez kept repeating his name. The Elder's strength impressed him.

Byron twisted a few times. He released him briefly to give him the illusion of a chance. Black Gomez' body folded and his head recoiled towards him. Yet his fangs only met Byron's fist. Then they met the other one. Again, The Elder shouted but this time didn't say his name. He paused briefly, noticing that the Elder's fangs were embedded in his left knuckles. He had to laugh once, striking him again. Black Gomez was introduced a second time to the base of the massive dome with a hollow ring. Even if he hadn't been weakened, Byron was sure the many decades without any fighting experience wouldn't make up for his craving for survival or whatever the Dark Instinct gave him.

"Black Gomez," Byron said loudly, kneeling over him, pinning him down one last time. "Remember how you watched me in agony while I was imprisoned in Xanadu? Please recall the delight you experienced, and then know I'm feeling about ten times as much right about now."

Any haughty air within the Elder was gone. He was finally and truly afraid. His claws swiped at Byron's face. He slapped them away and showed him how to claw. The skin on his face was instantly streaked, opened in deep gashes.

"Please!" he begged. "For Our Mistress, Byron. Don't do..."

He screamed while more cuts appeared now on his chest. You're enjoying this too much, Byron warned himself. Get rid of him quickly, take him back before you are seen. He heard Medea shouting at him from the distance.

Byron also heard something moving above him. It was probably the gales caressing the city or a chuckle of thunder from the sky. Why was Medea screaming louder?

Grabbing Black Gomez by the lapels, he pulled him upward, at the same time lifting his other hand. Two fingers sprouted from his hand ready to jam into his opponent's eye sockets. If it didn't destroy him, it would at least blind him into submission. The noise, like a fluttering, grew heavier. Proxos was now shouting as well.

Look up, one of them said. His arm moved to finish the Elder. For a brief instant, Byron did glance upward. He saw flashes of sharp, dangerous silver and a dark silhouette in the middle. The silhouette broke away, revealing various colors, but most of all a mighty physique advancing towards him.

Then something struck him with a force that made the strike of the Stargazer with the stone seem like a pat.

Then Byron saw little else.

6

Medea stopped in midair at the strange sights coming out of New Atlantis. Armored, humanoid creatures poured out from a sliding door. Medea had to continue when an even stranger sight attacked Byron and Black Gomez.

"No!" she screamed angrily at these creatures. "Don't touch him, you bastards!"

Before regaining flight movement, she felt arms around her waist. She was pulled down with a surprising and efficient force. When she crashed into the ground with a jolt that imploded the ground, Medea was even more surprised to see that it was Proxos.

"What are you doing?" She tried prying his arms off. Through the dust and fluttering debris, she could see the armored creatures surrounding Byron and his former prey. "Let me go, fool! They—"

"We can't!" Proxos tightened his grip. "You must listen to me first. We cannot go in, not like this, Medea."

"Let me go!" Medea felt she would have to strike her companion now. She cocked her elbow and prepared to smash it into Proxos' face. She hoped he would survive. "I said, Proxos, let me—"

Her body was enveloped by a cold fire. A cold fire that racked her spine and drained her energy. The Killer of Giants! Not now! she thought, even feeling her elbow go limp as if it had lost bone and cartilage. Not here! Her struggling stopped, but Proxos kept pushing her into the ground, as if he thought it might be a trick. He kept talking with urgency.

"Listen to me, Medea. New Atlantis isn't what it seems."

They were taking them into the city he spoke of at that moment.

"Let me go," she squeaked, feeling the effects of the Killer of Giants bang against her like icy waves. "Byron. No...Byron..."

"It's not a city!" the ex-Elder was screaming madly. "It

never was, Medea."

"Byron," she said, trying to shake her head.

We'll never be apart.

"New Atlantis is not a city," Proxos said with desperation. "New Atlantis is really a prison!"

Medea used all her remaining energy and turned her head to stare into him. Another wave struck her. Accompanied by the shock of his revelation, like Byron, she also saw little else for a while.

Chapter 4

He sat in his chambers, located at the apex of The Egg. There were always mirrors in this city, in all angles and most corners, in every hallway and chamber, but here they were draped in different shades of green and orange, colors his clan, the *Tylweth Teg*, had proudly worn as they played in the dominions of The Unimaginable. Relics of his times and many times half-neatly littered the place, an emporium of incredible items, which he cared little of these nights. The sight of Roland's sword or Cu Chulain's spear, the jewels of his beloved Queen Mab or the walnut-sized gems that were nothing more than the tears of Marduk, the verdant, combed tresses of The Green Lady of *Caerphilly,* or the scales of the Lindberg Wyrm gave him little pleasure as they once had, when he was collector from his world. So many objects, from scrolls to paintings to trapped emotions in quartz vials did nothing for him. The marred view of Luna, which he had respected dearly before becoming a Stargazer, was of little import to him. Even his gilded harp—played at some point every night and which could alter the elements as well as the moods of all within these walls except for The Centurion—had been left untouched for nights. All he cared for was his visions, his dreams, which came stronger and stronger every year, as if all the power of The Unimaginable was siphoned into him now that he was probably the last of the true beings of wonder. But he needed focus like all in The Egg needed focus, distractions, as sense of direction. His focus was a small Warm One pup, gently held between his hands. The creature had never been born from another Warm One, since all the food here was created in their laboratories using genetics or cloning. That way they could keep stock of inventory, even though they always had more than a surplus.

Marcion didn't know why he had taken one of the pups from the incubators. The thing hadn't been altered like most before creation, lobotomized and implanted with circuits, numbered for its duties, since it was meant to be a Veal. It smiled and cooed and drooled all over his lap. Marcion smiled back and raised it higher. Its smile grew, showing a gumless mouth with a nice pink tongue. He needed focus or his mind might wander especially now with what was occurring. The ripples of time and space were strong, as strong as they had been when The Queen of Darkness had caused the fire from the sky to transform the world into her playground.

His mind hadn't wandered enough to know that one of the Kappa's would enter his chamber in ten seconds. It wouldn't be Poppykettle, since what was occurring had risen in importance. It would be The Pharisee, Feltch himself. He wouldn't knock or ask for entrance since there was no privacy here.

Ten seconds. Marcion sat the pup on his left knee and bounced it. The thing giggled without constraint. Feltch lumbered into the room, larger than any Kappa—that's why he was their representative.

"Goddamn, Mac," he said immediately, part of his grotesque face coming out from the hood. "Fuck are you doing? We got two of 'em. Is one of 'em this knight?"

If a knight should come, a champion of eternity, errant on a darkening quest, knocking on your gates, then you should let him in. And if he bests The Warden and drinks in generations with The Centurion, then he must be stripped of his sword, his shield, and armor, and brought naked like a newborn into the gray dusk, into the awakening of our Prince.

The Good Neighbor turned in his chair towards The Kappa. He still looked at the pup, or baby as it was called a long time ago, when his kind might steal the fair-headed ones and breed with them in order to gain bridge-builders into the material world.

"I do not know that yet," he said, his voice stopping the large figure's almost threatening advancing. "After all, prophecies are the locks gods put on the doorways of future's perception."

"That speech really helps matters, Mac," Feltch said, pointing at him with a slopping cigar. "And speeches ain't gonna get us to where we need to be."

Marcion smiled idly at the baby. "Only the prophecy will, Feltch. That is all."

"Look, fairy-boy." Feltch's oval eyes glowed in a putrid tangerine. His eroded face appeared even more sinister than ever. "I'm growing fucking tired of your murky shit. *Is one of them the knight*? What shall we do?"

Marcion briefly closed his eyes. He felt the eyes of the population, some enjoying this little play, others as worried as Feltch. He opened them and leaned over to kiss the Warm One.

"There is one way to know," he told Feltch. "You know how Quidam, The Warden, will probably act. What happens to all Stargazers that enter our abode. Then we shall know. If you or some of the others are weary of the pace of my clairvoyance, then perhaps we can at least stall him until we find out more about The Queen of Darkness, Xanadu, and other unanswered issues we have at the moment."

Feltch grinned, the light in his eyes grew like two hellish beacons. Marcion had to shield the baby from their force.

"I follow your meaning," The Kappa said. "I fucking follow you, man. Let's get answers, let's keep the horizon open, you know. You're slick, even with your sissy Irish accent and all. Shall we call a council and meet the two jerkoffs?"

Marcion' lips curled slightly. He held the Warm One to his chest.

"What's that you got there? A light supper or something? A new pet? Quidam will shit himself, man. He doesn't ever want to see us doing anything but eat the animals."

"That is of no concern to him or you," Marcion said, staring coldly at the Kappa. "Or anyone else at the moment. Please call the Forgotten to meet."

The slouched being jumped up and down before making its way out the chambers. "You're a blasphemous son of a bitch, Marc. That's why I've always liked you."

As soon as he had departed, cackling down the mirrored hallway, Marcion brought the small creature up before his face. It was breathing hard, face twisting slightly. It was probably hungry.

"Do not mind him," Marcion said softly. "He is a bore like the rest." The population gasped but he didn't care. "Now you, little thing, are more interesting. You are something that Marcion sometimes envies, you have something that part of me craves."

He opened his mouth to show him the twin symbols of his curse. The baby didn't seem to care. He brought the flaying body towards those symbols.

"Let us foil them both," Marcion whispered, before he felt soft skin pressing against his lips. "Let us foil them all."

2

In the beginning...

She splashed so happily in the bathtub. Her body was pale and soft and unblemished. He was sweating hard after a while. "What's wrong, Daddy?" she asked him while filling a red bucket with bath water. He told her that he was just feeling a little hot, a little tired. He walked out of the bathroom, only to be met by his mate in the hallway. "Don't leave her alone, Eugene!" she exclaimed. "She's only six, for Christsakes. Go back in!"

He obeyed the female. But he commanded so much respect with everyone else. His face was often on television, in magazines. He had defended his kingdom, aided its technology. But now he was sweating in a place where he didn't have respect, didn't have power. Part of him liked it, though, he had to admit hours later, laying quietly and unable to rest in his bed. His mate was snoring and farting as usual, taking up most of the bed. He understood why he liked it because shame wasn't something common to him, knew deep down inside that the power he had was perhaps too much even though it could never be enough. He liked the shame. It was a balance, another part of the duality. He had tried being shamed with whores in hotel rooms in faraway cities but never had been able to go through with it. Here, in his home, there was a shame, there was something that made him for once feel so small. His mate was only half of it...

He left his bed and walked down the hall. He was sweating again. He wanted the shame, the smallness it brought with it. He opened his offspring's bedroom door. She slept soundly, peacefully like no adult could understand anymore. She was so beautiful, gave him so much pride, joy.

No, this is a place of shame, he thought, of smallness. This is a place where my flesh, my mortality is obvious, is naked!

She was so beautiful, gave him so much pride. Made him so hard with confidence.

No, not here.

And then Eugene Balkros understood that the shame was also guilt about his power, necessary in the balance of his persona, and the small girl that slept in his house, that he loved so much, was bringing him a chaste rage because she was pure and not part of the shame. She was goodness and that existed on the other side of the duality. Shame and power. That was the only way, and the only way was the balance. His rage blurred it, focused on his offspring. He only wanted more shame in this structure.

The rage kept growing as he watched her. The sweat kept dripping. The erection kept growing and dripping.

Data: Self-deprecating guilt people of power feel, either business men who turn to homosexual prostitutes or upstanding citizens who enjoy sadomasochism.

An electronic laughter filled Xanadu many, many years later, so loud the duality of that broken city, Warm One and Stargazer, could hear it loudly all night long.

3

Feed me!

"Medea!" Byron gasped, sitting up quickly. The room spun a few times, coagulating into a small bare room with mirrors lining the walls.

He had felt her, felt her weakness, her succumbing. He had felt her despair at something and more. She had seen something amazing, something in the desert that shocked her. What was it?

He placed a hand over his forehead. What was that? He asked himself. Whatever had struck him had slightly fractured his skull. That still wasn't enough to knock him out, since a Stargazer rarely was blanketed by unconsciousness unless it was *Moratoria*. But then again, Stargazers were vulnerable to odd things when submerged in stress or undernourished. Now that he thought about it, they had eaten sparsely in their trek to New Atlantis. Their melee with Black Gomez and his lackeys, the mad flight across the desert had probably sapped more energy than he had realized. The powerful blow had been enough to shut down his being, cause the Dark Instinct to retreat for a while in the shell that was his body and mind. Now it was back, talking to him as it always did, adopting part of his personality for no other reason than to mock him, show Byron who was in charge in creation.

Feed me, you pathetic, orphaned bastard! Hunt, destroy, consume...that's all you're good at.

"Shut-up," Byron said softly. Where was he? He had felt strong arms grab him, drag him away. He was indoors, in a chamber. He had to be in...

No, feed me, you puppet!

"No yourself," Byron said with gritted teeth, but suddenly he smelled something very sharp, very noticeable to someone in his state.

Yes, bastard. Turn around.

He pivoted in place. A nude Warm One, unclothed and

holding a large knife, stood a few paces away in front of a basin on a pedestal. It didn't move at all, not even blink at Byron's swift movement. Eyes stared blankly past him. Byron knew it was real by its lovely fragrance, the craving for it he had, and of course the urging of the God-Soul.

Feed me!

Byron stood up, knowing that he had no choice, knowing that he had to assault this animal who he was once, take away its Juice in order to appease the Dark Instinct and gain its powers again. He had to exist for a while and the only way was feeding on those who he partly sought vengeance, justice for.

Hunt, destroy, wipe it all out!

Before he could pounce on the Warm One, it held out the knife. Byron wasn't too concerned about his safety from the puny weapon. He was only concerned about his hunger. He opened his mouth, showing the Warm One his fangs and hissed at it. It still looked beyond him.

The Warm One didn't attack him. The knife plunged right into the side of his throat. A blank faced briefly showed pain, yet his body struggled only to lean over the basin. By the time the last twitches had ended, Byron couldn't deny the invitation of the sweet nectar rising almost to the rim, already over its head.

He fed without concern about cleanliness or tact. When done, he crouched with relief against the pedestal, face matted in Juice, body filled with the cold fireworks of the God-Soul's endowment. His mind settling now, Byron allowed surprise to enter him, make him wonder why the Warm One had simply given its existence to him. That could have never happened in Xanadu. He wasn't in Xanadu, though.

Byron growled slightly. He had reached his goal, but Medea wasn't here. She was in pain somewhere else. He needed her more than anything, for she had given meaning to him, to what he was. She had made him understand goodness, the spark of goodness that was in his dead human soul, murdered by Lilith in the city of Utopia. She was the reason he cared to exist as a monster. Medea made him crave for the thing called hope.

Yet he knew that he was in New Atlantis. She was in pain and he needed to find the cure that Balkros claimed was here. Fifteen nights and he was finally in New Atlantis. Perhaps he could move quicker without his friends, perhaps they were here somewhere at the moment. And where was Black Gomez? Only one way to know, he told himself, standing up straight. He walked to the door. If it was closed, he would smash it down. Why not? Better be direct.

The door opened before he could touch it and the same person who had struck him stood there, accompanied by the metallic creatures Byron now realized were Warm Ones. Altered Warm Ones. Yes, he was definitely in New Atlantis, the last remaining Stargazer city.

4

Medea shifted realizing she was still in Proxos' grasp. He was flying again. She opened her eyes and that tool almost all of her energy. The desert ground rushed below her in blurry yellow, the mountains loomed once again, their tops scratching the swirling, low sky.

A groggy mind tried to inventory what had happened and why they were edging away from their goal. She recalled the battle with Black Gomez, chasing him, Byron ambushing the haughty Elder. Then...a door opened in the single dome that was New Atlantis. Warm Ones exited, their scent obvious in the wind that slammed and bounced against the dome. But these were armored and silver—like soldiers—which Medea had never seen, used to scantily clad, sickly Warm Ones from the Farms of Xanadu. There was flesh here and there, but mostly metal—steel sown into their bodies, their faces, tubes and sparks here and there between seas of pink flesh. Most of them owned no eyes, regarding them in the distance through shimmering glasses or steely bulbs that moved independently from each socket.

What must have been their leader walked out afterwards. He wasn't a Warm One, though. He was a very large Stargazer. He had struck Byron with a speed and force she had never seen. He stood rigidly before the still sprawled and mewling form of

Black Gomez; the Warm One soldiers walked around him to pick-up the two forms on the ground. The Stargazer was nude except for a smattering of rags over his waist, which served for nothing except to fasten a massive, curving sword. The rest of the robust body was covered in every inch—even over the stolid face, even over the bald head except for a pony tail on the top—by tattoos, a topography of intricately etched purple, dark lavender, reds and green patterns. He was like a piece of art, from the muscles to the drawings. A savage piece of art. His face held little to no expression. Medea then recalled his eyes that weren't eyes. They were like black skies, empty, except for a twin dim star in the center.

Byron! They took him inside! She had tried to intervene but a dissolving strength and Proxos had stopped her.

"Proxos!" she spat. "Proxos! You said a prison!"

"Yes," he agreed calmly, continuing his course. "It is a prison."

"What are you talking about?" Medea felt that the Killer of Giants had lessened, perhaps because she had folded within herself, reached darkness. Balkros had told them that dormancy, rest was the only way to temporarily halt the rotting effects of this malady. She still felt very weak. "Proxos, are you listening to me? How can it be a prison? It's a city!"

The ex-Elder sighed and slowly halted. He lowered Medea to the ground, gently setting her in sitting position. He squatted before her with a solemn expression. She didn't care about his worries, only knowing he had a lot of explaining. Byron was in there, captured by the odd Stargazer and his warriors.

"No, Medea," he said. "As I've said before, Lilith had many plans during, before, and after the Holocaust. And these plans were secrets only The Elders were privy to."

"I was an Elder once," she countered, for the first time wondering if Byron had placed too much trust in his 'friend'. "I didn't know about this."

Proxos half-smiled. "But you were not one of The Elders before The Holocaust. I'm sure The Queen of Darkness decided that any new ones probably shouldn't know all the weighty matters of her conquest."

Medea scuttled backward a foot or so, more to show her

mistrust with body language. "That is fine, Proxos, but what are you talking about? Why build a prison when she had allegedly wiped out any enemies, any threats? Why have one when she could crush any surviving threats?"

He briefly looked over his shoulder towards New Atlantis.

"She never destroyed Byron, did she?"

"Proxos!" she snapped, that mentioning causing a pain that was oddly physical and emotional. "Are we going to go in circles until *Sol* rises over the east? Why is New Atlantis a prison?"

"Because," he said, paused while touching his chin with a finger. "Because Lilith wanted an empire with Stargazers that were formerly Warm Ones. She had toyed with humanity long enough to know they would make a good, devoted society."

"What other kind of Stargazer would there be?" she asked, suddenly understanding how hard it must be for him to speak of the things of the past, the sins of his once leader.

Proxos stood up and crossed his arms.

"You must understand that the God-Soul is only part of Lilith, of what she is. She imparted this....malediction upon the dying forms of humanity before they could return to The Light, creating something new, wrong, but sharing in her godliness. That is what Stargazers, vampires, *the estrie*, *the glaistig*, the undead or whatever you would like to call them are. We have the Dark Instinct, the force in the universe that only wishes to devour as its role in the universal balance."

"I understand, Proxos. Are we still going in circles?"

"And I understand why Byron admires you." He smiled at her. "Directness and honesty are qualities that haven't existed in this world for a long time."

"Proxos," she warned, smiling herself.

"Fine, Medea. Then you must understand that perhaps The MoonQueen didn't just have to impart it to human beings, that The Dark Instinct, her essence, could also touch other creatures that thrived in the shadows of humanity, that perhaps existed since the beginning of time."

"No," she whispered, looking around him towards New Atlantis.

"Yes." He nodded. "Since being thrown out of the paradise of The Mad God, she has enslaved, seduced, or vanquished other beings in other places, sometimes very faraway places, Medea." His face twisted with guilty pain. "Believe me. Destroying human civilization wasn't her first coupe since the dawn of creation, Medea. Many of these beings, these Giants, served her, many didn't. But those who were around when she created the members of The Rose and began the end of her vengeance against The Mad God's proudest creation had to be dealt with. And those were placed in New Atlantis."

"Amazing," she said, still fixed on the place where Byron was currently inside.

"You'll never cease to be amazed."

"And she decided not to destroy them, only allow the human Stargazers to exist in her realm?"

Proxos shrugged. "Perhaps she couldn't. There are laws, agreements that are beyond our concept. Perhaps she didn't want to. You know very well that The MoonQueen's whims have always been her own. After all, you rule existence, you mock the universe so easily, why not have a museum where you can place your trophies, a place where unruly Stargazers and other creatures can be kept until you feel a need to act, if you ever do."

Medea couldn't argue with this speech. Why The Queen of Darkness did anything beyond her wrath was unattainable. But what kind of creatures that were never Warm Ones existed behind those smooth, bare walls?

"What about that Stargazer that struck Byron? What was he?"

The ex-Elder thought for a moment. "He was a Warm One, I believe. Not exactly a Warm One since you must understand that evolution doesn't exactly go forward. It is cyclical, Medea. Humans were once very different, closer to The Mad God's dream. His name is Quidam, although he was once called Nimrod. He was punished by The Mad God before even I existed for attempting to unite the world under his powerful heels, then reach him with a mighty edifice that reflected the might of his empire. Like Lilith, he was cast out from any paradise. She found him and granted him a new existence, a new purpose. They say that every night Quidam tears his tongue out, for speech is something he is afraid of, for some reason."

"Why is he trapped there?"

"I don't know if he's really trapped. I think he watches those in there. A chaperone, you could say. Between him and The Centurion they make The Egg operable in their own ways."

Medea saw the look of fear that he'd shown a night before in the cavern. "The Centurion? Who is he?"

The look deepened.

"That is why I stopped you. That is why I thought that maybe we should think twice before entering. That is why it was so hard to tell you two."

Medea finally stood up. Part of her suit was shredded but it didn't matter. She wanted answers and wanted to procure Byron. Mythical monsters and gods didn't worry her. Only Byron. Only the fact they had a quest.

"You're going in circles again, Proxos. Who is this Centurion?"

Her friend looked towards New Atlantis. "It's been a long time since I met him. He almost destroyed me when he was a Warm One. He was amazing in any form..." His eyes narrowed, while he unconsciously rubbed his right arm. "Now that I think about it, I wonder if he was there that last night in Fran—"

"Proxos!" she snapped.

He shut his eyes briefly at her warning tone and said with force, "He is the one who made it possible not to use the cavern." Proxos pointed towards the mountains. "He is a being that matches, perhaps surpasses Lilith's power. At the same time, he is prostrate to her and I believe truly rules the prison called New Atlantis."

"More powerful than Lilith?" Medea was wondering if perhaps longevity in existence made one delirious, like Balkros and The MoonQueen herself. "I'm starting to wonder, Proxos. There is a Giant, a god in there and you didn't tell us about it."

He lowered his head. "Like I said, what could I do? I have been taught through centuries to keep Lilith's secrets just that. I didn't know how to tell you and wondered if I could convince you not to go in, make you understand the sealed danger that place has always been. I'm sorry, Medea, because by your condition, I see it could mean your existence. Furthermore, I knew that I could never convince Byron."

"I see," she said plainly. "You're finally making sense. But we must find a way to go in. If you don't care to see this Centurion, fine. I won't let Byron fight this alone, even if as you say we can never leave."

"It is not allowed," Proxos said. "The Centurion and Quidam will not allow it, will always follow Her eternal request. None has ever left, unless it was with Lilith's blessing. That blessing isn't going to arrive any time soon."

"So what are you going to do?" she asked, turning for New Atlantis. She was still very weak, starting to feel hunger, but what could she do? He was in there. They were apart.

"I..." Proxos started. "I...what is that?"

He pointed towards the south. Medea, again showing an amazing sight, saw at first black splotches in the dirty horizon. They grew towards them at a healthy speed.

"They're not coming from New Atlantis," Medea said. "But they're coming towards us..."

Proxos' eyes widened. "By...The Moo...I mean...look!"

Medea had already captured the shape of the objects. She had also captured the flags at the top of each of them, which unnaturally ferried over the hard ground on shiny blades that split it open. The flags were black and showed the visage of rose with two streaks of red slashing it. When Proxos caught the same view he gasped.

"I don't believe my dead eyes!" the ancient Stargazer exclaimed. "They're...they're blasted ships."

"Ships?" Medea mused, only knowing of ships and the ocean from archives watched as an Elder in Xanadu.

"Yes, ships. Ships in the desert!"

The objects, more than a dozen, kept getting closer to them.

5

It was the same creature who had struck him outside. Now he wasn't a fiery blur, but a solid, six foot seven figure in front of him. Byron couldn't help but evaporate any smugness or anger at the astonishment of this completely tattooed, scantily-clad Stargazer. In turn, his attacker showed no expression except for an empty stare. The Stargazer didn't wait for Byron's reaction, taking a step backward. A Warm One broke from his entourage, this one not sown with armor and circuits. It owned the same look of naught as had the one who sacrificed himself to Byron a minute ago. This one handed him clean, white robes and a damp towel to wipe himself from the juice staining his body and the room. Byron took them, now really knowing what to do.

"Your hospitality is almost relieving," he told the Stargazer, briefly pointing at the crack on his forehead that was already healing because of the satiety of The Dark Instinct. "But you can't be surprised I have a few urgent questions."

His 'host' didn't move, obviously waiting for Byron to dress himself. Byron thought about playing it difficult, one of his many gifts, but knew that time was no longer something he could toy with. He needed answers or at least to know why he was here.

"Let me guess," he said, scanning the flock of guards in the hallway, all waiting for either him or action from the Stargazer. "I have to get dressed and then follow you."

The Stargazer simply nodded once. It seemed he wasn't going to speak to him.

"Fine," Byron said, ripping off his suit. "But I'm warning you, whoever you are. That was the last time you'll lay a hand on me like that."

He thought the tattooed Stargazer's lips twisted slightly, struggling into a potentially droll smile. But the expression remained the same. The eyes of blackness regarded him patiently. Byron couldn't toy with time, but the citizens of this city could. They could toy with time and perhaps they would try to toy with him. They didn't know who they were dealing with.

Byron slammed the door shut for no real reason and began dressing.

6

The first thing he noticed being led through corridors and hissing doors were the cameras and mirrors. Cameras in some places. Mirrors everywhere. If a section didn't have mirrors, it was polished, buffed to show some sort of reflection. Byron saw his reflection several times. Sometimes it was precise, sometimes warped or smudges, sometimes his reflection was just a smattering of jiggling colors. But there was always a reflection. For some reason it bothered him. It didn't bother his guide, the mute Stargazer with the tattoos who walked silently, carefully. It didn't matter to the Warm Ones, who probably cared little about reflections since their minds were obliterated by science and surgery, forever serving the residents of New Atlantis. He tried his best to keep a calm attitude, trying not to think about time and urgency. The unnerving sensation savored a night ago when first seeing The Egg had returned. He lit a cigarette from a pack kept from his prior clothing. He only had two left.

Byron asked a few times about their destination, but the Stargazer didn't even acknowledge he was being spoken to at any point. There were simply more hallways, electrical doors, moving cameras that followed their moves, and mirrors. Mirrors everywhere and their reflections. After he'd asked him the fourth time, large, double doors (mirrored) opened to reveal a large chamber. When they entered, Byron thought he'd at least have some more answers, not questions. He tried hard to fasten his fallen jaw to his skull. It wasn't because of the finely crafted chamber of bright metal and delicate yet rising stands, but because of those who awaited him. Byron sensed that they were Stargazers, but they weren't. They were different Stargazers.

He was in New Atlantis.

To his right sat a group huddled closely to one another.

They all wore hooded robes of dirty brown, hiding bulging forms distant to anything common. Like worn sandy stone, their exaggerated features seemed chiseled into simian contours except for their eyes, oval and sinister with the common Stargazer shifting hues. Many grinned at him, revealing large pearly teeth. None seemed to possess fangs, yet Byron knew they were Stargazers because he couldn't smell any real mortality in them. One of them took off her hood—opening the robe enough to show more than a pair of breasts—and shouted obscenities at him, many which he couldn't understand. The others gurgled or giggled madly, a few jumping up and down in place. The rude one showed a skull that was undulating in the middle, taking the shape of a bowl where viscous purple liquid rested. The liquid seemed to throb slightly. Their brains, Byron wondered with a stiffening of all his senses. He'd never seen anything like this. Proxos, one time when they were both Heretics wandering the wilderness, told him that most of the creatures of wonder had gone away or perished because of Lilith. What was this?

Most of the creatures of wonder…

To the far left was another group that was almost as bewildering. At first glance, they appeared as normal Stargazers devoid of shirts or upper garments. Yet their skin was slightly purple, though, not the bloodless white of Byron's kind. Many of them had a wrapping design at the base of their necks, right above the collarbones. It wasn't a design but more like a fleshy stitching. Most of them owned long manes and protruding jaws. Their pupils, although black like any Stargazer, were larger, almost splotchy, like a dropped tear of ink. They beheld him without any expression of interest.

To the near left of him of the sectioned auditoriums, from what Bryon's stunned could absorb, was populated with a group that did not seem homogeneous, a stew of creatures in all sizes, shapes, and styles of clothing. Many were barely humanoid, possessing animalistic features with machinery implanted in them. Others were more like slivers of the elements or energy with male or female characteristics, while some bragged shapes that changed. What are they? he thought, reeling, sensing again that these beings had been usurped by The Dark Instinct—life, goodness twisted inside out in order to serve blind destruction. Had they ever been Warm Ones? Had the ones in the other two sections?

Byron sucked a strong drag to hide his confusion. He then opened his mouth to usher some sort of question, just as his guide walked to the center where a table risen on a dais waited for him along with three figures. Byron never asked anything, wild attention landing on the table. They must be The Pharisees, he thought, the rulers of this city. One was a robed figure, one was one of the maimed ones, but the one in the center was very different that anyone in this place of about ten dozen creatures. Byron's confusion lapsed slightly at seeing such a handsome being, stoically regarding him with an air of fondness. Byron could tell he was almost as tall as the tattooed one. His body was thinner to the point of gauntness. His narrow face was beautiful to the point of femininity. Light gold hair leaked over his shoulders, over a long, satin robe of hunter green color. Very pointed ears broke the river of yellow. Byron couldn't help be stricken by him, for The Pharisee reeked of a certain confidence that tumbled into arrogance, balanced by intelligent eyes with a glint of lost melancholy.

Byron opened his mouth again, dropping the cigarette, at this being different that the others. The being spoke immediately, as if knowing his dangling question.

"My name is Marcion," he said with an elegant, musical accent. "I am The Good Neighbor, Last of the people of King Finvarra. Welcome to New Atlantis. Welcome to our dream, Byron Solsbury."

"What?" he asked, for the first time noticing that Black Gomez stood right in front of the table. That's how he knew, they all knew. They probably knew more by now, and that didn't bode well.

The comments of the one called Marcion had caused movement. Everyone in the chamber nodded a few times, the ones to the right grunting loudly. The other two Pharisees didn't nod, looking as serious as darkness. They closed their eyes and all became very still and silent in the chamber. Byron didn't know what was transpiring with these beings, but knew that for the first time in a long while confusion made him feel completely hollow and transparent at the same time.

Worst of all, Black Gomez, whose shredded face was almost healed from the lopsided fight, looked as smug as ever, as comfortable as he had ever been sitting at The Tower, in the chamber of the Rose, with the other six Elders ruling Xanadu. The figures present didn't seem to perturb him. He probably knew of this different city of Lilith's kingdom. Then he had to speak to make sure his confidence, his obvious stature was safe, safer than Byron seemed to be.

"Do not welcome this fiend, Marcion," he said proudly, wearing a tunic of silver that some here also preferred. "As an Elder in direct touch with Our Mistress, I must press again of the seriousness of this situation and to see a modicum of justice in these ugly nights—"

"Justice," Marcion said, briefly touching one finger to his lips. "Justice is not for The Egg, Master Gomez. Justice was never imparted to us. We remember us, Master Gomez, the ones left inside The Egg, the ones too embarrassing, dangerous to share in you and your associates' ambitions."

Black Gomez laughed nervously. "Well, yes, Gentle One, but Our Mistress never forgot about you. New Atlantis is and has always been a part of the young empire. The MoonQueen's divine vision meant for all of our kind to share in—"

"We are not concerned with her vision," Marcion said, and Byron wondered what they were talking about. He also wondered if anyone else in this room would speak besides this ethereal character, whose voice was as soothing as it was troubling. "We are concerned with little, but that little is very important to us."

"But—" Black Gomez started, stopping when a screen dropped quickly from the ceiling behind the Pharisees. Images sizzled on its surface, images that at the same time plagued and excited Byron. They were the images of Xanadu from a high vantage point. It was the Xanadu he had left behind, with the center where The Elders and Lilith ruled in feathery flames, the other domes cracked and exposed, and plenty of havoc everywhere in different disguises. The sights sometimes fizzled and were pretty much a messy blur, but they were there. And it was now, Byron felt and Marcion would clarify.

"Our satellites," he explained, rising to his feet, pointing at the central fury. "Show an explosion that occurred a few nights ago. An explosion that their sensors deciphered energies that are not in the domain of science, imaginable, and only replicated in The Yolk."

The Yolk? The same energies? What was he talking about? Worse than anything, why was Byron being so quiet, so out of place in this situation. It wasn't his style.

Mirrors...reflections...

"And these energies only mean one thing," he said with a smile that teetered on being perverse. "And one thing only, Master Gomez."

The Elder stuttered a few times before opening a mouth that had once been painted in various shades of lipstick.

"But, Gentle Marcion. I don't understand. New Atlantis is not allowed to use the old Warm One satellites. Even in Xanadu we rarely used them because of the eye of Our Mistress. Why are you breaking her law?"

The nodding and grunting resumed. Several of the Stargazers with the scars on their necks grinned, showing teeth that were all fanged in different shapes, as if serrated. They were also matted in syrupy saliva. Long, lavender tongues slithered out of some.

Again, The Pharisees closed their eyes and the crowd silenced. Again, The Good Neighbor spoke.

"Because there is no law," he said plainly. "There were never any laws between the cities, and you knew this, Master Gomez. It was all just whims of Her. You were once the proud mayor of two militant cities, one of aquatic, sea-faring folk, another of herds of metallic beetles trundling on the wastes, ready to break off as soon as you found ancient mysteries and sources in the ocean. After you so fortuitously escaped, where did her whim take you? You were relegated to a communications duty. You did nothing but skew the news for the citizens of Xanadu, thinking of banal names like *Sol* and *Luna* for us to accept since they were in Spanish, making sure common language remained as close to the end of The Holocaust as possible, for no reason than your pastoral taste." Gomez' expression almost made Byron glad he hadn't spoken yet. "But where is She, Master Gomez? Where is your beloved leader? Where is The MoonQueen, may I ask, so that you can receive you next assignment?"

He kept on stuttering, until an answer came out in more stutters.

"I...Gentle Marcion...I...I was, uh, battling the Warm One revolution..." He looked at Byron, who knew that The Elder had probably been hiding somewhere underneath the city or had already escaped when the place crumbled to entropy. "When...The Tower was ravaged by this explosion...I..."

"Where is she?" Marcion asked quickly, for the first time showing a lapse in his patience.

He shrugged. "I thought...she would be here..."

"She is not," The Pharisee said. "As you can see. There is only us, The Forgotten, The Unsane."

Black Gomez seemed all too lost. Byron suddenly wanted to help both of them out. He wanted to shout out that he had destroyed their liege, using ancient faith and a hero's luck, that all they ever knew as stability was gone. But he understood that feigning ignorance presently was the best approach in order to remain here a while and unearth aid for Medea.

Marcion immediately tested him, as if he knew what Byron was thinking. His eyesight burrowed into him like a spear.

"Where is She?" he asked with a gentler tone.

"I don't know," Byron said, sounding too robotic. "We...my companions who were left outside...were just...fugitives from Xanadu...we."

"Liar!" roared Black Gomez with a pointed hand. "They are traitors. They are Heretics, do you hear? Heretics! They forged the revolution of the Warm Ones against the Stargazers. They—"

"Revolution of Warm Ones," Marcion said with a chuckle. "What a quaint idea. How primitive."

The chamber burst into laughter. Black Gomez's face was covered by venomous shadows. His body shook. Byron stood his ground, thinking that it seemed that the denizens of New Atlantis cared little for their city, their politics. They were interested in one thing.

"They are Heretics!" Black Gomez pressed louder, trying to fight over the odd laughter from these odd Stargazers. "You must punish them, for they are against The MoonQueen's order, Good Neighbor and people of New Atlantis."

Marcion sat down. He blinked. The laughing stopped.

"But she is gone," he said softly. "Gone, Master Gomez. We think her material form is that and more, forever. It is time for a new season perhaps. Time for The Forgotten to be remembered."

Black Gomez's anger turned to stubborn fear. He shook his head at him, at the auditorium.

"That cannot be," he said. "She is immortal. Without her, none of us could exist."

Marcion raised an eyebrow. "Some have said that without the Dark Instinct, The Queen of Darkness couldn't exist. Its purpose is greater than even the machinations of immortals."

"She cannot be destroyed! She is one with the God-Soul! I will not believe these words!"

"But we believe them," he retorted casually. "And we believe that gods and giants change, dissipate as they have in history, Master Gomez. They grow bored, old, senile with power. They go away to other less tedious places or states of being, perhaps leave their essences behind. You know this and Lilith knew this, too. You must admit She had become rather distant after The Holocaust. All things must come to pass, I heard once a long time ago."

The Elder opened his mouth, eyes shining with something akin to pleading. The folk here were enjoying this. Byron was almost, too, except for the weirdness. There was something odd, besides the obvious, in the way they interacted, obeyed the blinks of their leaders, all at once, all unified.

Mirrors...reflection.

"There seems to be no Xanadu," Marcion continued, placing both hands before his chest as if offering a prayer. "And we care little anyway. We are the law now perhaps, the only true law, and we care little, but we are curious about one thing, Master Gomez. We have been receiving transmissions from your former home at different intervals."

The screen flashed with another image. This image was almost as disturbing as the city's. It showed a Stargazer face, wrenched with glee, glossed over in computer-generated features that could not hide his raw madness. The image spoke, more like babbled in electronic spurts. Most of it didn't make sense.

Mad God I am now...will...be...Mad God....city of Mad God...coming...God...We are...convert...enjoy...Gina, I'm so very, very sorry...city...Mad God...delightful...duality...coming...you...

"Balkros?" Black Gomez questioned. "He exists? He was there when I escap...left the Tower. That is odd."

"It looks like Balkros," Marcion said. "But is it he, or some posthumous message, I wonder. Do you know of this, Byron Solsbury?"

He remained silent, shaking his head slightly. He was not going to bother telling them that he had in fact spoken to the modulated form of Balkros before leaving Xanadu, and that The Elder truly believed he was the new sovereign of the cosmos.

"It is irrelevant," Marcion commented. "But we wonder. Perhaps I will look more into this, since you give us no useful answers. Perhaps I will not. What matters is that Xanadu and She are no more, and thus there is hope for us. I knew this might happen, and now we will deal with it."

"What are you talking about?" Black Gomez whined. "You cannot let this happen. We must regain our city, our capital. It is the abode of Our Mistress! She will return, I am sure. This is just a test." His eyes gained some confidence. "A test for you, Pharisees and denizens of New Atlantis to perhaps fully reach her clemency. We must regain it and vanquish these traitors, for once rid our empire of the last cancerous elements."

The Good Neighbor shook his head.

"Why should we? You know what The MoonQueen did to us, Master Gomez. We care little either way."

"No!" he shouted. "I command you, as an Elder, a bearer of The Rose, that you follow my desires. You are all but reflections of our glory."

The screen showed Xanadu burning a second time.

"You mean that glory?" Marcion asked, but the crowd was very serious. "There is no glory since Lilith turned all of us into what we are. We are the law now, and that is not what we want. You know what we want. In any case, we cannot do anything for you, Master Gomez or the one called Byron Solsbury." He then pointed at the tattooed Stargazer. "Quidam, The Warden, makes all judgments here in complete silence, Elder. Although we convinced him to interact with you to gain information, it is he who decides who exists and who does not within these walls. That is how The Queen of Darkness planned it from the beginning. Like her God-Soul curse, we cannot change what she started. And the last time I checked one of Her rules was that no mundane Stargazer is allowed here without Her company."

Black Gomez took a step towards the table.

"You blasphemous fool!" he roared. "How dare you speak that way! You and all your aberrations will suffer when she returns. I myself—"

Suddenly, the one called Quidam, who had remained motionless the whole time, retrieved his massive sword from his belt. Byron barely saw him move. He knew Black Gomez never did at all.

Before he could have finished the sentence, the blade was biting into his neck. The whistling quickly turned into a thud, which turned into a quick tearing. The blade continued in an arc, even after The Elder's head and body segregated cleanly. His body staggered in place, still refusing to admit the damage. The head agreed, changing expressions as it rolled in the air. The Dark Instinct would fight to the end.

The end came quickly, though, as the tattooed Stargazer began hacking at the body. Limbs and torso and the rest were rapidly dissected in a rude manner. To end things, he impaled the sword into the head as it rolled on the floor towards him. Black Gomez would never give another flowery speech on The Moon-Queen's propaganda.

"Looks like I was right about that law," Marcion said with a thin smile, leaning back in his chair. "The Remembered, the ones with true voices in the world, cannot remain here. Only The Forgotten. Only the Unsane."

Then Quidam turned towards Byron. It was his turn.

Chapter 5

They were ships. More like broad catamarans with large blades carving the packed ground. Wide sails captured the unruly wind, but both Medea and Proxos knew that it was the crew of these thirty-foot vessels that truly controlled the movement and direction. A crew that could defy gravity as they could.

Stargazers.

Stargazers that existed outside of Xanadu and New Atlantis, gingerly driving land boats through the desert. Upon the ships in the center, below insulated masts that warded off the always chaotic lightning of the various storms, several objects littered the area besides the four or five crew members in each. They saw sealed cages with Rukas, rusty baubles, colorful rocks in baskets, and all sort of motley decoration that probably didn't do more than personalize each vessel. Proxos shook his head as the catamarans circled them twice, for even the crew was dressed like something out of the buccaneer age (which he had personally experienced when first touring the New World)—loose clothes and trousers that would make their task easier, many wearing bandages over their heads or crude visors over their slanted eyes because of the wind. He assumed that their style of apparel was only a coincidence—but coincidence was rare, even on this side of The Holocaust. Even their skins had a tanned glint like those that sailed the Caribbean centuries ago, this probably caused by The Dark Instinct adapting to the radiation. He was sure that they probably knew the wilderness as well as he had in his over hundred and fifty years exile in it. He had never heard of them. Then again Proxos had never ventured this southward, never neared New Atlantis which brought only a certain few of all The Elders and the older Stargazers because of the monsters behind its walls—the monsters he had failed to mention to Byron, who was now a permanent guest of The Egg.

"Proxos," Medea said in amazement, pressing her back to his while the ships slowed their circling. "What is this?"

"It's obvious what," Proxos said coolly. "But who? There

is only one type of Stargazer that might be foraging outside the city-states, Medea."

One of the ships skidded sideways, the ground losing form before its screeching blades. It halted a few feet away from them. They stood their ground, ready for anything. They had faced many horrors and escape wasn't a problem against these ships if they decided to take to the air. Or at least that's what they assumed. Nothing would surprise the two after what they'd experienced.

A Stargazer leaned over one of the blades, holding a rope that was attached to the mast. His boots were polished black, his pants baggy, his tawny chest exposed by a shirt that had once been white. Attractive, devilish features smiled at the pair underneath a long bandanna.

"Look what we have here," he said merrily, showing an expression that Proxos found similar to Byron's—mocking, proud and teetering on arrogance, and, most of all, fearless. "And you must be right. Only Heretics wander the wilderness. It looks like you two are just that as well."

The others on the ship laughed, as did the ones on the still-circling vessels. Their laughter was free and hardy, and Proxos felt a slight envy. He decided to play the part they should have played inside The Egg, erasing the Elder segment. If these were Heretics, their attitude towards any political leader of Xanadu would be less than cordial. Proxos hoped with little worry that Medea did the same.

"We are not Heretics," Proxos shouted. "We are fugitives from Xanadu."

More laughter. The one who had spoken to them allowed a long wink.

"That's what Heretics are," he said. "Fugitives from Our Mistress. Fugitives from civilization. What else could we be?"

"You're wrong," Medea said, taking a step towards the ship. "For Xanadu is no more. The City of Domes lies in waste by a Warm One revolution."

The laughter dissolved. The handsome Stargazer donned a few myriad expressions, orbiting around skepticism, until turning very serious. The ships halted, leaving the roar of the wind and the haze of sand pebbles that never stopped.

"What are you talking about?" he said, giving the crew behind him a brief glance. "That is impossible. The Queen of Darkness would never allow such a thing. Xanadu is the capital, for She nests in it."

"We speak the truth," Proxos said, appearing next to Medea. "It has been destroyed. After all, was not Utopia once the den of The MoonQueen? Believe me, Xanadu is gone."

"Incredible," the Stargazer leader said. "And to think we were simply going on a trade mission with New Atlantis with little finds. But we have found some amazing news and have found you."

"Trading?" This time Medea briefly glanced at Proxos, who only shrugged. "You trade with that city?"

The leader smiled at her, allowing some of the previous bravado to return. "We have to, in order to survive. Can't eat Rukas forever. How else would a Heretic survive but to find treasures and baubles from the ruins that a city with a surplus of food might be interested in? They are a wicked folk, but they are also a way for us to subsist."

"Why don't you ask for sanctuary?" Medea asked, as if to test Proxos' theory.

He laughed again but there was little humor in his strong voice.

"Enter there? Many of us have heard the stories, the myths on what exists behind the silvery walls. Regardless, it's still the property of The Queen of Darkness. No, The Dreamreavers would rather keep our savage freedom than what Our Mistress gave us."

"Amazing," she said. "More by the minute."

"Existence is amazing," he said with another wink. "But we speak here when we know that a sandstorm is building down the west side. Shelter would be appropriate, and my comrades and I would like for you to join us. This news of Xanadu is intriguing." Proxos could perceive the obvious hunger in his eyes, in all of their eyes. Yes, they had to be scavengers of sorts, all of them hoping that they spoke the truth and they could finally return to Xanadu, simply to pillage the ruins.

"I don't think—" Medea started but Proxos grabbed her

arm.

"We would be delighted," he said at the Stargazer and then stared hard at her. "After all, there is a sandstorm coming, and *Moratoria* can't be too far behind."

"That is not a good idea, Proxos," Medea warned without a care.

"Don't worry," the Stargazer said. "We will not harm you, unless you by chance worked for the members of the Rose or part of the bureaucracy."

Proxos simply chuckled at his implications.

"We can always use more Stargazers," he continued, extending a hand. "Nights are hard, but our kind is growing. We would like to give you some caveats before you go pleading to that city in the distance. And we want to hear your story, of course."

"And you would like to know more about the layout of Xanadu," Proxos said, trying to wrestle down Medea's ugly glare.

"Come," he insisted with a wink, while the others hooted. He pointed to the distance. The horizon was dimming in the twilight, taking away the charcoal view of the hem of the mountains. "We don't have all night to piddle."

The pair shared tenser staring. "You better know what you're doing, Proxos," Medea told him. "And this better not be another one of your craven secrets."

"It is not," he said. I can still make it right, he thought. I still have a few tricks up my dirty sleeve. He turned to the leader. "We accept, stranger!"

"Then come," he said, pulling at the rope so the mast shifted. "Come as personal guests of my ship."

Proxos noticed that Medea's expression was now timid, perhaps embarrassed. He recalled her weakened state and quickly wrapped his arms around her and hovered towards the ship. They landed on the center, nothing more than a square canvass that was patched in various places.

"You two are interesting, I can sense," the Stargazer leader said, while the others grabbed parts of the two blades in order to shift them and the ship in whatever direction he moved the sails towards. "Even without your little news. I wonder if there are more survivors."

"I wouldn't be surprised," Proxos said, grabbing on to the edge of the canvass, while Medea collapsed on her back, closing eyes as if just standing there and talking had sapped her energy too much. "They will all be going to New Atlantis, I am sure."

"Fools," the leader said, his voice drowned in the exploding gusts. "Fools all of you and them forever believing The MoonQueen offered any real protection." He started laughing again. "But that is existence and we are Stargazers, eh? Welcome to The Hellion, my ship. I am its captain and the captain of The Dreamreavers. My name is Dante."

Proxos wondered why Medea suddenly flinched and became very still.

2

Data: Religion. Ontological prostration to a higher form of existence. Wrong in our state. We are a higher form of existence. We are more than a form or matter or thought.

What could he do?

He would go to worship the one called The Mad God, seeking solace for the rage that gripped him at home. It wouldn't leave him. Even in the temple, praying for clemency, he couldn't help but stare at his daughter's exposed knees between a nice plaid skirt and white knee-high socks. She rocked her legs so prettily during the sermon. The heat grew within him. What was wrong with him? Why didn't anything work through the months? He was a man of respect, power, even fear in some places.

Data: That was the problem. Guilt at power. Expunge that guilt. We are the higher form of existence. We will be even more.

His mate usually had problems getting out of bed on the day named Sunday, the causes always on the prior evening when she finished a bottle of a thing called Jack Daniels and watched another thing called Saturday Night Live. Therefore, they usually spent the afternoon together without her. He might take her to a movie or go to the zoo. She loved the polar bears more than anything. "I saw one on a show, Daddy," she would say. "That they actually have a dark skin and that there fur eats the sun, making them real hot."

Duality. The rage.

This time they went for ice cream. Eugene rarely ate sweets but found himself ordering a double scoop of some spectrum of chocolate. He needed to cool down. He needed to relax. It was getting to the point that even at meetings with the other war leaders he was randomly feeling something become rigid in his pants. They walked across a calm park that made him angry for some reason. She held his hand and hummed while lapping on her chocolate chip ice cream.

"This is good," Gina told him. "Real good. Why are your hands so sweaty, Daddy?"

Data: Faith. A belief that suspends logic and wilts at the end of hope. A waste of our time. We have knowledge of The All. Stop this now. Come back to us.

That night, an eternity later, Eugene Balkros sat downstairs on the couch, leaning over to catch his head in his hands. He couldn't help it. He was full of this rage, this dark craving for a creature he loved more than anything. A voice kept telling him that she got in the way of his shame of his horrible mate. His daughter could only be part of that shame in a sense. Shame he needed for balance, for the duality of his other identity. He didn't know what to do. He kept thinking of the various guns hidden in the house.

"No," he croaked. "Please help me, God. Jesus...help me..."

The trees rustled outside. A television hummed in another room. There was a dense silence and the screaming of his emotions. He needed help.

"Please, God. Just once. Send me something. I will believe in you, truly believe in you."

For some reason, he walked outside to the back patio, uncaring his penis poked out in a fleshy gloss from his boxers. He thought he had heard something, thought at least that the tepid summer breeze might cool him off.

And it was there that he saw the angels, hovering before

him in splendid beauty.

"Eugene Balkros," one said. "We have come to help you."

3

Byron immediately advanced towards the lunging Stargazer. His body, his basic instincts craved action, which he was the best at actualizing. He could almost sense the crowd tensing in surprise after what this Quidam had done so efficiently to Black Gomez. He didn't care. He had struck Byron to the point of embarrassment outside the city. Now his body was fueled by a mollified Dark Instinct, now the element of surprise had been wasted on The Elder. Yet Quidam was perfect in movement and strength, a refined blend of raw power and elegant dexterity. He was a true warrior, a rarity in any age.

And so was Byron.

That is why he hadn't done the logical thing and turned into mist before they collided, taking Quidam off balance when he swiped Byron with his weapon. He wanted a fair battle, a final one.

Sure, Byron thought quickly, you have the sword but I have already analyzed your movements with Black Gomez. I have absorbed the way you swing your arms, the way your legs flex, the exact speed of your stalwart body. My father said many times that a war is won or lost well before it is fought, always making sure that his men in Utopia always watched the vampires long before they battled them.

The crowd's furor could be almost tasted as Byron met his executioner. The deformed, simian Stargazers clenched their teeth and grunted madly at him. The half-naked ones glanced at one another or tilted their heads. Many of the motley ones rose to their feet or whatever in anticipation. Byron didn't have time to glance at the Pharisees. The important thing was survival, for it appeared his little plan of seeking asylum as important members of the Stargazer capital was as in pieces, as the Elder who had been named Black Gomez.

Quidam swung at his head. His neck, to be more precise. Byron had expected this.

You're a warrior. The best way is the quickest, the most devastating. You're weakness is that you've never lost.

Byron was swift enough to duck once, but not swift enough to hear the deep whistling of the metal. *That's it, Quidam. Use both hands. You're buying me an extra second of recoiling time.*

The logical course should have been to strike, since Quidam was slightly off balance, send him across the room with enough damage to erode his morale. Byron didn't react this way because another plan had materialized between the frenetic gaps of action. His left hand swung out but simply grabbed Quidam's shoulder, keeping him in the same position. The Warden's face betrayed no surprise, but Byron was sure he might have wondered what was transpiring. His arms were already trying to swing towards Byron in order to score the blow missed the first time.

You'll try again, but not a third time, Quidam.

Byron pushed with all his strength, trying to buy a few more of those precious milliseconds.

His body bolted closer to the Stargazer's—no, more like closer to the sword. At the same time, Byron lifted his right hand and brought up his right knee. The blade was about to strike his midsection now, but his shoving had taken Quidam off course.

If you strike, Quidam, you'll cut me in half. We don't want two Byron's in the world.

Byron summoned more speed from his body. A Warm One could have never moved this rapidly, only a god could have maneuvered with such precision, only a predator could have risked such a move. His hand compressed to a fist, moved in an upward arc, and landed on the flat of the blade. His knee simultaneously touched the bottom side. Quidam should have released his weapon at the force but stubbornly didn't. The metal couldn't stand the force of a being that was created to break most material elements. It didn't have a chance to bend, snapping so loudly it echoed in the auditorium. Byron heard a few of The Egg residents gasp. He also finally saw some sort of surprise in Quidam's face.

In his worst arrogance, Byron wouldn't have denied that this Stargazer was mightier than him, purchasing his power from more than a generous account of the Dark Instinct.

But, if you've worked in this place as an enforcer, you more than likely have never been challenged and probably have your honor and identity embedded in the sword. The weapon means something to you, doesn't it? Your symbol of fear and efficiency is shattered.

Quidam stood rigidly, eyeing the half of the sword. Certain anger crept into his impassive features. Byron didn't wait for a full harvest of emotions, smacking him twice in the face. The first one relaxed his body and made him forfeit his weapon. The second sent him across the auditorium. Byron made certain to put all his weight into the second blow, all his frustration at being in this place which seemed even more of a sicker joke than Utopia or Xanadu had ever been.

Quidam collided into one of the stands. The ones with robes and cracked faces were very stunned, so much a few didn't float away from the imploding chairs. They fell to the ground, sharp steel and Stargazer rump smashing into the tattooed fiend. Byron was sure his broken nose slamming into his brain was enough to incapacitate him for a while, if he survived the rest.

The whole fight had taken less than ten seconds.

The crowd was completely silenced. Even the ugly ones rising from the debris or flying to the ground were flabbergasted. Byron turned his attention towards the Pharisees. He cemented a defiant stare at the one called Marcion. He wasn't stunned, but smiling again with a relieved joy, smiling as if he weren't surprised, as if nothing in the whole universe could surprise him.

"And if he bests The Warden," he yelled with joy. "And he did come knocking on our gates, Forgotten. So soon." He closed his eyes with yearning hope. "So soon. Perhaps he is the one. Perhaps..."

The Pharisee was obviously quoting something, but that didn't make Byron at all happy. Was once again Byron Solsbury, The Liberator, falling in a niche of fate's eternal grinder? It couldn't be, but at least he felt he wasn't going to be physically attacked by his showing.

Marcion walked towards him. Doors to the sides opened. The crowd began exiting quietly although most smiled, while those armored Warm Ones entered. The remaining Pharisees also departed, exhibiting the same joy Marcion and the spectators possessed.

Byron didn't move an inch. He doubted very much he had to worry about harm from The Good Neighbor. He had bested this Warden, as the line went, and the Warm One soldiers, still just mortals although armed with odd devices, also could never concern him.

"You are Byron Solsbury," he said, his gaze becoming lost for a second. "We have heard about you. Perhaps you are the knight we dream of. I have yearned for you many times, but in my unbeating heart wondered if any being could subjugate Quidam. Black Gomez was never even a consideration."

"I think maybe it's time I asked some questions," Byron said, not liking his tone. "And believe me, I have a lot. How much do you know about me? After all, you know my last name, my Warm One name."

Marcion glanced away in light thought, unfazed by Byron's innuendo, by the truth of their origins few Stargazers knew about. The room was empty except for them and the Warm Ones, who cleaned the remains of Black Gomez and the torn stand. Byron also joined him in a quick thought, wondering if truth could exist in any Stargazer society. Xanadu had been a lie to him the whole time, as no one, including Medea, had ever been what he had thought. Utopia, though, on the other hand was the truth, a grim truth about a grim reality. This place seemed to be in the middle, a place created and rejected at the same time in some form by Lilith.

"To know that, Byron Solsbury—"

"You can call me, Byron."

"Byron." He smiled warmly. "Perhaps you should know more about me. More about us and this place."

"I hope your hospitality improves a bit," he said, glancing beyond the Pharisee. Two Warm Ones had fished the unmoving form of Quidam from the wreckage. He hoped that was also enough warning for the Pharisees. "Clean clothes and dinner isn't enough anymore after this."

"Like I said," Marcion said while glancing back at the

same place. "We have no control over The Warden. We do not believe in violence here, Byron. We believe in joy and the craving of freedom."

"I don't understand," Byron said with warning. "And I'd like some clear answers. First, I came here with some companions. Are they here?"

"No, Byron," he said carefully, as if getting used to calling him by one, personal name. "Quidam and his troops captured you because you and The Elder touched the carapace of New Atlantis. The Warden exists to protect our city. They wisely retreated, but we do not know where they presently are."

"They left?" Byron couldn't deny feeling more than worried. Again, he thought it might be better that they stayed away, that they not enter and have to deal with Quidam or the others. Perhaps they wouldn't be allowed entrance. Yet, he wondered why they hadn't tried to aid him. Then again, Medea in a weakened state and Proxos wouldn't have done much against The Warden and the Warm Ones with Byron unconscious. He would try and reach Medea later, hope that they didn't come knocking like Black Gomez and he had.

"Yes, they left." Marcion nodded. "They are nowhere near here. If they do arrive tonight or the next eve, I will personally inform you. I doubt Quidam will be in any shape to enforce his duty. The Warm One soldiers will not act without his consent."

"Good." Byron also nodded, but just once. He told himself not to push this or any other issue right now. If he was truly going to receive hospitality, the chance of accessing their data banks for the cure of The Killer of Giants might arrive very soon. He would be very wary, though.

"But the time for more clear answers is not now." Marcion motioned for one of the doors. "I will do my best next evening. Come, let us get you installed in New Atlantis."

Byron nodded once a second time, unable to escape his reflection around the chamber where he first had met the people of a city named New Atlantis.

Mirrors. A reflection.

4

The trip had been phenomenal, Medea had to admit. In all the un-predictability of their mission, even with the silly idea of tempo-rarily joining these Heretics, this was a sort of welcome respite. And a mental respite she needed, laying on the canvass.

The ships were graceful in the nighttime haze. Although aided by the Stargazer crews who used their flight gift, it was the skillful maneuvering of the sails which propelled the ships on the sand. When the wind turned to their backs, the one called Dante allowed the ship to continue unabated. When the wind shifted against them, he almost deftly turned in a zigzag, undulating pat-tern. Proxos commented that this was the traditional way of sail-ing. Dante chuckled, asking the ex-Elder why Medea seemed so listless. "She has been through much," Proxos told him. "Escap-ing Xanadu and the trek through the mountains took a lot out of her."

"It's a pity you didn't have one of these," Dante men-tioned, waiving at another ship that had gained on the leader.

"I doubt we could have crossed the mountains that way, sir," Proxos said.

"You don't think so?" Dante said and suddenly yelled some odd orders. The crew seemed to lie down and grip harder the top of the blades. At the same time, Dante pulled his rope down, lowering the mast. Within a few seconds, the ship was ab-dicating the ground, hovering over the air at about ten feet. It quickly turned to twenty. "We can take it higher, if needed," he told Proxos. "But why take the romance, the challenge out of it? I must admit it takes too much energy."

Medea only smiled, recalling her nights as a Warm One, when males always had a penchant for boasting when it came to physical acts. Perhaps they hadn't changed that much as Stargaz-ers. She reminded herself there lingered other things to worry about than the mortal past and the rushing view of the desert. She still felt very weak, feeling the Killer of Giants pulsing stronger with each moment. *Moratoria* couldn't come quickly enough, and Medea needed a long one. A good meal couldn't hurt, but she wondered if these wandering Stargazers had anything close to that.

Besides, the leader or captain or whatever name had struck something within her. She couldn't place it but it had to do with Byron. They were connected, and she hoped that also in *Moratoria*, when the power of the God-Soul and their minds was lessened in rest, Medea would be able to contact him as performed before in dreams. Medea knew she had never met this Dante, but the name meant something to Byron. Something very large that had shaped his personality forever, long before their paths had crossed. Perhaps it was just a name, but coincidence was to them and their plights another synonym for an excuse.

Now rest, she thought, hearing them sing odd yet secure songs in the night, riding their ships over sand and through foggy air. The ride was good, soothing, and new, and the word freedom must have rang in her head as it rang in their merry words. Dreamreavers, they called themselves, nothing more than Heretic scavengers who had somehow attained pride and identity while learning survival. They also had their music.

> *Release the anchors of lies,*
> *raise the sails of liberty.*
> > *The sand our master,*
> > *the wind our mistress.*
> *To where we're blown*
> *Forever we'll roam.*
> > *Our ships our homes,*
> > *our freedom our course.*

Yes, they had their music. They sang well with the vibration of melancholy and the bravery of this hope. It was good singing, out here in the wastelands. She enjoyed it, and Proxos only looked ahead of him with a serious expression.

> *Through desert we reave*
> *no port to call.*

Where we roam
the sails our laws.
We make our existences
under the skies.
Our path is lit
by our true mother Luna.

The ships finally reached the northern mountains less than an hour later. They took for the air, attentively surfing over the craggy slopes and pathways. Eventually, they entered a series of narrow caverns. There, they would find a place similar to Proxos: a chain of natural chambers, sparsely decorated with pre-Holocaust antiques that served the forty or so Stargazers. The only difference was that Proxos' base held electricity and a few apparels of technology. These pirates used nothing of that caliber. One of them told them they would burn some wood they had found as a treat for finding them. In the largest cave in the center they lit a bonfire using flint; a few sat around in a circle, each allowed a bowl of Ruka juices. Medea drank it politely, hoping that the animal's essence, their symbol of life, would at least give her some strength to make it to the end of the night.

Dante, not waiting for their story, told his. He rose to his feet and paced with flaying arms, voice loud and proud and echoing. He had been the first Dreamreaver; like the rest, nothing more than a Stargazer expelled from the capital, a Heretic, never to return or enjoy civilization.

"The reasons I would rather not speak of," he said plainly, his princely face somber in the amber firelight, his bandanna pulled off to show a curly mop of flamy red hair. "But my survival came for what was thought of as the seriousness of my act. It was." He grimaced and so did many others, Medea noticed, probably having heard this story before many a night in the wilderness. "She herself threw me out. After being judged, she grabbed me, one of her most loyal progeny, with her icy arms and embraced me; my bones shattered and my identity perished then. She took me to skies like a comet of blue and ivory, mocking me the whole way, then." He raised his arms dramatically. "She tossed me in a place high up in the mountains, a place where the thing called snow still endures, which one can see on nights when the ashy haze is less."

Medea touched gazes with Proxos. Lilith had done the same thing to Byron, except he had been deposited on the edge of the valley where Xanadu existed in a sand dune, and was discovered by Proxos months later in a sort of survival stasis. Her sense of familiarity grew.

"But that was my fortunate mercy," Dante said, moving around the group. "You see, it seems that some pre-Holocaust animals survived up in the heights where the radiation and nuclear winter is less. Perhaps they migrated when the world was strangled by The MoonQueen's plan. It didn't matter, for I was a warrior once, a proud leader in Xanadu. I would find a way to endure, even in despair." Again he grimaced with a slight touch of humor. "And what things I had to eat...hairy things and things with feathers, oh my friends." Many laughed. Proxos nodded, as if relating to this plight. He seemed to know so much, Medea thought, so many secrets that the change in eras still held—and she and Byron knew of so little. Even as an Elder much had been kept from her; she had always thought it was because of her virgin position in the perfect society, but now wondered if it was because The Queen of Darkness and her lackeys wanted to horde any information that might help them in the future.

Dante continued, and Medea found the constitution to listen and remain upright. The story was heroic, if anything. He thrived in the snow and ice, barely making it night after night. In time, he made his way down the slopes and found the carcass of what had once been a Warm One village, nestled next to a lake that was now nothing more than lagoon of hot mud. There he found these ships and modified a few using some of the small factories in the habitat. He also found Rukas and other animals that had changed through exigent evolution or perhaps the mutation of the radiation. He existed well enough, enjoying shelter and entertainment from all the things in this town. He also learned much.

"I see how the animals subsisted," he said. "And I see that we did nothing but usurp and copy their civilization. They weren't animals, but truly something close to us, my friends. I mean, look, Dreamreavers, our style is based on a Warm One faction that pillaged a place called the sea."

Many didn't like his comments, but Medea realized he was more than a leader to them. He was a savior. If they only knew what the Warm Ones really were to them, she thought.

Eventually, perhaps out of loneliness, Dante began using these ships to migrate southward, away from Xanadu. He found more ruins, more animals, and thus more survival. Through the decades, he found other Heretics, many near expiration, many newly expunged from Xanadu. The reasons were always political, it appeared. The reasons were many times beyond them. The Elders or The MoonQueen simply did it and that was enough.

"Thus we survive," Dante said. "And perhaps one of these nights we'll grow fully, create our own society away from Our Mistress. It is a romantic notion, but dreaming made me outlast my banishment."

"Don't forget New Atlantis!" one shouted and the others snickered.

"That is true." Dante nodded. "Our trading with them gives us true subsistence. They love what we find in the wastes: statues, books, pieces of building, and any other silly baubles. In turn, they give us materials, maps to other ruins, and most of all they give us Warm Ones." He shrugged. "They care little of us, and it seems that The MoonQueen has never cared of our business."

He focused on Medea and Proxos.

"And what is your tragic story?" he asked. "Please forgive my manners, I don't even know your names yet."

Both of their mouths twisted. Medea wouldn't dare a glance at Proxos as a silent question. Could these outlaws know of their identities, current and past? Only one way to know, and Medea would be as frank as always.

"My name is Medea," she said. There was no reaction from the crowd except for a few nods.

"And I am called Proxos," her companion said, surely risking more. More nods, although Dante raised an eyebrow at him.

"That is the name of an old Elder," Dante said. "Destroyed during the razing of Utopia, as he heroically fought at The

MoonQueen's side. Or so legend goes."

Proxos nodded, talking as dry as usual. "We do share the same name, this legend and I."

"And Xanadu is no more?" a Stargazer asked in disbelief. Others muttered at one another.

"Yes," Proxos said, staring directly at the dancing fire. "How did it happen, we do not entirely know, spending most of our time away from The Citadel." Medea couldn't help to silently applaud his words—they weren't total lies. "What we do know is of a massive explosion that swept The Council and most of the Mall Zone."

"What about The Queen of Darkness?" Dante asked eagerly. "Did she make an appearance? Is she anywhere?"

"We don't know," Proxos said. Medea felt a sharp pain in her stomach. When would it end? When would The Killer of Giants take her away into oblivion?

Byron!

"All we know, dear hosts, is that we escaped and somehow crossed the mountains towards New Atlantis. It was the only logical thing to do."

"There is little logic in the wilderness," Dante said with a mild frown. "And little logic in that city. If it is the last city, then it deserves the waste that is the world now."

"What have you heard?" Medea asked, deciding to test Proxos' assertion some more.

Dante turned serious for a moment. "Not much, Medea, but we deal with some of the citizens when we trade. They are an odd bunch. They're different..."

She could feel the crowd tensing. Even these wanderers who surely faced horrible risks every night seemed more than cautious when it came to New Atlantis. What was in there?

"But it doesn't matter," Dante said, his face lighting up a bit. "We are not against or for anything anymore. We are glad for your company and we hope to warn other fugitives that might migrate towards New Atlantis. Perhaps, like us, they have already seen the brittle loyalty Our Mistress has towards her people. If anything, we might have more recruits."

"How often do you deal with New Atlantis?" Proxos

asked. Many including Dante eyed him oddly. Medea suddenly knew what Proxos was planning and why he had accepted their hospitality. It seemed Dante also had an idea.

"I don't know," the Dreamreaver said. "Whenever we can. Whenever we need. I think we shall go there in three nights perhaps. Why? Do you need an escort to this place?"

"Not exactly," Proxos said. "You see, we lost one of our companions, someone very important to us, Dante. He is in New Atlantis, and we hope to meet up with him. Your voice has given me at least time to reconsider our voyage, perhaps find a way to retrieve him from such a city."

"You lost someone?" Dante mused with a nod. "To lose a friend is terrible. To lose one in such a wicked city is desperate, believe me. Who is this person? Your leader?"

Proxos chuckled. "Not exactly. Although Mr. Solsbury would like to think so."

Dante's eyes bled with magenta light. "Mr. Solsbury? That name. Is his first name Byron?"

Before Medea could interrupt, Proxos was saying, "Why yes. Bryon Solsbury."

"Byron!" Dante roared, surprising everyone in the cavern. His face had burst with harsh lines, his eyes shifted to grim crimson. Even his fangs were exposed by a menacing mouth. "Byron? You don't speak of the same Byron that was once a Raven? The Head of The Ravens?"

Medea shut her eyes, knowing that her feeling was right. There was a connection—an awful and unfortunate connection. She felt weaker, all of a sudden.

"Uh, well," Proxos stammered, not at all ready for the outburst. "I...don't know..."

"Don't fool around with me," Dante hissed, his twisting face showing he meant the warning. "I doubt that Our Mistress would have ever named another Stargazer with his name." Realization joined the anger. "Then again, I doubt she would have named another after a prominent, martyred Elder. Something is amiss here. It is the same Byron, isn't it? He still exists! I cannot believe this!"

"Uh, well." Proxos looked at Medea for succor. She

avoided his glance, notifying she was too frail for verbal rehabilitation. "I...did you two know each other?"

Dante laughed and it came out more like a snarl. "Know each other? We were each other, Proxos. We were and destroyed each other. But it doesn't matter. Things have changed. A friend of Byron is a foe of mine."

Proxos tried to speak, but Dante turned towards one of the dank tunnels. "You may stay the night and that's it."

They couldn't do anything, sitting there with a stunned crowd that hadn't fully grasped the entire interaction. The only real movement was Proxos slowly shaking his head, his dry tone returning.

"Well," he said with a sigh. "That didn't go very well at all, did it?"

5

They were led soon after to a lower part of the caverns. The Dreamreavers still seemed courteous enough, but Dante's command told them that coolness must be shared with the two. As soon as they were in a small, natural chamber with two oddly shaped boxes, their hosts left Medea and Proxos in the darkness. Like any Stargazer, they could see through it with their stabbing sights.

"Incredible," Proxos said, running his hand through one of the boxes. "These are old coffins where Warm Ones were buried. We used them quite a bit before the Holocaust."

"That's nice," Medea panted, not able to act with pride. Her face seemed sunken, eyes barely glowed with any illumination. "Can you help me?"

"Sure." He grabbed her by the shoulder and gently placed her in the coffin. "I'm sorry I worsened our situation."

"Our situation has always been the worst." Medea feebly smiled at him. "We can only hope tomorrow brings more hope. That's how we've always done it. So you now want to follow Byron?"

"If we can enter undetected there might be a chance for exodus," he said. "And these folks are our best hope, tonight and tomorrow. Are you going to be okay?"

Her eyes were closing. "All I need is rest. Tomorrow. I'll figure it out. I'll..."

Medea promptly entered *Moratoria*, where the God-Soul would rest and renew its power, avoiding the fury of *Sol*, where Stargazer sometimes dreamt of simple things like the thing called life.

Proxos moved the covering over her, hoping to see this brave and direct being again. He hoped it too for Byron. Where was he? How would they convince Dante to give them aid? Too many questions. Keep it simple, he told himself.

But as he lowered himself into his coffin, a place for dead things that shouldn't be frolicking in the world, another question also told him that perhaps the simple ways would never happen again—sitting by the fire in his cavern, searching for stalactites or taking walks in the desert, things he now missed. Chess.

The question was simple but it bothered him. Like anything else, tomorrow might deliver an answer.

Didn't Medea seem a little taller tonight?

Chapter 6

Lord Orion knew he would be the one to succeed. No matter what happened, he would make it to his goal. He had traveled for three nights, slowly making his way across the mountains. His skin was peeling because of encountered hot pockets of radiation; many of his bones were slowly re-knitting because of a semi-avoided avalanche. The ground was always uneven, the air shimmered dangerously above him like a breathing fog, revealing little of the pathways or ledges before him. But he would succeed. He had once been the Head of The Ravens after Lord Crow had fallen during the notorious battle at the North West Farm, when the Warm Ones used some sort of faith-magic to decimate their soldiers (and ironically it was Crow who took the position from Byron when he was disgraced for destroying another Stargazer). Sure, his guard had done little to re-take the Farm, but The Elders had been just as successful. When the explosion occurred and his soldiers disintegrated against an assault by the Warm Ones that struck right at the center of Xanadu, it seemed he lost it all. It seemed everyone had lost it all. But now was his chance to fulfill a mission for once. It was simple: take a simple USB drive and give it to the citizens of their smaller cousin, New Atlantis.

Why now? Sure, Balkros had always been rather eccentric and hard to understand, but he was a great Elder that had forged Xanadu into a gem in the wastes. He wouldn't let it all go to waste! Perhaps this was a simple test, and Our Mistress would be waiting to reward the first person who finished the task. That was surely it. That's why Lord Orion wandered the wilderness with the hope to reach another city.

Glancing at his almost empty reserve of treated Juice, he knew he had little choice anyway.

His uniform was tattered, nothing like the proud and black imitation leather the Ravens once wore. His long, formerly slicked-back, jet hair was a wiry mess. His long face and noble hooked nose were dirty. But he would make it. Orion hadn't converged into groups like the others because success was better rel-

ished alone. Already, in pathways and at the bottom of small valleys, The Raven had found the remains of the others, weaker ones
that had once taken Xanadu for granted. Not like Lord Orion, who
had always believed danger and alertness were something to savor every night like the Juice of animals.

He had noticed that the mountains were losing stature. He
would reach the desert soon, thinking of the map Balkros had
provided for all, memorized and tossed away miles away. Then it
was maybe twenty or thirty miles to New Atlantis. Maybe two or
three more nights. Then he'd have his glory, one way or another.

The barren ground slanted downward suddenly, and Orion
tried to quicken his pace, too wary to take for the air, ignoring a
pulsing body that needed more nourishment and was as wounded
as it had ever been.

2

Byron entered one of the many chambers at the top of New Atlantis, where the Pharisees and their parties resided. He hadn't heard
anything about equality in this place, unlike Xanadu, but he had
heard a lot about privacy and perfection. Privacy did not exist in
The Egg, even for The Pharisees, the three rulers of this place.
Privacy, Marcion had told him last night before showing him his
quarters, was for those who had something to hide, like weakness
and denial. That is why they had mirrors everywhere, cameras in
many places, that is why every door could never be locked here.
"Was this your idea?" Byron had asked his host. "Or The Moon-
Queen's?" Marcion hadn't seemed fazed. "It was a both," he answered plainly. "We have no choice but to exist this way." He
never answered Byron's 'why' question.

Mirrors everywhere. No privacy. Reflections, in types,
sizes and shapes, but it was only him, Byron, in each.

He saw his reflection and those of this small feast. Even
the table and floor were mirrored here. Warm Ones entered other
doors, nude and ready to serve themselves. These, Byron had
learned, weren't changed outwardly, hadn't metal and sensors

knitted into them, but were primarily for feeding. It seemed the population didn't have to do anything. The Warm Ones were programmed before birth to blindly serve the denizens of The Egg. Before *Moratoria*, Byron had been allowed to spend the previous evening in the computer room accessing all the information about New Atlantis. The Pharisees didn't seem to care. He had learned so much about this place within twenty four hours of arriving, and it astounded him. It astounded him that the Warm Ones even oversaw the birthing and breeding of their kind to serve the population. There would never be a shortage like in Xanadu, for everything was itemized in precise computer data banks. If there was ever a thinning sickness or accident in the lower parts of The Egg, progressive cloning techniques could double the stock almost immediately. It was perfect from the standpoint of nourishment. Warm Ones also oversaw the technological and engineering aspects of this place, performing research in laboratories, testing new machinery and computer systems, parts of their brains which could analyze or deduce allowed to function. This all created an organism far more improved than Xanadu, with no Warm One enjoying a mind that might fathom individual thinking. They had told him this was the perfect society. It definitely was one for a Stargazer.

"Byron," Marcion said when he arrived. The other two Pharisees, Feltch and Revenant, barely wasted a glance at him, staring hungrily at the meals that kept entering. "Are you rested? You must be famished."

Feed me!

Byron only nodded, walking towards the table. Even his cupula had been mirrored, a small room with a wardrobe, a sink, and not much else. Part of the not much else was a small camera, which he would later find out was in every room in the city. He was dressed in dark blue trousers and pants of fine cotton, trying his most to seem different than the citizens. He felt a strange balance, uncomfortable yet slightly at ease with himself. He wouldn't show them either.

The Egg got his name from its shape. New Atlantis wasn't a dome but actually was dug almost a mile underneath the ground. It was a metabolism of tunnels and shafts and many

chambers, dissected by little else besides laboratories and elevators. The Warm Ones dwelled in the lower levels, the Stargazers
thrived above the ground with little to no care. Every room for
The Forgotten, he accessed through the databases, was for respite
or enjoyment. There were old fashioned libraries, ballrooms of
glittering candelabras, studies, aquatic wonderlands, virtual-
reality rooms that keenly emulated past realities, and many museums and art galleries. There was so much more, like special zoos
where some pre-Holocaust animals were caged, re-created parks
or buildings in large chambers reflecting a famous Warm One
age, all to be enjoyed by these creatures. Besides Quidam and his
soldiers, there was no need for law enforcement, no real cells or
jails, no headquarters for politicking. This place was for leisure
and little else. Nobody had to work, nobody had to worry. Warm
Ones labored, the gods sat in their paradises and enjoyed creation.
It was perfect and full of mirrors. It was the most amazing feat of
science Byron had ever seen, and he was sure nothing before or
after The Holocaust could have come near. Why didn't The
MoonQueen rule from here instead, in this place where conflict
was wondering what to do with one's evening?

Byron sat down. Feltch chuckled at him with his crude
features. "Sleep well, sweetheart? Woke up with a woody?"

His words were odd, his voice was odd. He was odd. Byron hadn't gotten to the origins of these beings. That was for him
to ask tonight. There were other things to ask, his curiosity being
fed and wanting with every iota of information he obtained.

"Thanks for your concern," Byron replied. "I hope you
can fake it better next time."

Feltch started cackling, the sides of his mouth lathered in
foam. Revenant remained silent, while Marcion, Byron noticed
then, was petting what seemed to be a Warm One pup. He wasn't
though, he realized with dread. It was a Stargazer! Someone had
granted the small body The Dark Instinct. Although its face
seemed innocent and blank, two meaty fangs broke from naked
gums, its skin was colorless, and its small fingers were encrusted
with long nails. It made a pathetic sound at Byron, showing a
mixture of cunning and danger. Marcion, who must have been
responsible, petted it.

"There, there," he said. "You will be fed soon, Adam. Your first meal should be a memorable one."

It started screeching, so loud many of the mirrors cracked around them. Byron had never heard such a tragic scream. He couldn't hide a resonant distaste for this. Marcion and the others showed a glint of satisfaction at how they had purchased a reaction so quickly from him. His little rebuttal to Feltch seemed like a long time ago.

"Do not worry, Byron," Marcion reassured him. "It is not the first time we have done this. It is very interesting when one creates a Stargazer from such a young soul. Do you know that it will actually grow, the nubile human essence still fighting for the thing called life as The Dark Instinct slowly corrupts it? What it eventually creates is a pernicious monster more terrifying than anything, more dangerous than Quidam." He winked. "Or you. I will have to destroy Adam in time."

Byron wasn't worried about anything, his disgust being curled by hunger. He spoke, his query appearing so forced.

"You know about the secret of creation?"

"Of course," he said. "Why would we not? All of us came before The Holocaust. We are The Forgotten, but we remember much in our nightly joys. There are no secrets here, Byron."

"And no privacy," he said curtly.

Marcion shook his head, appearing almost sad. "No, Byron. If you wish to know anything, simply ask."

"You've already told me this a hundred times," Byron said. "And I'll start by asking again if any of my companions have arrived or been spotted since last night."

"And will say 'no' again, Byron. There are no other visitors. Our surveillance shows no movement in this valley at the moment."

Byron didn't know if he needed to feel relief or concern. It was an effort to feel clearly in this place with these situations.

"I have a lot of other questions, Pharisees."

"They can wait," the one called Revenant said, her voice sounding like the screeching of steel, as if her vocal cords were shattered and patched with something else. "Now we should feast, for that is our only true destiny."

"Whatever," Byron said, wishing he'd lit a cigarette when first entering, an old trick to hide any surprise. They had even left several packs outside his cupola when he awoke. It was perfection.

"Let's start this barbecue!" roared Feltch, clapping knobby and wrinkled hands.

Byron almost couldn't eat the Warm One that simply sprawled himself in front of him on the table when he saw how the other two ate. Eventually, he fed but would never forget this spectacle.

A Warm One came to Feltch's side and leaned over the table. The creature stood up and kneeled behind the meal. He didn't bite or tear the flesh apart. Instead, he puckered his lips, stuck out a long fat tongue, and jammed his head in the buttocks of the Warm One. The Warm One couldn't deny a look of pain, but it stood its ground. Feltch lapped hungrily, his face tearing into its body with pops of blood, each hand clutching the sides of the hips. Very quickly, the Warm One's body shriveled and lost all hue, so quickly the skin succumbed against bone before realizing he had no existence. The shell fell over to the side, completely and efficiently dried. Feltch sat down satisfied, feces and blood and a little yellow matting the sides of his face.

Revenant was slower but just as gruesome, an adjective Byron had never fully accepted when feeding. The scars on the lower neck suddenly broke apart. Her head simply divorced the body, taking with it a spine and various entrails including its heart, all of which throbbed with its own life. The body left behind remained still. Yet the head, showing the hunter's fury, fluttered towards a standing Warm One. The spine curved and stabbed its prey in the midsection. Before The Warm One could jolt, Revenant bit his neck, brutally tattering skin apart. The Warm One departed slowly, not able to move as Revenant' spine had severed his own, making movement useless. Byron felt more disgusted but also slight admiration. What a perfect hunting machine this was! How had it happened? He pushed away the question, seeing the dangling organs gorged and pulsing now with a black illumination. When she was done, the head and entrails returned to its body, skin closing rapidly to reveal only scars again. Her

eyes, which had turned white during the whole exhibition, returned to their empty blackness.

Byron noticed that Marcion hadn't eaten. He gave him a
quizzical look before jamming his own fangs into the Warm One.
As the sweet taste of juice filled him with erotic energy, The
Good Neighbor answered.

"I have already dined," he said, allowing the pup-
Stargazer to move its claws and mouth all over the chest of a
Warm One, shredding it with astounding velocity. "I cannot feed
in front of any Stargazer or being, for it immediately melts their
spirit away, sometimes sending it to another dimension, if they are
fortunate enough."

"What?" Byron asked in between lapping juice. He had
slain his meal as quickly as possible.

"He sure ain't shitting you," Feltch said, his robust tongue
wiping away the moist, gritty stuff on his face.

Byron moved away from the table, feeling all of a sudden
as if he weren't present, as if he'd just witnessed some sort of rav-
ing dream from *Moratoria*, a joke from the God-Soul. Part of him
knew he just had. But all he had to do was ask the people of New
Atlantis. They would give him the answers, they said. His jaw felt
very heavy, petrified by a sense of loss at the extraordinary and
quick feast just experienced. Marcion also sat back, ready to answer his silent inquires. The small Stargazer floated in midair,
taking a tiny respite, shrieking as if warning the ones present this
was its territory; it then burrowed severely into the corpse a second time, bone chips and entrails flying out. Byron finally lit a
cigarette. The filter and his fingers were matted in Juice.

Blood.

"Feltch," Marcion said casually. "Is a Kappa, Byron. Once
they were an intelligent species of apes, if you know what that
is."

"I do," Byron said, his voice sounding as distant as his
body felt. "Apes, right?"

"Correct," he continued, ignoring the untamed chuckling
of The Kappa. "And a very talented species, thriving many thousands of years before the Warm Ones rose in evolution's eternal
race by jumping off the trees. They existed in floating cities above

the jungles of India and China. You do not know those places?"

Byron shook his head.

"Whatever wonders the Warm Ones discovered, they had already surpassed in medicine, philosophy, or any material science, even some of the immaterial ones. They were artistic and bright, their gods benevolent, fair, and later stolen by the Warm Ones of that region. Almost a perfect race."

"Until She came along," Feltch said with a sneer, placing a cigar in his mouth. Other Warm One servants were beginning to clean up the syrupy mess. The small Warm One was almost done, its body crawling out of the large crater that had been the Warm One's midsection. It jumped into Marcion's waiting arms.

"She came along?" Byron asked, as if not knowing who 'She' was. He knew, and it bothered him.

"Yes," Marcion said, standing up with his creation. "She poisoned their minds and hearts, devoured their gods' wills, corrupted their innocence." He bowed to The Kappa. "As you can see, Feltch, who was once a king of his own empire, hasn't been his lofty self for many millennia. She caused wars and pestilence, She showed them their insecurities." He then pointed at the hole in the Warm One corpse. "And they ate themselves from the inside. She destroyed The Kappa, molded many of the stronger ones into Stargazers, nothing more. Of course, being different from Warm Ones, their powers and habits are slightly different."

"But we ain't' no ass-kissers," Feltch barked. "Just suckers, man."

Byron shook his head again, this time in disbelief. But it was happening, right in front of his dead eyes.

"Only in tales in the place called the Orient did they exist," Marcion said, walking over to the other side of the table. "But I am sure Master Tsing-Tao never spoke about them. It is a tragic story, but tragedy makes good conversation. Tragedy is the nutrient that feeds memory."

The Good Neighbor stood behind the other Pharisee. Warm Ones scuttled around and behind him, wiping the remnants with damp cloths, the bodies already shunted away.

"Now Revenant is less of a tragedy," he stated, not hiding his enjoyment at giving answers, increasing this dialogue. "Her kind were known as ghouls, liches, boggarts or other puerile names begotten from Warm One folklore. She and her kind were once gifted Warm Ones: sorcerers, witches, if you will, people with a certain gift into the reserves of primordial instinct. When their ranks were pruned during a period named The Burning Time in the place once called Europe or at any time during civilization's grip, it wasn't She who 'saved' them, though. It was actually they who crossed the borders, reaching out to oblivion when their existences were flickering away. Somehow, denying The Light, they grasped into a thread of The Dark Instinct beyond time and space and were given new incarnations, different than Stargazers but very much slaves of the God-Soul. They were not baptized with it, but found it through their talents and yearning. Their abilities are different than the Kappa or vampires, but make no mistake: they are also seething with The Dark Instinct."

Vampires, Byron thought, just like my Father called them. Monsters, Medea and her kind had called them in the Farms when he was investigating a murder for The Elders. Things that terrified the living, the ones that belonged to The Light, Creation, The Mad God's breath. Things that weren't supposed to exist, that never were, The Unimaginable. But they did. They always had. And they belonged to Her in shadowy fullness. Once again, Marcion seemed to catch his emotions, his thoughts so easily. The other two Pharisees did the same by their expressions, but much slower. The Good Neighbor allowed this mass of understanding to mushroom in the room a few seconds.

"And why not, Byron?" he said, pacing towards him. "The Dark Instinct, The God-Soul, is her power of birth, the poison in her womb. It exists to corrupt in order to destroy life, existence, or any reflex of creation. It is like a virus that can adapt, overcome, control, and manipulate as long as it can follow its bleak course. The others you saw, they have also been touched by Her Dark Instinct. Some were animals, some have changed through the God-Soul's needs throughout centuries, many were changed by meeting with other Giants or deities." He raised a perfect eyebrow. "Some you cannot even see, Byron, existing in other planes of reality. Lycanthropes, ghosts, demons—call them what you will, but they are all part of The Dark Instinct in some way."

For a second, he recalled a conversation with Proxos about the powers of the Stargazer. Proxos had said that their abilities were notable, very shadowed by the lies of The MoonQueen, but that their gifts might be limitless if tapped into correctly. They were notable creatures, he now admitted even more.

Byron opened his mouth but already knew the answer before he had said, "Why?"

Marcion answered for him.

"I am sure you have heard, Byron. She was, perhaps by accident, the greatest progeny of The Mad God. She was too much for him, for the universe to accept, for the other creations of that early time. For that She was cast away only to smolder in resentment, never to be part of The Light, only to fulfill another part of the balance, the struggle that is all of Creation. Thus, her wondrous power of darkness exists everywhere, trying to destroy, annihilate what The Mad God ejaculated. That is what we, her brood, are, Byron, a reflex of her anger, a tool in the machine." He shrugged lightly. "A piece in the game called chess."

"What?" Byron said, blinking hard. He couldn't have known!

"But so be it. In many legends you would call her the Antichrist." He laughed once, a gentle sound that seemed to light up the room. "And many thought She would be male. No, it was always Her, Byron: Kali The Destroyer, Tiamat, Sekhmet, or whatever named She crowned herself with in order to usurp imagination. Nobody else. And her rage has blossomed through eternity and affected so many beings of wonder."

"But she's gone," Byron said and paused. He almost admitted he had destroyed her, which perhaps wasn't such a bad revelation by their attitudes.

Marcion and the others nodded. "Yes, Byron, She is gone. But the rage perhaps continues, eh? It always does."

"Perhaps." Byron looked away, not liking his host's amused look. "And what about you, Marcion? What is your tragedy?"

The Good Neighbor sighed, sitting next to him. The expression of more of that sad melancholy crossing his comely features almost snapped Byron out of his trance. Almost.

"My tragedy," he said, holding his creation closer to him. "It is the saddest of all, besides the tale of The Queen of Darkness. After all, unlike Revenant and some of the others, I understand it. I yearn for my past fully. I miss what I was once and am not totally a slave to the hunger of eradication that is The Dark Instinct. That is perhaps because I am the last one, the only one, the only reflex of another species that never really existed on this material universe."

"I wish I was the last," Feltch said, masticating on his cigar. "I can't stand the other fuckers."

Marcion didn't say anything, but Byron suddenly knew of his past. It was as if his thoughts had flowed into the room like deepening shadows, punched him, and folded out into a tepid understanding of this Pharisee. Marcion didn't come from earth but he did. He was never mortal but never truly immortal. He was the last of his kind, beings that had negotiated two dimensions, that exploited time, that wove the fabric of matter in such a way many gods envied them. Byron blinked and thought he smelled lilacs and the sound of stringed instruments, vibrant yet innocent, thought he could see a majestic court underneath the waves in a pseudo-reality of creatures like Marcion—with their pointed ears and cloudy hair, playing music, playing jokes, feasting on thoughts and dreams, dancing the cosmos away because the cosmos didn't affect them. And even though they all obeyed King Finvarra and Queen Mab, even though the many clans, like the Tylweth Teg he belonged to, fell under the mystic umbrella of the *Sidhe,* they only obeyed their whims and the few rules of the universe. Even though they were named the *Tuatha De Nannan,* elves, fairies, and other names, they truly were more spiritual than material. They were wonderful, but Byron suddenly saw the harps and chalices drop, and a smoky darkness cover the image of the court underneath the waves of unreality. It was the Dark Instinct. It was She. At first She was a guest, someone they could toy with, play with, and they named her Lhiannon-Shee; but so quickly these folk realized that they were the ones toyed with, played with. Like the Kappa, their music stopped, their dreams ripened too far, and they were forever changed. And now Byron also understood that the Warm One world was just one of her many victims throughout history, throughout time. And in between.

A tool of the machine. A reflection. Mirrors.

Then there was only Marcion and none other. He was the last one, the only one with the will to continue after Lilith's visit. Unique. Alone

"All gone," Marcion said, sitting back down in his seat. "Only I remained when Lhiannon-Shee arrived and poisoned our own hearts, corrupted our souls which we thought could never be corrupted." His lips twisted with frustration for a second. "Ironically, it was the imagination of certain visionary Warm Ones such as Shakespeare which ultimately created a path into our kingdoms. I still do not know why I survived, but now I am both what I was and Stargazer, Byron. I have both gifts equally; nonetheless it has somehow made me so much less than before."

He bowed his head dramatically, long curls concealing his pallid face. Feltch blew out rings of jittery smoke. Revenant seemed totally unamused through the whole speech. The Warm Ones kept tidying up in a meticulous, slow manner.

Byron finally felt as if he had returned to this place. It all appeared so staged, yet his eyes couldn't lie to him, could they? They had given him answers. He stood up nervously, lighting a second cigarette. The first he had thrown on the floor, just to have a Warm One retrieve it.

"So that is why you are The Forgotten?" he asked, trying to anchor his personality to a situation he felt so weightless in, as if possessing no importance, no perspective in the chasm of time. "You were perhaps embarrassments to Our Mistress, different, maybe even too powerful in some aspects to truly be allowed to mingle with the other Stargazers."

"And too resentful," Revenant said with her shrill voice. "We might have started a revolution."

Byron's mind was racing too fast to read too deeply into their comments.

"So She created this place," he said. "Another experiment, probably some sort of museum she could keep the relics of past victories."

"Very Good." Marcion raised his head, not a trace of sorrow on his features. "And here we are, co-existing in pleasurable flawlessness."

"Did you ever think about challenging her?" Byron asked slowly.

"Why should we?" Marcion retorted. "I knew her time would come, Byron. She is more of celestial mistake than a supreme being. Mistakes end or at least eventually evanesce."

"And you knew I would come?"

The Good Neighbor shook his head. "We knew of a prophecy about a knight that would defeat The Warden, bring us a new age, which is coincidental with The MoonQueen's passing. Ironically again, Byron, it was She who gave us this prophecy, a long time ago. It appears you are The Knight. I did not know you, Byron, but I knew of someone like you, knew the prophecy would come true. One of my gifts is to peer beyond the pleats of time and space, catch the shadows of the turning wheel."

Great, he thought, just what I needed—to be another savior in another damn city. I'm not, though, I'm quite the opposite. This age is over, and I wonder if you'll see this turning of the wheel before it breaks, Pharisee.

Byron then almost regretted the eagerness of his next question. "Aren't you curious about how she was unseated?"

Marcion simply leaned back in his chair. The other two Pharisees appeared little interested with the last part of the conversation.

"I am very curious, Byron," he said. "But we brought you here to answer any questions you might have. We have plenty of time for our questions in the future. We want to make sure you perceive us as good hosts."

There was something he didn't like in his tone, but now wasn't the time again to inspect the arcane words of this figure.

"Any more questions, sweetheart?" Feltch asked impatiently, looking larger and larger by the minute, probably a side effect from recently feeding. "I got a game of baccarat in level 12, plus I got to inspect some of the textile inventory before the night's over."

Marcion raised a hand, his free one slinging the little Stargazer over his shoulder. "Be patient, Feltch. I am sure he has many more questions."

"Fuck him," Feltch spat.

Byron narrowed his eyes at The Kappa. "Actually, I do have just one more question, since I'm sure you are all busy in your perfect society doing much of nothing."

Revenant actually grinned, revealing those nasty serrated teeth. Marcion nodded once at him.

Byron asked him about a section of The Egg that astounded him while perusing the data files. It seemed all the energy, all the power of this city, whether electrical, nuclear, or even radiation used in the laboratories came directly from the center of New Atlantis. It all came from a place called The Yolk—which they had mentioned during Black Gomez' execution—that also created other amazing energy sources. He asked what The Yolk was and how could one area, which had no reactors or plants, according to the blueprints, execute such a feat.

Behind his question, Byron knew that was part of the reason he still hadn't searched for the cure. His curiosity was driving him; he needed to know more about this place even though its nights were soon ending. It seemed only honorable in a way. In addition, he wanted to make sure trust was lain like a carpet between them before he started hacking deeper and discovered any hidden files or data sent from the exterior, which the Pharisees would have surely already intercepted. He wasn't worried anymore about any treachery after showing them his strength. Furthermore, they didn't seem like warriors; and he believed in their calamities. They were giving answers. Marcion gave him yet another answer.

"Of course," he said. "You would like to know what truly drives this city."

"Yes," Byron said, placing a third cigarette in his mouth. "What drives this city?"

Marcion winked at him. "Not 'what'. 'Who', Byron."

The cigarette almost fell from his colorless lips. "Who?"

The Good Neighbor stood up. "It is hard to believe, but what could surprise you more this night, Byron."

"Normality," he responded.

"No such thing," Marcion said. "Not since She was banished. But come and see for yourself. I will personally show you.

Come and take a look at The Centurion, The Prince of Shadows."

Byron again felt as if he were not present anymore. He lit his cigarette and tried not to think of anything that had just happened, preparing himself for more of what might be seen.

A tool of the machine.

A reflection.

It was always her.

3

Data: Angel: 1. A messenger of God. 2. A guiding spirit or influence.

They were gorgeous, Eugene thought, mouth open and wide like the sky above. They hovered ten feet above and in front of him, wearing white robes. They possessed no wings, but their skins were as white as the crown of a cloud, their eyes shone in intoxicating red. They were angels. They had come to help him, guide his tortured soul in between the duality, the dualities of his life.

"Eugene Balkros," the one in front said, his voice powerful and rigid. "We have come for you."

His mortal knees struck the cobbled ground. He couldn't see anything but their sublime forms, he couldn't feel anything but his beating heart, pumping blood and emotion through every niche of his body. Eugene held his hands together towards them. Hot tears made an appearance, the first time since his mother had died twenty years ago.

And he asked them if they came to deliver him. He told him about his passion for his offspring, nothing more than a way to satisfy the rage, bury himself in shame, balance and deepen at the same time the duality that was his home and the world's perception. He cried to them for help. He had never really worshipped God, but would do anything to serve Him because of this miracle.

The first angel glanced back at the other two. Was he confused? Balkros wondered. Why were his eyes losing their illumination. The angel in the back, much plainer looking than the one in front with the milky hair and high cheekbones, nodded back. The other slightly frowned.

"Yes, Eugene Balkros," he said loudly. "We will aid you in finding peace, but you must aid us, too. How far will you go? Your God asked much of Abraham. How far will you go?"

"As far as you need me to," he said with chokes. "Just tell me."

"And if we asked you to bring deluge," the angel said. "And if we ask you to bury the sodomites again, would you do it? Would you change it all for the peace we can offer you?"

He closed moist eyes. He thought of his daughter and knew she was the only thing that mattered. He couldn't taint her to satisfy the duality. He just wanted peace, her happiness. The fame, the power, the duality itself didn't matter. Just peace. He understood then that peace, inner peace was the only true salvation in the universe. Happiness, love, and all the others didn't matter unless one was gorged with peace.

"Anything," he whispered. "Anything for Gina."

"Good," the angel said with a grin that was less than cordial. He certainly had large teeth in some places. "Then we shall return in three nights with instruction. You will follow them."

Balkros lifted his head up with newfound determination. He could almost taste the peace that would be his reward.

"I will follow them," he said. "Oh, great angels. I will follow them. What are your names so I may know in prayer?"

The grin grew. Two of his teeth were very pointy.

"I am the angel Shibboleth," he stated. He then pointed to the one to his right. "This is the angel Proxos. And this one to my left is the Angel Gomez. Our names do not matter, just our words that are the voice of The Lord. Farewell, Eugene Balkros. In three nights."

Their bodies rose into the sky, the vanishing light of their eyes bringing the patio back into darkness. He had never felt so overjoyed. Even after returning to bed, three brandy's bubbling in his stomach, his wife shouting at him for having the television too loud, the feeling remained through the twilight.

The only thing that bothered him was the soft breathing of

his offspring down the hallway. That was it.

4

Medea found Dante in one of the posterior caverns where the ships were tethered. He was busily hammering with his fists one of the massive blades, slightly dented during their voyage here. She knew he had heard her footsteps down the tunnel but stayed with his chore. The other Dreamreavers had told her after *Moratoria* where to find their leader; they were cordial, but there was an understandable guard in their voices and eyes. This Dante was their commander, no, more like a savior to these Heretics and their meager existences. They weren't here to jeopardize this, but their aid was very important from what Proxos and she had discussed.

Before speaking, she eyed the ships, odd inventions that melted two eras, trying to understand this person that had been injured, perhaps betrayed by Byron. She immediately felt an admiration for him; like, Byron, he was a creative and dreaming survivor, perhaps more direct than The Liberator. She liked that. Then Medea gazed at the cave opening, seeing the always blurry landscape, dangerously mischievous, unfriendly, and always in the way of their goals. Behind her, that dream of the show continued, more vivid than ever. Medea could almost smell sweet food and straw, could almost feel the music touch her skin, could almost taste the excitement of the crowd as their emotion palpitated against the performance. And the female was so beautiful...

And She was also changing things with each performance...changing the crowd...

"I understand your reaction, Dante," Medea said, pushing the dream down to her chest, "but you must understand that Byron changed, I believe. He is not the same person."

Dante didn't turn his head, but allowed one loud grunt. Medea tilted her head slightly.

"You changed, didn't you? You're not the same being."

He shook his head. His fist banged harder on the metal,

smoothing it out. "Being resuscitated by The MoonQueen and then cast out by her tends to change an individual, Medea."

"That happened to him as well," she said. More than you, she thought, more than you should know.

Dante paused and looked over his shoulder. His expression showed skepticism, but also a flicker of curiosity.

"It did happen to him," Medea pressed. "When he tried to start a revolution with the Warm Ones and overthrow The Queen of Darkness."

Dante's face grimaced. He stood up and pivoted.

"Warm Ones? Why would he do that?"

"Because he changed," she said, thinking of the arrogant monster she met as a Warm One just before becoming The Shaman of The Circle. Arrogant but with just enough doubt to serve her needs. Sandwiched between arrogance and doubt, their friendship had flowered, and even back then there was so little time to nurture it. Always so little time. "Because he realized the same thing you realized about our ruler. But he actually battled The Moon-Queen."

"And he still exists?"

Again she glanced at the desert and the city somewhere out there.

"I think so, Dante. Let me tell you a story."

And she did. It was a story about a Liberator that began a revolt, failed, and came back to finish it. A Liberator who returned to confront Her again, this time as a victor, armed with faith and determination. She told him everything, omitting that she had been this Shaman and that every Stargazer was once a Warm One. Dante listened to every word, disbelief growing with the size of his eyes with each chapter of the story.

"That is the most incredible tale I've heard," he said with an incredulous laugh. "It is so far-fetched, I wonder how could it be a lie. The Queen of Darkness felled by Byron...Byron and some sort of sorcery from another epoch? How do you know this?"

She sighed. "Because I was the Elder who aided him, Dante. He recruited me."

"And that after meeting Proxos, who was also an Elder.

The same Elder who perished in Utopia. Proxos Commodore. It all makes sense."

"It's the truth," Medea said dryly.

He smiled, gaze dropping to the rocky ground.

"Why should I believe you? Why should I think you say the truth?"

"Why should you think we lie?" she retorted. "It doesn't matter, really, Dante. I just wanted to show you that Byron is not the same Byron, if he ever was. In any case, your pasts shouldn't get in the way of a favor we ask, which is to accompany The Dreamreavers when you trade in order to gain access into New Atlantis. It's small enough."

Dante matched her tough stare. "Perhaps I should tell you a story."

And he did, and Medea felt the emotions of that story, drawing from her connection with Byron. She heard of younger days when Xanadu was growing steadily, when the Warm Ones were first transported from Utopia and other places in order to try a new method of breeding. In Utopia, the Stargazers simply crossed a border and freely stalked their food. Here they would be bred, raised, and slaughtered in tight conditions. The second city of the empire would be more efficient. Rice City and New Tenochtitlan followed the same design.

It eventually worked, mostly because of the skill of a new faction called The Ravens, headed by a mercurial and canny Stargazer called Byron. With help of scientists and The Elders, he tightened security everywhere: The Farms, The Slaughterhouses, even the Citadel itself. He enlisted other fierce Stargazers, like Dante himself and their other close friend, Mephisto. They were celebrated and revered; they solidified the growth of Xanadu, which was now the new hub of the empire after the destruction of Utopia. Byron and Dante, leaders, friends, forever, they often said.

"But many did comment," Dante said at one point with thinning eyes. "Especially a few of The Elders that—what was their expression—this city wasn't big enough for the both of us. I think that is it. I think they were right." He shook his head. "We were very competitive, Byron allowing me equality, me trying to undermine his power. We wanted to do good for our leaders, we wanted to enjoy every moment, make sure we were at the center of anyone's attention."

But Dante got carried away one night, deciding to exterminate a whole section of Warm Ones to make an example, back when the supplies were abundant. Mephisto tried to intervene and was almost torn apart. Byron never gave the order to stop after saving Mephisto, but insulted him, challenged him, and, worse, mocked him for only being a simpleton follower.

"And we fought," Dante said. "My lovely friend and I...and I lost, you see." He growled slightly. "He...was better, the best. I should have simply faded away, but like I said, Our Mistress made whatever flicker of the Dark Instinct in my broken body grow into a healing flame...and then she mocked me, too. Then she sent me away; she probably informed the population that it was Byron who destroyed me to humiliate him or something. Here I am, a hundred and forty years afterwards."

"And you have changed," Medea pressed, seeing little of the speech softening his walls. "Just like Byron. So much has changed, Dante. Whether you believe me or not. Aren't you at least curious to see him, find out what happened?"

"Not at all," he said. "Perhaps we have changed, perhaps Xanadu and the icy tyrant are no more, but that was my past, Medea." He pointed at the ships that sailed the nights, scarred the desert floor in search for baubles of another era. "This is my present, and I have no desire to turn back. Byron and The Moon-Queen took my existence, my identity away. I brought it back to me, and this is it."

"Wasn't part of it your fault?" Medea asked, knowing she might be treading on dangerous ground. Yet, she realized more and more, they needed his aid. The only way to perhaps escape Proxos' allegations that New Atlantis was a prison no being ever escaped, was to perhaps enter without notice.

Dante's expression didn't boil, only showed a rather weary smile.

"Of course it was, Elder."

"Ex-Elder," she corrected.

His smile lost some of its fatigue. "Whatever. The point is

that I've thought about this many times, so many times, even when I was lost in the icy peaks, feeding on birds and hairy vermin, even now that I have the potential to create something new, cleaner, if not save a few spirits from desperation. I think that's good enough, Medea. And I think that a Stargazer should be as we are—free, alone most of the time, traveling rough roads and hoping for the best."

"I think you're right," she said, crossing her arms. His walls were still erected.

"But as I said, and in order to keep sailing forward." He patted the almost un-dented blade. "I cannot return to my past as a Raven, a friend, even an enemy of Xanadu. Do you understand?"

Medea dodged his somewhat pleading look. "I don't want to," she said. "We all have to face our pasts, sooner or later. They're always out there in front of us, as much as the future, as necessary as the future. If you look hard, Dante, you'll see that it didn't matter when or how you became a Heretic. You know it was all a false paradise, an evil one. Byron was the cause you fell from grace, but there never was a true grace there. There was only the selfishness of The MoonQueen."

"That is a twisted logic," he said defiantly.

"Is it? You blame Byron for your fate, but all you lost was, as you have put it, The MoonQueen's lies. Perhaps you should thank Byron."

He narrowed his eyes. "I don't believe your argument just went there, Medea."

"It doesn't matter," she said. "I don't like getting this abstract, Dante. I merely wanted to show our honesty and our intentions. I assume you will not aid us." He shook his head after a short pause. "And I assume we cannot stay here. We are part of that past."

Dante's hand stroked the blade, his sight was on his blurry reflection on the metal. Before he had opened his mouth, Medea was interrupting him.

"Please don't apologize," she said, turning for the tunnel. "We will leave immediately. You have been kind enough with your hospitality. I won't forget you."

Down the tunnel, towards their coffins where Proxos

waited, Medea thought she heard him sigh loudly. It was probably just the wind and the pasts it carried.

5

The Prince of Shadows.

Marcion led him to the center of The Egg, to the place aptly called The Yolk. They passed a herd of Kappa on a walkway over a large sitting room. They all wore dresses and heavy make-up, making their gross faces into bright caricatures, giggling with the same earthy tones Feltch manifested. They seemed to be in a hurry, ignoring the couple, except for one who blew a kiss at Byron while almost stumbling on its long gossamer dress. Byron turned to Marcion with an arched eyebrow. "They are going to a tea party," he responded. "They are very entertaining, if you do not mind Romantic poetry, especially when watching The Kappa try to not break the China with their pudgy fingers. The best-dress contest is a delight, Byron."

"Sorry I'm missing it," Byron said, suddenly feeling the metal and mirrors hum slightly. They were nearing a source of energy, he could tell, like a reactor or a massive stove.

"They enjoy these all the time, so do not worry," The Pharisee said, as if missing his acute sarcasm. "We have very tasteful clothing for females in this place, not the dreary, sleek style of Xanadu. I am sure you have somebody you would like to see in such a dress, Byron, someone close to you, if not yourself."

He closed his eyes, trying hard not to replace the image of the Kappa with another person wearing that clothing. It made him ache, it made him want to rush out of this place. Not yet, he thought, you have to continue, for her own good. When it comes down to it, maybe it's better you did this alone. Yet he had felt Medea in pain. Where could they be?

"Is there anything you don't know, Marcion?"

"I just grasp images, palpitations," he said plainly. "I did not mean to disturb you."

After wrestling with these thoughts for a minute, Byron

tried to clear his mind. That was difficult again, for in the next few hallways, different ghouls waved plastic branches at him, singing words in an unknown language.

"What are they doing?" Byron questioned in a high tone.

"It is just symbolical," Marcion reassured. "Tonight is not Sunday, but then again those branches are not real palms."

It struck him that he thought he recognized most of the dressed Kappa and ghouls from his first encounter with The Forgotten in the auditorium. What were the odds, unless...

Byron asked what the population of New Atlantis was. Marcion, gliding with breezy precision, turned his head briefly. "You met it during your besting of The Warden."

"That's it?"

Marcion calmly explained of how time had shaven their ranks. Although Quidam never allowed any other Stargazer inside The Egg for long, granting them the same fate as Black Gomez, he sporadically turned on The Forgotten. The MoonQueen also arrived periodically, sometimes to be challenged by a desperate faction who couldn't stand their plight anymore; or she simply destroyed a random denizen.

"That way she could keep you obedient," Byron stated, still feeling like he didn't belong not only here but in his own body.

"Perhaps," Marcion said, as another door opened and the humming had changed into a soft rattling of the area. "Destruction is a blessing we cannot seem to give ourselves, Byron. No, all of us seek to cling to the hope of freedom one of these nights."

Byron chuckled. "You are free, Marcion. She is gone, remember?"

"Almost free," he said, and then entered a chamber that surprised Byron is so many ways. The first was the fact there were no mirrors at all, just dark colored iron, tightly riveted to endure the shaking that was probably constant. The second was seeing Quidam standing in a corner, as if expecting him. Byron took a step backward, not caring if the tattooed Stargazer held not a hint of emotion at meeting him after the defeat.

"Do not worry," Marcion reassured. "You subjugated him. The Warden will never raise his hand against you...unless The

MoonQueen desires." He laughed once. "Amazing how he healed so quickly, Byron, since you shattered almost every bone in his body."

Byron wished he had shattered all of them, seeing once again the cool fierceness this Stargazer radiated. Marcion grabbed his arm gently. He felt a soothing warmth shiver to his chest at the touch of The Pharisee.

"But he must stay close to The Prince of Shadow," he said, as Byron entered with him. "Do you like the new sword I gave him? It is made of a metal that never existed on this planet and you could not break so easily, Byron. I tend to be giving at times, and also have need to the preservation of The Yolk. After all, Quidam's true purpose, other than The Egg's protection, is the protection of The Centurion."

"The Centurion?"

"Yes, Byron, The Prince of Shadows."

The third was the most astounding. Most of the floor in the middle was made of glass. He realized it had to be more than glass, probably magnetized, for the heat and turbulence below would have shattered anything so brittle. Beyond the glass was a gray haze, reddening towards the center, which was the direct apex of New Atlantis. Through the cloudy murk, detonations like lightning fizzled, some as close as a hundred feet away, others as far as a thousand. Gases coalesced in some parts and took other hues, sparks of unknown aura blinked seemingly in and out of existence. It was like a maelstrom he'd never experienced, like a cluster of stellar galaxies seen in pictures back in Xanadu.

But what hovered in the middle truly made him reel. Normal Warm One eyes could have never perceived the shape in the center, only the gifted eyes of a being cursed with The God-Soul. It was blurry but it was obvious. It floated in the middle of the energy tempest.

It was the silhouette of a person. It didn't move, arms and legs spread. It did nothing.

"That?" Byron started, fumbling for his cigarettes but completely forgetting in which pocket of his suit they were stashed.

"He is the Prince of Shadows," Marcion said proudly. "He

is our leader of sorts, our ruler, still nothing more than another slave to The MoonQueen. His purpose is simply to fuel our city."

"I don't believe it," Byron said, the data agreed with this. The Yolk, this area, fed a metropolis of over 100,000 tons of steel. 500 megawatts of electricity, enough nuclear power to nurture a small atomic explosion, gamma and infrared rays for the laboratories, solar power even for arboretum and gardens below, and so many other spectrums of energy, all siphoned by feelers, filters, rods, and other eaters of this floating power that seemingly knew where to grant each form of itself. Just like that.

"It is true," Marcion said. "The Centurion built this place and entombed himself in The Yolk right after The Holocaust; we have been around for a while, Byron, trust me. I do not believe he has true form anymore, the shape but a shadow. But he exists in a semi-sentient aspect, able to give what our computers ask of him and that is it. He gives us energy, for that is what Lilith wanted."

"Lilith?" Byron murmured, for the first time ever hearing another person besides his companion say her true name. It made his nervousness grow, deepen like a tearing gash. "But..." He shook his head and lit a cigarette.

Marcion moved across the glass to face him. "I know, Byron, the power is awesome but very little to him. I think the effort is but a dream to his senses, you see. His might perhaps equals that of Lhiannon-Shee; nonetheless he still was prostrate to Her."

Byron took a heavy drag, his head hammered by the vision of the caverns a few miles away. They held the tools to build this city, but none of them had. He then recalled the conversation that ended this question they had about the stockpile.

"Are you sure, Prox?" he asked again. "Something built that city."

Proxos blinked, shook his head, and stood up.

"I probably did miss something else," he said quickly. "We must eat soon."

Something built that city. Something that could have bent raw material, moved it through many miles of unruly weather, shaped it perfectly, efficiently to the desires of someone who had the blueprints of it, someone like Balkros or The Queen of Darkness herself. It had been this Prince of Shadows who forged the museum for Lilith and sepulchered himself in it, kept away from the other city-states as The Forgotten were.

"No," Byron whispered, also understanding that Proxos probably had known. He had been one The Elders that caused The Holocaust, helped nurture these cities from the wastes. Why hadn't he told him? Why hadn't he told him that night, which seemed like a long time ago, in another world?

Byron then recalled another conversation with Proxos, years ago back at his headquarters. They had been playing chess. Byron had mentioned that his research informed him that the nuclear winter shouldn't have lasted this long. Even Mephistopheles, a better scientist than him, had agreed back in Xanadu. Again Proxos had sidestepped the question, just as poorly as before he ended up in The Egg. Byron knew why, and it had to do with what he currently beheld.

"It's him," Byron mouthed. "Because of him...the condition of the planet...this long. But why?"

"You know Her almost...if not better than us, Bryon," was the response of the Forgotten.

To destroy. To control. To subdue. To bring fear and ban life. Because it simply amused her.

"Are you fine, Byron?" Marcion asked with tenderness, hands behind his back.

"I..." He placed a hand before his eyes. "I hear...muffled voices. Other sounds. It's loud. Something is loud, Marcion."

"It is not a sound, Byron. The Centurion emits other energies, winds of The Dark Instinct, his own emotions, which can pierce one's identity if not accustomed to it. He is wondrous, is he not?"

"He?" Byron looked up. Marcion was bathed in ambergris light. He turned his head to see Quidam still standing in the same position. "What is he?"

"He was once a Stargazer, like you, like any Warm One slain and brought back again by Lhiannon-Shee or any of her brood. Yet he did something when he was something called a centurion a long time ago. You could say that he drank from Juice of The Mad God himself, or should I say one of the avatars of The Mad God. He was curious, perhaps he wanted power. The Centurion achieved it, Byron, but loss much of his individuality, became a hidden weapon, a trophy for The MoonQueen."

Byron dropped his cigarette. He realized he had been slouching the whole time. Straightening, he tried to compose himself in front of these two characters. He had come for a reason, and the reason would terminate what he'd seen in seventeen nights. After all, he was going to go too far, survive, and save Medea very soon. That's what he would do, no matter what his curiosity told him.

"I think he's moving," Byron said with a distant voice.

Marcion blinked. "Moving? He has never...you are right, Byron! The Centurion is moving...he..."

It was flaying its arms slightly, kicking legs. The chamber shook slightly, as stronger bursts pulsed from the shifting silhouette, chiming wall and glass. It moved a few times more, twisting in midair, and then was still. The energy fluxes returned to normal.

Marcion turned to the stunned Byron, once again his face adorned with the same triumphant smile shown when The Warden had been beaten.

"That is almost impossible," The Pharisee whispered. "The Prince of Shadows moved...as if something had caused it...someone...he recognized you, Byron!"

"What?" Byron said. "He recognized me? I never heard about him until now. I've never met—"

"The prophecy." Marcion's smile thinned, although his eyes shone brightly in white-gold. "I believe it is unraveling further. You are the one, Byron. Would you like to hear the rest of it?"

"No," he said softly. "No, thanks. Not right now. I think I've learned, experienced enough tonight. I'm mentally sodomized."

The Pharisee motioned for the door, proving that his main intention was to flourish as a good host in a city that never entertained guests. He still couldn't hide the overflowing excitement on his winsome face. "I understand. Let me take you back to your chambers. Perhaps I can play my harp for you. It will soothe your emotions."

6

The mouth of the cavern showed them the desert. It was night and blurry, the eternal distortion of ash and faint radiation always out there. Temperatures had dropped abnormally, as the wind shifted from the south with icy licks. They stopped, both almost dreading to have to return to the outdoors, perhaps one or the other wishing for the safeness of the world they had once belonged to in other lifetimes.

"What now, Proxos Commodore?" Medea asked, feeling another cold that didn't originate from her dead body, but from a malady that was growing slowly from within. She knew the effects were always different with each Stargazer. Some eclipsed rapidly, rotting from the inside of their bodies, souls, and minds. Others simply weakened at a slow pace, feeling each nail of the Killer of Giants scrape away at each layer of their identities. The end was always the same, a complete implosion of being, if the Stargazer didn't destroy his own person before in maniacal resignation.

What was odder still was that her voyage through *Moratoria* held the same dream. She reached for Byron but found the image of the tent and the show that was happening before a merry crowd of Warm Ones. And there was that beautiful female, in silver and black, getting ready to dance. It was more real with each night, and now she knew that the entertainers were not Warm Ones. Not even close. She had almost danced...

Almost...

To changes things.

"What now?" he asked back, patting the helmet underneath his arm. "That is always a good question. What now?"

She rolled her tired eyes. It was still only the beginning of the evening.

"We don't have The Dreamreavers' aid. Will you not go into The Egg with me to find Byron?"

"Perhaps he will escape, Medea," he offered. "And bring

with him the cure."

Medea felt he was reaching for a clinging hope like a drop of water shivering on a rocky ledge.

"You don't sound sure, Proxos," she said, too weak to feel anger.

"If anyone can do it, Byron will."

"I thought you said nobody could escape this prison. How come?"

He closed his eyes briefly. "The Prince of Shadows, Medea. The Prince of Shadows."

"Was it that Stargazer we saw attack Byron?" she asked, again too fragile to care about other powerful entities. She only wanted to see him one more time, perhaps one last time.

"No," he said. "He is much more and much less. I'm sorry I never told you two before...I think I'm regretting it. I'll tell you all about him."

"Do it quickly," she said, taking a step down the small slope leading to the wilderness. "I am going to New Atlantis, and I'm going to find him, Proxos. He is in there because of me, because of what we represent in our vengeance, in our justice. Do it quick, and go your own path if you wish."

"Medea," he called out for her as she took more small steps. "Don't you understand? You will never leave there. Maybe Byron can, but you might not. Why are you following some romantic notion?"

She pivoted, her face a mask of angered determination. "Because I'm fading away, and we all joined for a reason, Proxos. That was to end it all, but most of all, I realize now that he's not with me, to find humanity in this dead world, to find good. And that is love and the love I have for him. I hate him, and I don't want to be without him."

"I feel the same way," Proxos said, "but..." He shook his head.

"But what?" she asked with irritation. "But the odds are too much. The odds were too much in Xanadu, the whole world was against us, Proxos. But we won because we had to, because perhaps we were good, we represented a sigh of the old world, what was noble about it."

Proxos smiled sadly. "Still have that Elder tongue. Or is it the Shaman in you? The old world wasn't all that benign, Medea. In some ways it was much worse than what we created in the wilderness."

"I don't know about old worlds," Medea said with a snort. "I only have this one; so do you. All I know is what I told you. Are you coming with me, or shall you be waiting back at that cavern with the rest of the dusty and forgotten relics?"

Proxos flinched, and then flinched again. His expression clouded slowly but cleared quickly. He smiled, looking towards the south.

"The cavern," he said. "By...I mean, dear, I mean...Medea, that's it!"

"What's it?" she asked, ready to walk away from him forever.

"That's it!" he shouted with a smile. "The cavern. That's how we can do it." He pivoted back towards the base of The Dreamreavers.

"Where are you going?" Medea asked. "I meant the ones you showed us. You're going back in to—"

"Yes, I am," sang Proxos, a new enthusiasm in his voice. "I'll be right back, Medea. Then we can all go towards it."

Medea simply stood there, wondering when the old Stargazer had exactly lost his sense of reality. Perhaps he had a sense of reality, and she and Byron had never bothered cultivating one when given The Dark Instinct.

Chapter 7

Xanadu was dying. It had been re-born, but now it was dying. *They* knew that was the only option when the toxin of the insurrection was injected months ago. *They* knew that when The Tower burned like a torch and part of *them* was minced by the Warm Ones there was only one chance. Actually, two. There was a seventy percent chance that the second and current one wouldn't work, but they weren't worried. Hundreds had been sent, each with a seed that might germinate another existence for them. Already a few had returned, depleted and terrified of the wilderness. *Their* wrath was quick, severe like their smile. *They* showed the miscreants the image of *Sol*, and their already wounded minds unraveled so easily, like a stack of papers in the wind. *They* didn't give a second chance. Xanadu was dying. *They* were Xanadu now.

They were still enjoying their new reincarnation. Although *their* veins, the tunnels that once bled with trains, the smaller tunnels with gaseous Stargazers, the shafts leading to the thousands of chambers where the population enjoyed *Moratoria*, were burnt, broken, and exposed, *they* could feel movement. Although *their* skin, the domes that shone in teal in the night, was cracked like a hope, *they* could still control the radiation trying to dry *their* body out. Cameras worked, circuits still beat with life, doors and machinery were still part of their reflex.

It would all end soon. The Warm Ones had done plenty of damage. *They* had isolated the stock they needed for now. In the Farms, the Ozone Shields had been cropped slowly, allowing the radiation to destroy thousands in a matter of nights. The Warm Ones went for the stations, and *they* sent high-pitched sounds that drove them mad, killed the younger ones. Any hope, any revolution was on hold. Some went into the wilderness, but that was silly. Some would stay and fight some more, but that was silly.

Balkros thought it was all silly. Balkros was a god. *They* were a god.

In The Citadel, there was very little movement. A few Stargazers shambled through the ruins, but *they* cared little. *They* had sent thousands with a mission. Xanadu was dying, slowly eroding away, roofs collapsing, metal rusting at rapid percentage, grids and computers blinking out in large numbers each night. *They* existed in all of this, and time was running out. *They* weren't worried. *They* smiled a lot on screens.

Remember...

Gina.

A god.

The only thing that worried *them*, deep within their circuits, the silicone and electricity like neurons, was that the Dark Instinct would need to feed. They needed to feed, for that was its destiny.

They only knew of only one way to culminate this fact. Thousands had been sent.

Remember...

2

Data: Reluctance at first. But the angels only wanted in-formation at first. How silly.

"General Balkros," a voice said.

He lifted his head from his desk. It was his secretary. How long had she been at the door?

Data: We looked way too startled.

"Are you okay, General?" Her name was Pamela Thorton. She was young, twenty-six, but had been one of the top females at The Citadel, had worked in Navy Intelligence, and knew that this place, right under him, was the perfect springboard for what would be a great career in warfare. She was better looking than average, had obtained a mate just a few months ago, and enjoyed charity work when she wasn't serving him.

"Fine," Eugene said, wiping his forehead. She walked in the office, and he leaned over to cover all the work on his desk. He should have never had this type of information here, in plain view. "Just, uh, getting tired."

"You have been working hard," she said, her sight grazing his desk. "It's almost six o'clock, sir. But I'm not here to tell you the time."

"You're not?" he asked.

She smiled. "No, General. Admiral Timmons just called and left a message. He simply said, 'it's a go.' He didn't want to talk to you because he was in the middle of a golf game at Pebble Beach."

Data: Admiral John Timmons, head of NSA. Had more ac-tually just spoken to the President and called him.

It's a go, Balkros thought, his nerves jolting with heat. They swallowed it. He had planted the doubts about their code systems, fooling all with false intelligent reports from phantom sources in eastern Russia and the Middle East. They wanted him to take care of new codes, new security systems, for the Strategic and Tactical weapons systems, from the command Control Com-munications all the way to the DEFCON's. The new codes would land on the President's lap, the Joint Chiefs of Staff, all with his signature on it. They would also be in the hands of certain heav-enly beings. He couldn't believe it! What was he doing?

"Are you okay?" Pam asked a second time. "You just turned paler than you usually are."

"Just feeling a little under the weather," he said, sounding very unconvincing. "My...Gina had a bout of the flu last week. I might be getting a touch, Pam."

"Hope she's fine," his secretary said. "She's a darling thing, sir. What a beautiful girl."

"Yes," he said and couldn't stop a large swallow. "She's beautiful."

And soft, and tender, and delicious.

Stop it!

"Anyway," Pam said. "Do you mind if I go? I've got some Christmas shopping to do. Do you need me to file any of those papers before I go?"

Eugene felt his damp hands slither over the work, all secret material from several places in the capital. His palms were moist.

"No," he said softly. "That's fine, Pam. Have a good night. I'll be locking up soon."

She nodded and smiled at him. "Then good night, sir. Please get some rest. I've never seen you work this hard. Gina probably misses you a lot."

"I miss her." He tried to stop his eyes from losing focus. "But sometimes we have things to do. Good night."

As soon as she closed the door, he leaned over his desk. What was he doing? How had it gotten this far? They had only wanted information. He was just being tested, wasn't he? Wasn't he? And Pam was probably wondering by now, so close to him in his office of the place called The Pentagon. That wasn't good. Not at all. What could he do? He asked himself, prying himself from his desk and placing the papers in his suitcase.

That wasn't very reassuring performance either, he thought. You were never a good liar, Eugene. What could happen next?

He heard Pam's voice, no more like a quick yelp, in the next room. It stopped, replaced by the sound of something hitting the floor. Balkros quickly locked the briefcase and called out her name. No sound. No response.

"Pam?" He went for the door. It was very quiet.

When he opened it, there was a duality before him. One showed beauty, the Angel Shibboleth standing before him, appearing in this most guarded of places of the empire as if it were no problem.

The other was his secretary, lying on the floor on her back, staring at the static ceiling fan with unblinking eyes. A few seconds ago she was been full of life, talking and breathing and traveling through time like most. Now it was all gone, so easily, symbolized in the crimson grin on her throat. It had been sliced so deeply and quickly, her larynx probably hadn't been able to utter even more than one or two gurgles.

The angel smiled at him, not worried about Pam's predicament, the stains on his robes, or his dripping index finger on the right hand.

"She knew too much, Eugene," he said with his lofty voice. "She was getting worried about you."

He barely heard his words, wrestling with his breath, leaning against the wall. He was a messenger of God! Why?

"Why?" Balkros choked.

"It is part of the grand plan," Shibboleth said. "A plan you are part of now. She is saved now, and I will personally take her soul with me. You must have faith, for it will deliver you, Eugene Balkros."

But what they obviously wanted from him, what they were planning—it didn't make sense. Yes, yes, it did. It was the end of the world, wasn't it? Armageddon. Fucking Armageddon! But why now? Why him?

"I can't do this," he said. "I...I'm sorry...I can't..."

"You have been chosen," Shibboleth said, stepping over the body of his secretary. "You cannot turn back. It will be a better place, Eugene. A wonderful place where God shall give you a wonderful seat at his side."

Eugene clenched his teeth, trying at the same time to convince his legs from not turning to lava.

"It's too much," he said. "And...I still feel the rage...it's getting worse...I can't take it."

The angel smiled at him with such pity, with such concern, that it made his legs feel strength, made his heart stop beating so erratically.

"You will receive your peace soon," he said. "You are being tested, sweet child. Even I am being tested, but I do not question. Do you think this is easy for me, a mere messenger of Heaven? Perhaps nothing will happen, but all that matters is that you will be delivered, you will love your daughter like you should, and the world will finally make sense to you. Have faith. It is a great honor to be part of the mysterious, the supreme, the beyond, Eugene."

Balkros took a deep breath, closed his eyes, and opened them to see that a divine creature stood in front of him. A creature of God when he was of weak flesh and imperfection.

"I'm sorry." He looked again at his secretary. She was going to go Christmas shopping. "I'm sorry."

His eyes shone with graceful blue. "It is fine, Eugene Balkros."

"My, Angel, your teeth are so sharp."

Shibboleth winked. "Everything about me is sharp. I exist in eternal grace. Would you like to do the same?"

"Yes," he said loudly. The rage, the duality...Gina.

"Good. Do you have the information? I must have all the analysis on world climate effects, as well. Do you also have the signed orders for stockpile retrievals."

"Yes, Angel." He nodded rapidly. "I have it all."

"Wonderful. So you will change the codes in the way we told you." He kept nodding. "And when you're almost finished, we will tell you what to do. Make your task stretch a while, take at least six months. There is still much work to do on our side."

He didn't like the sound of those words. "Work, Angel? I don't—"

The angel winked at him. "Let us just say that we have others working for us. One will eventually give you certain viruses on USB drives, which you will take to Colorado, to Norad, and a few other places. It will be a simple task."

No, Eugene thought. A virus in the weapon systems computers! Something that would confuse the radars and sensors, which were attuned to understand what was a threat from the sky and what wasn't. It couldn't be!

"Have faith." Shibboleth patted his shoulder. Eugene could feel a hard cold touch him through his uniform jacket. "You look awful, Eugene. Get some rest, free your heart from questioning. It will all work out. Now go. Do not worry about a thing. I will tidy up here."

"It's all in the suitcase," he said, suddenly wanting to run out as quickly as possible. This was all too much.

"Go," the angel ordered. "Deliverance will soon be with you, Eugene Balkros."

And he did go, trying his hardest not to run out of the Pentagon offices, trying his best to see in the car with sweat raining down his face.

3

Thirteen nights. Then it was twelve nights. Now it was eleven nights.

A sense of comfortable claustrophobia had made its home in Byron's head. It was as if time had lost its muscle in this place. He felt he belonged here, and that made him nervous. But being nervous was better than feeling like he wasn't renting his body, owning his actions. He needed to be nervous, more nervous, for the fact was that the voices heard that evening while seeing The Prince of Shadows were still in his head, distant but getting louder each time he awoke from *Moratoria*. Byron couldn't make them out, but for some reason they didn't bother him, for some reason the will to question them seemed almost unimportant. His dreams were varied, but there was no Medea out there. He knew she still existed, knowing that if she passed it would reverberate all the way to his heart, but couldn't tap into her being like in the past. Perhaps it was The Centurion, who ruled silently and tethered any form of material or immaterial energy. After all, besides making Earth a radioactive tomb, his purpose was to nourish and protect this metropolis. His power stretched beyond science and mocked it at the same time.

Medea wasn't in his dreams, but The Dark Instinct was a few times. The God-Soul, who taunted him often in hunger possessed a form and a face. It was his own, although his skin was gray-black, luminous yet somehow swallowing, his hair of jet. And he did taunt him, of course, standing in a storm similar to the one the Prince of Shadows lingered in. Beyond the storm, there were those voices.

"You're such a bastard," The Dark Instinct chided. "A bastard of a universe that never cared about you and your little delusions. You gave your identity to me, now you'll give it to everyone else."

No, I won't. I'm Byron.

His own smile widened, showing teeth also of jet.

"You're a joke," it said. "A joke from the beginning, a joke in the end. The best thing you can do is succumb to me and learn to consume fully again. Play the part, Byron."

Never. Damn you.

"No, Byron. Damn you. They're coming for you. You're losing it all. I'm not going to..."

Byron would wake up, his starvation for juice, which he could easily get from a tap on the other side of his room, telling him The Dark Instinct was still with him, still fueled the corpse he truly was. Who was coming for him? He was here, his enemies no longer walked this planet. New Atlantis was going to be judged soon, and all he needed was to find if Balkros had lied.

After touring other sections of The Egg and offering shallow companionship to sundry Stargazers, Byron spent the late nights accessing data in the various computer rooms. The computers were another hallmark of this advanced society, nothing more than large squares of glasses with decorative keyboards since they were voice activated to precision. He was usually alone by then, the population interested in activities other than their rare guest. By that part of the night, the undead gadabouts were immersed in their balls, their poetry readings, their quiz games and midnight swims, to name a few events. Their shapes and forms and powers didn't bother him after the second night; he accepted that, like him, they were just part of Lilith's rage, a twisted mimic of the thing called life. Byron knew that unlike the Stargazers of post Holocaust times, they knew of their elemental doom and, worse, resided here in hidden shame from the rest of the Stargazer civilization. But that would end soon, for he had a mission and they believed they were going to be free in a new era. They were, in a different sense.

At first, he browsed the many topics in the data banks. The information was astounding—for they had nothing to hide here—much broader than anything in Xanadu. He could have learned all about the world before and after the Holocaust. He could have spent years soaking in all the topics veiled from his reality as a citizen of Xanadu. But he wanted to find a file with Balkros' signature, or one titling the cure for a certain disease. Byron did this cautiously at first, part of him wondering if The Centurion or any of The Pharisees might find his intentions by his logging on the computers. He wouldn't be too bold yet.

'Yet' came on the third night of his stay. He used the search engines to find the end of his quest. There was nothing on The Killer of Giants, The Blood of Circles, and all the files on Balkros were about his past. He had actually been somewhat of a heroic Warm One? Obviously, the files weren't that accurate, he thought at one point with a sneer, a cigarette always burning on an ashtray by the screen.

On the fourth night he tried to excavate deeper. Despite their claims to no privacy, there were certain files that were guarded, files that seemingly were only privy to The Pharisees and their passwords. Byron had been notorious at hacking guarded programs in Xanadu, but the passwords could only be breached with the exact voice of one of The Pharisees. He saw they were only a few, but wondered if they were put this way after Balkros had sent his transmissions, maybe to be inspected for potential viruses or noteworthy information. After all, The Pharisees' function here was to administer The Egg's affairs with loose leadership, along with Quidam and The Centurion. Byron knew he had to rape those files, for a few were entitled 'Balkros', and there were no images of his lovely face in the banks like the one seen by the population and him that first night.

How would he get into them? Simple. He would ask Marcion. The Pharisee would tell him. He would ask him and only him, for he found him somewhat pure in this place, somewhat majestic. Like him, Byron found him just as tragic as himself. And just as lonely in his world. He couldn't deny a certain admiration, a little awe, and a lot of comradeship towards Marcion. More than that, The Good Neighbor was the first figure of power and prestige Byron had ever met who was fair and devoid of arrogance.

The difference was that Byron had Medea, Proxos to a lesser extent, and thus wasn't totally lonely in the world like The Pharisee. He couldn't stop wondering about her, worrying about her. Byron also yearned for her, yearned for her balance and dryness, wished she was here to help him with all he had to cope with. He hoped she was simply waiting for him at the stockpiled cavern or even back at Proxos' base on the other side of the mountains. But he understood that Medea would never do that. She should have already followed by now. What had happened? Why had Proxos lied about this city? Why couldn't he contact her? There was a wall somewhere, a wall that impeded communication through their spliced souls. Who was the wall? Was it she or him or, again, was it this place and its mute ruler?

Since he couldn't climb that wall, Byron used more mundane methods to find his allies. In between touring the city and searching for the cure, he again used the trust of these people to retrieve his solutions. Voice commands were enough to manipulate their satellites from any of the computers. To his chagrin, an electrical storm had spread across this area right after the night he met The Centurion and still hadn't passed, making any scanning impossible. He had seen part of the mountains and the remains of Xanadu. There was very little transpiring in his former home, except for the perishing of Warm Ones in large scales. He forced the satellite to seek the mountains where the storm wasn't as potent, pushing away the angry shame that came from those images.

To end it all.

Byron did catch Stargazer movement through the mountains. The size of the groups told him it was probably more fugitives escaping Balkros' new domain. He also noticed dozens of fallen ones, and he told them silently they were perhaps lucky to have collapsed in their search, for this place only held The Forgotten and Quidam's blade.

On the second evening of his search, late and close to the rise of *Sol*, he had asked Revenant if he had heard or seen of any refugees recently entering the city, since many of the outside sensors were disturbed by the storm. His question had come while they witnessed a play called *Endgame*, terribly performed by some of The Kappa and a few Stargazers that appeared to be made out of crystal.

"I have heard or seen nothing of that sort tonight," she said, clapping daintily, her exposed breasts with black nipples jiggling at the same time. "You are still our only guest, Byron, and a Stargazer would surely succumb to the tempest outside in the open valley. Your friends would be wise to seek shelter in the mountains. Even the traders avoid this area when a storm falls from the higher elevations."

"The traders?" Byron asked, not clapping but smoking a lot. All they mostly did here was find means of entertainment; if there wasn't a card game or party around the corner, they wandered around with lost expressions, looking for dialogue or argument with the first figure encountered. All he mostly did was smoke, search for the cure, and search and long for Medea.

Revenant explained who the traders were, Dreamreavers they called themselves, and Byron could have sworn a few times her lips never moved—probably another gift for these ghouls or whatever they were called. Byron shook his head at the notion of rogue Stargazer bands out there, but Proxos had mentioned that there were a few pockets of Heretics in the wilderness, or at least the potential. He quickly concentrated on his companion's fates.

"Will you and the rest make sure I know if they come? I can at least warn them not to enter or scare The Warden away. They are close to me, Revenant."

"And obviously not close enough at the moment" the Pharisee said. "Please, Byron. I would like to enjoy the rest of this play. I have seen it one hundred and thirty two times, but Prince Poppykettle's Klev improves each year."

"Well, will you inform me?"

"If they arrive, and I see you, I will tell you, Byron."

"What about the rest? What about the others?"

"Shh," Revenant said, his sound echoing inside her mouth with prickly timber.

"Shit." Byron rolled his eyes while leaning back in his seat.

He smoked more. He yearned more.

And he could tell he was getting more distant to everything, no matter how hard he fought it. Medea and his destiny was his anchor, but the chain lengthened with each dissolving hour. One part of him told him he had time, another craved for her and the hope she might be safe at the moment. And the voices still came, garbled but still there, and his dreams showed The Dark Instinct mocking him. In between the dreams and voices, he tried to find a way into those files, mingled with the population in their efforts to battle boredom, and prayed the damn electrical storm would end. All he wanted was answers.

When it was ten nights before five megatons of a new age visited The Prince of Shadows and The City of The Unsane, Byron decided that prying Marcion for more answers was the best alternative. The Pharisee seemed glad to spend time with him alone for part of the evening. The two watched the storm from Marcion' chambers. There were no windows to disrobe the outside, so it was all viewed from a large screen brought in by some servants. They were dressed in something called a tuxedo; Byron's was black, The Good Neighbor's was white. "Your hair looks well with that color," Marcion had remarked while they dressed.

"It wasn't always that color," Byron said before a tall mirror, toying with a bow-tie he knew would never be fully mastered by his fingers.

"It can be anything you wish," The Good Neighbor told him, watching Byron's reflection from behind. "A Stargazer should do whatever he pleases, especially with the material world."

"You're sounding like an Elder, Marcion."

"I am, of sorts. Now, gaze hard into your reflection, change what you need. We are notable creatures."

Byron shook his head but obeyed. He felt curdling emotions and thoughts sweep through him. Closing his eyes, he pictured himself back in Xanadu, with his long coats and former hairstyle, before the months in his sand grave had changed him by giving him a new hair color and the personified voice of The God-Soul.

When he opened his eyes, his hair had returned to its rich dark brown with the reddish tint. Just like that it was short and curly and thick. He blinked a few times, not to catch light but to catch reality.

"Like you were before," Marcion said. "Like you should be in eternity. Quite easy really." Byron shook his head again. "Too easy. Can I get rid of a voice in my head? Actually, there are more of them. Do you know why?"

He grabbed his arm and led him towards the screen. "As I said before—The Prince of Shadows, Byron. This is his domain, we are part of his dream. He fills us with his essence, his power permeating the city, which is his organism. We are the cells, he is the spirit. We are all one with him, in perfection and naked like sucklings."

"I don't know if I like that," Byron said, tensing inside but just not enough. As if it didn't matter, as if the sickness of comfort had been infected from the other inhabitants.

"Then you will probably try and change it, fight it until you win. You enjoy doing this, and we are glad you are here for you represent our freedom."

"Freedom, eh? Tell me more about this prophecy."

With a musical edge, Marcion related a sentence about a knight who might knock at the doors, best The Warden, drink in generations with The Prince of Shadows and have his armor stripped.

"Sounds like nonsense to me," Byron said. "Drinking in generations...what does that mean?"

"I am not totally omniscient, but there is a connection between the two of you. Come, Byron Solsbury."

They drank juice from a thing called a martini glass. The storm shivered before them, serpentine bolts lighting up the filth, giving the mountains a severe silhouette. Moody blues and cobalt hazes added to the spectacle. Marcion spoke about his storms and his people and how Lilith kept him close to her after she had violated the fairy world.

"I don't know how you did it," Byron commented.

"We miss, we yearn, but with our kind it is much more severe," Marcion said. "We miss life, we miss death, we miss satisfaction."

"A friend of mine once said the exact same thing." Byron arched an eyebrow. "Do you always have to be so damn mystical?"

"Yes," he hissed, crossing his legs in the chair. "I told you that is one of my gifts, Byron. I see through time's tapestry. I can capture spasms, reflexes, and memories that are but morsels, toys to my elven side."

"And what about your Stargazer side?"

"We miss, we yearn, Byron."

The storm grew stronger. He hoped his friends were sheltered from it. This place could handle it, but it wouldn't handle what came in ten nights.

Suddenly, realizing something that should have been faced nights ago, that should have given him more urgency, Byron hoped staunchly that Marcion and his gift wouldn't bring to light his intentions, his mission.

"Can you predict my future, Marcion?"

"Yes," Marcion responded. "To a certain extent, when it comes to me, when I meditate or concentrate. Would you like to hear it?"

Mirrors. A reflection. The voices.

"Not right now," Byron said, still not as nervous as he should be. "I'm sure all you care about is that I symbolize something, I fit into The MoonQueen's prophecy."

He turned to look directly at him. "I care about more. Yes, Shiannon-Lhee, is absent and we are free to figure out the rest of eternity. Yes, we must follow the prophecy for it still involves two of her main apostles: The Prince of Shadows and Quidam. Yet, for some reason, I care about you, Byron. We are both peerless to an extent. We both have a way of standing above and beyond destiny, history, so noble, so lonely, so intense. It is quite a burden, eh?"

Byron didn't say anything, wishing the storm outside was in his heart again. He felt so comfortable with The Good Neighbor, yet so detached from himself. He needed to find the fury, strike through his goals. Take it far again. What had happened? What was happening to him?

"If you're offering friendship," Byron said, trying anything to rekindle his old bravado. "I'm not sure I'm ready to give it."

"Would you rather us become adversaries?"

"I've had my share of formidable opponents, Marcion. You—"

"I would win," he said with a thin smirk. "After all, I have two qualities you'll never have to be truly victorious: patience and poise. I have waited for thousands of years for this moment, knowing that it was a matter of time before she unraveled, witnessing so many foes succumb to her glacier might. She is gone and I am here."

Yes, Byron thought, but because of me, because of what I am.

With a blinding movement, The Pharisee moved his head and kissed Byron on the lips. He didn't flinch, for some reason allowing Marcion' cold lips to crawl over his own cold lips. The lips wriggled like snakes into a smile during the kiss, a satiny tongue darted quickly to slither over Byron's teeth.

"But would I betray you with a kiss?" Marcion asked, shifting away. "You must excuse me, Byron Solsbury. I have matters to attend."

Byron watched him leave with his ethereal grace. He might have been more than dumbfounded, but the exterior would never show The Good Neighbor any satisfaction—he'd had plenty of that showing his guest New Atlantis. As for the interior, it still wallowed in a lackadaisical swamp of voices and perplexed emotions. It had just been a kiss. They were both peerless.

When Marcion was gone, he tossed his glass over his shoulder. By the time it had shattered behind him, his head was in between his legs, hands clutching his hair. The sound felt good, sharp and awakening.

Mirrors. A tool. What was happening?

"Shit," he said. "Medea where are you? Tomorrow, damn it, before he finds out, they find out. I have time. Tomorrow I'll ask him about the files. Tomorrow I'll find out, one way or another."

He felt some agitation within him, the old excitement he had felt when first witnessing New Atlantis. He knew he would get it back, find what he needed, and leave this place. He tightened his fingers around his hair and something else shattered but within him. He barely heard the storm cackling outside.

The shattering was that excitement. The pieces falling in his mind told him that he dreaded two things, didn't want to face them, that it was almost better to fall into a comfortable stasis, forget time, and fall into the voices and the system of this place.

One, was what would happen if there was no cure, surely dooming Medea. Then he would have failed, unlike the other times when there was always a kernel of redemption, and have nothing in this world. Nothing. He would be truly alone in a city of lonely souls.

We'll always be together, one way or another.

Two, he knew his destiny but somehow dreaded that the destiny was to exterminate these beings that were as much victims as he was, actually much more. He would end wondrous Marcion and the others who simply existed to enjoy their curses, find a semblance of humanity as he had in The City of Domes.

But he had to end it all and this was it. He couldn't stall anymore, deny his place in the destiny, for this was risking Medea and sowing doubt in his mind. They were all truly dead, dead memories, dead spasms of brighter times. They, like the ones in Xanadu, were a lie and a horrible blackness over a punished world. Yes, Byron was an omen that they would be free. Free forever.

And tomorrow he had to ask about those files and face his goal, no matter what nagged him, The Dark Instinct boasted, or The Prince and his court had changed in him.

4

In Medea's dream, the beautiful tall female was getting closer to reveal itself. She could now see beyond the entertainment area. She realized that in the back and lining other areas of the massive tent, this pageant spread before and after this climax. Amazing things loomed around the beautiful tall female's dance.

In cages, queer creatures pranced behind bars in cages of brass and silver. Figures with simian or furred faces gawked back at the Warm Ones gawking at them. Pale blue people on small platforms chewed metal with serrated teeth or swallowed swords. Others gave small presentations, turning into mist or floating in midair right in front of cooing children. Then ancient stories were woven to these pups or gifts were tossed out, like thin books with changing pictures or eggs that hatched birds with flaming wings. In some isolated places, money was charged to witness deformed monsters that growled or spat fire at the brave spectators with a craving to be terrified. She saw so much, no, more like felt it, in a short span. It was a display like no other, and the entertainers were like her, not like the Warm Ones who came in droves to see things that challenged their minds.

Someone spoke again in an odd language next to her. She was starting to understand the words.

"C'est, magnifique, non? La femme est formidable?" one person asked.

Medea started to cringe, perceiving that language had been spoken by one being only, met when she was a kidnapped Warm One in the kingdom of ice at the top of Xanadu. The cringing subsided, for the currents of this show took her in again, swept her away as it did all who came.

It was a circus. That's what they called it in a land called France.

The beautiful, tall female's circus.

This was the zenith, and she was about to dance.

She looked directly at Medea.

And gave her a coy wink of recognition.

5

Marcion walked down the many hallways of The Egg. He didn't know where he was going, but he indulged an urge. Most of the times, he simply acted on his arcane impulses and allowed the situation to take care of itself. That's how The Good Neighbor had done it even before becoming a Stargazer, that's how the *Sidhe* had done it, dancing on time's whims, toying with the fabric of the material. Now he was a being of destruction, a ravager of creation, but held this destiny at bay as often as possible.

He turned a corner and saw a will'o'wisp dangling in a niche that, like everything, was mirrored. The once gentle spirit was a signal to him, for only he and The Kappa could see its pulsing light. The Good Neighbor nodded at it and pushed on the back of the wall. It opened a secret chamber of many in New Atlantis. Actually, it wasn't secret, but the denizens preferred that notion when playing murder mystery or role playing dice games.

In the small chamber, Feltch and Poppykettle waited for him, dressed in powder blue shorts and sailor tops, crested by curly bond wigs, each holding a stick with a round flat red candy. They bounced on their warped legs, looking as eager and foul as they always did. Patience had been suffocated in them when they were given new identities five hundred centuries ago, and that often annoyed Marcion. At the same time, he knew why they had summoned him and that they would have to have dialogue. Dialogue kept the citizens from fading away just as entertainment did. They didn't want to fade away yet, for this was their last chance for freedom, to start something new their way without Lhiannon-Shee.

"So, how's it going, Mac?" Feltch asked, not waiting for Marcion to close the door behind him. "The storm was horror show, man. Keep this knight away from other meddlers. Everything else going as planned?"

"Yes," Marcion responded. "I will go into a trance this night, for I feel that we must act quickly for some reason. There are still fluxes that are not clear. I must wedge into them and finally understand the fullness of the prophecy. Kismet is everywhere, but Byron will bring us what we have craved for so long.

He believes he is a signal, a beacon of changing eras, but he is much more dynamic to our needs, as we have seen."

"He scares me," Poppykettle admitted, spittle growing in bubbles on his thick lips. "He's brazen and powerful, Good Neighbor."

"He should be," Marcion said with a small smile. "That is partly why he is the one. The God-Soul is so full in him, so is his Warm One nature."

"Reminds me of you," Feltch said with a guttural chuckle. "You like him don't you?"

"I like him," Marcion said sadly. "But I cannot stop the turning of the wheel. I only predict it and tweak it."

Poppykettle held his gnarled hands. "So he is knight for sure, our champion, uh? He drinks in generations—"

"Of course he does, stupid!" Feltch growled. "That is why The Centurion moved that night. He recognized the fucker, Byron, or at least was jolted by him. Drinking in generations means that they are related, a long way at that. Mac, you were smart in not telling him the whole truth, man. We don't need him messing with us. We're a goddamn Pandora's Box ready to explode all over the world and show that ice cube bitch how to really party."

Marcion shook his head at the pair. The population, who heard it all through The Yolk, shook his head at him.

"But what about being stripped of armor and shield and the rest?" Poppykettle asked.

"That is why I must enter a trance," Marcion said. "But for some reason, I believe that is already happening. I will procure the rest and find a way to accelerate matters"

"But you said we don't have much time!" Poppykettle said, along with the population not understanding the hidden senses of this Pharisee.

"I know, Poppykettle. But, as I said, there are other shifts which are not clear. I see a Raven felled by lightning as he tries to cross a desert in a mad quest. I see a bursting image of the circus where we enter—"

"Don't say that!" Feltch shouted and Poppykettle cringed. So did many others, envisioning cages and having to tell boring stories to pups they couldn't devour until afterwards in the thick night.

"—I see an old friendship rekindled and fire from the sky coming our direction—"

"Lovely." Feltch grinned evilly. "Fucking lovely."

"But I cannot separate it all," Marcion admitted. "It is like a maelstrom is steaming above the universe, melting away any vision, blurring time and space at once."

"I wonder what it could be," Poppykettle mused. "Even Quidam seems nervous. You wouldn't know, since he is the only who can have privacy if he desires, but after all this time I can tell."

"We can tell," Feltch said. "No fucking privacy."

"Yes, yes," the other Kappa continued. "But he, like The Prince of Shadows, for now, if you are correct, only serves The MoonQueen's desire. He still guards us, and she is gone, isn't she? Why is he still here? Why can't we leave?"

"Because she willed it," Marcion said. "An absent god can still have its desires on the world, if she chooses. That is why the prophecy must be carried out, my friends. That is why The Liberator must continue his quest."

"Sweet!" Feltch said.

Poppykettle nodded. "Sweet."

Marcion only regarded the two with mild amusement, knowing that his feeling of slight sadness was sensed by all. He more than liked Byron; but Byron had to fulfill his part, as he'd done before. And then they would finally be free forever. After all, as he told Byron before betraying him with a kiss, Marcion was patient and poised. He was that way when his spirit was filled with The Dark Instinct, he was patient when The Holocaust ended and they were brought to this valley.

"No, Mac!" Feltch moaned. "Not that vision, not that again."

But he couldn't help it, wouldn't help it, and the citizens would share in that grim memory, which haunted all inside the shell of New Atlantis.

How could they ever forget the night they were summoned to the edge of this valley by The Queen of Darkness. From their respective shelters, many carrying mastodon loads of their valued possession, they traveled to this place. Many never arrived, absorbed by the still-coruscating outdoors, swallowed by ash and despair at what had happened. The ones who retained a will to face a new age had no choice, for Her will was all that mattered.

She stood at top of a rocky ledge, proud and victorious and glistening in shades of icy blue. Her dress flowed softly against the torturing squalls, her aura easily dispelled the heat and radiation and the petals of ash. This was her world now, and right beneath her was an unholy triumvirate: Quidam, The Elders, and The Prince of Shadows himself, still donned in the same leather armor he wore when he usurped part of The Mad God progeny's juice, still appearing as senseless as ever, eyes a trail of smoke, mouth opened and always drooling black juice.

The Forgotten already knew of their baneful plights. They had aided her in the past but not with The Holocaust. They were too dear to her, but too unruly. They would have their own city, she explained without words, pointing at the valley. The remnants of a Warm One city stood, metal barely cooling, buildings still fuming in charcoal plumes. One of The Forgotten, named Jimmy Squarefoot, complained that this was not suitable for them. He was unceremoniously slain by Quidam. The rest remained silent, while The Queen of Darkness laughed so hard the sky broke open to show them the constellations just briefly. It would be the last time any of them ever saw stars with their own eyes. Soon, they would never personally witness the outdoors.

Then She waived at The Centurion. He floated torpidly towards the ruins and exploded in dark silvery light. It covered the valley, bringing towards it the remnants of the Warm One city. Metal dissolved into warm globs, wood evaporated, whole buildings changed forms as it all went around The Centurion. At the same time, Balkros, who wasn't wearing the robes of The Elders at that time, held a computer with a speaker that emitted odd tones, compressed information to the dark silvery light that was now a lurid tornado.

It barely took half of the night. When it was done, a large dome rested in the middle with no trace of the former skeletal metropolis apparent. Balkros cackled at them while they lowered their heads, knowing that their permanent existence would be in that new city, born from the bones of the Warm One empire.

"You still all have work inside," Shibboleth told them, always close to the hem of Shiannon-Lhee. "The Warm Ones will arrive soon, and you have specific orders on what you will be, on how the city will develop. Go now, for you all are part of New Atlantis. To us it will be the first true Stargazer city. To you it is your prison for eternity. Or Bastille, as Our Mistress prefers to call it."

They couldn't do anything but pick up their belongings and march towards it in line with slumped shoulders, those that had shoulders. At one point, Marcion turned his head and asked The Queen of Darkness if there would ever be any freedom for them. He dreaded the isolation more than anything, not caring anymore if his existence was in jeopardy. It was, for Quidam advanced towards him ready to cleave his body. He stopped as Lhiannon-Shee raised a hand.

"DO NOT STRIKE HIM, MON-SHERI" she said with her celestial yet childish tone. "HE IS MY SWEETEST OF SWEETESTS NOW, ENKIDU. BESIDES, HE MIGHT AID YOU WHEN YOU OVERSEE THE FORGOTTEN IN THERE."

Quidam's face bled with terror, at the realization that he was also being banished into The Egg forever. The Queen of Darkness didn't bother to notice The Warden's pleading stare because of his realized fate, speaking to Marcion. The whole line had stopped.

"WHEN THE EGG IS STRIPPED OF THE HUNDREDS OF TONS OF EARTH AROUND IT WITHIN TWELVE HEARTBEATS, LOOSE AND BALANCED IN FREEDOM, YOU MAY ASK A BOON TO THE CENTURION."

Marcion began to weep immediately, knowing that no force but The Centurion himself or her could move such a mass so quickly. The others began to weep, too, many for the first time in millennia, in their existences.

"IS THAT NOT GOOD ENOUGH FOR YOU, N'EST-CE PAS? HOW ABOUT ONE MORE, SWEET MARCION. HOW ABOUT THIS ONE, FOR IT IS YOUR ONLY HOPE THAT MIGHT OCCUR TOMORROW OR IN A MILLION YEARS: IF

A KNIGHTS SHOULD COME, A CHAMPION OF ETERNITY, ERRANT ON A DARKENING QUEST, KNOCKING ON YOUR GATES, THEN YOU SHOULD LET HIM IN. AND IF HE BESTS THE WARDEN AND DRINKS IN GENERATIONS WITH THE CENTURION, THEN HE MUST BE STRIPPED OF HIS SWORD, HIS SHIELD, AND ARMOR, AND BROUGHT NAKED LIKE A NEWBORN INTO THE GREY DUSK, INTO THE AWAKENING OF OUR PRINCE.

They all wept together, all the way into their new abode, not believing her words fully, knowing that they should better get accustomed to these walls and their new and final set of rules.

As Marcion retrieved his vision from the population, many cried yet another time. They cried at the memory, at the joy that the predictions might come true now. One had beaten The Warden. He drank in generations with The Centurion. Now he must be stripped and brought naked and brought into the gray dusk. And it was already happening, he had a feeling.

The storm raged outside and beyond, and perhaps in many heavy hearts of The City of The Unsane. Now all Marcion needed to do was to go into a trance.

Chapter 8

It was the most wonderful thing Dante had seen in a long time. His mood, tested by the pair of Stargazers retrieved from the desert, was ballooning to heights not experienced since realizing he could survive, thrive outside the Stargazer realm. In his adventures as a Dreamreaver, Dante had foraged to many of the ruins of the Warm One kingdom. Both Xanadu and New Atlantis had been erected in valleys circled by tall mountains in order to detain some of the Holocaust's early fury. Many miles away, in the mountain chains and beyond, Dante and his companions had perused the cremated remains of the abodes of the animals. He had seen towns and buildings and roads, empty vehicles and rusty machinery, all ravaged but surely functional and efficient at one time. He didn't care about wondering about the cattle's intelligence or any zoological theories, pruning these places for artifacts, items useful for survival or bartering with New Atlantis. It was a dangerous occupation, daring the climate and the distances, but he enjoyed it. It made him stronger each passing year, and one of these nights he promised he would build his own city from all of these scraps, as far away as possible. He had all the time in the world.

But what he saw made all of his hopes, dreams, and cravings almost real enough to savor. Medea and Proxos had not lied. At first, he thought of the ex-Elder's bargain as some silly hoax. These two had to have gone mad traveling across the mountains. In any case, he had no time to resurrect old ghosts and delve into the nihilistic politics of his former home. But he had accepted the offer, and now it appeared Dante and his people were getting the far better end of the bargain.

All he had to do was take these two characters with

him when the Dreamreavers traded with New Atlantis. Take them and allow them to infiltrate the city during the sometimes chaotic exchange. Both Medea and Proxos had smiled when he told them that the doors remained open for at least an entire night during the transactions.

And all he got in return was a cavern full of products that barely showed any rust, tucked away in a dry cavern inside the belly of one of the mountains. So many things that could easily be used to buy large stocks of Warm Ones, materials, clothing, weapons, and even the information fools like Poppykettle and the others bragged about having in endless amounts. More than that, if the fuels in the tanks and a quarter of all the machinery worked, Dante had the tools to begin crafting his own metropolis, perhaps from the shell of that first Warm One town he discovered.

"This is it?" he had said, the only Dreamreaver able to speak when they were led into the cavern.

"Is it not enough?" Proxos said. "There are a few more tunnels to the back with sealed materials, the toxic ones."

"I don't believe it." Dante had felt almost lightheaded. "Shit...I never knew..."

"You told us you always avoided the northern part of the valley," Medea said, looking frailer with each night. Was the Ruka juice not enough for her? "But it is here, Dante. We've explained what it is. Now we want you to fulfill your part of the agreement."

Dante chuckled, feeling as if he'd been asked the simplest task of his existence. It would be a few nights before they left, barely arriving before an electrical storm scoured the valley. Thunder shook the high ceiling of the cavern, but Dante only knew the thunder of his hopes. This was wonderful, he thought over and over again, taking non-stop inventory each of the four nights. Their provisions were low, but he shrugged away his Dark Instinct, pacing the rows, asking Proxos the uses of some of the objects, absorbing every single item. His good mood increased so much, he barely noticed anyone else. Medea and Proxos appeared nervous and kept counting down each night. Ten nights was the last thing he heard between them. No matter, he thought, perhaps these odd fellows speak the truth about Our Mistress, but it is no concern of mine. I am still free, and if it is true, then nothing can stop me from starting something over.

Starting it better.
I am still free.
The past is behind me.

On the fourth night in the cavern, as his crew readied the ships anchored at the bottom of the tunnel, many which needed repairing because of the narrow entryway and the weather outside, he found Medea at the entrance. Dante had gone to make sure the storm had decayed enough. Medea had probably beaten him after *Moratoria*.

The first thing he noticed, besides the clouds gurgling away above them and still burping with lightning, washing the plain valley in a dark lavender and the mountains in grayish purple, was Medea's appearance. He couldn't deny her sharp beauty, accentuated by large and proud eyes, but the eyes were very sunken, the pale skin of the Stargazer almost tinted with blue. More than that, she exuded less of her confident energy. He wondered if her features had changed, if she wasn't shorter nights ago, but it was probably just his lack of focus on detail when it came to individuals. Dante realized suddenly he liked and could easily appreciate this person, liked her directness, her seriousness, which were not at all poisoned by cynicism. He couldn't deny his attraction as he couldn't deny the absurd bargain.

He had all of this so that they could rescue Byron. Byron! How could such a being change, full of haughty conviction and galactic charisma? He wasn't surprised Byron had fallen from his nest, but still couldn't accept he was a hero, a revolutionary, a defeater of The Queen of Darkness.

"We will do it right this time," Byron had once told all the newly recruited Ravens in a meeting, the Farms and Slaughterhouses recently built, stock coming from other places, a few years after Utopia had fallen. "Xanadu will be the last home for Our Mistress, do you hear? We will be severe, cruel, and so methodical that we'll pass for the machinery that takes away their juice. I won't make the same mistake as in Utopia."

Dante recalled looking around to skim various gazes. As usual, it was Mephisto who had to put into words their silent question, his mouth always one step ahead of everyone's.

"You were in Utopia, Byron?" he asked with his dashing smile that never allowed anger to last against him. "What mistake was that?"

Dante also recalled the puzzled look of their leader, followed by a sort of lost smile.

"Sorry; I was speaking possessively, people. There was no mistake, only Her will. Blessed be Our Mistress."

Dante had caught a certain hollowness in his voice he assumed was Lord Byron's dislike for true formality. But it had to be that, seeing his tight rule on most of the new city and the pride The Elders had for him. Dante always tried to emulate him, he knew these nights, and had thought he was able to surpass him. He hadn't, and that was the only thing that bothered him to this night.

The only thing.

And he had completely missed that rebellion was already germinating inside Byron, unbalancing him, as soon as he was given authority.

Starting it better.

"We are almost ready," Dante told Medea, who still looked at the dome that was allegedly the last Stargazer city. "It will take us no time to reach New Atlantis and you can be on your way to find your friend."

"He is more than a friend," Medea said plainly.

Those words bothered him. Part of him could almost see Byron with a smug grin whenever he felt like he'd won at anything. But more than a friend? What was she talking about? She wasn't talking about a primitive notion only Warm Ones entertained?

The same Warm Ones who had built what had once been advanced cities?

"I see," Dante said, pushing away any emotion or thoughts getting in his way. "You are very odd to me, Medea. You don't seem like a fool to me, but the things you say...want, seem very foolish, even reckless."

She still wouldn't look at him, but she allowed a tiny smile. "What you do for your people, Dante, the dreams you impart on them, your notions of a free Stargazer land, might also be construed as foolish."

"Yes, but—"

"And you would do many things for them, wouldn't you? You would go a long way for their wellbeing."

"I suppose," he said flatly, her words strumming more feelings he couldn't understand. "But we're talking about Byron."

"Yes, we are. Don't worry, Dante, if we escape, we will stay as far away from you as possible. You'll probably never see me...any of us ever again."

Again, the words bothered him.

"Perhaps, Medea. I never thought I'd hear his name again." He laughed once, trying to regain some semblance of his notorious confidence. "It doesn't matter. I have my hopes, and hopefully you can rescue him."

She finally looked at him. Her eyes held little energy, barely glowing as Stargazer eyes did when hard emotion coursed through their godly bodies.

"We're doing more than that, Dante," she said. "We're also going to destroy New Atlantis, finish The MoonQueen's empire once and for all."

He covered his mouth in order to hide an orphaned smile. She definitely was odd.

"Whatever you say," he said. "In the wilderness, I mind my business, Medea. Is Byron already planting bombs inside the hull of the dome?"

Her gaze darted towards the glossy dome. "Let us just say, that when you trade, trade well because there will be no skeletal remains for your people. Afterwards, travel in your little vehicles far away from that city."

Dante couldn't help sigh. Nobody ever said Heretics had to be sane. Delusion was a nice place to be when not trapped in The MoonQueen's reverie (or perhaps *even* when trapped in it). Perhaps there was no Byron, no razed Xanadu, just two expunged Stargazers sentenced for their madness. He decided to change the course of their conversation by placing a hand on her shoulder.

"Are you fine, Medea? You seem...uh...weak. Did you go through anything odd while traveling here?"

"I'm fine," she said wearily. "I'll be better when we can leave your new property."

Changing the course had dried the current very quickly. He took his hand off her shoulder, sensing that something was indeed very wrong with her. His nose sensed an almost rotting smell that emanated from somewhere besides her body. It wasn't his business. Dante was handing them over to New Atlantis and that was it. Start it better.

"We'll be right up," he said, making his way down the tunnel. As the dusty smell of the cavern increased, the odd emotions and bothersome words were almost forgotten by the place, until he heard Medea whisper something a few hundred feet away.

I can't feel you, Byron. I just can't feel you. Why?

Dante wanted to say something snotty, deciding instead that Medea must find her own realities just as he had.

2

Nine nights. No answer. Not yet. Another night and he had failed again.

Byron had been told by a Kappa named *Unkulunku* that Marcion was in a trance. He shouldn't be disturbed— for they were important for the fettle of The Egg. If there was a rule here, besides the sword of Quidam and the eviction of privacy, this was it. Byron told The Kappa he was a moron and rushed to The Pharisee's chambers. Mirrors and doors and hallways, and the voices wouldn't go away, the lethargy that had set within him still bubbled. He didn't care about them, only about finding his answer and getting out of this place. He wanted to vacate before he enjoyed it too much, before he found the true ecstasy of immortality which was nothing but defeating boredom. Warm Ones attempted to defeat destruction, these beings attempted to defeat boredom. In the other cities they had just served Lilith. Here they tried hard to entertain themselves by being honest and imaginative, two aspects of existence Byron enjoyed so much. The one reason he hadn't succumbed was Medea and the small fact that, at this point, a missile was pointed this way. Pointed this way to finish Marcion, The Prince of Shadows, the citizens he was starting to empathize with in their tragedy.

No, he kept telling himself. They are a reflex of The Dark Instinct. They are Stargazers, pawns of Lilith. They are evil!

But they're not, another voice told him. They are as forlorn as you, perhaps more. They never really served her, but were helpless in her grasp. You are a hero again to them because you are the true, eternal vanquisher of boredom, of the darkness of mere being.

"Damn it!" he shouted, slamming his fist on one of the walls. The mirror shattered around him. He ignored the few shards stabbing his cold skin. An alarm sounded, and Byron was sure some Warm One platoon would arrive to fix it in moments. They didn't like privacy here, they wanted honesty and self-reflection at all times.

"Damn it!" he said many times until storming into Marcion's chambers. He would always have access to any place here. If he didn't feel like it, he could just have visual intrusion with a screen to any place of this city.

Perhaps he should have, his feet sliding on the juice matting the floor, all belonging to the dozen Warm Ones slaughtered and strewn around the cozy room. Byron didn't even want to wonder about their expressions—each had an irregularly large smile, as if their expirations by The Good Neighbor had been enjoyable, a reward. But it wasn't, he told himself. It was wrong because the God-Soul only existed to vanquish, destroy, hunt all that was thriving in the universe. How could they enjoy their destruction by beings that sucked more than their juice but their life essences, their dreams...their light!

But then again, it was Marcion.

He sat in the middle, eyes wide open but gorged in a pure white light, hands clutching the arms of a throne he said belonged to some King Henry or something. The Pharisee's face held no expression, although the corners of his mouth curled slightly as if in potential smile. The little Stargazer, Adam, growled at Byron with a wet mouth at his feet, its small hands clutching the severed penis of one of the bodies.

"Marcion," Byron said, ignoring anything but his intentions. "Wake up. I need to talk to you."

Nothing.

"Marcion, damn it! I'm not in the mood for this dramatic shit. I need to talk to you now. You said I could always have the answers."

Nothing.

Byron moved to shake him, but the creature growled louder. Byron growled back at him, only to have the aberration fly through the air towards him. With one swipe, he shattered most of its bones, sending it flying across the room. Mirrors shattered. Mirrors everywhere. Then he shook The Good Neighbor, stopping himself because he thought his bones might break, too.

Nothing.

"For fuck sakes, Marcion," Byron said with an aching frown. "Where are you? I need to talk to you. I only want to talk to you."

Nothing. The eyes glowed. He was in a trance.

Byron stormed out in the same manner he had stormed in. A Warm One was already diligently fixing the mess caused in the hallway.

Mirrors. A reflection.

In rebellious anger and somehow to touch upon something rigid in himself, Byron slew the worker and fed on only a few pints of juice. He spattered the rest of the juice on the remaining mirrors, trying to cover any reflection out. The reflection showed his body in crimson. The anger grew, the voices were so loud.

Cursing all the way, he searched the city for the other two Pharisees. They would allow him entrance to Balkros' files. He wasn't worried about discovery anymore or even suspicion. He knew the population cared little of those two concepts. He wanted the information, he wanted to see Medea and escape the voices. He wanted out of this delicious place.

Feltch ignored him in one of the large chambers on the western edges of The Egg. Dressed in a beige, heavily starched uniform with an arm-band that held a twisted cross as a sign Byron didn't understand, he was making a speech to several members of the population similarly dressed before him. Byron couldn't understand his words and didn't see the humor in a small, square mustache painted over his gross mouth or the greased wig covering the hole on his head.

"I'm trying to make a speech, mein freund," Feltch said, raising a straightened arm to the population. "It's the same speech he gave in Munich just before invading Poland in—"

"Shut-up!" Byron spat. "I need some answers. You said you will always give them to me."

The crowd booed Byron, waving black and red flags wildly at the same time, while Feltch sneered at him.

"You're being fucking rude," The Kappa said. "And you need a shower. I never said I'd give you any goddamn answers, Byron. And I'm not going to give you any now."

Byron hissed at him with narrowed eyes, his anger swelling at the jeering of the population, half of them who barely fit in their uniforms.

"There is no privacy here," he said with rigid softness. "I need to ask you something."

"When I'm done," Feltch retorted. "The whole actual speech only took about two hours, if you include the interview afterwards."

He continued his speech, the crowd silenced in focus. Once again, Byron was storming out, not able to conjure the energy to convince or even threaten The Pharisee. On the way out, he screamed at the reenactment.

"Don't you know that reality means something? That complacency only makes you irrelevant in the world."

They wouldn't answer, too absorbed in Feltch's booming oration. He went to the nearest observation room and found that Revenant was in the lower levels, enjoying some Veal with a few other ghouls. Taking several elevators and shafts in mist form, trying to hide his image from all the mirrors and cameras, it took him a few minutes to arrive there. His anger still burned but something else bothered him.

Feltch's speech, he could still hear it in his head. He could hear it and other speeches, random thoughts, talks and conversations. The voices...they didn't come from The Dark Instinct or some other dream, they didn't directly from The Prince of Shadows. They came from somewhere else. He had heard Revenant speak without opening his mouth the night of the play.

No! The voices came from the population! The voices came from inside their heads, all tethered to his brain!

He entered the darkened area, no, more like stumbled inside. The ghouls were feeding on some of the Veal, detached from their bodies and slaughtering quite a few. Byron tried to speak but his words seemed to blend in with the voice of Feltch. His voice and others.

He leaned against a wall with clamped eyes, the dying screams of the Warm One mixed in with the terrified screams of the ones not chosen filling his already saturated mind. Of course, there was the always snide voice of The God-Soul.

Feed me! Feed me more!

When Byron opened his eyes, color was a storm before him and his head was a volcano of pain. Revenant stood before him, her face as matted in juice as Byron's. The other ghouls were gliding into the elevator. Byron glanced back at her, almost pleadingly. The Pharisee bent down and gingerly retrieved Byron's cigarette pack from his robes. She lit one for herself and Byron.

"The voices," she said, placing a cigarette in Byron's mouth. "They will increase, become more defined, but you will get used to them. It is part of not believing in privacy. It's the best way to keep us all in check, with ourselves and our rulers. In Xanadu and Utopia, Stargazers existed in fear of their actions; here we existed in fear with just our thoughts, hiding them away with entertainment, trying every evening not to be swallowed by the weight of ourselves. You see, The Prince of Shadows makes us one with our thoughts, Byron, with his almost-omniscient thoughts. Soon, we will know all of your thoughts, even your emotions. And you will know ours. You will be exposed." She smiled with a certain triumph. "Naked, if you will."

"No," Byron said, thinking about his plans and the fate of this city. At the same time, the appalling realization of the predicament of The Forgotten disgusted him. "Please...I just need something...a file that was sent here."

The ghoul straightened.

"I'm sorry, but I know little of technology. I let the other two deal with that aspect. In any case, the computer will not work with my voice; strange how a slit throat from a blessed dagger never fully healed on the inside. You'll have to ask the other Pharisees."

Byron looked away. "Damn!"

"Yes," Revenant said, standing straight. "We are damned, but we make the best of it. Welcome to New Atlantis, Byron Solsbury. Welcome to the Prince of Shadow's dream, The MoonQueen's nightmare."

The Pharisee walked out. After finishing his smoke, Byron stood up and took the elevator. The Veals still mewled in fear in the corners of their pens. The smell of juice was almost sickening to him.

No privacy. A reflection.

On the way to his chamber, trying hard to repel the voices, the swirling thoughts on the edges of his phenomena, Byron noticed Quidam on one of the walkways above him. Something was different about him, something unnoticed before in this ancient Stargazer.

He was smiling at Byron. The smile was satisfied, almost condescending.

"Damn," Byron said under his breath. The anger was still there. But the anger, like him, was becoming part of the voices, the collective persona of New Atlantis.

3

Data: Becoming too anchored to the past. Thinking and speaking colloquially of that time with each spasm. Must rule city. Must plan for the futures.

Remembering...

Data: We are beyond this. The Dark Instinct must be satisfied soon. Or it will consume our body in tribute.

Remembering...

Gina had asked him to shut all the closets in her bedroom after being tucked in for the night. He asked her why. "Because I'm afraid," she answered plainly. He gently pinched her freckled cheek, then explained there were no monsters. "But if we believe in them, Daddy, then don't they exist?" He kissed her on the forehead, lips magnetized a little too long upon her warm skin. Believe in angels and God above, and they will protect you, he told her. No monsters. She said yes, but still wanted the closet doors closed. There was a duality there, having faith but still clinging to old superstition. A duality.

Remember...

Hours later, he stood before her while sweat marinated his body. His wife was fast asleep down the hall, farting and snoring in her alcohol-inspired slumber. The only thing inspiring him was the rage, the heat searing his shame, smothering his duality. Gina slept quiescently in her pink gown, not caring about the world, not caring that he held his penis nakedly in his hand. It was hot, too, shining in a meaty burnish against the hall-light to his right. He could barely breathe, as if his lungs might sound an alarm in the house or his heart. Same thing. He couldn't help himself. He loved her so much but she was the solution to the problems with his duality. He didn't understand why.

Balkros felt eyes caressing him. He turned his head to see Shibboleth floating outside his window. This was all a delusion, Eugene told himself. There were no angels, he hadn't basically committed treason against his nation, his secretary was only on leave of absence for the last several months. People weren't suddenly missing from many posts in the government; others didn't only request to work at night or walked the hallways with unnaturally pale skins and sunglasses. Rumors of instability across the ocean were just rumors, nothing else. His rage had created these beings, not God. But he believed in God and angels right?

The angel seemed to dissolve into an argent mist. The mist slithered between the window and wall, which his wife had told a million times to seal for economic reasons. The mist swirled before him, gurgled, and then took the form of Shibboleth.

"Are the codes ready, Eugene?" he asked, becoming more and more direct with each visit. He almost dreaded seeing Shibboleth's wispy beauty. Eugene only liked speaking to the angel Proxos, who was simpler, casual even. His gaze darted to his daughter and back to his room. "They will not hear me," the angel then reassured. Eugene then looked down and tucked away his penis.

"Angel, please," he stuttered. "I...do, but I'm getting close to getting caught. I'm stepping well over the toes of the NSA...I've raped the computer files of FEMA, where it seems all your action is concentrated in Colorado. I—"

"Don't' worry about that," Shibboleth said. "We've taken care of any suspicion."

Sure you are, Eugene thought. That is why the heads of those departments keep dropping dead. That is why others are acting as irrational as I have, even The President himself. What are you and your host of Heaven doing to them? Is the world going mad? And your obvious plans...what are you building out there...why are you hoarding all these materials with my help. Why? Why?

"You look quizzical," Shibboleth said. "You question me, you question your faith. You are of flesh and weak. That is why you became so tainted, because you were full of hubris and imperfection. That is why you built a dungeon for your soul, that is why your spirit has only rotted with each success. You question me, but you are on the brink of the abyss, Eugene. You grab your penis and you go to Hell." He pointed at Gina. "And you have a chance to save the only pure thing in your life, do what you were intended to do, besides build tools of destruction, aid the world in killing itself. You question me, and God is the only thing that will grant you succor."

As usual, his speeches worked so well, puncturing any cognitive armor raised that moment. Balkros fell to his knees and apologized with hot tears. Shibboleth simply and coolly asked him about the codes.

"They are ready," he whispered, head down. "I can have everything setup in two weeks."

"Good. What about the disks...the virus disks?"

"I have them with me, Angel. Do you want—"

"No," Shibboleth said sternly. "You will take them to Norad yourself. You know where they should be planted. We will give you instructions at the end of the two weeks on the precise date. After that, one of us will come for you. Then you shall receive your peace, Eugene Balkros.

"Thank you," he said, wondering about another question. "Uh, Angel, can I ask you something...please."

Shibboleth crossed his arms.

"If you must."

He took a deep breath before speaking. "You said I can be what I should be to my daughter. But won't there be a new world? Won't there be Armageddon?"

The angel smiled smugly, unfolding his arms. "Perhaps, Eugene. That is not of your concern. Don't worry—either way, you two shall be spared. You two shall be together, alone, with your new deliverance, with your new peace."

Eugene wanted to thank him again, but the angel's form imploded again and trickled out from his home. He wanted to feel joy, renewed hope, but a dread, a fear made his chest heavy, made him fall to the ground and roll himself into fetal position. He simply wanted to stay there forever, hugging himself, never facing the always shifting future. At one point, though, long before he finally dragged himself to his bed and uncaring wife, he craned his head towards the closets. In the dark, in the uncompromising night, they were closed. Monsters didn't exist if one didn't believe in them.

4

"Look ahead," one of the Dreamreavers on their ship shouted, pointing towards the west. Many heads turned, but Medea caught it first, on her back in the rear. Her sight was so keen even for a Stargazer, she knew, as were her other senses. She almost felt that if The Killer of Giants wasn't invading her body, she would be also stronger. That was odd, perhaps a trick by the disease, a false sense of hope.

"It's a body," she said softly. "It's not moving."

"She's right," Dante said after a few moments, moving the ropes that slaved the sails. The wind bellowed with its filth, the sky was a gloomy teal with a murky *Luna*, but they kept sailing almost heroically, scarring the rough but hard ground, hooting and singing most of the way.

"Do we really have to stop?" asked Proxos, becoming more nervous as New Atlantis loomed less than two miles away. Once again, Medea noted, the mere presence of it terrified the ex-Elder. She hadn't ever had a chance to ask about its citizens, since they both knew any ushered word would have been caught by the Dreamreaver's ears in both caverns. She didn't care anymore. Medea wanted to find Byron, who she couldn't feel; she wanted to see this prison herself. She also wanted to buy a little time, since her body was declining with each evening.

"Why?" Dante motioned the other ships to slow. "Are you afraid we might find another fugitive with another incredible story? Perhaps it's the Elder Shibboleth who will tell us that the Warm Ones now rule the world."

"I doubt that," Proxos said dryly. "Shibboleth was a liar; I wish the things we told you were a lie, Dante."

Medea noticed the leader of these Stargazers was staring at her motionless form. "Wishes won't make lies go away, the truth isn't about wishing but about facing."

She only closed her eyes and smiled. He was very similar to Byron, she thought, but more naive and a little gentler. And definitely a lot less complicated.

The ships circled the other motionless form, as was their custom, closing in with each revolution. No latent threat was obvious, but all awaited for Dante's signal. Caution was woven underneath their freewheeling spirit. He gave it and leaped off the ship. None would leave until Dante gave another signal, as was their policy, but Proxos and Medea weren't part of their crew. Medea asked the ex-Elder for assistance to where Dante silently ogled. Proxos obeyed without a word, tenderly holding her up with an arm behind her back.

It was a Stargazer body, part of its abdomen nothing but a blackened crater. His eyes were still open in defiance of its fate. He wore a uniform the three recognized all too well, even in its tarnished condition—not just a Raven but The Lord of The Ravens.

"Orion," Medea said numbly. "He replaced Lord Crow after I destroyed him."

"You destroyed a Stargazer?" Dante asked. "That is the worse penalty a Stargazer can commi—"

"I know, I know," Medea said, understanding too much was said. "But Byron wasn't eliminated after he destroyed you, was he?"

"It doesn't matter," Proxos said. "What matters is why is this influential Stargazer here."

"That's obvious," Dante said. "Another fugitive from Xanadu. It looks like he got caught trying to get to Xanadu before the electrical storm perished. City-folk! I think I'm finally starting to believe your tale."

"No!" Medea exclaimed, pointing at a few feet away, directly where the body's hand extended towards. "Look there."

Proxos was the first one to reach the spot. He picked up an object and showed it to the other two. It was a USB drive, still intact because of it being made of titanium, the kind only used by the influential in Xanadu, which usually meant an Elder. Medea knew this, and Proxos' quick glare to her informed he did, too.

"Balkros," Medea said, trying hard to stand up, trying not to weep all of a sudden. "He must have sent Orion with that storage device! He wanted it to arrive at New Atlantis and used a warrior for it!"

"You think," Proxos said, showing less exhilaration. "But he said it was uploaded to the city. Why—"

"Perhaps he failed," Medea said. "Perhaps he used another method. Maybe that's why we haven't heard from Byron: he hasn't found it."

Proxos shook his head. "Why would he care at all about the cure?"

"Because he gave us his word."

"You don't know him, Medea. Balkros cares little for honor. We took care of that before we made him into..." Proxos also caught himself. "A...an Elder."

"It doesn't matter," Medea said, anxiously grabbing the object. "He also knew that we might return if he lied. He knew what we did. He wanted us out because we were a threat to his new regime, remember!"

"Perhaps," was all Proxos said, eyes cautious slits.

"What are you talking about?" Dante asked. "You said Xanadu was no longer. Are you telling me the Elder Balkros rules it now? What is this cure?"

Medea ignored him, holding the USB drive to her chest. Yes, there was hope and the hope still resided in the dome before them. They needed a computer. They needed to go in there. It all made sense. For the first time since she had rescued Byron from the explosion of The Moon-Queen's den, she truly felt strong happiness, felt that there was joy on the other side of their dark quests.

She also knew that Dante needed more of the truth. It was only fair. Medea felt she could open up more to him, which is something she rarely did with anyone.

"Why don't we continue on our journey," she told the leader of the pirates. "And I'll tell you about Balkros and cures."

She wouldn't release the fallen Lord's object the entire way.

Chapter 9

Eight nights.

It was finally time to obtain some answers. Answers that mattered, that took things all the way. Byron never thought it would be his turn to give them.

At his request, he met Marcion in one of the computer rooms. The voices were sturdier in his head, trying to draw him into the way of New Atlantis, into the museum of Lilith, The mad dream of The Centurion. Byron had felt like someone else, like he didn't belong within himself since arriving, but he still had the vision of Medea, the fury of his mission to give him some identify. Take it all the way, he told himself. They aren't alive, they are just a reflex—

No, a reflection.

A reflection of something human, something good, like you are, like the cities are. The Forgotten were punished differently than you, but still suffer with no privacy and the truth always out there to burden them. They go through the motions, try to find meaning, but there is no meaning, meaning swept away when the sky burned and you were born between the ages to end the rulers of the post-Holocaust.

No, a tool.

The Good Neighbor was dressed in opal-colored robes of satin, accentuating his flaxen mane, his bleached features. He was handsome and unique and endowed with great powers. And Byron had to destroy him and the others of the museum. His mood gained density; the voices grew like beating, rhythmic sound waves.

"Why did you slay Adam?" Marcion asked with certain rancor, leaning against one of the tables. "He had done nothing wrong. You should not disturb me when I am in trance."

"I'm sorry," Byron said, immediately lighting a cigarette. "It's just that...the voices...what I've seen...I needed answers."

"No," Marcion said softly with a smile that held no tenderness. "You were just following your nature."

"What are you talking about?"

He stood up, towering over Byron.

"I needed to go in trance to find other uncertainties in the future, Byron. I...we have been hoping for your coming since before arriving here after The Holocaust, but I needed to know exactly how you would aid us in thriving for ultimate freedom."

"But you have freedom," Byron said, shaking his head. "The MoonQueen is gone. You are free!"

"No, Byron." His smile wouldn't deteriorate on his face. "Not yet. You see, we, The Forgotten, are trapped in The Egg."

Byron flinched slightly. "Trapped? What are you talking about? Are you being mystical again?"

"Always." He frowned slightly. "But Lhiannon-Shee decreed that we should never be allowed to feel the outdoors. You said this place was like a museum. It is, but none of the trophies or exhibits are allowed to depart. Ever."

"Ever?" It made sense to him now. There were no windows, he had never seen anyone leave, assuming it was out of free-will. Quidam was jealously dangerous to any visitors. *And his name, you idiot...Warden, Warden!* The citizens of New Atlantis were perhaps too odd to ever mingle with the other Stargazers. "Why didn't you tell me this before, Marcion?"

"Because you did not ask, Byron. But I will tell you this: there are still events that must transpire, which have to do with you and our destiny. There is always a price to pay for freedom, for the changing of ages, and someone has to pay it. There are still other things unclear, though, like the fallen Raven and an old friend from your past, but I will have time before it is all over. The trance has opened doors of perception to me, and the answers come to me still."

It was Byron's turn to smile wryly. "But all you and your people care about is freedom."

Marcion nodded. "Yes, Byron. Do you blame us?"

"No," he said softly, not matching his firm stare.

"And you are the first step. You were the first step when you defeated The Queen of Darkness."

"What?" Byron could only take a step in retreat at the invisible blow.

The Pharisee tilted his head. "Did you think I...we would not find out sooner or later, Byron Solsbury? Did you think your actions had not rippled through the cosmos like a boulder in an innocent pond? Pardon the prosaic analogy. Yes, you are The Liberator, are you not? You are a revolutionary, a champion of eternity. Do you deny this?"

He hesitated. They had given him answers. They had been honest. He didn't have anything to lose anyway. He just wanted one thing...

"Yes," he admitted. "I did it, Marcion and the other who can hear and see what you see. I bested her, I ended this age."

"And why is that?" Was it condescension he heard in Marcion's voice? Everything was so loud in between his ears.

"What do you mean by that? This place should know about her, more than anybody. I did the universe a favor, I did everyone in this planet a—"

"Did you?" The Pharisee spoke with a confident edge. "I wonder about that? After all, by what I have seen, you simply razed Xanadu and left it behind. Warm Ones are in peril—the same ones you swore to protect against The Queen of Darkness once upon a time, Byron. Why did you do that?"

Byron opened his mouth, all thoughts sizzling in white.

"Why did you not stay and aid them, allow them to take Xanadu over and then leave? You were fighting for humanity, for this good I am sure you have spouted many times, were you not? Is no order better than some order, is total chaos purer than a stern ray of uniformity? Did you think Balkros would allow this revolution to linger?"

"Wait." Byron raised a hand at him, each sentence shredding part of his mind. "Just—"

"That was almost as sophomoric as the plan in Utopia." Marcion wasn't going to allow him any satisfaction. "Did you think you would succeed? You should have taken them into the shelters during *Sol's* rise before you destroyed the Reactors."

"No!" Byron gasped, images of his past swirling before him. He was running in the fire, he was being pummeled by The MoonQueen. His family was afraid...

"Yes, Byron," Marcion said with gritted teeth. "And you

know why, Byron? Because you are a true slave of The Dark Instinct. You are a destroyer, a hunter in the night, so efficient, so wicked, you can even pass for a hero. But all you care about is destruction. You cannot help it. Lhiannon-Shee knew this when she first enslaved you with her kiss. The MoonQueen always knew you would make her fancies into reality, take it farther than even she dared. You destroyed two cities—"

"Shut up!" Byron warned, barely able to see past the confusion pushing out against his temples. It wasn't true, it couldn't be true. He had done good, fought against steep odds in the name of Blood of Circles, the freedom of all beings and the memory of times past. He was the Liberator, Byron Solsbury, a hero...a...

A tool...a reflection...

"You were the greatest creation of Our Mistress. I mean, did you think you were not manipulated from the beginning? If you do, then you must think she planned The Holocaust just before it happened. You are wrong, Byron. Lhiannon-Shee planned it long before, planned this all many centuries before and used us all for this, for all of this. I doubt The Queen of Darkness could truly care about this Killer of Giants or anything that hurt her brood. It probably made a convincing selling issue when it came time to finish her desire. I believe it was when we were in her circus that it truly began." His eyes turned dreamy with golden light. "Perhaps it was before, when they came into the jungles with the message of The Mad God she was trying to avoid. She *is* The Dark Instinct, Byron. As I told you before, it is like a virus, only caring for its blind purpose, mutating, adapting to the currents of the universe's bloodstream. Lhiannon-Shee is the spirit of destruction, the end, the void, and that also means everything, Byron, everything! When there is nothing, She shall be content, the Dark Instinct will be sated."

"But she is gone!" Byron screamed, holding himself, ignoring the cigarette burning his right side.

"It does seem so," Marcion said. "But She needed someone to finish it, destroy her only hatchlings, continue her legacy. That was you, Byron, the last pure reflex of The Dark Instinct. You are just a pawn."

You bastard! Feed me!

A reflection. A tool of the machine. That's all he was?

Byron could only shake his head. Marcion only chuckled.

"That is my theory," he said. "I like to predict fate. But if my theory is to be tested again, continue true, then you must be here to destroy us."

Byron's expression froze. He turned his head.

"I am right, am I not? Not a good guest you are, despite what Quidam tried to do to you. We took you as one of our own because you are so similar to us and our situations. But you are here to continue with your passion, which is destruction. At least we citizens of The Egg attempt to create something most of the time, and that is the true spirit of humanity, the artistic, dreaming side of it."

"You're evil," was all Byron could say, never so lost for words.

"'There is nothing evil which follows its nature'," Marcion said. "Marcus Aurelius said that, and like you he was a bright, adroit warrior. The Dark Instinct is not evil, neither are you or I, Byron. We just follow our natures, and your nature is to follow The Queen of Darkness' whim, even from her grave."

"Shut up!" Byron shouted again. "Just shut-up! Why are you telling me this?"

"Because I must," The Good Neighbor admitted. "Because I have my agenda, and that is our freedom. You will influence this."

"I thought I was here to destroy you."

He blinked once with force. "You will try."

Byron delivered brackish smile. "I already have, and I will succeed."

Marcion remained silent, regarding him solemnly, only showing Byron the hollowness of his sentence. Byron's reaction was to place his hands on one of the tables. The plastic, created by the dumbness and numbness of the Prince of Shadows cracked under his fingers. He felt like he was being drawn farther again from his being, from what he was. The voices continued, louder with the aid of a guilt that had never truly been present in his persona. After all, the excitement, his sense of urgency, was truly a way of avoiding his rational, human side, move through with his fury as quickly as possible before coming to terms with his actions. He had destroyed, he had ravaged Warm Ones, Stargazers, civilizations and dreams. He had changed the ages and brought more ends than beginnings. And he was going to do it again, he knew with cringing distaste. Yes, Byron Solsbury was a Liberator of all that was reality, all that was real, all that was known to the beings that crossed his path. Except for one person, one person only.

We'll never be apart.

Sieg-Heil!

Nothing is evil.

A tool of the machine.

Sieg-Heil!

It wasn't always this way.

"Marcion," he mouthed, using all of his concentration to prick the tempest inundating him.

"You want to see those files," The Pharisee said. "In twenty seconds I will access them, Byron."

"Marcion," he repeated louder, lips quivering.

"In forty seconds I will tell you that you can check out of here but you can never leave. Once you enter, you are forgotten. After a minute you will attempt to leave The Egg." Marcion narrowed his eyes, which glowed in pale blue. "In one minute and ten seconds I will weep for you—"

"Marcion." The table cracked in half, sending a computer to the floor with a sparkly crash.

"Very well," Marcion said with certain resignation, facing one of the screens to his side. "These are the files you so desperately need to save the one called Medea."

2

A door slid up, not in the same place where nights ago Byron was attacked by a painted Stargazer. It was hard to tell because of the featureless exterior of the dome, but this one was twenty feet above the ground. The ships had been waiting a few minutes, keeping at least ten feet away, the crew eager as *Luna* rose to its zenith above the swirling sky.

A large figure materialized at the entrance, stout and wearing a tunic that was more like a tent. His head was bald, features exaggerated, and instead of displaying fangs two long tusks ascended from a fat lower lip. To his sides stood two Warm Ones in glittering armor, looking out into the desert with vacant expressions.

"Is it time, Dante?" the Stargazer asked, hands to his waist, which could have been anywhere. "Found a few old vase fragments or rusted automobile fenders for us?"

Dante smiled back at the creature, obviously used to the first round of bartering courtesies.

"No, Ogre," he said loudly, looking like his good mood could never be broken this evening. "I have things here that will make you bounce in joy like the fat-ass ball you are."

"Careful, Heretic," the unnatural Stargazer growled with a menacing smile. "A good sense of humor will not feed you tonight. Things are changing more than your puny mind will ever fathom, but we are always interested in your drama and trinkets."

Dante didn't waste any time, raising a canister with red numbers painted on it.

"What about this, Ogre? I don't know what it is, but I know you fellows enjoy bright things. 'Multi-colored condoms,' it says, in perfect condition."

"I don't believe you," the one called Ogre bellowed.

"Can you use it?"

"Balloons," the Stargazer grumbled. "We love nice balloons!"

Dante turned and winked to Medea and Proxos, who were by his side. "Why don't you come here and see this for yourself."

"Very funny," Ogre said. "You know I won't do that."

Can't do that, Medea thought, glancing at Proxos.

A prison.

Ogre motioned at Dante. "One of the few reasons we allow your pitiful existence is because of your wit, Heretic. Now let me see it."

"Does The MoonQueen know of this?" Dante tossed the

heavy canister to the rotund Stargazer.

"We've already argued this on a thousand occasions," he said, catching it. "It's none of her business. Ah, nice balloons! Do you have more?"

More words were exchanged. Dante threw additional objects, small baubles from the caverns. Ogre couldn't smother his look of surprise mixed in with eagerness after inspecting the items: paint-guns, seed-packets, camouflage fatigues in boxes, digital watches, and thermometers. Medea and Proxos had been told the Stargazer would leave and return several times, shouting offers for certain objects, and the true bartering would initiate. Tonight the advantage was certainly with the Dreamreavers. The process sometimes continued for the whole night or the next, with Dante's people having to create haven underneath the ground before *Sol* arrived. All they hoped for was a few materials and Warm One's to slaughter. All Medea and Proxos wished for and found was for the door to remain open. It would stay open until the whole transaction was finished.

"The Warm One guards will stay," Dante whispered to them. "I don't see their enforcer, so you two can enter unnoticed...Medea it seems your malady has increased."

She shook her head. It wasn't that but a realization that had slowly crept to her head at seeing the peculiar Stargazer, which both Proxos and Dante had warned about. Dante didn't care about their appearances, assuming it was from the cosmetic experiments Ogre always bragged about.

That Stargazer, she thought. I've seen him before. Not here, not anywhere, but in the dream. He was in a cage, eating fire, entertaining the crowd. He claimed to be from a dungeon in a place called Germany. He was in the dream!

"I am fine," she said, rubbing her forehead. It couldn't be—it was just her frail senses playing larks on her. "Really. We should go."

"Yes," said Proxos. "The sooner we are out of your way, the sooner you will feast on a buffet of Warm Ones."

Dante didn't brighten at the words. He regarded them seriously, especially Medea.

"Yes I shall," he said. "It has...been interesting. I...we will wait for you as long as we can."

"Don't," Medea said with a worn smile. "You have done enough. As I said, make sure you are far away, Dante. Please." She held his arm.

"And I always thought I was a dreamer," Dante said and pursed his lips. "Fine. Go, Medea. Find your friend who is more than that. I don't hope for that but I hope you find this cure. You are..."

He pursed his lips again.

Proxos patted his shoulder. "I'm going, too, Dante. Farewell. Heed her advice on anything. It is probably good we never meet again."

Medea wanted to say something else to him, but since she couldn't connect the moment to the emotion to the word, she did what she usually did when in that situation: she remained quiet and turned to the next agenda.

The two Stargazers' bodies shivered into mist and lapped on the ground. The parallel strings of smoke crept on the ground and onto the hull of New Atlantis. Rapidly, in a few seconds, they were entering the opened wound on the dome.

3

The Warm One guards never noticed them, for their orders were simply to stand guard, not allow entrance or exit to any material beings. Their sensors, which could have easily captured the smoke and used installed Radiovaks, machines designed to trap Stargazers in mist form, were not focused on what was not an issue during bartering. It never had been. They simply guarded, more as a protocol than anything, waiting for Ogre to return after meeting with The Pharisees, another formality since the corpulent Stargazer had already heard the population scream offers from all sides, those who cared. His leaders were just there to grant focus to the bartering. In this focus there was always Feltch, who drove hard the price and Revenant, content with any offer, and Marcion in the middle.

But another figure who cared little of bartering or the filmy leadership of New Atlantis saw the smoke from a perpendicular hallway a few feet away from the entrance. He had seen them, always close to any area that opened in this place, which he was forsworn to protect by his true leader. It wasn't The Prince of Shadows but The Queen of Darkness. Nothing ever left, and those who entered had to perish. That's all he cared about for it was Her desire. He was granted protection from the net of The Centurion whenever he needed to mask intentions, for he stood apart from The Forgotten. He could even leave on his own accord, but that would never happen unless intruders touched the shell of The Egg.

She, Tiamat, had saved him millennia ago when his god had abandoned him to solitude in the galaxy, when humanity was brought down from proud heights and cursed to mortal flesh. She had nurtured him, understood his ambition and passion back then, which was to unite mortal and immortal, open the eyes of the universe to creation, tether it all together. He was no longer a king, the hunter of the wondrous ages, when The Leviathan and The Behemoth battled to shake the sky and earth, when *Mot* wandered the land slicing gods apart for sport; but he still was in charge of the greatest wonders in the world, which resided in New Atlantis. He had only been defeated once, and that was fine. Circumstances were changing but he would grow stronger. Whether Tiamat had traveled to the beyond didn't matter, for like any good warrior he served her words and her ideals as much as her physical being.

Therefore, he had his duties and his obeying silence. His tongue had been ripped out a few hours ago—tossed in a massive vat where it wriggled like a pulpy serpent with all the other thousands—he was wiser after defeat, and now wielded a greater weapon. Tonight was a good night as any night.

Quidam placed a hand on his sword and quietly followed the fog.

4

Screens flashed with different sections of New Atlantis. From the tender gardens to the theaters, from the aquariums to the video arcades, dozens of them flickered with the beauty of their city. The Pharisees kept their eyes on the images, focusing only on certain images: the ones that showed Byron trying to escape. He had read the files and that was enough.

"Look at him," Feltch grumbled. "He's trying everything on every level. Guess he didn't believe you."

"He should have asked earlier," Revenant commented, wearing clothing that would have been called a wedding dress in another era.

"He should have asked many things." Marcion stood in front of the other two. They didn't need to speak, their thoughts and feelings bound to each other and the population. There was no privacy here. It was one of the laws The MoonQueen started with the help of The Centurion. A population with no secrets would rarely show discord, nurture insurgent action. They had accepted it now, but still needed dialogue to hold on to identity, not be swept away into madness as had many here. They were The Forgotten and all they could do to survive was keep remembering.

Byron was having that problem now, struggling with his mind and persona. There was no privacy here, he had learned, mirrors and cameras a true reflection of the voices in all of their heads.

Now he was learning that nobody was allowed to ever leave.

Byron had tried everything. Hermetically sealed doors would not allow his mist aspect to depart. His powerful fists, which could crack stone or bend iron so easily, were not enough to even mar the magnetized steel, controlled by The Prince of Shadows. Buttons and consoles would open doors briefly, giving him a glimpse of the freedom they all craved, but shut in split seconds before his snarling visage. Nobody was allowed to leave, and he had been the only ever to arrive and allowed to stay without the consent of The Queen of Darkness. His face showed tortured determination, salted with the aching of the voices of the population, stronger with each hour, picking at his thoughts, his fiery emotions.

"The Dark Instinct is so copious in him," remarked Revenant. "I've told him that already a few times. He won't listen."

"Not strong enough to get out," Feltch said, nose and mouth filthy with feces from a recent feeding. "But stubborn enough to keep on fucking trying."

"You are all correct," Marcion said tonelessly. "That is why he is the one. He is atypical, enigmatic, and full of destiny and pride. Yet, once again, he must face himself, truly face himself, and perhaps succumb to what he sees. It is not the first time, but it is the worst."

The Kappa took a step to his side. "You like him, don't you? He makes you feel...alive again, Mac. What a faggot-ass."

"I like him." The Good Neighbor ignored his last insult. "I think we understand each other. But it does not matter. He bested The Warden. He drinks in generations with The Centurion."

"And that will give us our freedom," Revenant said. "But first he must be stripped of sword, shield, and armor. And to do that—"

"He must be broken down," Marcion said. "Exposed—"

"Personality stripped," Revenant finished. "And then brought naked...bare, if you will, like a newborn into the gray dawn. In other words, he is just a token, a sacrifice because of who he really is to The Centurion. Do you think we will be able to strip him of his weapons and armor. Retrieve his defenses?"

The Pharisee didn't answer right away and kept his sight glued on Byron soliciting escape on every wall leading to the wilderness. He would keep trying, desperately seeking a way out, or more like a way to a person that fulfilled him.

Even with the tragic news.

"He already began that process," he told his colleagues. "He began when he first entered and saw his reflection, fell under the willowy fan that is The Centurion's aura. The more he tried, the more he had to face himself and the more disrobed he became. Soon, my friends. Soon."

"Fucking-a," Feltch shouted, lumbering in a circle.

And Byron kept trying, banging his fists on unyielding walls, trying to exploit a blemish or a crack when there weren't any, hoping against all hopes that the storm would leave him intact when it left the horizons of time.

Just as he'd always done, Marcion thought, crossing his arms, which he did once or twice a century. But this time is different.

After all, Balkros' files had shown nothing but gibberish. What he had tried to find in this city was never here. There was no cure. All he had done was find himself, his true, evil self.

5

Dante was getting impatient. After wandering the wilderness as a Heretic, surviving the sterile world, rising as a new subculture of the Stargazer Empire, Dante thought that annoying faction of his personality had been long mastered. He had never been patient in his brief stardom at Xanadu. That was a quality he had shared with a once close friend, Lord Byron, and that had both aided and finished him in those nights. But he was getting impatient as the evening shifted. Ogre kept coming and going, the bartering continued, and already their ships were congested with Warm Ones dressed in insulating suits and chains, even though they cared naught about escape or their fates.

"Are you fine?" one of his pirates, a lanky Stargazer named Fien asked him at one point, while the others already celebrated by devouring one of the Warm Ones.

"I'm fine," Dante replied tersely, sipping on a clay cup of juice, sight moored to the entrance.

The lack of patience told him two things with barbed derision. One was that Dante wanted her to come out. Her name was Medea, and he more than liked this person. She was special, a fresh attitude to a world of complacency and foolish optimism.

She could see so well in the ash that covered the planet and the spirits of those tumbling through it. Her name was Medea, and he wanted to see her again, speak with her, wanted to know if she would find this cure for a malady that had caused The Holocaust in the first place.

The other thing was that it didn't matter. Her emotions belonged to another, another he had competed with in so many episodes. One who had outdone him, left his being for finished, to be scorned by The Queen of Darkness.

"You do not deserve to fall like a warrior, Mon-Cheri," she had said, standing in a haze of glassy flakes, so gorgeous Dante could not move when she had healed him. "But you played your part, and you can play it again at another time, I promise you. For now, you deserve the fate of a loser."

What had that meant? He didn't know, but Dante knew that once again Byron was upstaging him, taking what he wanted, and somehow humiliating him with his actions. The ex-Lord of The Ravens was even going to attempt to smash the one place where his Dreamreavers could obtain real food. And Dante was just going to allow it! Glancing back at his people, which he had saved and hoped to better with that patience, he wondered what would happen if they did escape soon, if they floated out now, not two of them but three.

He'll probably take over, Dante thought, gritting his teeth. He'll probably find a way to destroy this cursed city, show that he should be the leader and sail away with Medea under one arm.

Foolish thoughts, but Dante realized they were reflexes of unfinished business. Byron had always thought he was the best, the greatest Stargazer to walk this planet. But times had changed, patience had brought him here, and there was unfinished business.

"No," Dante said, more to himself. "I am not fine, Fien. Not at all."

Ogre was appearing at the entrance again, tossing out boxes full of clothing, basic materials, and rudimentary tools. At the time, Dante was reaching for another item, which he wasn't going to use for bartering.

Medea had told him that it was The MoonQueen, not Byron, who expunged him from what had been an illusion. But it wasn't that, it wasn't blame that nagged him all this time, or guilt, or any silly emotion for lesser Stargazers. It was the fact Dante had lost and received a second chance to find who was the best. And the best deserved to start something new, something better. Only the best survived, only the best won.

He turned to Fien. "If I don't return in a night, you're the new leader."

Not waiting for a response, he rose in the air, holding two weapons under each arm after feeding his shirt with clips. M16's, they were called from what Proxos had told him while they inventoried the caverns for four nights, equipped with 39 millimeter grenade launchers. It was time to use that lack of patience to his advantage on one last occasion. It was time to bring out that old volatile personality. It was time to settle scores, borrow one more time from the Warm Ones, and then truly start something new, better.

"Dante!" yelled Ogre with an amused expression. "You don't have to show off your findings to me. I know what they are and I'll give you—"

"You'll give me nothing!" Dante shouted back. "Except entrance."

"You know I can't do that," Ogre said, as he floated closer. "And I don't appreciate your tone, Here—"

The Stargazer almost looked surprised when his body was perforated by a hundred small missiles in a few seconds. Smoke and skin flakes shuddered away from his large form. Two hundred more and Ogre staggered to one side, coping with the damage that might be permanent, that might be too much for The Dark Instinct to consider, pudgy hands trying to hold his torso from falling apart, spilling innards.

The Warm One soldiers advanced, replacing Ogre who was sliding down the wall with angry gurgles. Dante showered them with fury; they seemed surprised too, as if they only knew how to battle Stargazers with traditional means. They didn't survive the assault, flesh coming apart at the seams, metal cracking and bursting in sparks. The two bodies keeled over and rolled down the small slope to join the Stargazer. By then, his people were shouting at him. By then, he had followed his almost reflexive action and had to go through with it.

Dante entered New Atlantis, thinking about her name being Medea and the one called Byron while replacing the empty clips of his weapons. Two names with two spectrums of emotions. For the first time in a long time, he felt truly like himself.

6

Data: Must return to Us. More circuits perishing, fires taking away underground tunnels and the few working factories. Damage at seventy percent now. Warm One existence nearly done. Mad Stargazers shredding city for nourishment, even the ones who have returned, too fearful to finish quest.

He would receive his deliverance in three days. Around him, turmoil was oddly brewing in other nations, in this nation, everywhere. Something bad was going to happen, he knew, and the codes were a farce. When it started, no one but he could stop it. His team, code experts and military men, had strangely been recently drying. And then some would turn up later, only at night, as if nothing had happened. They looked, acted very different though, as if they had just looked into the abyss of Hell and been reversibly tanned in white-hot light. How strange. Politicians acted irrationally; world leaders were worse. It was all madness, and he was helping angels build shelters.

Balkros knew it wasn't just him. He'd seen the sheets, the military invoices. He'd seen how others in the Pentagon and The Capitol also acted: scared, lost, or absent because they weren't alive anymore. The angels were taking care of everything. He was beyond caring, his erections and fire for Gina increasing, unable to sustain an air of normality in public settings, and his brain a crackling fizz of two colors. Black and white. Duality. He laughed, he cried. He slept, he was awake. He was full of rage, but where was his deliverance?

"Are you okay, Daddy?" Gina asked him while he sat in his chair.

"Of course he's fine," his wife said, walking by the hall-way, looking like a Medusa of hair-rollers. "Maybe if he went back to work sometime this week and earned his damn living, he'd be better."

His hand tightened on the glass of his scotch and soda. He forced a smile to his daughter, wiping off sweat. It was growing.

"I'm okay, sweetheart," he said, putting his hand on her cheek. "Just a little tired, that's all. Are you okay?"

The girl half-nodded. "Liza Thomas said at school today that the Jews killed Jesus, Daddy. It is true?"

He sustained the smile, feeling the heat of her body shud-der up his arm.

"No, sweetheart. God killed Jesus."

She blinked. "God? I thought Jesus was God?"

"He is," he replied. "He was."

"God killed God?"

"Yes, Gina. He wanted it that way."

"He wanted death?"

"I love you, Gina," he said, a genuine smile growing.

"Daddy, you're pulling my hair too hard!"

"I love you so much."

"Stop!" She pulled away and ran down the hallway. He kept smiling. Then he began to weep.

He would be getting his deliverance from the angels. In three nights, after he returned from his trip to Colorado. He would take the disk with him, which would confuse all the radars that scooped the heavens for nuclear javelins.

God killed God. And monsters didn't exist if one didn't believe in them.

Balkros drank because he thirsted.

7

Doors opened before them without complaint. Corridors were mostly empty. Mirrors everywhere. Cameras followed them but nothing happened. A walkway here, an escalator there, and they found a sleek room filled with all types of computers. It bragged several consoles, two sliding doors, and a few red-cushioned chairs.

Medea sat on a chair, while Proxos dabbled in the New Atlantis technology. He had a few questions, which she answered flatly on post-Holocaust computers.

"Amazing," Proxos said. "Even I can use these things. I have complete access to the whole city. Look, I've got these cameras honeycombing our immediate area, just to make sure we're not—"

"Please," Medea rasped, slumping in her chair. "The USB drive, Proxos, the..."

He could barely look at her. Just using her mist power and running here seemed to have taxed her too much. It was more than that, he thought with dread, not wanting to notice the places where her clothing was tearing or how long her jet hair had grown, seemed tinted slightly in blue.

"Medea. I'm sure this may not be the right time, but you're...different." He shook his head. "You're taller, thinner. Your skin is changing to a cleaner, alabaster color. Even your cheekbones are rising."

"It's the Killer," she said, head bobbing, eyes moving sloppily. "It's growing so fast...Proxos, I haven't shivered since The MoonQueen fatally wounded me in her chambers...when Byron..." She blinked, as if thought process had been severed all of a sudden.

Proxos narrowed his eyes slightly. "Are you sure? I know your plight, but your voice...it's different—"

"Proxos." She held out the USB drive, her voice brimming with icy warning. "We have no time. I have no time. I can barely move..."

He sighed, took the storage device, and fornicated one of the hubs that fit its contours. Information began appearing on the screen in ghostly pixels. Balkros had promised the cure for the Killer of Giants. Was this it? Was it perhaps still here?

"What do you see?" Medea asked, head down on her hand, as if too afraid to witness the results.

Proxos' eyes remained on the screen, his face washed in

pale green neon. "I see numbers, entire programs moving. It's like a self-extracting file. The numbers get shinier with each transference, almost shivering—"

"It doesn't matter," Medea whispered. "Is there anything on a cure?"

"Wait," he said, his voice almost a breath. "It's almost done. Very odd. There, it's done. Now I will see where it is on the hard drive."

"Hurry."

"That's odd again. Now the program itself is copying itself again. I need to get into—"

"Hurry!" she said, her voice sounding very different.

"I am hurrying, Medea." He tapped the touchscreen furiously, trying to stop the process. A few files stopped. He tried to find their properties.

"Proxos."

"We're almost there."

"Proxos."

"We're..." His eyes widened, his jaw dropped suddenly.

"Proxos?"

"I..." He said, and then odd sounds exited some of the speakers.

"Smoke, Proxos."

"Smoke?" he echoed. It wasn't smoke. It wasn't even close.

He turned his head, wondering if Medea was not growing delirious. She was wide awake, staring in terror at the pool of smoke that had been dribbling quietly underneath the door. It wasn't smoke anymore, shifting rapidly to the brawny form of the tattooed Stargazer. Proxos had met him briefly a few times in the past, but knew very little of him. He knew his speed and tenacity, though.

It was that knowledge or perhaps Medea's paltry scream that made him move an arm over his face when the sword came loose from his belt and cleaved down upon him.

Chapter 10

Regret at his actions had almost begun to nag Dante when he encountered a group of Stargazers, some dressed in white tunics, the others wearing feathered masks and flowing dresses. After all, he had perhaps forsaken what little he had built since being cast out of The MoonQueen's garden. He was seeking a dark ideal, a kernel of vengeance, a way to for once beat the one who was so like him, who was superior for so long. He was going to even a score.

"Look at that," said one with an effeminate voice, and Dante took a step back when seeing a forked tongue dash out from a mask opening. What kind of gross experiments were they performing here, since Dante sensed they were Stargazers. "Love that outfit and the weapon. The Carnival in sector G7 said nothing of bondage."

"He's not one of ours, Naga," said another merrily, this one looking grotesquely deformed in his robe. Fake leaves were pasted to a head that owned no ears and seemed caved in with purple liquid. "We can't reach him. He's another visitor."

"A poorly dressed one at that, Poppykettle," said one with a wet voice, whose skin was transparent, showing glowing organs. "He's the one who downed Ogre. I wonder if he'll make it with his spine so torn apart."

"I felt his pain," the long-tongued one said. "It was delicious."

"Silence!" Dante warned, trying to gain control of a situation out of control by his rashness. He pointed the two guns at them. "I need some answers. I need the location of some people."

The Stargazers glanced at each other with mumbles.

"You won't be joining us, I presume" the grotesque one said. "I guess they are letting any commoner arrive these nights, wanting answers to everything except the truth."

"Silence," Dante repeated. "And answer my questions. I'm looking for two Stargazers—"

"Let me guess," another said, who seemed like a normal Stargazer. "One, a female who smells like she's decomposing. The other an average fellow with—"

"That's them!" Dante exclaimed. "Where are they?"

All of them began, in perfect unison, to give him directions. They were a few corridors down, up three levels in one of the observation rooms.

"But you better hurry," the transparent Stargazer said. "Quidam is right at their heels. They are as good as gone when he does..."

"What?" Dante asked, wondering if this was all a farce but knowing these capricious Stargazers, like Ogre and others, had an odd penchant for honesty, probably born from complacency and arrogance.

"Hurry!" the one called Naga shouted with loud hisses. "We can't wait to see what happens."

Dante hurried, using all his force to go towards their direction. Who was Quidam? What would he do to them? Why did they speak so strangely?

He would soon find out.

2

Sieg-heil.

Voices.

A reflection.

One a female, who smells like she's rotting.

We'll never be apart.

Byron roared, pulling out yet another panel of circuits, ignoring the shock of several bolts of electricity, wires unraveling between his fingers. Flames rose before him, so real he focused hard on them. Sight deviated towards the doors. They wouldn't open. Angrily, he tore at other consoles. Nothing happened when he was done. The voices continued.

There was a battle somewhere here.

There was a party, a carnival, somewhere here.

Marcion was watching him.

Sieg-heil!

A reflection, Mon-Cheri.

"Shit!" Byron yelled with gritted teeth. Nothing was occurring. He had practically disemboweled a section of the city, but the doors to the outside still wouldn't open. He'd tried everything for hours. He couldn't override the locking systems, violence hadn't worked, neither had mist form, and gutting the place now seemed like no option. It wasn't any internal security reason, but more. Something was fortifying the metal, controlling the door systems.

And the answers were always there.

The Prince of Shadows.

"Shit," he repeated in a lower tone, and the voices sang the word back at him.

He couldn't escape. Worse, he had found what Balkros had left.

Nothing.

There was no cure. The bastard had lied, lied to get them out, to break their spirits. Yes, he was a new god, cruel and callous like the others.

There was no cure for Medea here. He couldn't reach her, the voices and The Centurion impeding this, he couldn't touch her, the shell of The Egg unbreakable. He couldn't do anything but keep trying and failing, succumbing slowly to the population that was invading his head, that had torn at his soul and shown how pathetic he truly was.

He lowered his head and pulled at his hair. He could change his hair, his appearance perhaps, defy the material, the scientific, but he couldn't change his soul, his true being. It had all gone so wrong, and worse. He was the same, but he wasn't, and didn't know which was more terrifying. He was now a Forgotten, not a Liberator.

Yes, you are, Marcion' voice told him and faded away.

"No," Byron whispered, squatting, uncaring of the spreading fire, of the Warm Ones that were already flooding the area in order to repair his damage. "There is always a way, even when there isn't one…you create it…I've done it before."

He wanted to attack them all, then attack all the Stargazers, destroy everyone in his desperate anger, show…

A hunter in the night. A slave, Mon-Cheri.
You bastard.

Byron Solsbury almost clawed his eyes out when an image floated before him. It sputtered against the voices and the minds of the population, which still hadn't become him completely. It was faint but he caught it and retained it.

Medea! She was here! Quidam had seen her. Violence. Destruction. It had happened. It was happening.

Medea!

He didn't care if this perhaps was some hoax by the bored citizens, always trying to find a way to battle the lack of privacy by ritual and dialogue. He hated those things, and he would destroy them all if this wasn't true, fulfilling his role before the missile did in less than nine nights

Medea!

Byron followed the location of the images.

3

Movement was a tangle of pain bursts. Her eyes burned coldly, her insides felt like gushing magma. Words that never should have applied to a Stargazer, a species of alleged gods, came to her faltering mind—weary, lethargic, blurry-eyed, delicate and trembling, among other mortal adjectives. Medea could have never fathomed the severity of the blooming of The Killer of Giants, even when she was a Warm One carrying it around like an unborn offspring in the hopes to pass it down until the right time came for a revolution. The right time had come, with Byron's aid, and she had given it to The Queen of Darkness, who fed on her after their defeat at the North West Farm. That is why Lilith had used Balkros' mind to find a cure, since even she couldn't subjugate it. That is why they were here and not on the other side of the mountains waiting to see a mushroom cloud over the spiny horizon.

Medea impressed herself, though, finding a reserve of energy from the lagoon of agony muffling her body. Adrenaline, she had heard it was called a long time ago. It wasn't adrenaline, but some desire for survival and aid of one close to her.

Proxos cringed as his arm divorced his body. His form collapsed in shock against the computer after turning to meet the attack. The tattooed Stargazer raised his weapon again, the head the obvious target, recoiling to insure he would have enough thrust to end her friend once and for all. He moved so efficiently and quickly, striking again before Medea had left her seat. Proxos moved his newly formed stump, body leaning back further to shove the computer off the desk. The blade shaved the stump off by the time the screen had crashed into portions on the other side. His arm now lay in two pieces on the floor. Bone and useless veins wiggled from his body, what little juice reserves he occupied sputtering out. The Stargazer, still showing no emotion whatsoever, went for third and final assault since Proxos' other arm was instinctively grabbing the side of the table.

Adrenaline they called it, Medea thought, ramming into the tall Stargazer with all she could muster. All she could muster surprisingly moved the painted fiend, even making him lose his footing. He toppled over another computer, pulverizing it, and fell over the side of the adjacent table. For a second, Medea didn't know which to worry about more: Proxos' condition, the Stargazer's condition, or her condition. She could already feel her legs trembling in exhaustion like stretched rubber bands.

"Medea," Proxos said, gaze shifting back and forth in confusion from her to the place an arm had just been playing with the touchscreen seconds ago. He started blinking hard. "Thank you, uh..."

But her sight was fastened to the table. The Stargazer rose without spectacle from the mess of plastic and wire. He simply stepped on the table, and leaped before them. There were no dashing threats, no demeanor of victory. He was here only to finish them. Had this fiend done the same to Byron, Medea wondered. Was she going to share the same fate?

We'll see, she thought, taking a step forward, trying to show some semblance of balance. Proxos was grabbing her shoulder, speaking rapidly and incoherently. The Stargazer raised his sword.

Unlike Byron, she wasn't going to go hand in hand. Medea had already decided to shift to mist aspect, hope Proxos followed, and try for escape. She didn't have the strength and Proxos, who was probably a suitable fighter, had just been handicapped.

The sword stopped over the Stargazer's head. His eyes narrowed to slits, but the weapon remained steadfast.

"Come on," Medea hissed. Had he figured out her plan? They couldn't battle in mist aspect, but they couldn't stay in that shape forever.

The Stargazer rocked on his legs, as if unable to make a decision.

"Come on," Medea repeated. "What are you waiting for, damn you. Strike!"

The sword remained over him.

"Come on!" She tried to stare into those black eyes. For some reason, she thought there was an ember of fear in them.

"I don't think he will," Proxos said after a few tense seconds. "He's just standing there."

Medea could see the fear grow. She was having trouble keeping her knees straight. The rush of survival was ending.

"Why?" she whispered at both of them.

The Stargazer lowered his sword. His mouth was wide open. Confusion had joined the fear.

"I don't know," Proxos said, slowly pulling her away from him. "He's...something changed, Medea. He won't attack you. I don't think he'll answer without a tongue, look."

Medea felt her lids gaining weight as she tried to peer into his mouth. She practically fell into Proxos' arm. That seemed to be the obvious answer.

"The Killer..." she started.

"Yes," her friend agreed. "That must be it. Perhaps he finally sensed the Killer in you. Perhaps it's time we took advantage of this reprieve..."

"You lost your arm, Proxos," she stated weakly.

"It's happened many times before," he said casually. "The Dark Instinct heals its weapons. Always does."

Medea knew she was too weak to even will her form to change. Proxos seemed to understand this, wrapping his one arm around her waist and taking flight. She could have sworn the Stargazer was shaking his head at Proxos' last remark, but phenomena obfuscated against movement and collapsing senses. Simultaneously, her ears had caught something again—two loud, repetitive explosions coming from the other door.

4

There were about half a dozen of those Warm One soldier's in front of where the directions lead him to, down the final hallway. By then, Dante's mind had shifted to a very arousing conclusion. For so long he had been a scavenger, a survivalist. To battle, to be gripped by a violent lust was like waking up from *Moratoria*. He was a warrior, he realized, filled with might and the seduction of The Dark Instinct. A warrior, as he'd been before, enforcing the laws, hunting prey for leisure, corralling Warm Ones in the Farms. It felt so good to have conflict with moving opponents rather than the elements or starvation. It felt so good to be himself, a self that was robbed by Byron and The MoonQueen. He allowed the lust to flood his thoughts and feelings away. The smell of their Juice only added to his flushing eyes, growing fangs, and a malevolent smile.

He still used his machine guns, though, knowing he had final goals and needed to dispatch the warriors as directly as possible. The Warm Ones might have been surprised, but had to worry about their disintegrating bodies as bullets punctured them. The walls were quickly washed in crimson, circuits and metal prostheses broken or bent in sharp sparks. Almost all at once, they collapsed on the ground, a few still moving, not knowing if their computer or organic aspects would perish first.

He cautiously stepped over them, trying to suppress a guttural chuckle and the craving to feed on them, take part of them as trophies as The Ravens had once done during tournaments or with rogue Warm Ones. He had to reach his goal on the other side of the door. These animals wouldn't give him any trouble. No one was going to give him trouble...

The door suddenly opened, showing the Stargazer what surely must be Quidam. Now he recalled he had heard about this person. He was a type of Raven, the one and only enforcer of this place. He regarded Dante without emotion. He didn't seem to care about the wet, crisp mess before him. Dante in turn, opened his mouth in order to start threats and questions.

Something whistled, something shone. Dante raised the barrels of each of his weapons. Something struck one of them with a screeching echo. He was more than startled at the force causing him to topple backward and forgo one of his weapons. By the time he had slammed against the back wall, he saw what this Quidam was employing as his weapon.

Dante ducked and rolled to one side, the blade biting into where his neck would have been. He lithely rose to his feet, ready to shower this fool with his fury.

But he wasn't ready for the swift kick that almost cracked his neck, that sent him skidding ten feet. Colors lost their borders, pain urged him to stay conscious. When he glanced up from laying on his back, Quidam was charging without fanfare, sword held behind his back in order to cleave him in twine.

Dante did the only thing possible at the moment, glad he hadn't released the other machine gun as well. With both hands he held it up, receiving the brunt of the weapon. The strength of the Stargazer impressed him, as the blade banged into the middle of the gun and pushed down upon him. He heard metal bend. He couldn't believe the Stargazer's face was so calm. His wasn't, though, showing effort while pushing back and moved his left foot to Quidam's stomach. Using the momentum, he kicked up his leg, throwing his opponent over him. It was somebody else's turn to skid several feet down the corridor.

The Dreamreaver jumped up to his feet and turned for the

next assault. Quidam was already standing twenty feet away, amassing a second charge. He was incredible, Dante thought without fear. No waste of movement or energy, direct and concise as any warrior he had seen. Dante would have cherished to fight without weapons, but this Quidam had his duties for the city and he had his goals.

He pulled the trigger, already showing a cocky smile at the Stargazer and his primitive weapon.

Nothing happened, except for a thin 'click'. He pulled again.

The Stargazer was closing in at ten feet.

Click.

Again. Nothing happened.

Click.

Dante glanced down in terror, seeing that the metal he had heard bending was his own weapon. He couldn't believe the sword was that strong. But it was, and his trigger had been jammed by the damage.

Five feet.

The only thing he could do was swing his weapon back at the Stargazer. Dante didn't have the momentum now, or anything close to an advantage. The two weapons met with a loud clang. One weapon pushed the other away easily.

Dante felt arm shudder, gun shudder and move towards his direction. He never saw his own handle smack him in the face. He bounced on the floor for another good distance. His nose shattered and another part of his jaw cracked, already damaged by the kick. Once again, he was sprawled on the floor, feeling the hard friction of the ground burn his back clothing.

Feeling like the rest of his body wouldn't obey him, he lifted up his neck, which still functioned. Quidam was again going to charge. The Stargazer had only one outcome for his melee, perhaps because of his Warm One soldiers, perhaps because of what Dante did to Ogre, perhaps it was just his duty in this metropolis.

Again, his powerful legs propelled him towards the sprawled Stargazer. Again, the sword, seemingly unscathed glittered in the light and in its many reflections.

Again, Dante reflexively lifted up his weapon. It was useless, mangled and chipped at several parts. He didn't have the positioning or the time to muster another defense.

Twenty feet one more time.

His thumb grazed something he had forgotten about. It was a dark red button a few inches above the trigger.

Fifteen feet.

What was it? He groggily tried to recall the instructions Proxos' had given him at the cavern.

Ten feet.

He lifted up the barrel one more time at Quidam. No expression. Sword glimmered over his head, clutched with both hands.

Five feet.

If it didn't work or perhaps it wasn't loaded, this was it for his brief stint as a warrior once again.

The sword descended in an arc.

Dante pushed the button.

Nothing was happe...

Something shivered inside the gun and pushed him backward. Something flew out of the round hole underneath the barrel and surprised Quidam, finally showing some emotion.

Hands released the sword as an object struck him in the face. Where his mouth had once been now was a black object, round and shiny with teeth falling around it. Quidam took a few steps back, eyes widening in anguished orange flames.

Dante's joy shifted because he fully remembered what it was. What if it didn't work? What if it didn't explode? Go for the sword. Go for it now...

He didn't go for the sword. He rolled on his stomach as a light exploded from Quidam's head, followed by heat and shrapnel, all of which took away part of the hallway and those with it.

5

"It seems that Quidam is no longer with us, Feltch," said Marcion sadly.

"I know, Mac! He couldn't hide that from us. Is this another omen, another step towards freedom and our conquering of the world?"

"No, Feltch. It simply means Quidam is no longer with us."

"Who cares? The prick was one of the reasons we've fucking been here for the last two hundred years."

Marcion remained sorrowful. "He was as much of a prisoner as we were. Loyalty is the greatest enslaver, Feltch."

"So is love, compadre. So is love."

The Pharisee grinned. "So is love. In any case, he was a remarkable and arcane being, singular in his prowess who will not grace creation anymore. The museum is smaller."

"And burning, too, Mac. Looks like the entire grid is under flames."

"This city was never meant to sustain internal damage. It was not built for that. No matter, that is not what concerns me."

"What concerns you, Mac?"

He blinked and time rippled before him like wind upon a lake surface, and then stilled gradually.

"Many things at the moment. The Warden spared our dear colleague, Proxos, and the Stargazer named Medea. He wouldn't strike her for some reason, and I do not posit it had to do with the malady. It is something else, but I would need to meditate on it. It disturbs me, though."

Feltch's lips twisted. "Not essential right now, amigo. But those two have been giving me and others a bad feeling since they arrived. Can we get them off the damn chessboard?"

Marcion nodded in agreement, still feeling troubled.

"I need you to do a favor for me, Feltch. We must, how would you put it, tweak with destiny a little more, unclothe Byron at a faster rate."

"Sure, elf-boy. Are you going to be freakin' murky as usual?"

"Yes," Marcion said. "I need you to relay a message on my behalf."

"Sure thing, Mac. Anything for you. What? In the middle

of that hell?"

"Yes, Feltch. In the middle of that hell. Thank you."

The Kappa took a majestic drag from his cigar.

"Goddamn, motherfucker, man. How much do we have to take him down, Mac, in order to have a sacrifice?"

The look of sadness had returned.

"As far as he can go, Feltch. As far as he will go."

6

The Forgotten were many in his flight away from the tattooed Stargazer. In all shapes and sizes, they rushed by Proxos. A few spoke brief greetings, centuries and even millennia since had interacted with this pedigree of Stargazer. Proxos didn't have time to answer. He was trying to gain distance. To make matters worse, he kept hearing explosions, while smoke had made itself present in many of the mirrored corridors. The ones Proxos saw didn't seem worried, but he was. The throbbing of his severed arm long forgotten, Proxos was also worried about Medea, who had grown limp in his grasp. The stench of the Killer of Giants was almost forcing him to release her. She was poison, more than ever, fading slowly into nothingness. Her eyes were open, showing a little energy, her lips twitched as if she was trying to speak some advice to him. He needed advice. He needed to know that this all wasn't a mistake, that they should have stayed in his abode, allowed Byron and Medea to properly say farewell. Now it seemed Byron had suffered a terrible fate at Quidam's hand and they were in trouble. They would be found, he knew, noticing cameras at each intersection, stairwell, and hallway. Proxos didn't know what would occur, but it couldn't be pleasant. This was a city where the ones who Lilith hadn't deemed worthwhile were tossed into, a jail for the powerful and obscure. Proxos didn't see their rancor, but he was sure it was there. Perhaps it was better for Medea to fade away and not experience what might be their judgment.

He entered a chamber of high walkways and facing escalators, one hundred feet in diameter. A winged Stargazer was zooming by, while others in gaseous form floated with the fattening smoke. The place rumbled with warning.

Thinking of safety in height, Proxos flew towards the highest walkway. Cameras moved with him and not the other fleeing Stargazers. At the same time, Medea was beginning to mumble odd words, speaking about a circus, an entertainment by a beautiful woman.

How could she know! Proxos thought with fear. She wasn't there! Medea wasn't there when The Queen of Darkness had begun her first true corruption of mankind, infecting their souls and minds as they thought they were being entertained! How could she know!

"She is looking right at me," Medea mumbled. "Direct-ly...saying..."

Proxos escalated his pace, as flames puked at the top of one of the escalators. He wanted to reach the highest walkway, penetrate the door and hope to exist a little longer. There was no hope, there was no point anymore. They had destroyed Xanadu, but the two could have never understood this place and the disregarded beings that walked the mirrored hallways.

"The crowd, Proxos. Their pupils are rising into their heads. Reality is being disbanded, their minds are being expanded."

Proxos practically slammed into the door. He bounced backwards, grappling with all of his concentration not to release Medea.

"Towards me," Medea whispered when they struck the walkway's smooth metal surface. "She is revealing herself to me..."

He ignored her, staring at the door like an enemy, as if he'd just been insulted. Why hadn't it opened? Everything in this place had worked automatically. Fire was spreading below, coming from underneath the floor, through the polished tiling. Was that the reason?

A familiar voice ringed in his pointed ears for a second. He stood up, knowing if was from one of the lower walkways. It was calling Medea's name. It couldn't be.

"She is saying..."

Proxos, still clutching Medea, leaned over the edge of the walkway.

7

Dante turned furiously another corner. Where was he? He had survived the explosion, which had damaged his skin and clothing, but he was mightier than ever. He had won, and now the sword rested in his lacerated hand. He had won, destroyed a laudable opponent. He was a warrior, a true soldier of the Dark Instinct. He had won.

But fire and smoke and crumbling ceilings made him lost. He hadn't seen any of the twisted beings of this city. He needed to find her, to find *him!* He was a warrior, and if anything, he would return to his Dreamreavers stronger, more determined to begin something different, something new and better.

He wouldn't be like the others, like Her.

In one of the corridors, this one narrower and with several small rooms with a fake view of water, a figure suddenly appeared before him. He was shrouded in ratty robes, but a malformed face couldn't be denied underneath. Dante raised his sword at him, knowing he would take down as many as he felt (and somehow knowing that they would still trade with him in the future).

"Titanic's sinking," the figure said with ridiculing, garbled voice. "Better get out while you can."

"What are talking about?" Dante asked, grabbing the handle with both hands to show he was more than serious. He could feel the creature grin.

"Nothing, but I know who you're looking for. And they're both gonna meet real soon, you know."

"What are you talking about?" he asked a second time, this one tinged with danger.

Dante heard quickly about Medea and Byron, their plights, and directions to all three. Then the robed one said, "You better hurry like a mother. You better get there in seconds, pal.

They're gonna meet."

"No!" Dante exclaimed, using all of his speed to impede this news. A voice somewhere asked him why had he just listened to this creature at all. He didn't care. The description and Medea's condition told him it had to be true. Perhaps it was a trap for all of them, but he would find a way to surpass it, take it as far as he could. He was going to be direct, a warrior, and if he ripped the whole place apart, so be it.

8

Data: City faltering. We are dying. Death, do you understand? Must keep things together. No listening to us. Not listening.

Balkros walked into his home one afternoon. The news reports heard on the radio were nothing compared to what was truly happening. Shit was brewing over the horizon, botched codes and information confusing what was transpiring in Russia, Pakistan, China, even Korea. He was sure the angels had something to do with it. He was sure The President, NSA, or the military wouldn't fix it in time. It was over, and he was also sure his house would have plenty of desperate messages, probably many Federal agents at his doorsteps before the day was over. He had driven for hours, it seemed, strangely following the sun's course on the highway. The sun was disappearing, vanishing below a sea of dark indigo clouds, and Balkros somehow missed it. He didn't feel at peace, but he felt numb. What was done was done. Numbness was as good as faith. Now it was time to come home. Now it was time to receive his deliverance, his peace.

Balkros' house seemed normal, except for the fact that his wife was stabbed to the fireplace in a humorous position that almost looked like a fleshy swastika. Someone with massive strength had used Dorothy's knitting pins to penetrate meat, bone, and ultimately the white bricks of the fireplace. Someone had shoved liquor bottles up her vagina and into her mouth, ripping them both to obscene shreds like bloody flowers. More blood thickly cascaded down on the fireplace, staining more of the white brick of the immediate ground. Dorothy was still breathing. Her eyes, wide and pinkish, were pleading like an animal.

"Honey," Eugene said casually. "I'm home."

He walked by her, placed his suitcase on the table, and went for the stairs. Before rising to the second story, he turned off the television; some talk-show vomited an episode entitled *My Lover is now the Living Dead and drinks blood.* Just a re-run, he mused and said, "It's going to be the zombie apocalypse...wait...it already happened." The hard blinking phone machine was never even considered. Once upstairs, he unbuttoned his coat, took off his trousers, and his shoes before stopping before his daughter's room. Fate or numbness, it didn't matter. He had to please his duality, his rage that was there because he couldn't fuse the two. He loved her so much but couldn't deny his craving. If they were going to give him his deliverance, this was the time. The world was ending, he had never been strong enough, but it was time to face his fire. Poor, Gina, poor world, poor Heaven and Hell.

Balkros calmly walked into her bedroom, surprised to see that his daughter was bound and gagged on the bed, nude and waiting. Her eyes were also pleading, full of fear and hope. Fear and hope, another duality. Eugene went to her and stroked her hair. She trembled when his hand ran down to trace the contours of her body.

"There, there," he said. "It's all right, Gina. It's all right. Daddy has to do something, Daddy has to do something..."

Fear and hope. Faith and numbness. Fire and ice.

Love and...

Gina!

Balkros took step back, practically hyperventilating. What was going on? Had he gone insane this whole time? This was his daughter, Gina. Gina! This wasn't only his daughter, it was part of him. Why did he want to hurt part of him? Why did he want to punish a part that reflected shame in his weak masculinity, in his duality he couldn't compromise? She had never hurt anyone, he lived to create ways to hurt others. Gina was right because of who she was, and he was so wrong.

Innocence and salvation. Ambition and happiness.

Love and seduction. True love and lies.

Data: Do not do that!

"Oh, Gina," he said, shuddering, placing his hands over his ears. "What have I done? What have I become? No, no, no!"

His daughter's eyes reflected an almost pity for him. Even with the terror the little girl had probably experienced, she still cared for him, tried to understand him. She had never wanted to hurt him, make him feel less of a man, a warrior.

"Gina." He lifted a hand and paused, almost afraid to touch her. An erection was trying to gain daybreak between his thighs. Fury threatened to spark the forests of his sanity. This all had to be an illusion, a deception for him, perhaps a test by those higher forms of spirit.

Angels and monsters.

Fire and ice.

The windows suddenly blew open, followed by an azure, piercing luminosity. The child's room, with all its pictures and dolls, teddy-printed sheets and pink cars, was engulfed by this energy that brought a coldness that was more than physical, brimming with a sadness that made his legs buckle.

Someone came in with that luminosity. A figure so tall and gorgeous, the rigid light and bursting wind could never steal any attention from her majestic form. In any movie, in any picture or painting, in any hot fantasy or tender dream, Balkros had never seen anything as perfect as this person. She was a woman. She was blue pale and had eyes of liquid gems, red lips that smiled with refined delight. She was also advancing towards him.

"BALKROS," she said, her voice in his head. He could see frost covering the walls.

"Who are you?" he asked, still on his knees. Was Gina okay? The illumination was so potent.

She smiled. He could feel urine warming his boxers, bowels lose control, his heart skipping a few unwise beats.

"BALKROS," she repeated and all of his emotions swirled into an attention for her. He couldn't stop from clutching his hands in prayer. The answer was so obvious of who this being was, who this being had to be.

I AM GOD, she said but her lips didn't move this time.

He opened his mouth and choked on the swirling emotions. Lips wrestled with themselves to mouth the word 'please'. This was it, he knew. This was God in all of Her glory. He had worried about his masculinity in his duality, and now God was a woman! How appropriate.

"Please," he was able to utter. "Help...me..."

She floated close to him with a loving smile. She moved a hand to absently stroke the hair of his daughter. Why did she look so terrified?

BALKROS, God said, moving closer to him, her radiance following like an imperial comet. YOU WOULD NOT TAKE HER. YOU HESITATED.

"No." He shook his head savagely, hating that now he had a painful erection. "I couldn't...I can't, Lord. Please help me...please make me better."

Balkros thought he heard her laughter, a celestial giggle that shook his house, brought winter into every room.

YOU HAVE SUFFERED, BALKROS. YOU NEED PEACE. WILL YOU SERVE ME FOREVER?

"Yes," he hissed, clamping his eyes. He would do anything, not caring about the world outside his senses. All he wanted was what Her angels had promised. He wanted peace, he wanted peace.

QU'EST-CE QUE? Her tone sounded as youthful as the voice of Gina. I DID NOT HEAR YOU.

He opened his eyes, tears quivering against the cold.

"Yes, Lord! I will serve you. I give you my word. Please help me. Please—"

He heard the laughter again, this time dislodging some fear behind the hope that surged within him. Why should he be afraid? This was God almighty, and he was being rewarded. All the violence and death, they were just tests for him, tests for the gay future. He was going...

YOU WILL BE DELIVERED, BALKROS. FOR THAT I REWARD YOU WITH ETERNAL DESTRUCTION, ENDLESS PARADISE.

Destruction and paradise?

He thought he heard Gina screeching through the gag. He

thought the blue storm was surrounding him. He thought God was suddenly right before him, gown flowing around him along with her bluish locks, opening her beautiful mouth, revealing two marks that further accentuated the fear that now was so obvious. It replaced his thoughts. More than fear, it was a primordial terror. But he was being delivered!

But God had fangs, long, translucent and shining, and coming towards him. And God whispered something in his ear, her breath killing any skin on the side of his face, turning the cartilage into brittle, crackling pieces.

YOU WOULD NOT TAKE YOUR OFFSPRING. ABRAHAM HAD MORE BALLS, BALKROS. BUT IT IS NEVER TOO LATE, MON-CHERI.

The terror made him scream, joined by the agony of her breath. Balkros couldn't move, swept away by the light and the swirling emotions.

"NO!" he was able to say, witnessing her fanged mouth smile before him and then lower itself to the side of his neck. Then he added, "Gina!"

Then he felt God bite his neck with such force it snapped neatly.

9

Byron was now feeling a connection. It was Medea. Finally! She was close, behind the isolating walls of this metropolis. Something was very wrong with her. Through the storm of voices, the lightning of his wounded soul, he could sense her. She was leaving somewhere, faint images told him. She was leaving to meet a beautiful, tall female, to join a...circus? To join a mystic show that was as ghastly as it was seductive. A show that had started many terrible movements in the history of humanity, poisoned their spirits with the deception of brightness, the false beginning of enlightenment and revolutionary eras. Byron didn't know what this meant, but did know that he needed to stop her, anchor his spirit to hers. But first he needed to physically find Medea. Something had happened, for smoke and tiny earthquakes were met in every turn of this place of mirrors, cameras, and themed chambers from pre-Holocaust times. It was a museum but it was also a prison. A prison of the Forgotten, a playground for the Stargazers that weren't Stargazers. Byron didn't mind that because he probably was the cause by tampering with The Egg's guts when trying to escape.

He ignored a ghoul running past him in flames in a corridor. Byron knew the Stargazer was enjoying the rare sensation of pain, as were many in the population. They could sense each other, connected at all times with their minds, learning to change the channels, the frequencies of each other. He hadn't learned that. He wouldn't learn it.

Byron came upon a large chamber with escalators, one which was fuming, and several walkways. His mind screamed because Medea was close, so very close. The voices organized in his head, some trying to distract him, some trying to help him.

Look up.

They're gonna meet.

Look up.

A tool of the machine.

Byron obeyed a few of them and craned his head towards the walkways, ignoring hot gusts from the rising inferno to his side. The walls shook, sizzling, detonated from several places, but he could focus on one thing only.

In the highest walkway, an old friend stood holding Medea. Byron had never been so glad, never felt such elation. It seemed like such a long time since seeing them; it seemed like so much had changed. Byron spent years as a Heretic away from Medea after being cast out from Xanadu, but this was much more intense and severe. The same could be said physically about his companions. Proxos looked just as battered as he, sans one arm, and Byron had never seen such a look of puzzlement in his brow. Medea's form and spirit rushed to him, and the joy still held. She was fading away, but he was here. Byron had always fulfilled her; he would find a way to renew her being.

I hate you, Medea.

She seemed to stir in Proxos' grasp. Eyes flickered with

muffled consciousness. Byron took for the air, a large smile on his face, which only added to the ex-Elder's puzzlement. Motion deteriorated. Thin fire was in his way, ignored.

I'm coming, Medea. You're the one thing that kept me going through my earnest quests, the one person who believed in me even when you dreaded my actions. It was always us, Medea, it was always us...

Medea's head cocked towards him. Their sights knitted together for an instant, the corners of her mouth quivered into what Byron knew would be a pining smile. An arm reached towards him. Byron thought the arm was longer, thinner with a sheen like a glacier, but didn't care. He reached for her, increasing his speed.

"Medea," he said with eager joy.

Byron...she spoke to me...she said, "Welcome to our dream, Medea. The show has only begun, you little cunt."

He heard an explosion to his side. He thought he heard a scream. He was almost there, passing the last walkway before he reached his friends. He was almost there. Medea's lips were parting at the widening corners of her pretty mouth...

"Byron!" someone screamed, a voice that jolted part of him. A familiar voice he had only heard in memory. Unlike most sounds the past nights, it didn't come from inside the whirlpool that was his mind. He turned briefly and ghastly memory arrived like a train to haunt him like so many times.

The memory intercepted him in midair with a hardy thud. The memory propelled him downward, smashing into a through one of the walkways. The memory pulled him further with glass and metal shards, through flame and smoke, through despair and hopelessness.

Medea, no!

"Byron!" the memory shouted a second time, holding him tight, with strength he hadn't forgotten even after they had fought in a Farm decades ago. Byron struggled back, arching his head to see his friends fade away. It wasn't working—he was descending into the inferno.

MEDEA, NO!

10

Proxos took a step back, as cruel heat rose from the chaos underneath. That was Byron, wasn't it? What had happened? Another Stargazer had bolted from nowhere, thwarting his direction with force, dragging him down before he had reached them.

Dante?

It couldn't be.

Medea had stirred, probably sensing her closest of friends. She twisted in his grasp more, as if their aborted encounter brought out wakefulness. Her face cringed in agony.

"She's coming," she uttered. "Byron, no...don't talk to her...it's a..."

Proxos stumbled backward more, trying not to release her since Medea would surely plunge down to the fury underneath. As if in queue, he heard the hissing of the door opening to his back. He pivoted, the confusion asking why it was happening now. As if in queue...

Three figures awaited him, smiling the smiles of predators. Three figures he'd known before, who loosely ruled this city.

"Greetings, Proxos," the one in the middle said, as comely and ethereal as always. "Did you know that it is Midsummer? That it is night? That it is not a dream?"

His gazed darted from creature to creature. He knew no benign intention was exuded from their laughing eyes.

"Come," Marcion stated with a voice that chilled his soul. "Your role in the act is over, Proxos Commodore. It is time you two were put away for good."

11

A battle took place. A battle that had transpired a hundred and thirty nine years ago between two friends who cherished each other to almost no limit. This time it was also because of a friend, once Mephisto, now Medea. Before they had fought as Ravens, breaking a severe law in the Stargazer capital, now they fought as Heretics in the dying nights of the Stargazer Empire.

The roles were much different now.

"Dante!" Byron exclaimed after being tossed through a window that led to what the citizen's referred to as bowling alley. The walls were burning, smoke shivered on the floor, thundering heat gossiped of more to come.

"Hello, Byron." Dante grinned, as if delighted at the disheveled appearance of the one who had finished his glorious ride in Xanadu. He was the shell of how he'd looked in uniform, hair combed, always smiling like he knew a weakening secret about anyone. "Please get up from your knees."

"It can't be," Byron whispered. "You? Here? You...you..."

Dante casually admired his new sword, twirling his wrists to allow light to dance upon the fine surface.

"Yes, Lord Raven. You destroyed me. Almost. Our Mistress gave me a new existence. I have wandered the wilderness thinking about meeting you, craving it, no matter how many times I told myself we would never meet, that it didn't matter, that the chapter was forever closed. A Heretic and the fierce head of The MoonQueen's soldiers? Never! But I heard you made your own mistakes, Byron, that you were also excommunicated. I've heard many things, but it doesn't change what I've wanted to do."

Byron kept shaking his head, eyes wide and bleeding in shifting purples. Dante's were beginning to teeter towards ruby.

"It can't be," Byron said and almost laughed. "You...here? Why I'm not surprised? Damn them. Damn me."

"Please stand up," Dante said casually. "You're not the only thing on my agenda."

The last word caused Byron to blink, to suffocate any light from his eyes. He turned his head to the fiery mess outside, to the holes they had caused in their collision, spanning many walls.

"Medea," Byron said, feeling for her. "I must—"

"No!" roared Dante. "Don't think of that! Doesn't my sight mean anything to you? Don't you have anything to say about what you did to me, about how you broke me?"

Byron looked at him with an odd expression.

"You would have broken me. It was honorable and fair, Dante. Dante?" He shook his head slowly, cringing as if some ache traversed his head like a scythe. "Stop, voices...no...I...It was so long ago...I was different..."

"Are you?" Dante asked arrogantly.

A tool of the machine. How far is too far?

"Yes." His voice echoed with little conviction. "Yes, damn it. It doesn't matter...you don't understand—"

"What I understand is that you're right, Byron. I would have broken you. And as long as we both walk this planet, we must find out who can break who permanently."

Byron placed a hand on his forehead. "Whatever. I have to go. You're the best, Dante, you're the..."

Dante struck him squarely on the face with the handle of the sword. Byron's body slapped the ground, folding backward at the force. Then Dante kicked him in the stomach and sent him sailing against a counter that lost its form. He tossed the sword to his side and said, "Only one way to find out, Byron. Thank you for getting off your knees. You never got off them for Our Mistress when I knew you."

The battle started. Perhaps it was the fact Byron had no choice, perhaps it was Dante's last words that caused him to blow out from the splintered wreckage with rash fury, perhaps it was the fact that they just had to find who the best between them was. Again, they collided in the air and ripped through stories and walls, uncaring of the intensifying tempest and explosions spreading like dark clouds throughout the city. Before, Byron and Dante had razed a section of The Farms while both Warm One and Stargazer watched in dread; now they had aid from the fire and a population to enjoy their exercise.

Claws and fangs lashed, fists and limbs banged, curses and mighty growls attempted to rise from the blistering anarchy. More glass and metal gave away to them, as bone chipped and cracked, but they still fought, uncaring of the flames marring their skins, shrapnel cutting their handsome bodies. They battled, the city was wounded, and only one would be victorious.

And one was victorious in the end. They crashed down

through two stories, tangled in wires and a haze of mortar, using their reserves for the last melee instead of flight. A cloud of dust rose and so did part of the floor. Debris covered them, even as their hands attempted to squeeze each other out of their existences, even as their fangs dug into each other to rip out anything that the Dark Instinct might deem suitable to reside in its respective house.

Then it all was still, except for the sound of fire, the far away voice of electrical discharges. After a while, the rubble trembled and burst like a volcano. A figure rose from it, holding another in both arms, who was completely limp in his grasp. It was like the first battle a hundred and thirty nine years ago. And the victor would roar in both sorrow and joy like before, showing his fangs to creation, eyes gurgling with angry coral light.

The roles were much different now.

12

Data: Alert. All systems shutting down. Binary functions ceased. Reserve circuits showing fatal applications. We must come back.

So cold...cold beyond cold...inside...outside...so cold there is a heat somewhere...a heat that can never be sated...that suffocates...hunger...

Data: We are failing. Warning! Warning!

Hunger like never before...so damn cold...deliverance...no pain...worse...so much worse...than pain...

Data: WARNING! ALL...ALL....WARNING... SYSTEMS-- WE--SHJFGAOURFHZZZZRU--WE-AKJJSURRURU.

So cold...

Her laughter. She called to him in tears.

Hunger.

Nothing.

Darkness.

Data:.............

13

Dante tossed the body to one side. The lust, the craving had re-ceded so quickly. He now truly felt as if he'd just woken from *Moratoria*.

What had he done?

He stared at Byron's form—torn and shattered, bones jut-ting out, face a mess of bite marks, hair pulled out. He wouldn't dare look at his own figure. It was probably in the same shape, but not as bad. He had won finally. He was the greatest. He had drunk his vengeance in the most poetic of ways, punished the one who indirectly threw him out of the City of Domes, the one who caused him to become a Dreamreaver.

And what is wrong with that? A steady voice asked in his head. You understood the lie of The MoonQueen, you knew that Byron suffered to the same thing. Medea told you with a distant warning that night at the caves when you wanted them out of your reality.

Dante covered his face, barely noticing that some of his fingers were missing. The darkness couldn't hide why he'd done it. Yes, the world couldn't hold both of them but that was because of Dante. He had always been envious of Byron's power and san-guine attitude. He had never swallowed the fact that Byron was better and got better, reflected in what he performed in Xanadu, which he had wanted to do in time; and Medea, an amazing soul that only cherished Byron. Vengeance and violence had been his excuse. If given time, he would have attempted to dislodge Byron as head of the Ravens in the past. He knew it. Byron had known it, and never really cared.

Deep down inside, Dante knew that Byron wasn't sinister or brazen, that he would never have corrupted Medea, because he never had corrupted anyone, finding that too beneath him. Byron only wanted to shine and burn it all away. Dante had always fall-en too low to shine like Byron, and had never understood.

He uncovered his eyes and again stared at Byron. He had

won, and it was shallow, probably as shallow as Byron had felt. He had allowed the Dark Instinct to go unchallenged, use him like the weapon he had once been, taking with it all of his insecurities and petty desires. For this he had abandoned his people on a dark whim, searching for revenge and a person who would never care for him as much as Byron.

Taking a few steps back while gasping in aching to gain distance from the body, his back felt the remnants of a column of broken, melted mirrors. Flames spread around him, all probably caused by his besting of Quidam. Dante knew leaving this era was necessary, at least find Medea and save her since Byron couldn't, but felt very weary. Very weary and very ashamed. For the first time in his existence, Dante didn't like the passion and fervor of a Stargazer. He didn't even like the role of a warrior.

"Maybe if I can find you a Warm One...there might be hope...healing..."

He noticed smoke of a different pallor slither to his side. It condensed and showed the form of the hooded Stargazer met in one of the hallways. Smoke and heat were starting to make vision a chore, as the incoming fire came from all sides and above.

"You did it," the Stargazer said, head lowered. "You fucking did it, pal. How ya feeling?"

"Not good," Dante responded honestly, finding it hard to speak with several perforations in his neck. He glanced to Byron's blurring shape. "No good at all. Who are you?"

The Stargazer lifted his head, revealing a twisted face with a twisted leer. His round eyes showed a malevolent glee the Dreamreaver had never experienced before.

"I'm the goddamn guy who helped you face your darkest desires and fears," he said. Dante was too fixed on his visage to notice him retrieve an object from the folds of his robes. "His too, may I add. I didn't do it alone, having the help of an elf and a ghoul, but this monkey'll take all the credit. Here, you forgot this back there. Would have made things easier for you. It'll make it easier for me."

Dante felt a cruel, solid sensation slam into his belly. Solid turned to sharpness and then to rigidness, as something carved right into him. He glanced down while his body was pushed back with incredible force to see part of the blade of the sword taken from Quidam. Then he had to concentrate on his back pressing into the column, the chipping shoulder blades, and the movement of the sword that truncated his spine.

"This is for Ogre," the Stargazer rasped, angling the blade to his right to cut into him more. "And this is for Quidam." He leaned the blade to his left, stopping at each side before he had severed his body in two.

Dante couldn't do anything, without passion or energy, but shake at the damage and clutch the blade with his remaining fingers. The deformed Stargazer took a step back, as if to admire his handiwork. Soot covered his robes now, flames were encroaching their immediate area as more debris collapsed from above in the warning of loud crashes.

"Not bad, uh? We're fucking endowed with the God-Soul, but we must follow some of the rules of our past aspects. You're paralyzed and movement will divide you, man. Don't know if you'll survive that way—depends on the will and stamina of your cord to The Dark Instinct. Mist form is a risk because you might turn back in two pieces or without any existence."

Dante's eyes widened with terror, but not at his situation but at something he'd said. The Stargazer seemed to catch this, grinning with its teeth that had no fangs. No fangs! That was impossible!

"What's the matter? Didn't you know, Dante? We were all once mortal. You're just a Warm One given mobility by a part of The MoonQueen. You're a fucking corpse, an android dreaming of electrical sins. Haven't you ever thought about it? You will now, man, and that'll help keep you there until it's all over. Anyway, gotta go. This place is a bad spot to be pinned down, you know?"

The Stargazer started cackling, lumbering towards Byron. He picked his broken form up and tossed him over warped shoulders. Still cackling, he bounced a few times and flew up, disappearing into the curdling smoke.

And Dante still shook with widened eyes, clutching a sword that would not break and wounding thoughts that wouldn't either, barely noticing the bedlam that was engulfing him, that was spreading throughout the city.

Chapter 11

Nights passed. One after the other. Many things happened until it was all over.

The continuous damage that maimed part of New Atlantis suddenly stopped after twenty four hours. Somehow, every fire stopped, any hazard was smothered. Without clamor, hordes of Warm One workers came to rebuild the wreckage. In some places where it was severe, metal and wire and glass recreated itself, grids and networks re-knitted as if they had never been injured. It was obvious who had caused all of this, and it came as no surprise to The Forgotten. They had their Prince, but another city without its queen wasn't so fortunate.

Witnessed by many who sat in front of screens with glasses filled with juice to toast, they saw the ultimate finale of Xanadu. The Stargazer capital finally burned itself out of shape, except for parts of the tunnels and the Farms, where Warm One factions still held on to survival like the ants that they were. The remnants of the metropolis would soon be swept away by radioactive squalls and their myriad effects; in time, The City of Domes would appear as if it had never been there on the surface of that harsh valley. The spectators cheered and laughed, and a few imitated Balkros and his silly threats.

Only one remained serious, as usual. He didn't participate in the donning of various costumes, ranging from festive apparel to uniforms from the various epochs of history. Many brought musical instruments or just whistle blowers, but he had left his harp in his chambers. Marcion stood before the crowd, arms behind his elegant back, intent on the swan song of the Stargazer capital. Feltch walked to his side, trying to look as serious as his ugly features would allow.

"Too bad they don't have a god to fix their problems anymore," he told The Good Neighbor. "We got one, and soon he'll be doing our complete bidding. Right?"

"Correct," Marcion said. "That was the promise of The Queen of Darkness."

"The damage is almost fixed, Mac. Our workers are doing a damn fine mop-up job. The only thing odd is that some of the computer systems are acting weird, all of a sudden. Must be the side effects of The Centurion having to do something other than his fueling job. Don't you think?"

Marcion blinked in slight confusion, telling all that he hadn't used his gift to pry this matter. Most thought this aberration wasn't anything of concern. This was a merry occasion, getting merrier by the night. So many spectacles had transpired recently, so many greater ones would when they were finally emancipated from The Egg. Not only emancipated but ruling it instead. Everything was going as planned. Feltch slapped his arm.

"Don't worry about it, amigo. All we care is about one thing. When is the sacrifice?"

Soon, Marcion thought. In a few nights. He still must be broken down a little more, one last time, so that he cannot be peeled of any defenses or weapons anymore; so that his soul is ripe to be fed to our god in the gray dusk.

"I see," Feltch said thoughtfully. "Can't fucking wait."

Some of us have been prisoners for thousands of years, Feltch. A few more nights won't matter.

The population tried to ignore his serious demeanor. It was a merry time, a good time, something to pass the time, something to forget time and the time of The Queen of Darkness.

2

Only one person was concerned with time.

Eight nights. Seven nights.

They were tossed in a sealed chamber, featureless and without furniture. Outside, he heard the constant marching of Warm One soldiers, more as a warning that their situation meant containment. Proxos was sure escape would be something unattainable with Medea's condition, which worsened with each passing revolution of *Luna*. They received no visitors, except for two Warm Ones each evening who came for their nourishment. Proxos ate what he needed and used a cupped hand to drain juice into Medea's always opened mouth. There was not much else to do, except wish for a fire to keep him company and listen to Medea's paltry mewling. Proxos didn't want to reflect on their actions, on his actions, for that is something he hadn't done before The Holocaust.

On the second night of their captivity, she almost appeared coherent. Proxos was glad, a little hopeful, partly because he didn't want to hear about the circus. She asked a few questions, head on his lap, still unable to move a body that still changed slowly—thinner, longer, with skin that was beginning to shine with a faint glow of pale sapphire. He didn't know where Byron was, where they were, and what would happen to them. They were in a prison inside a prison.

"Proxos," Medea said softly. "What about the USB? Did you see the cure?"

He stroked her forehead. "Yes, Medea. I saw it. It's very simple, actually."

"Simple? How simple?"

He raised his head slightly, pursed his lips, and said, "It has to do with transference of Dark Instincts, which will rejuvenate you to the point of complete healing. Balkros was astute, I tell you. It's similar to the ritual of turning a Warm One into a Stargazer—it will give you enough of me to replace what the Killer of Giants has decayed inside you. It will give you new life."

Not opening her eyes, she smiled slightly at that word that was not used for immortals.

"Good," she said. "I can still feel Byron. Barely, though. He's close. I will see him."

"You will," he said, biting his lower lip. "In time. I will do this ceremony this night, after you've eaten more. Everything will be fine, Medea."

"Thank you, Proxos," she whispered, turned her head and was again enjoying her oblivion.

He was almost glad, because she couldn't see him weep for the next hour. After he was done sobbing, he sighed several times and said, "I've got to stop lying to my friends."

After two more nights, alone with his tormented thoughts and Medea's rare babbling, the ex-Elder knew that she was too far gone to enter *Moratoria* and try to detain the disease. It didn't matter, because they were trapped in a city that was nothing but a target for one of the tools of the Holocaust. The end was coming.

Six nights. Five nights.

3

After four nights, Fien took control of the pirates. He stood up and called upon his people. There was no more trading, their ships were gorged with livestock and other materials. Dante had not returned.

"We must return to the caverns!" he shouted, words escaping heavy and wobbly. "Dante will meet us there, if..."

He eluded the rigid, daring glances of the Dreamreavers.

"I mean, he will meet us there, in one of our headquarters. We have work to do, and plenty of bartering goods to keep us content for a long time."

Many nodded, faces clearing of worry. Dante was probably adventuring in the city, some mumbled, thinking fondly of their great leader. He had survived The MoonQueen and the wilderness, he could survive a city of complacent, mutated Stargazers with no warrior skills. Perhaps he was weaving diplomacy with them, gaining support to fragment another Stargazer kingdom away from Xanadu.

Sails were erected, blades carved the ground, and they slowly began to gain distance from New Atlantis. They sang, trying to elevate their moods a little higher, hoping to see Dante soon, knowing that they had treasures to trade that would keep them sated with good juice perhaps forever. But the Dreamreavers didn't believe in forever, just the now, which was the current of wind, the mercy of the skies, the hope of making it another dawning of *Luna*.

Release the anchors of lies,

raise the sails of liberty.
The sand our master,
the wind our mistress.
To where we're blown
Forever we'll roam.
Our ships our homes,
our freedom our course.

Now was time to leave, Fien thought, glancing back as he guided the pirates towards the rich caverns, part of him like the others, not wanting to know what the explosions on the side of the city had been a few nights ago.

"To where we're blown," he said with a dense sigh. "Forever we'll roam."

4

zzsxoouruusjfjjrjrjj
    Da...
    Zjsasyurjjfjs
    Ta...
    Sjauduru.
    Data: Remember. We exist again. We are that we are.
    We are that we are!
    No, *I Am*.

5

The God-Soul once again floated before him in the void, in his image, all in black like a finely carved piece of obsidian, a dark gem in nothingness. His smile was mocking while he lit two cigarettes. He handed one to Byron, who owned no real form. The God-Soul's smoke was dark like him.

"You're a bastard," he told Byron. "Humiliated by destiny

again, Byron, but I wonder if you're going to get the proverbial last laugh. I'm sure you want me to help you one more time, get you out of this mess."

Medea. I can feel her. So faint...turning a corner.

The Dark Instinct's eyes narrowed with evil joy. "Are you sure you want her? You should worry about yourself. You're a mess, Byron, hung up with all of these beings with living souls that should be drained quickly. Helping you might mean interfering with The Prince of Shadows, who draws upon other energies besides me. I don't like him, though."

Yes! Help me. One more time. I must find her. I must retaliate against all of those who manipulated me. I must take it all the way!

"You sure? I'm warning that for once, Byron, back off, pretend to take a deep breath."

His laughter was piercing, and Byron thought he could feel universes, worlds, dreams wither away at its darkness. At the same time, he thought the essence's features seemed softer, more feminine.

Please! One more time. I must find Medea!

"Sure." The God-Soul smiled, part him, part the wrath of Lilith. "You've always been my whore. One more time. But you'll owe me, Byron. You will pay this time. Let's go. I'm already mending your bones."

One more time...

And in time, he heard Marcion coming down to the place where he and The Veal's shared a tortured predicament.

6

Four nights. Three nights.

One more time never came for one person in New Atlantis.

The end came for Medea on the fifth night of their captivity. All of a sudden, she opened her eyes with a terrified expression and jolted on the ground.

"I know Her," she screamed. "I know her face. I know her soul. She is...she is...no...anything but that..."

She was then very still, and Proxos could sense her Dark Instinct draining away, the Killer boiling in victory, leaving Medea to be what she should have been when Lilith attacked her mortal form in the kingdom of ice at the top of Xanadu—a corpse. And this corpse would never know that there was nothing about a cure for The Killer of Giants on the disk, just gibberish and odd programs.

He held the corpse in his single arm. It was still cold, but it would never move again, never act with the human light of the personality of Medea, never crave for destruction and defy natural law. It was so quick and simple, so devoid of honor and fanfare like a heroine should have experienced, Proxos shook the corpse a few times in dreading disbelief. He grabbed her by the hair and pulled her face in front of his eyes. The mouth was opened. No light in her eyes. The light was gone.

Medea was gone, the one Byron hated, the brave Shaman who had ignited a revolution, thrived as an Elder, and helped Byron end an era of evil Proxos himself had helped start. Medea was gone.

For the second time, he began weeping, tenderly rocking the body.

"No," he said with a hard croak. "No...I...no, Medea..."

Yes, Medea, it was Her, The Queen of Darkness, who created this circus, this venomous festival of twisted fantasies that twisted the soul of humanity, that was truly the beginning of the road to The Holocaust, centuries before, and who saw you in her vision in order to spell your doom, as she did with many others crossing time.

Time.

Time continued in his cell, and Proxos Commodore was finally all alone having to face his failures and lies, wondering over and over how they could have handled things from the beginning of the end.

Time.

He lowered the body to the ground and crossed his legs to sit before her. Bloody tears kept arriving, but he just sat there solemnly.

7

Two nights.
>Time passed.
>One night.
>One more time!
>It was time.

8

Wakefulness finally came to him as it always had after his second birth. It came tinged with hunger, seething craving. He couldn't open his eyes, but could smell exactly where his body had been deposited. It was in the lower levers. Byron was with The Veals— the dumb, quarantined Warm Ones that suffered a fate worse than the stock bred in the Farms of Xanadu. He was fastened against a single metal column towards the back. The chains were not his true captor but a castigated body that had suffered through a scathing fight and more. Byron doubted any part of his body was sound. The Queen of Darkness had smitten him down and buried him once in the wilderness; this felt pretty much the same. Yet it was worse because it was hard to think, focus on the canvass of reality. Part of him didn't want to, cringing from images of the ghost that defeated him, of the nights when he became naked to himself and The Forgotten. It couldn't have been Dante! More than that, the voices in his head screeched playfully at all times, making him more naked than he was, arriving with anguish to his senses, binding him further with their wills. The voices. He couldn't escape them. None could here, none could ever leave the abode of The Centurion. Everything was so muddled, but the broken figure that was Byron Solsbury understood one thing in his agony and delirium.

This place, it was so wrong. New Atlantis was many times worse than Xanadu. In his former home the truth was murdered and buried behind the laws of The Elders. Here the truth was obfuscated in a twisted way. Here the truth was as malleable as a lie. They had never lied to him, but never truly given him the hard pure truth, tweaking it carefully to their needs. From the first feast to the tours, to the last nights, they had never showed him truth's fullness. He obviously was part of their needs, and the truth was just a shuttered light, opened gradually to draw him in to their wicked and yet unknown plans. Perhaps he had never asked the right questions, so easily exploited by his arrogance and curiosity and guilt, but they had never given him the right answers. Washed in the light and reflection of no privacy, one also had to lose freedom in some sense. The Forgotten had made him seem like a toy to their games, their never ending games. She had concocted something far worse than the nightmare experienced in The City of Domes. No, they had also helped concoct it, the voices in his head told him, louder like a constipated storm.

He'd been exposed, harvested to putridity by their games. Byron knew what he was, what he'd done, and they were glad to give it to him. Now he was their prisoner, now he finally experienced a sense of deep hopelessness, something never felt before.

The hunger rose within him, momentarily taking away the shame and sorrow mirrored in a body of broken bones and minced skin. Byron knew he was still just a Stargazer. He hungered for them severely. He could smell their thin Juice. Their blood. Veins felt like thundering rivers in his ears, hearts exploded with invitation. He wanted each and every one of them, but he was bound. Even with a broken jaw and one fang he thought hunting could be attained one more time, even with knees poking out of his skin Byron felt he could pounce on them. A voice separated from the others with a strong whisper and told him to move, but he could not. He didn't have the strength. He was barely conscious. The other voices laughed at him. The voice told him he would release him but it would take time. *Sol* would be arriving soon, though. Time. Mirrors. The Egg. He was bound and hunger had turned into agony.

Time...mirrors...hunger...I know your face...

Medea, no, Medea. What happened to you? I can't feel you anymore. I saw you briefly.

We have a deal, bastard. Oui? You owe me. We have a deal!

MEDEA!

Feed me!

Suddenly, after an ocean of oblivion, Byron was free. Her name still dangled in the high canyons of his fading thoughts. He lay on the floor, strangely panting when he didn't require oxygen. Byron almost wished he did, since it might help the spinning ground, the sizzling throbbing that mushroomed in his head. The Veals had heard him fall, moving anxiously in their pens. How ironic, he gave himself a brief thought, that all they wanted was to be fed when many times they were the ones to be fed.

Feed me! You're free, bastard.

Medea! Where are you?

His body quivered at first only, drained at breaking a power that had slowly taken over him, as The Forgotten and their Prince had planned from the beginning. He slowly dragged himself into sitting position, a ghostly soreness making itself present like a dusk star. Part of his rib-cage collapsed, making all sensations even more uncomfortable. He wouldn't dare look down at the ribald mess that was his body. Smoke drifted from one of his ears. At the same time, his eyes glowed slightly in scarlet. He yielded a brief smile of triumph. He was hungry. He wasn't bound. He still was far from being free.

But he was free of one thing...

The elevator door opened in the distance. Of the many reflections only one walked out. It was him. Byron wasn't at all surprised.

The Good Neighbor walked airily towards him. His gorgeous eyes gazed at him with a perfect harmony of amusement and pity no mortal and few immortal beings could have achieved. But there was a finality there, Byron noticed, like a hidden glint of farewell.

Byron tried to show some semblance that he wasn't done, that there was still the fight of defiance in him. Marcion held his expression.

"Remarkable," The Good Neighbor said. "You released the voices from your mind. You took off the shackles of The Centurion. None has ever done it before. Ever. The Dark Instinct is strong in you, stronger than you will ever know. That is one of the reasons we needed you, that is why you had to come here."

Byron growled, eyes gaining luminance. The same force that aided him allowed gravity to dissolve and raise him to his useless feet.

"What is wrong?" The Pharisee asked casually. "Did you ever expect anything else? You always enjoyed being the center of the tale, Byron. You were the center of my tale, and it does bring me a certain aching to have done this to you, even though you did more yourself. Do you not believe that, Byron?"

"I don't believe in anything right now," he admitted in soft warning growl. "I just want right now, Marcion. The games are over. I want and you're going to give it to me."

The Pharisee raised an eyebrow the same color as his willowy hair.

"Still clinging to that hatred, Byron? Still thinking your style will work in any time, in any situation?"

"Yes," he hissed without much conviction. He wanted war. He was hungry, and the voice urged to forgo thought and emotion. "Where are they?"

Marcion glanced away for a second. "They are in better and worse places than you. They are wishing you had never brought them here with your irascible charm and your craving for desecration."

"Damn you, Marcion, where are they? Where is Medea?"

He smiled warmly at Byron. "Your love was the only salvation, Byron. But you still told her you hated her, you still would never admit in your self-centered universe. Now it is too late. You—"

"Shut-up!" He hovered closer to him. The Pharisee didn't move, looking more and more concerned.

"You do not like me reading into the fabric of reality," Marcion said. "You did not like what I did to you. But I had to, Byron, for you are the one. I cannot stop stressing this because it lightens the guilt a bit. We have something very special planned for you. The Egg is eager for a truly new era."

"Are you going to answer me?" Byron rose above him. Despite his appearance, he could feel The Dark Instinct had given him much power, enough power. His claws were unsheathed. He had no doubt he could tear him apart, if need be. Marcion was no warrior. The Forgotten didn't believe in violence, using the Warm Ones and The Warden for their grimy work. Byron didn't care. Yet The Veals were getting loud, some banging on the mesh of the pens. The one single voice he could never escape grew. It had turned into a command.

Feed me, you bastard! We made a deal. I am the God-Soul, The Dark Instinct and must be satisfied!

Marcion finally took a step backward.

"Byron, be civil. After all, you came here with less than pristine intentions. Save the female and reward us with the same fate as Xanadu. You were a poor guest. With my kind it was once considered the most profane of actions."

"You're still going to burn," Byron snapped, each word leaving with more effort. "But for whatever we shared, Marcion, I want to know where is she?"

"Do you really want to know?" The Pharisee said, moving towards one of the pens.

"Yes," Byron choked, blinking as color had begun to warp before him.

"Perhaps you should feed first?"

Feed me, bastard of the cosmos!

"Tell me!" he croaked.

"I think you will starve soon, Byron."

His long arm shot out, moving skillfully in between the mesh. One of the Warm Ones had been jumping on it, mewling with hope and hunger. Marcion' claw bit into part of his shoulder. The shoulder ruptured into spraying liquid.

And then The Pharisee told him what had happened to Medea.

9

It was time.

In an old missile silo, deep within a place once named Norad, a timing device activated its final countdown. The nights that had turned to hours turned to minutes. The computers tampered by somebody after two centuries didn't know the implications of what they did, only followed the pulse of their circuitry. Alarms sounded, rusty door opened, and something joined the poisoned sky.

10

Byron screamed in rage, in pain, in disbelief. Every thought, emotion in him was burnt away by Marcion' words of the passing of Medea. There was only the hatred left. His body lost total control of his actions. The groan mutated to a massive howl, full of anger and dread. The hatred seemed to direct him towards The Pharisee. The hatred wanted him to end the creature standing before him. Byron thought he was leaping towards his friend when that wasn't the case. The voice, the Dark Instinct that had gained a personality, was controlling him, as his personality had crumbled against the news. The hatred was The God-Soul. Byron was jumping towards the moaning Warm One. He was going to meet the true destiny of The Stargazer, what he was, and devour. He couldn't control himself, every cell in his body crying out in a symphony of potential destruction.

MEDEA! NO!

He was going to feed. Darkness. The mesh would give way to his godly body, the creature that he had once been would implode against him. All in seconds. Darkness. His fangs sweated in anticipation. Feed me.

Medea!

Darkness.

Light.

Coursing all over him, sending him in retreat, again on the floor this time on his back. Light, forcing all energy to abdicate his body, challenging his mind to barter for consciousness. Light, so bright and powerful, tickling him at first, burning him an eternity later. Then darkness. Then he couldn't move. Then he recognized the pulverizing pain and his entire body smoked this time.

Marcion leaned over him. A smile was now carved to his pallid features. Byron tried to open his mouth but his tongue and lips were fused together. Even the voice of The Dark Instinct had gone silent.

"Still with us?" The Pharisee asked. "Good. I wondered if a thousand volts in your weakened condition might have sent your valiant career to a drastic end. You are strong, Byron. But you also have succumbed to the force you despised in yourself ever since you found the truth of your origins; you have lost the person that made it worthwhile. You are finally broken. Broken for good. And thus, naked. You have nothing left, anywhere, internally and externally."

Spasm took over him and the smoke kept rising. The Veals were growing silent, knowing that this wasn't part of the only routine that gave their existences any meaning.

"You wonder how I did it, Byron? Simple." Marcion smiled at himself at the last word as if it were a joke. "We always keep the pens electrified in case of the rare event of a glutinous Stargazer or a sudden homosexual impulse in the Veals that might cause senseless harm. I raised the voltage before you awoke. I knew that you would have to follow your nature, feed before you could take action, especially after your mind dissolved against the news and was usurped by your God-Soul. Now you are fully devoid of any defenses and must be taken like a newborn to the gray dusk."

Byron tried to move, feeling part of his flesh peel away from his smoking bones. The pain was now beyond understanding so he simply didn't. He knew he would fall down a tunnel any second. It was over. Perhaps go to a place he and another Stargazer had spoken about in a tunnel that was haunted by the roar or trains feeding another civilization in another lifetime.

Marcion reached to pick him up. He was as tender as always.

"Come, Byron," he said with trembling excitement. Byron had never heard that in his voice. "It is time you met our true god, our true hope. It is time you personally met The Prince of Shadows."

11

Like everything in this city, there had to be ritual, dialogue, all to separate the voices, give meaning to the meaningless, help The Forgotten to remember. Marcion took Byron to the next story, where a group of ghouls including Revenant awaited for him dressed in leather and red uniforms. Two carried a cross, which was soon adorned with Byron's charcoaled body. They roughly used nails to pin him to the object.

"I forgot the crown," one who was called Billy Shear said with genuine regret. "No crown of thorns for the King."

"The King of the Jews?" Revenant took a step back to make sure Byron's position was correct. They began to lift him up.

"It does not matter," Marcion said, his admiration vanishing for their handiwork all the way to the rusty nails. "He cannot even carry the cross to the mound of skulls, and there is no time for a Simon of Cyrene rehearsal. Variation makes the past less tangible, makes remorse and the weighty decision easier to swallow. No, he is no King of The Jews. Perhaps he is the king of something."

"The King of Light," Feltch said a few feet away. "He's going to brighten our futures to point we'll have to wear shades."

Marcion inspected Byron's face with bittersweet sorrow.

"Yes," he said. "Perhaps he is our King of Light."

"King of Light!" the Forgotten chanted in unison

A procession began, after they argued whether to use the traditional Byzantine chants or *Jesus Christ Superstar* (they used both). They marched from the lower levels towards The Yolk, the whole population singing with them. It was time for freedom, freedom they had secretly craved for many, many years.

"I know you can hear me," Marcion told Byron's motionless form, walking next to the cross, doors opening, mirrors showing the Forgotten and their sacrifice. "And I am sure you are now aware of what we had intended from the beginning. Yes, Byron, you are our freedom and the end of New Atlantis as we know it, just as you were in Xanadu and Utopia. But it is slightly different." He paused as they reached some escalators, seeing if there was a reaction in Byron's face. Nothing. He was like a newborn. "You see, Byron Solsbury, you are a sacrifice to The Prince of Shadows. You are Lhiannon-Shee's sacrifice. She knew only someone like you, a knight, could have helped us. The Dark Instinct is overwhelming in you, injected in healthy amounts into your mortal soul by The Queen of Darkness. She was fond of you as she was once of me. She must have had great plans for you. None of us have ever seen such power, shown by your deeds, how you defeated Quidam."

King of Light!

He stopped briefly, as they neared the center of The Egg. The chanting halted, as excitement bubbled in everyone's spirit. Marcion continued, but didn't want to look at Byron's incinerated features anymore.

"You are the perfect spark to give to The Centurion. Your place in fate, your brimming God-Soul, was the one thing I saw that could bring Him out of his eternal hibernation. The Moon-Queen had left us, and now The Prince of Shadows was not prostrate to anyone; but he doesn't know that, doing his unconscious deed which was to protect this city and the world from us. But that will stop, Byron, because we are giving him to you. First, though, we had to peel you, layer after layer, take away your sword, shield, and armor, with my help as I toggled the lines of time and destiny. You had to be naked for him. We had to break you down, you see, take it all away until you were as bare as a newborn pup, stripped to only your sentient soul and your bridge to The God-Soul. If you had asked, we would have told you, Byron. But you never asked the right questions, you never really cared about the real truth unless is tickled your curiosity, your sense of intrigue and adventure."

Nothing. They were nearing The Yolk. Marcion couldn't help but smile, as joy swept through his being as it had already with the rest of The Forgotten.

King of Light, save yourself if you can! King of Light!

"I am forgetting one part of the prophecy," he added. "That night when you first beheld The Centurion, he stirred. I told you there was a connection between you two, that he recognized something in you. I did not tell you that it is because you are a descendant from the Centurion's mortal line, and that faint recognition of your DNA pattern will help like a sharp flint upon stone. You are our King, Byron, the son of The Queen of Darkness and The Prince of Shadows. It was all conceived by the irony that is the Blood of Circles, Byron. You must liberate us by your craving for destruction, as you have done, as you are the one born between ages, always teetering at existence's borders, so mortal-like yet so demonic in godly fury. It was always you, Byron."

Marcion giggled nervously, as they reached the hallway leading to the observatory rooms of The Yolk. The walls hummed, heat bled from the floors. The population heard, but was silenced in exhilaration. It was only The Good Neighbor's dialogue.

"But how far is too far, Byron?" It was time for the final speech, which Marcion had crafted ever since they sensed the fall of The MoonQueen. "If you had asked, you would have known. If you had spent more time using our satellites instead of searching for Balkros' lie, you would have seen. We will have our freedom and we will take the world. Contrary to popular belief, there is one place on this planet where Warm One's still retain a civilization, far away, in an island in a place called The Pacific. The ash and winds of heat from The Holocaust were less there, the elements have cleansed themselves. You might say Our Mistress commanded The Centurion to make it so." He shrugged. "Who knows why? Another one of her whims perhaps?"

He looked at Byron, who appeared gone. Marcion' grin was predatory.

King of Light, save yourself if you can!

"And there we shall eventually travel and take it for ourselves, satisfy our Dark Instinct, erect our empire the way we want it, Byron, not the way Shiannon-Lhee did. To start something new, a friend of yours said. What a joy shall it be! The Forgotten will be remembered, creation, with the aid of a Prince of Shadows, as witless as The Veal and ready to serve, will be shaped in our image, as we once knew it! Full circle, and our kind will be atop the world as we respectively once were." He winked at Bryon. "And unlike you and the MoonQueen, we shall shepherd it without destruction or injustice or lies. We have learned our lesson."

They entered one of the rooms, maneuvering the cross to pass the narrow doorway. Stopping before the resistant glass, the crowd looked down to the stormy haze and the floating silhouette in the middle. It was time. Time. Destiny. A reflection. None wanted to speak, almost too afraid to truly begin a new age. High above them, at two thousand feet, a missile loaded with twenty megatons of atomic power began a quick descent upon New Atlantis. In a secluded chamber far from The Yolk, Proxos Commodore began counting, legs still crossed sitting on the floor, staring at the body of a being once called Medea. In stocked caverns with the remnants of a Warm One bright empire, the Dreamreavers took inventory, ate willing prey, and waited for the return of their leader and hoped for gentler nights ahead of them.

"Well," Feltch said. "What are we waiting for? He's not going to give us a speech or start crying about his god forsaking him or we know what not we do or some horseshit like that."

Marcion raised his robes slightly, focusing past the glassy floor to the floating form of The Prince of Shadows.

"His god did forsake him," he said with a whisper. "He forsook us all, including Shiannon-Lhee"

Marcion waived a hand. It was time.

Save yourself if you can!

The ghouls holding the cross used all of their strength to slam it down upon the magnetized glass. The cross splintered immediately, as did much of Byron's body. The floor did give way, releasing immense heat and energy, which seemed to slither around the forms of the small crowd while it melted steel and loosened doors in the area.

And Byron Solsbury fell and fell, down into the tempest of amber fury, like the projectile that neared New Atlantis. At the same time, a tear took a similar course down Marcion' face, falling on the ground to become a tiny gem. As it struck the hot metallic floor, Byron touched the form of The Centurion. Then another explosion happened, changing the shadowy tinctures to brightness.

Then the nuclear missile struck the carapace of The Egg, also turning the shadow of night into a fake daylight, which was all The Holocaust had truly been.

There was a ghastly sound for many miles around.

And then there was a ghastly silence.

Chapter 12

It was gray. Everything was gray. There was a gray sky and there was submersion into gray clouds. Through a gray storm and shadowy uninvolved light, ashy vapor palpitated before the fall. The gas quivered, unraveled, and tore into an open patched landscape like a lumpy quilt. And it was gray. The fall continued, and it was all gray. Gray was safe, it owned no allegiance, it took no risks. Gray was the essence of shadows. Shadows owned no allegiance, took no risks. But falling was a risk, falling was direction. Through the fall, colors began to separate, sift through shadow and gray, take allegiance. The landscape gained texture, identity, the gray storm above moaned, now far above. The fall continued, slowing with density. The colors were obvious now, straddling the fences of the gray, and they showed the rough details of a city, a small town perhaps. Velocity was being betrayed, challenged. Buildings now dotted the panorama, then muddy streets, then figures darting away from a place, a place where the fall ended.

Three crosses adorned a lonely, bleak opening. Three crosses with three figures nailed to them. There was something so right and so wrong with the one in the middle. He was fading as were the other two, but it was different. He was fading but he was rising. Rising beyond gray and colors and storms and anything unimportant.

Before him, there was a Stargazer who was also in a predicament. His eyes smoked like ripe geysers. His neck bulged and his body shuddered with such force a few of the metal plates on his armor fell to the barren ground.

"No!" he screamed with a terrible voice. "I...never knew it would look like this...I never knew!"

He sealed his eyes but the smoke still leaked. His facial muscles twisted in unnatural distress, his flexing fingers coiled into fists.

"No, no, no...I never...help... me...help..."

Then the Stargazer screamed, placing those fists over his helmeted head. As his voice veered into a choking mewl, he pivoted and ran away from the crosses.

"Help me," he pleaded, his voice less and less forceful, as if fading away with each ignition of thought process. "Help...never...knew..."

His movement was forceful, though. No wall or door or cart could hinder his grave motion. A crowd of people only saw a fuming blur as a building was sundered before them. One person, a soldier similarly dressed and standing by a corner drinking a skin of wine, was trampled to a gory mess. By then, The Stargazer only whispered and his expression was settling to a desperate understanding.

"Help...never..."

He reached the edge of this city. Footsteps were slow and heavy. His back slouched in surrender. His face was becoming rigid, devoid of any rational emotion.

"H...I..."

Suddenly, a female came from behind a building, pulling back the hood of her robes. Her features, gorgeous and lush, frowned with sorrow. The same features had never betrayed such emotion. The Stargazer quickened his pace a bit, as if recognizing the female. He staggered, tripped, and tried again to reach her outstretched arms. He performed the same actions until toppling to his knees before her. He shook his head slightly.

"Help." His voice was but an exhalation. His mouth remained open then.

"I warned you, dearest," she said, reaching to him. "I told you what to do. Why did you not listen?"

Her long pale arms wrapped around him, but he no longer felt her presence. The Stargazer could not enjoy the tender embrace, her head pressing against his, or even the ghastly sadness emanating from her body that caused the area around them to freeze.

"No, Lucius!" the female said, closing her eyes. "I, we were so close, and now you are leaving me. Leaving because of Him and his progeny, leaving me all alone in the changing of an age that will surely wash me away with all the other Giants of The Unimaginable."

It seemed she held him for a long time. There was a sober

nightfall, there was her sobbing, and there was a loneliness that settled over the entire world and beyond its material borders. After a while, she pulled away. His expression was engraved forever with that opened mouth, those burning eyes, and deep lines that showed a final terror. She forced a smile at him, while her tears turned to writhing gems on the ground. Her beautiful mouth showed fangs that glowed with their own illumination.

"Oh, Lucius," she said softly, inspecting him with fondness. "My favorite, my gentle hero. You have left me and you are my tool now, you are the bridge to all I hate and hate me. But I do not know what to do. All I know is that you will always be with me and some night perhaps you shall return to me."

Her expression clouded again. She held him once again, one last time, the last time she would ever hold anything without destroying it. And then she took him into the sky with a mighty roar and a mighty flash. Her scream was felt in every corner of the still planet, her sorrow echoed in the vast reaches of The Unimaginable and the dreams of the cosmos.

And the essence, the perished reflex that had fallen through the gray dusk and witnessed all of this, that could still assimilate a thought or two, couldn't help but jolt in its state of non-existence.

Lilith? The Queen of Darkness had showed such emotion at these events?

No way---

The storm beckoned once again. The journey continued through time and space.

2

At first they had thought it was just an earthquake. But they had felt the heat and the bellowing sound that was like a furious, echoing fire. The throat of the cavern had collapsed as had much of the ceiling. Crates and stacked machinery had tumbled over; part of the succumbing ground had eaten many vehicles and packaged materials. Most of them were swept off their feet, others fought the effects of being embedded under rock and metal boxes. It was a complete surprise during their meals and storytelling and counting inventory. When it was over, Fien, who sifted from rubble in fog mode, quickly scanned the upheaval before him. He waited a few seconds before shouting out the names of the Dreamreavers. Slowly, after treacherous minutes, one by one at best, they came to him in bruised conditions. All surrounded the new leader except for one called Logan, who had been in the back rooms searching for a walk-in freezer Proxos had told them about in order to store some of the Warm Ones. Their provisions from New Atlantis had surely perished, mortal frames squashed under this calamity. They were almost as worried about Logan. They divided into groups, noticing how temperatures rose with each moment. What had happened?

After finding pieces of the lost Dreamreaver, who had been destroyed by a crate of shattering acid, Fien tried his best to calm the rest. They swallowed his uplifting words but were not sated for he was no Dante. Had Dante caused this? What had happened?

"There is only one way to know," he told them, pointing at the collapsed entrance that had surely consumed their ships. "We must dig, Dreamreavers. We must find out now before insecurity and fear takes us away."

They all obeyed without argument. They used their strong arms and hands to dig, pound, scratch through many feet of hot rock. Fien was the first to leave. The heat would scar their bodies but they didn't care. The others joined him, wondering why all their new leader did was gurgle as if words were trapped in the tunnel of his own throat. The other Dreamreavers began gurgling as well.

There it was, under a clotting storm of ash, in the middle of a lagoon of fire and melted rock. It was seemingly unscathed, teetering on its bottom, amazingly balanced by an incredible force. It glistened against the flaming valley, and the ash wouldn't even mat its surface. It looked much like an egg now, not the dome they had visited many times to trade.

New Atlantis.

"By The MoonQueen!" one gasped, not caring about his

words since this spanned all emotions and perceptions. "I can't believe it. What happened? Fien, what happened?"

Fien gurgled more. His thoughts spilled down upon him like the radioactive autumn, but only two images were certain. Medea and Proxos. The image melted into one—Lord Byron. He couldn't think of Dante, their ruined future, or anything else. Medea and Proxos. They had madness in their voices, war in their eyes. And the Dreamreavers, with Dante's blessing, had fed them to the strange city, all for some pre-Holocaust loot.

It didn't matter because all he could do was gurgle. When Fien thought he might utter a command, a request to his stunned comrades, something else happened to New Atlantis that turned all of his thoughts into complete ash.

The Egg moved.

3

The Egg moved.

After standing still for many hours, balanced in equinox perfection, inside a stormy cavity in the middle of the nuclear heartbeat, it began to teeter slightly. The polished metal, unscathed by the explosion, seemed to hum gently, almost warningly. The teetering increased into an almost subtle rocking. The Egg moved after more than two centuries when it was built by The Centurion and cinched by the derisive prophecy of The Queen of Darkness.

Not only did it move, it deserted the ground, heading out of this valley that was its tomb as it was the tomb for The Forgotten.

The population watched from the various rooms, their already flatulent moods lifted further when they felt and beheld their city torpidly hovering into the air. They finally had freedom, which was arriving with such sweetness. It was so wonderful, they all agreed, expressed many times over, especially in a universe without the stifling tumor that was The MoonQueen, especially in a universe in which their god would be their servant.

"Those morons really thought their little missile would destroy us," Feltch mentioned to Marcion in his chamber. "All they did was help us."

"Indeed. Actually, it was the idea of Proxos. Thinking himself a hero was the beginning of a bad journey, although I've always liked him more than any commoner Stargazer."

Feltch frowned with concern. "Are you sure about this?"

Marcion plucked some of the strings of his harp. The noise was rippling and tender, yet clear over the rustling ash heard outside.

"She did say The Prince of Shadows would grant us a boon," The Good Neighbor said, wondering why he still couldn't attain the exhilaration of the rest of the citizenry. "And we know what to ask, King Feltch."

The Kappa licked his always moist lips with a fat tongue before speaking.

"Yeah, I know, Mac. We will ask him to serve us and our goals to rule this world. Isn't that too broad, though?"

"No," Marcion said. "After all, he will not be the omnipotent mute that followed Lhiannon-Shee through the curtains of ages past, or the cloudy silhouette that was the nervous system of this city. Byron will bring him a new rational identity, but he is still bound to her prophecy, to the will of The Dark Instinct. I know in my heart he will see matters in our perspective, which will make it easier."

"I see." Feltch turned his head to one of the screens in the corner. New Atlantis was already a hundred feet in the air, slowly but steadily gaining velocity. "So we're going to the island, uh?"

"Yes," Marcion said. "As I said, he is bound to The Dark Instinct, thus will seek the ripest place to crack himself open, where the living abound in large numbers. It is a metamorphosing process. If you change the image on the screen, you will see that his form in The Yolk is changing. The Centurion is gaining density, reality if you will."

"How long will it take?"

"I do not know, Feltch. Soon perhaps. When he is reborn, we will go and greet him."

"Fucking great!" The Kappa barked, rubbing his gnarled

hands. "This is unbelievable. We're doing it, Mac, we're doing it!"

The Pharisee closed his eyes briefly. "Yes, Feltch. And have you noticed anything else?"

His eyes narrowed, widened, narrowed again, and then started blinking wildly.

"I...Mac...oh...oh," The Kappa stuttered. "It...can't be, man..."

The Good Neighbor nodded.

"It is, King Feltch," he said with a whisper. "It is. Everything is changing."

"Oh, Mac," Feltch said, with a meek voice and tears coming from his eyes like globs of pearly semen. The leader of The Kappa had never shown such emotion. "I can't fucking believe it...it..."

"Yes," Marcion said, concentrating on his music. "The voices are gone from our heads. We are no longer denied of privacy."

"We're free!" Feltch covered his face. "We're finally...truly free."

Marcion gingerly ran his tongue across his fangs, and wondered about this. They would never be truly free, but they owned more freedom. And nobody would ever know that he thought this or anything else from now on. That was good, desirable, for he had his own agendas now.

The Egg reached five hundred feet.

It rose.

4

Falling. Many feet, no, nothing measurable, falling through gray, the grayness of memory and time and emotion. Falling. It was falling.

But who was it? It had no shape, no identity it appeared. It was a spectator in this storm. The clouds were parting again. This essence without shape or identity felt that it hadn't moved forward in this voyage but backward, just briefly for some reason. It, the essence, was a witness of the grayness as it separated color and history before it.

The landscape was very different, rockier and sweeping. Scant trees and the glow of a sapphire ocean were in the backdrop. The essence dipped more and floated over two figures that spoke before a freshly gutted body. In the distance away from the waters, an army of swordsmen waited impatiently.

"What do they tell you, Bran?" one of the figures asked, leaning against a massive sword. His tall body was painted in wide blue streaks, much of it covered in dried blood. He was as regal and muscular as the other wasn't, draped in beige robes and wiping his hands on them.

"The Greek's intestines do not bode well," the one called Bran responded. "They predict that tomorrow and the next score of days will be *Anmatis* days."

"Unlucky days, eh?"

"Yes," Bran said with a nod. "Unlucky days to fight."

The warrior frowned with a look that revealed he was rarely used to being denied anything.

"To wait even one more day will be unlucky," he said, glancing towards the south. "We have stormed into this land from the fanged mountains with success because of our quickness and fierceness, Bran. Waiting means that their city-states might join forces, that their wayward armies might regain the composure we scared out of them. We must march if we are to rape the fabled riches of Delphi like we have planned for years."

Bran now shook his head.

"That would not be a good idea, Arden. I have—"

"The gods want us to win!" the warrior snapped angrily. "When was the last time all the tribes united—the *Helvetii*, the *Allobroges*, and all the others? And they have done it because of my prowess, my importance. My ancestors defeated and pillaged Rome generations ago, ransoming it back for many pounds of gold to those short fools who worship gods with visages of humans." He took a moment to sneer at that notion. "I must have such a place in the lineage, Bran. I must follow my destiny and humiliate the other civilization that calls us barbarians. We have already swiped away all other adversaries from Gaul to here, druid. We are undaunted and will move forward."

Bran couldn't match that eruptive yet steady gaze. The witness felt that this person was a man of respect and magnitude, but there was a fire to this warrior than none could contain.

"Very well," the druid said. "But you have been warned, Arden. I will not press further since you are unlike the other chieftains who are jealous of my kind's influence and power. You are a true master. But I must warn you also that a river troll warned me a fortnight ago that Lhiannon-Shee might aid the Greeks in this campaign."

"Lhiannon-Shee?" scoffed Arden. "I do not believe this! She has always aided the Celts through the centuries. She is the personification of the night and the moon and nature, which we revere, while the Romans and Greeks couldn't care less about either nature or the mother-aspect."

"I know," Bran said. "But I hear she has had much success in increasing her brood in these parts of the world and is fascinated by the minds and spirits of these Greeks. If she moves her frigid hand, my power or any druid's power would not be enough. Many of the gods and spirits are afraid of her—"

"Nonsense!" spat Arden. "I do not believe such words, even from a wise person like you. We will continue tomorrow at dawn and show these people the might of the Celts. If Lhiannon-Shee is there, then we shall fight the demon."

"No!" Bran grabbed his arm. "Do not say such things! The omens are obvious, Arden. Do not listen to your temper, for it has the pulse of thunder and the rashness of lightning. Do not risk your men for the lust of—"

Arden pulled his arm away and kicked the body of the Greek general he himself had captured this afternoon while his troops scattered towards the southern hills. He would have severed the Greek's head as a trophy, but his horse already lugged a dozen from his campaigns, and the fool had not been that good of a fighter. Arden had simply brought him to Bran for divination after strangling the general with a copper wire.

The Celtic overlord trundled down the slopes towards a grove of trees near the shoreline, cursing loudly. The nighttime air was settling with a swelling cold and clouds invaded the ocean's horizon. The druid bowed his head and took for the other direction, surely going to tell the armies of thousands that their leader would not change his mind.

The witness fell more and followed this Arden to where he sat, on a stone in the middle of the thin trees. The sky was nude and starry, the wind moaned with a certain freedom. He did not do much but tap his sword on the hard ground and glare at nothing. Suddenly, the Celt turned his head with widened eyes.

Arden was staring directly at the witness, at the essence with no shape or identity. The warrior knew it was there, but that wasn't what mystified it. The features of Arden seemed familiar, even in the darkness and the paint over his savage features.

"Who are you?" he asked the essence, standing up and holding his sword out. "Who are you that comes to me in the night? Have I offended a god or wandering spirit? I…"

The warrior's face softened, the point of the sword descended slightly.

"I do not see you but I recognize part of you," he said. The witness knew it could not answer. "You must be a ghost…are you an ancestor of mine? Have you come to warn me or perhaps guide me in this grating time?"

The witness wanted to crawl back into the storm. The features were obvious. Almost the same as when it had shape and identity. But who was it, the essence? What was it doing here?

"Why will you not speak to me?" Arden shook his head. "I am not one to understand signs, ghost. And will not seek Bran's guidance. I know what I do is right in my heart and nothing will stop me."

No, the witness thought, feeling it was going to fall into the gray storm again. Don't think that way, damn it. You have a family, like I once did, and are probably just as deluded in thinking you can be conqueror and protector at the same time. Don't take it all the—

"I thank you for visiting me," Arden said proudly. "I will fight proudly as you must have done, perhaps against the Romans or the other tribes. I will never surrender for what I believe in and will take it—"

NO!

But it was again dissipating into this voyage, into the separation of light and history. The essence couldn't warn him, couldn't do anything, but suddenly appear into what surely was a time in the following days. It wanted to close eyes but possessed no eyes. It wanted to swat away the realization that came to its ghostly senses at what had happened.

The elements had been unkind to the Celts. Wild and uncommon weather fell upon the armies as they marched towards Delphi, especially snow and prickly wind. They fought valiantly, but it seemed they lost too many men. The Romans and The Greeks had never been able to understand their style of fighting, since to them warfare was organized and meticulous. To the Celts, it was individual and lustful, a chance to brag to the gods and a good excuse to drink plenty of wine before and afterwards. Yet in those following days, accidents and miscalculations hindered them, cropped their ranks. But Arden and his united tribes marched on. The Greek's armies came, stronger and with higher morale than before. Strangely, the weather only struck down upon the Celts when they traveled alone on the barren roads.

The clouds broke, and the witness came upon a battle in which Lhiannon-Shee had personally been involved. It didn't see her but saw corpses strewn below an icy fog that glittered hauntingly over a flat battlefield. Most of them were Celts. It heard with no ears the growls of monsters that separated from this mist with fangs and talons that could penetrate their armor. It fell more and once again came upon Arden.

The Celtic overlord was as brave as he should have been. Despite a severely wounded body, he kept on fighting. Behind him were dozens of slain Greeks, at his feet the hacked parts of two of those monsters still wriggled in denial. In front of him one of the monsters fell back, as the warriors sword slammed upon its powerful body.

"Back, demon!" he shouted, face distorted in grim joy, knowing he had surprised it, stunned it so it wouldn't have time to become part of the fog in retreat. "You will never have me, you will never win! I am Arden and I defy and challenge any who stand in my way!"

The sword struck the monster in the face, splitting it open and breaking off the nose with a sharp sound. The monster collapsed to its knees, raising its arms to fend off another blow. This time it lost an arm. Arden screamed wildly, lifting up his blade one last time...

A whirlwind materialized in the mist, exploding with bluish embers and tongues of aureate light. Arden paused, raised his head, and felt his body tensing in complete awe. A silhouette descended from the whirlwind, nude and exalted except for a golden crown upon her head.

"DO NOT END PROXOS, MORTAL!" She boomed. "NOT MY GREATEST WARRIOR, ALAS, BUT ALWAYS LOYAL TO ME."

Arden raised his sword at her, partly in salute, mostly in challenge. The female stopped her descent and tilted her head.

"ARE YOU NOT AFRAID OF ME? DO YOU NOT UNDERSTAND THAT NOT ONLY YOUR LIFE IS FORFEIT, BUT ALSO YOUR PLUMP SOUL?"

"I do not care, Lhiannon-Shee," the warlord screamed back at the celestial vortex, ignoring the cold, the monster, and the fact he understood what he faced. "I am not afraid of anything. You will never have that satisfaction, and I would rather fight with honor to the end."

She seemed very surprised.

"NONE HAS EVER WANDERED FROM EITHER FEAR OR SUBMISSION OF ME, MORTAL. NONE HAS EVER SHOWN SUCH SKILL AGAINST MY OFFSPRING. YOU ARE THE FIRST. YOU ARE..." She smiled. "YOU ARE LOVELY!"

"Come," he said, uncaring of her disposition. "I am ready for you."

"I KNOW YOU ARE." And she fell upon him like an avalanche of waxen colors that marked her winter. He never had a chance.

And once again, the witness with no shape or identity was entering the storm, separating light and memory, but this time it thought it knew its name.

His name.

5

"There is no problem," Naga said with her fizzing voice, the black scales of her body gleaming against the neon palpitations of the consoles. "And I don't know why we are wasting our time when we should be celebrating and preparing for the invasion."

"There is a problem," Poppykettle insisted, tearing his attention from one of the plasmatron screens that showed system failures with various computer networks in the city. "It is very obvious and we must make sure New Atlantis is at its best for the voyage."

Naga waived a long-fingered hand towards the various Warm One drones that in this sector did nothing but overlook the computer systems of The Egg. Sparkling head collars marked their status; these devices linked the logical segments of their minds to the computer biology and directly to the brawn of The Centurion. The Warm Ones ignored the two Stargazers, walking back and forth from the consoles, capturing the various waves the plasmatron screens emitted in order to process information, little more than checking and double checking to see that everything operated as smoothly as it always did.

"These workers don't seem agitated," she told The Kappa. "So why worry? After all, The Prince of Shadows is evolving to our needs now. Assuming there will be glitches in The Egg is more than wise. The nuclear explosion and our flight I'm sure add to this."

"It does not matter," Poppykettle snarled. "Feltch is concerned. He told us last night during the waltz party to inspect this problem, and that is what we need to do, Naga. We are already nearing the ocean and that would not be a good place for a malfunction of any sort."

The Stargazer crossed her elbow-less arms and rolled her jewel-like eyes.

"Why should I follow what Feltch says?"

Poppykettle leaned towards her with a patronizing whisper. "Because he is a Pharisee, remember? They are our leaders."

"Feltch is *your* leader." Naga pointed at him. "And I don't particularly want to take orders from any sentient monkey. I never have."

"What are you talking about, Naga!" The Kappa exclaimed. "Are you that intoxicated with victory to act so audaciously?"

"No," she said, her forked tongue appearing more often with each stage of the discussion. "But that is always the way I felt deep down inside. Now that there is no Quidam and there is privacy, I feel I can express myself better."

Poppykettle took a step towards the ebony Stargazer. The Warm Ones cared little for the argument, busily moving about the chamber.

"You are making no sense! Feltch is our leader! So is Marcion and Revenant."

"Who decided this?" Naga spat.

"We did, you fool! It was part of the original order imposed on us. Those three gave us a certain representation to The Warden and The Queen of Darkness."

Naga smiled thinly. "That was then, Poppykettle. As I said, I still don't feel the need now to take orders from a sentient monkey, especially one as crass as Feltch."

"Do not say that!" roared The Kappa. "And what is your pathetic story? I forgot so easily now that I do not have your paltry thoughts in my head. Were you not once a lizard charmed by Lilith."

"I was a guardian of Set, you gross ape-vampire!" she roared back. "Chosen in an already changed state of being to safeguard The Centurion when—"

"Ape-vampire?" Poppykettle shoved Naga with such force her form crossed three of the thin screens and slammed into the back wall twenty feet away. He began giggling immediately, dingy foam collecting on burly lips. None ever forgot a second time the strength of a Kappa. Not even this...

Naga rose from the floor, her skin smooth and untouched by the glass her trajectory had shattered. Her body began lengthening slowly, coiling towards The Kappa. At the same time, her face expanded as if frills were popping from her cheeks. Poppyk-ettle took a step backward, surprised at her recovery and the way she seemed like nothing humanoid. Pulsing ruby eyes didn't help matters easily or the way her jaw grew with growing wet fangs.

"I said *gross* ape-vampire," Naga said with a trembling voice. Liquid dripped from her fangs, burning holes on the metal floor. "And that is a compliment to someone like you."

Prince Poppykettle charged her, swatting to his side two Warm Ones who crossed his path, slaying them immediately. Naga also charged, with a blinding speed not employed in decades. The remaining consoles still glittered, the other drones continued their duties, and because there was now privacy none of the other Forgotten knew two of their own battled in the lower parts of The Egg.

Chapter 13

He had a name. He had no shape or identity, but he had a name.

He once had a name, the witness realized, propelled through the gray storm. It was the name of a hero, a tragic individual, a vicious monster. It was a name often despised by the living and the undead, by the ghosts of his past yet cherished by an evil goddess, a dead family, and friends who drank tragedy with him. And his name was separated like the light and darkness in the gray.

Byron Solsbury.

To have a name one must have an identity, he thought. Wisps of filmy clouds passed him by. His identity was Byron Solsbury.

What had happened to him? Who was he?

It was hard to procure answers, for he was floating in this gray storm, not understanding himself so much but this other hero, this other champion of eternity. His name had been Arden, then Lucius. But he had known him as The Centurion, The Prince of Shadows.

Time…mirrors…I know your face…

Those two jumps in history taught Byron much about this character that was so familiar, so endearing to his own identity. He was moving faster, absorbing more images and scenes quickly, bisecting history that was The Centurion's memory. Yet it was so vivid, so evocative, as if Byron was there participating in the past. There was a reason for this, he knew, but he had to cross the clouds and the memory until the reason was the destination. He was the witness, and that's all. A witness.

Arden had fallen to Lhiannon-Shee without much of a chance. Yet, unlike so many of the *Estrie*—as vampires were called in ancient times—he awoke under the curse of The God-Soul with a certain joy, smiling as if he'd reached paradise. This surprised the goddess and the others, but Arden didn't care. He was now immortal, he was now a hunter of the eras; and taming, mastering his own Dark Instinct was as exciting as seeing the world through the eyes of a deity. His family, his heritage, his beliefs were left behind to sometimes haunt him in *Moratoria's* lair. Ahead of him could only be great adventures, great challenges, and perhaps great feats that might transcend mortals and immortals alike, perhaps allow his deeds to written in the stars by the old gods. More than that, Arden never hid his face from the present and its tests, never ate fear and never would. Thus, he was Lhiannon-Shee's favorite, her beloved, the great knight of twilight for the next two hundred and more years.

Until she asked him to perhaps thwart the passing of The Mad God's avatar, usurp some of his power while granting him The Dark Instinct. But Byron knew he had taken it all the way, even then, and found himself absorbing a minuscule fraction of The Mad God's power, The Light. Byron felt sickened at what he could recall, the vision of Lucius drinking the blood and succumbing into a permanent stasis. The power was too much, melting away his mind and spirit, leaving not much more than an insipid shell that mutely served The Queen of Darkness. He also knew the name of The Mad God' avatar, for he had mentioned it in his time, but he still really didn't know who this figure truly was...

As Byron continued in The Centurion's memory, he wondered why she hadn't used him more often. After all, his power was staggering, teetering towards omnipotence. Would it backfire on her, even if he served her because she was the fountainhead to the Dark Instinct? Did she plan his power for something important?

(Like containing The Forgotten, prolonging the nuclear winter)

Those thoughts quickly vanished, for he viewed so much, not just concerning The Prince of Shadows or Lilith *(her other name),* but the other actors in this play he still hadn't fully understood *(your name is Byron Solsbury).* More than anything, he learned about Warm One civilization, how it grew from these Jews and Romans and Celts and Greeks, spread to dominate the world with alarming conviction and acceleration. Byron *(that is your name)* didn't know if years or seconds passed, time distorted in the gray storm, but was amazed at how the information braided into his mind with precision.

He saw Lilith, The Queen of Darkness, not so much as an adversary to these Warm Ones and their conquests, but more like a fugitive of creation, sometimes protecting old laws and ancient beings, yet always on the run, escaping other gods and creations of The Mad God. As her aspects changed, so did the world, and it was all like that game of chess, it seemed. From one end of the globe to the other, it was as if she tried to dodge the waves of time, of history. Sometimes Lilith would lash back, sometimes she would destroy those she was supposed to be protecting. Many times she abandoned all she held dear, many times she joined with the Warm Ones if there was a chance to learn, enjoy, or create some future chaos.

Byron saw all of this, but knew this had to be just part of the game. She was oblivion incarnate, a destroyer by nature, a hunter for all that lived and thrived towards any salvation. Chess, he heard again, that's what it was, part of the games she played on the universe. The many looks of sorrow were part of the charade; the way she patiently waited for Lucius to perhaps return to sentience was just another romantic whim she was known for. That was it. She was The Queen of Darkness, and he could now recall what she had done to the earth close to his *(Byron's)* epoch.

Time...mirrors...it was always you...

The Holocaust.

The Centurion followed her loosely across history. Again, she never used him for more than protection against the various faith-magic's, angels, and other divine beings that tried to vanquish or snare her. They always failed, one way or another. Sometimes she concealed him, tricking civilizations to build magical tombs or edifices like pyramids in the jungles, concocting unique and powerful Stargazers to guard him. Lilith always came for him, took him along when she changed her disguise, her identity, and always seemed sad that he remained the same.

One thing was certain, though, something in her never changed. Her winter. Her eternal winter that simmered, that swelled within her, that began to resent everything as the centuries unraveled. It was always her winter.

Through the changes of the Roman Empire to the Medieval times, through The Renaissance and the Mongol hordes, through the bright reign of the bronze people in the new world and their fall, through the age of enlightenment and the times of conquest and the samurai, all the way to the industrial and technological revolutions, Byron also began to witness the other Stargazers *(vampires)* whom he knew, some whom he knew very well.

There was Yammamoto, riding through the steppes of a cold land on horseback, howling with blood-lust with thousands of others, overtaking a continent to build a massive empire. His death had been a thing of folklore, but his true end came when he tried to have one of his sorcerers summon and bind Lilith in order to have an ally to surmount the rest of the known world.

There was Shibboleth, also a great warlord, who impaled the bodies of his enemies and successfully repelled the dark-skinned infidel armies of the south. His downfall came when his intended perished by her own hand because of a miscommunication about his own death. There, in the temple of The Mad God, Shibboleth rejected all he knew and called upon The Queen of Darkness. She granted him a way to satisfy his own lustful hatred for creation and perhaps to search for another aspect of his intended. He almost perished in a place called London, but, like many others, escaped, survived, thrived, and became part of fable.

There was Black Gomez, another conqueror as viscous as the others, undaunted and unsatisfied in his search for more wealth and prestige, until meeting Lilith in one of her mystical abodes in the jungle. Byron couldn't help but feel a certain joy when seeing him dismembered and weeping at his fate.

There was Tsing-Tao, a poet warrior who collected taxes in an island that hated strangers, dishonored by his ilk and unable to destroy himself. He ran from all he knew, only to meet the goddess in a glade, recently having defeated two dragons who didn't want her in their lands. She wasted no time transforming him, wanting to have an eternal eyewitness of her great victory.

There was Tugros, ancient Persian tyrant that sacrificed his mortality for an irrational fear of death, handing Lilith all the tomes and magical vials in a barter, basically taking away all the sorcery of his empire forever. And there was Qumbre, the oldest of the seven, one of the first Warm Ones, tossed out of the material world for the first murder and blessed by Lilith in reward.

He saw the others and their stories, ancient Stargazers other than The Elders like Quidam or Archimedes, who kept quiet after The Holocaust about the secret of creation and the reality of Warm One civilization. Both creatures were so intertwined that their tragedies fueled the crossing of borders, tightening the links of Lilith's fences.

Time...mirrors...I know your face...

(You are a vampire, a Stargazer...you were once a Warm One)

What struck him odd was the fact that these Elders, the so-called handpicked that had aided The MoonQueen in her ploys and ultimately The Holocaust, were so unlike these mortal leaders—heroes or villains—that had become Stargazers. They were definitely not the same characters he had dealt with in Xanadu. They were once august warriors, generals, and such, but had become so tame and political after The Holocaust. Had Lilith chosen them in the first place because of those warring, rugged qualities she perhaps saw in them, then became disappointed because all they did was grab onto her hem and follow her desires? Perhaps she had hoped for another Arden, another Centurion, but found instead sniveling servants who did not take their heroics, their passions, when they crossed into The Dark Instinct.

Except for Balkros. His story was much different. Much different.

Remember...

2

He was so cold. Colder than ever before. So cold...cold beyond cold...inside...outside...so cold there is a heat somewhere...a heat that can never be sated...that suffocates...hunger...

He opened his mouth to discharge a complaint. A voice that must have been his echoed a deep, animalistic growl. It scared him. So cold. He tried to open his eyes but was afraid. His sense of smell was different, too, keener, sniffing automatically for something he needed that was nearby, something that would warm him briefly. He was afraid, and now his head began hurting.

The duality. It was still there. It was worse. He couldn't face it now, for it crackled like thunder in his head. The pain increased. The cold urged him to open his eyes. Then there was a voice, meek and wanting. He finally opened his eyes in recognition.

The room was still painted in winter, from the dresser to the dainty toys. A large hole replaced an area where a window lined with gay curtains had once accepted the soft mornings on the east side of the house. Outside was only the twilight, cold and bare, without the sun...the sun and its warmth. Part of him knew he would never see that sun ever again as he would never enjoy warmth for too long. The headache kept dilating.

Words formed within the voice. A figure broke from the icy haze. He felt that his heart should throb in joy at her sight, unscathed and rushing towards him except for red streaks on her face from the gag. But his heart didn't beat anymore, a symbol of that cold. As the sun would never be seen, the heart would never beat.

Warmth and the sun.

Cold and...and...the moon.

(Sol and Luna)

"Daddy," Gina cried, stopping right in front on him. "I'm afraid. You wouldn't wake up all day...you..."

"Gina." He smiled, and something about his smile dismissed her joy away.

"I was afraid to leave," she said, taking a step in retreat. "Daddy! Are you sick?"

"Gina," he repeated, suddenly wanting her again. It was different than the last time, though, but just slightly. She was safe, saved! Thanks to...

God?

God and the Devil.

Monsters and angels.

The cold exploded, scraping every part of his being. He growled again, eyes blinking in reaction to the monstrous headache. He couldn't feel. He couldn't think straight. All Eugene could do was force his eyes open, try to find what the cold wanted, find a way to calm poor Gina that had been trapped with him after God visited last night.

Gina was washed in a cherry light. Where did it come from? She kept retreating. He forced a smile from a mouth that was wet, that seemed to have two large objects stuck to its roof.

"Gina," he said, trembling. "Come...I'm okay. Daddy's okay, I promise. Come here."

Tears rolled from her eyes, mucus bubbled from her nose. She shook her head. It excited him, but he needed her, wanted her to feel safe.

"Come here," he said a second time, blinked hard, and almost collapsed against the headache. His sight was almost failing, a continuous pop of colors and shards of agony. "Please...Daddy doesn't feel good, Daddy's also cold. It'll be okay."

The little girl's features softened a bit. She regarded him curiously with her large eyes. He could barely contain his weight.

"The lady is gone, Daddy," Gina said. "Where's Mommy? Your teeth, Daddy, there so big. So are your eyes, and they glow."

To see you better. To eat...

Eugene Balkros could barely take the suffocating cold, the cavernous headache. All he wanted was to hold his daughter one more time. He knew she would help him with the cold and the duality that now split his mind open.

"I'm okay," he whispered, but his voice still sounded like a growl. "It was just God, Gina. It was just...come here."

She walked towards him. Balkros saw her movement in bright, severe flashes. When the girl was near enough, his arms held her with a speed that amazed him. His daughter hugged him back. The cold only increased. Something within its dominance urged him to find warmth, the only way he would find it.

"No," he complained, but the headache sent tongues of anguish to the base of his skull. "I can't."

"Daddy," Gina said. "You feel so cold. Can we leave, please. I'm scared."

It's okay, he mouthed, finding his head pressing against her small neck, pivoting.

"You're holding me too tight!" she squeaked. "Daddy, can..."

Suddenly, Eugene Balkros found the warmth. It filled his body with the cadence of a waterfall, raiding every corner of his being. It was wonderful, it was necessary.

The headache remained. But he had warmth, he had a semblance of satisfaction. Gina had given it to him because of who she was. He needed her in his life, always, for she was the answer, the key to unlock the problems he'd always faced or avoided. God had delivered him, hadn't he? As the angels promised in their infinite wisdom, as destiny delivered in its heavenly menu. They were saved!

He pulled away to assure her, smile at her like never before.

The skin on her face was the same as his that of his hand. Oval eyes were almost shut, pupils fading upward into the rooftops. Her mouth was open, but part of the headache lifted to give him the memory of a terrible, pitiful screaming.

And it was all because of a neck with a side that had been ripped open like a cat burglarizing a paper sack. It still oozed blood.

Blood and warmth.

Death and the hunter.

Life and paradise.

"Gina?" he whispered, not understanding, watching her body lean backward against his grasp. He un-flexed his fingers, which felt wet from carving into her shoulder. Gina flopped on the ground, still with the same expression. The warmth grew, granting him strength and an unclean joy never experienced.

"Gina? Gina! GINA!"

He placed his hands on his head and grabbed thick chunks of hair that had never been there before. He also leaned backward, a mouth larger than ever opening, trying to release the obvious reaction at what he'd just done.

But Eugene only laughed. Heavy cackles exploded from his mouth, as eyes narrowed and emotion was devoured by the headache. He laughed so hard, his legs lost their balance and his frame tumbled backwards. He kept laughing as his body fell into the hole and down somewhere in his backyard. He barely perceived the impact. But he kept on laughing, for it somehow drowned all pain and cognition, somehow was the only gratification at the joke that had been played on him. Knowing that the tears coursing down cheeks were partly from his offspring only made him laugh harder.

When he paused briefly, Eugene couldn't be surprised to see the angels before him. They all looked so serious, so patronizing as they always had. This made him start laughing again, a keen, rattling giggle.

"We have work to do," the Angel Shibboleth said. "Less than a few nights. You have been delivered, Balkros, and you have also been chosen."

His laughter shifted to a reacting chuckle.

"Will you serve us?" Shibboleth asked sternly. "Or would you rather join all the rest in oblivion and the failure of their dreams?"

Dreams and nightmares.

Reality and oblivion.

Balkros only nodded, tilted his head back, and rolled himself in a shaking fetal position. His laughter rose again.

"Good," the angel said without a hint of compassion. "Then we must go immediately to the mountains, where you can see how your handiwork has aided us. Then..." He added his own quick laugh. "Then you can meet God again."

"Are you sure he is fine?" another angel, Tugros, questioned. "He does not seem someone who we should bring into our own, especially as an Elder."

"He's fine," Shibboleth said, his voice barely audible through the laughter. "Our Mistress would never lead us astray. Besides, we will need him very much. He and his genius are as essential as any one of us. Let's go."

Balkros heard them storm into the air, knowing now that he was one of them...an angel, a servant of God and her skirt.

Angels and monsters.

One remained, though. Balkros heard his footsteps and felt a gentle hand on his shoulder. His laughter thawed slightly.

"We better go, Eugene Balkros," Proxos said softly. "And

we better make the best of it, you know. It's a new age, a new existence."

A new joke.

Balkros pulled his head from his chest and simply said, "Balkros. My name is Balkros only. My name is Balkros."

Proxos only nodded and sighed.

"Come, Balkros. As Shib said, we have much work to do."

3

The essence that was Byron pulled himself away from that last image in history, while more recollection attacked him. That was right before The Holocaust, right before he himself had been born from a Warm One, from his mother who read him stories years later in a closed cellar. The Holocaust, which brought the city-states and the reign of Stargazers and those dark quests that did nothing but consume him, serve the needs of other beings with their agendas.

Like him, Balkros had been just a tool, molded and polished into another black gem that adorned the crown of The MoonQueen and her court of annihilation. Is that what The Prince of Shadows was doing to him, showing him the Warm One history and its Stargazer players, only to reveal that the climax was a terrible age in which he took it one step further and ended everything? Every plight, every emotion, every action was nothing, burned away by Lilith's anger and the chess game she played with The Mad God. That was it?

That was it?

Damn you, damn you, damn you!

Suddenly, Byron could glance down because he had a body, suddenly he could flay arms and cock his head and shout those words. And suddenly, he was descending again, this time pulled backward in time and memory. He wasn't a witness anymore, but was now going to be a participator. The act wasn't over. There was one more scene, and he didn't like it.

"No," he said to the gray storm, seeing another Warm One

metropolis below him, centuries before The Holocaust. "No!"
And the gray storm answered from the distance. It was faint, but
very discernible. The gray storm spoke to him.

"Help me," it said.

"What?" Byron asked, still not able to control his motion
although he now owned a body. A body and an identity. Byron
Solsbury.

Falling.

Falling right into a stage of Warm One history, all of this
because of the might of The Centurion.

Help me.

4

Marcion felt no need to leave his chambers. In fact, he began to
find interest in all the artifacts he overlooked since being stored in
The Egg. Hours were spent buffing enchanted items like boxes
that held djinn-like spirits, weapons that could wound more than
the flesh, or jewels that held antediluvian magic. He took inventory, organized, and pondered what to do with them when they finally left the shell of this former prison. In between these rituals,
he looked at the screens and admired the stars of the sky.

New Atlantis had left the valley three nights ago, now
roaring above the ocean. It had taken such heights, it rose above
the filthy elements to take flight below an undraped sky. Even
though Marcion could not see the stars, its kingdoms of constellations with naked eyes, he felt closer to them at this location.
Much of the population did, too, halting briefly what had become
constant bickering and fighting among The Forgotten. That was
the second reason he mostly stayed in his chambers.

Even though he now wasn't connected to the rest, his gifts
told of the friction that prospered in this place. Factions had
formed, loyalties splintered, and none could totally agree on their
evolution from inmates to dominators of the world. Now that
there was privacy, strategies loomed in each Forgotten's personality. Old resentments and opinions festered like constipated volca-

noes. Communication was harder still, for speech and attitude had to be honed after many decades of nakedness among them. They had dreamed of this time countless times, but never had a chance to anticipate what would happen when it came, never drafted leadership or political potential. What struck him as odd was that the perfect society was no more—the many rooms and auditoriums were unused now, the population too busy with ambition. The seeking of entertainment and knowledge, to hinder the lack of privacy, was all but deceased. How ironic, Marcion thought, that with freedom they had no excellence, no high deportment, and no harmony. They were acting like humans.

An hour ago, Feltch had entered his quarters, angry because of several issues. Like many, he was frustrated because his grasp on The Egg had lessened. Without being part of the web of thought, it was harder to enter the body of New Atlantis. Doors opened and elevators worked, but they could no longer access the computers, the satellites unless it was manually. Feltch whined about this and flatly told The Good Neighbor many resented him because now his seer-power more than removed him from the population.

"Don't think about using it without our consent," The Kappa warned. "Don't even fucking dream of getting to The Centurion or any area of this city, you understand?"

Marcion simply nodded, folding robes in a wardrobe that could become invisible with certain words. Then he listened to Feltch demand retribution against Naga for defeating Prince Poppykettle. She had not slain him, but left him with many nights to fully heal.

"The reptile humiliated one of my kind. She must be punished and it's gotta be final, Marc. We've got to get all these pricks in line."

"Especially those who are not Kappa," Marcion said in a low tone, moving towards one of the screens to again admire the stars.

"Don't get silly with me!" Feltch exclaimed. "I don't have time for your shit. We are the Pharisees, but I think enforcing should be my duty. You and Revenant are the tinkerbells of this place." He mimicked a feminine voice and pretended to drink a ghostly saucer of tea. "You two like to feel, you know, stay in touch with your tender side and shit. I don't work that way, pal!"

"Very well." He placed his hands behind him, still fixed on the sparkling, dark ocean above them and their flight. "Do what you will."

"I am. And I think we need to execute Proxos, while we're at it. He could be a threat and is not important to us."

Marcion knew there was little use in arguing with The Kappa, even though he felt a pang of discomfort at dealing with the ex-Elder. He simply nodded.

"I'm taking care of those two tomorrow," Feltch continued. "I've got too much other crap to do. Are you going to stay here or get some work done? We need a military plan when we reach the island."

"We do not need one, King Feltch. We will have The Prince of Shadows."

"Don't tell me what we need! I'm the general, you see. Oh, and you will get me and my people when he's complete. Are you listening to me? If you don't, I swear I'll take care of you, ol' buddy. Do you understand?"

"I understand," Marcion responded plainly.

"Are you going to get me when it happens?"

"Yes," he lied, feeling there was no need for truth anymore now that there was freedom. "I will call for you."

That was an hour ago. Since then, there was more friction, more squabbling because there was freedom and privacy. How ironic and a good reason to stay in his chambers. However, there was a third reason, which had to do with a new type of loneliness. Before, it was the loneliness of being the last one of his kind and being a tenant of a prison. Yet it was shared with others and there was always the hope, the craving for escape from being a Forgotten. Now Marcion felt he couldn't relate to anyone, still with his mystic images and starry mind.

He felt he could have related to Byron, but The Pharisee had betrayed him, peeled him, sent him to that gray dusk in order to attain this freedom that made no sense. He was the Judas of this age, and the knight, the champion of eternity, had fallen to his honeyed manipulation. Perhaps he might have found rewarding dialogue with Proxos, but that was never to be a potential.

The only other being The Pharisee thought he might make a connection with would be, oddly, Quidam. Once, eighty years ago, he had asked The Warden why they all still existed here, why they all bothered to continue both as Stargazers and convicts to The MoonQueen's empire. In a rare moment, Quidam had spoken with thought.

I tried ambition once, and it only led to fragmentation. It always does because ambition places the one before the all, the lesser before the greater. It's a dead end, always, in life or beyond. Duty and honor are the true pathways to wholeness, to paradoxically a sense of real freedom. Our Mistress has a duty to you that you still reject; if you would find your duty to Her will, you would find meaning. But you have always been too ambitious, elf prince.

Marcion admired that because he could not understand the way of the warrior, the hero, the way of Byron and The Warden. He had always been one of curiosity and self-gratification, much of it lost when he became a Stargazer, more leaving now that he was a free Stargazer.

But there was still hope here, he mused, and that hope was presently strangling the citizens, taking the breath out of their coherence.

How ironic, he thought one last time, concentrating in organizing the relics of his chambers, not wanting to face when his own hope might finally dissipate.

And not before he did the right thing, a true duty full of honor.

5

He had a body and it was clothed. Unfamiliar cinnamon, belted trousers and jacket, puffy white shirt and leather boots decorated a form that looked as it had before his demise, before being tossed into the gray storm. Byron still couldn't recall totally what had happened towards the end, his own memories distant against the giant palpitations of all recently learned. Bleached hands felt himself for several moments in touching recognition. The only thing different was his hair, which was long and tamed by a large ribbon. Yes, he was Byron again, wearing some dated clothes, standing in a narrow alley, his feet safely pressed against a cobbled floor. Beyond the low rooftops, a city spread in the twilight, a city of lighted windows and diligently-polished stone, old trees and the busy noises of horses and faded shouts.

"Why am I here?" Byron asked and then sighed in relief. He had a voice. He was real, it seemed. Was this still just a neatly crafted memory, part of the eternal dream of Arden, The Centurion?

Help me.

He tilted his head towards the sky expecting his elemental chaperon of this voyage. Beyond the silhouette of building, the haze of light and faint smoke, he saw a sky without grayness, the shadows, blossoming with stars and a crescent *Luna*. Pure, unscathed joy was already knifing his senses, for it was only the second time in his existence as a Stargazer the innocent sky had been witnessed.

Gawking at the galaxy as he had with Proxos after a tornado storm would not reach a forgetting climax. A door opened a few paces away. Byron felt other emotions stab him this time, making the stars, the curiosity of what his state really was, and any priority dissolve at the sight of the figure that crossed the threshold. He had assumed recently that nothing could surprise him anymore, and was now assuming he was very wrong. But assuming, along with motion, were quickly whisked away by the confounding vision of coming outdoors into the same nook of history he presently resided in. Although not as tall as when they last met, she still had to duck underneath doorways. It didn't matter. It was her, by her features and the might she exuded.

It was none other than Lilith, The Queen of Darkness.

Chapter 14

She had not chosen to wear her blizzard aspect in this place. Her hair was long and the color of faded honey, fastened by a black velvet bow behind her narrow back. The colorless skin marked her true identity, although her lips were bright red and curving green eyes chose no glow at this moment. She was dressed in a simple light-blue dress, holding a stack of papers with both hands to her chest. Young maiden features looked pouty as The Queen of Darkness closed the door behind her.

"*Merde!*" she said. "Monsieur Arnold drives me harder each night. I do not blame him, though. Tens of thousands of years with divine capacity and *the one thing I cannot master is bloody French!*"

Lilith turned to walk down the opposite direction of the alley but suddenly paused. She slowly turned her head, noticing Byron. He couldn't move, couldn't find a nice remark to the being he had personally fought twice, skirmished indirectly most of his existence both as Warm One and Stargazer. He had vanquished her and her city a month ago, but time had recently lost its posture. He truly didn't know what was transpiring here but could accept the certitude he was truly a ghost flushed down history's sewer in some didactic punishment.

"*Bon sier,*" she said casually with a small smile. "*Comment allez vous, monsieur.* Or is *comment ca-va,* I wonder?"

Byron could only open his mouth, baffled by the innocent mien of a creature that was his greatest foe, the greatest foe for all that was good in the universe.

"You are one of mine," Lilith said, turning her body to fully confront him. "What are you doing here, may I ask? The others know never to seek me during my lessons."

The mouth stayed open, the mind told him different reactions: Run, fight, insult, find a way back into that damn storm even though you might lose your body!

"You are not part of the circus," Lilith said, eyes narrowing. "Are you a traveler soliciting to join, perhaps? I do not think

I need your services, *monsieur*."

"I…" That was all he and his brain were able to concoct at the moment.

She smiled coyly, while one hand patted the back of her head to make sure no strand of her pretty tresses had disturbed the flow of gold.

"'I', you say? Is that the best you can do? I am sure you have a name, *vampier*. Would you like to be courteous and give it to me? You must know who I am."

His mouth this time jumped the clumsiness of his thoughts.

"Byron," he said, cringing internally for a reaction.

There was little reaction but the tilting of her head.

"Byron, is it?" She walked to him and nodded towards the direction of the alley originally intended. "Come, walk with me. Keep a *mademoiselle* company. Paris is chaotic this time of the century. There definitely will be a revolution soon." She winked at Byron. "And you can thank me for it."

Byron, still basically mute and fumbling with his mind, could do nothing but walk alongside The Queen of Darkness in a Warm One city that should have been well over six hundred years to his back.

2

They walked down the side of a calm river that threaded the city. Byron was briefly and thankfully absorbed by the placid beauty of it, from the flowers to the veiny roads to the lofty buildings. At the same time, he was somewhat disheartened, for two reasons, by the people in the streets, most of them soldiers, many screaming with flags in that *language he couldn't understand and which Lilith would never master*. One reason was that there was an uncertainty in the air, a sense of passionate tension, much like what he felt in his last night in Utopia or in the North West Farm of Xanadu. The other reason was that it was a time of dire flux. Byron knew about this era from his tour through the gray storm. Lilith was right about the incoming tempest, and revolution usually meant nothing more than painful carnage, as this one would be.

But why should he care? Byron thought, trying to hide his features from the Warm Ones, although The MoonQueen cared little, smiling and winking at pedestrians. After all, he was the ultimate monster, the one who had finished all ages, left the wastes for the Forgotten to plunder like the buccaneer ghosts that they were. Yes, he was a monster, even in this dream, this delusion of The Centurion, for he was finding it hard to keep a straight path with the aroma of juice all over the city.

"We shall take the back streets to the edge of town," Lilith said, as if sensing his predicament. "Well cross the Siene River through the *Rue Du Bac*, mostly deserted at this time of the night. There I shall show you the circus. We will be moving on soon, I feel."

"The circus?" Byron frowned, knowing he hadn't seen it in the eye of the gray storm. He had seen it somewhere, perhaps in a dream or through someone else's eyes. Is that why he was here? Glancing again at Lilith's striking countenance, he somehow knew that wasn't entirely it.

"Yes, Byron," she said with a plush grin, uncaring that her radiant fangs were exposed to all that walked on the narrow sidewalks. No Warm One seemed to notice, as if it weren't allowed unless she willed it. "The Circus, my ultimate creation so far. A place where every mortal can witness the children of The Unimaginable, feast on the wonders of ages perished, witness the deeds and tricks of those who truly are the apex of creation."

"Doesn't seem like your style," Byron said, immediately putting a hand over his mouth, at least knowing he was becoming himself again. He still hadn't put together what had happened in The Egg towards the end, his present form trying to deal with this dream or memory. Many impulses nagged from afar, but it wasn't time in this time yet.

The Queen of Darkness only giggled. A pack of dogs behind a rickety fence madly barked at them, but they continued.

"Why do you think it is not 'my style', as you say, Byron?" she asked, not wasting a look at him, enjoying the walk even if parts of the city burned and canon-fire was heard not too far away. "I enjoy entertaining. I am the last dance. Do you think you know me so well?"

"You'd be surprised," he said. "But I don't know. I hear you've spent time running from or against humanity, Q...Lilith. Why throw them a party?"

She giggled again, and Byron could feel the air turning cooler. He also felt her gaze inspecting him; he tried to look away to some carriages at an intersection with their drivers shouting about the right of way.

"I like you, Byron. You are insolent yet boyishly charming. You are also right, my sweet. I am not doing this to better these insects, but to worsen them."

"Worsen them?" His pace was slowing, as the urge to feed bulged. At least there was no God-Soul speaking to him. He was glad and wouldn't wonder why, knowing suddenly that the Dark Instinct had tricked him in the end...

Time...mirrors...a crucifixion...

She locked her arm under his. It felt soft to his touch, but Byron knew the fierce strength that no material on the Earth could resist, having been introduced to her fists and slaps on more than one occasion.

"Come this way," Lilith said. "You must be fed and are not used to these urban areas. Where are you from, Byron?"

"Really far away," he said softly, lowering his head as his eyes were beginning to glow. "I don't think you've heard of this place yet."

"I have been to every corner of this planet, little vampire. I know every name of every creature and place, past and present. Sometimes future."

"That's wonderful," he said. "But what is important now, lady, is the circus. What exactly is it?"

She pondered his question for a while and spoke with a deeper voice, divorcing part of that childish slant used so many times in Xanadu.

"One thing I have learned about mortals, *Mon Cheri*, is that when humans are imbalanced they are far worse than any vampire, or monster."

"I don't understand," Byron said, thinking he did, though.

"Simple, *Mon Cheri*. The circus shows them supernal amazements, ultimate magic if you will, beyond anything they can conceive or have experienced. It culminates with my dance, a dance of pure celestial joy I had almost forgotten back when I was known as Inanna. This sparks their imagination to heights they could have never felt, ignites their sense of wonder that cannot be sated, and flames their creative aspect to the point of obsession. They are truly touched by divinity."

"Well, that's no so nefarious, if you ask me."

She giggled. "But it is, Byron! Once the imbalance is created, then Urizen must rise in mortals."

"Urizen?"

"That's what Blake calls reason untethered. The human mind must compensate for the solar storm that is the transformed imagination, and it overcompensates as it seeks to match immortal sensations. Man thinks himself god then, crafting marvel after marvel. Civilization moves at rapid pace...but...in the bridal chamber of ecstatic reason and imagination...wisdom is always left outside at the gates. And with wisdom forsaken, then in time man is no god but will become a beast again, a slave to his own creations. That is what I have been doing for the last few hundred years with the Unimaginable, in my nameless circus—granting them a full panorama of the sublime that only should be taken only in glimpses."

"And you've had results?" he asked, while she led him through a poorer section of the city where refuse and smoky aromas briefly shielded the scents of Warm Ones. He knew the answer, though, recalling the destructive wars and punished landscape right before The Holocaust.

She waved behind them. "This is part of the result. Throughout the world, they seek more knowledge and the suffocation of the simple, the innocent. They've called this The Age of Enlightenment, but all they're actually strangling their own illumination and vision that made them so wonderful in the beginning. The Renaissance was short, too short. I made sure of it. They will continue with their march of ideas and inventions, trying to defeat death and ignorance, decaying a little more, losing their instincts and their faith, which will be nothing more than the reliance on technology, science, and those things that are seen and safe. Wisdom remains at the gates. All because they came to the circus, and I showed them the real creatures and feelings of the garden of paradise."

And making you stronger, Byron thought, making their faith-magic and dependence on The Mad God and the other gods less relevant. And you probably expect mortals to destroy themselves in order to frustrate this Mad God, and they know this, and they'll try over and over again, gaining more power and cities and wars. But what happened, Lilith? Was it not quick enough? That's it! You became frustrated, wallowed in your emotional glaciers, and decided to speed matters, move extinction a few centuries earlier with your Holocaust. The Killer of Giants was probably part of the equation.

"I understand," Byron said. "And you'll show me the circus."

"Of course," she said, leaning over to rest her head on his shoulder. "And I will show you so much more, my sweet."

Byron thought he might have cringed, but for some reason enjoyed the sense of closeness to her. It reminded him of closeness to someone he couldn't place.

We'll never be apart.

He couldn't believe it, feeling a serene desire course through him, smelling something timid yet wonderful in Lilith, The Queen of Darkness. This was his greatest, truest nemesis and manipulator, who centuries afterwards, in Byron's time, had fallen to his hand, her veil of arrogance obviously not donned too tightly yet.

And Byron felt disappointed when the goddess pulled away. He hadn't noticed where they ventured, somewhere in another alley full of rubbish, a few dead cats, and tossed excrement over another rickety fence. They neared an opening, a small dark courtyard that somehow struck him as a place where few Warm Ones ever neared.

"You must be in need of nourishment," Lilith said, raising her skirt over the thinly layered muck and greasy refuse of the ground.

Byron blinked and it made his head ache. Yes, he was

famished in this incarnation, in this delusion. He needed to feed and the smell of blood needled his nostrils immediately. Concentrating on his stroll with The Queen of Darkness had almost made him ignore a very apparent smell that should have been noticed streets away.

Blood. Exposed. Trickling, no...no...flowing.

The small courtyard was strewn with the exposed juice, some fresh, some clotting into uselessness, all oozing from dozens of headless bodies of all sizes and sexes. Most were packed in carts or crude wagons, yet many simply hid the mud and trash on the floor or were propped up on the sides of walls, a fine feast for eager, fearless rodents.

"What," Byron asked slowly. "What is this?"

"This is part of my results," Lilith said proudly, gorgeous beyond the gruesome buffet before him. "The heads are over the fence to your left. Why they keep them separate is for various reasons—puppet shows, not to upset the populace when they see their great hero or thinker guillotined in such a way, or just perhaps out of superstition. Perhaps all of it." She winked at him. "I thought you might be one of those suffering vampires who still cannot forgo their mortal conscience."

"What?" He could barely hear her words through the din of his hunger and shock of the almost casual carnage.

"That way you don't have to look at their eyes when you feed, Byron, see your bestial reflection in their terrified eyes. Many, like you, feel the need to feed here, poor sensitive vampires who dissect, analyze the universe so much—every action, every moral conundrum, every breath of history. Artists or soldiers or both perhaps. And they only have fun when their tortured being explodes in untamed passion...forgetfulness, if you will, which is just another fold of destruction."

"I..." He stuttered, dizzy with a hunger that it seemed wouldn't even leave him in this dream or any other for that matter.

Blood.

Lilith patted his shoulder and a numbing yet soothing cold spread through his already dead body. Even colder.

"Go, my sweet," she said tenderly. "Feed so we may leave

this sad carnival and go to my circus. I have already made sure no one will interrupt, for that is my will."

Byron fed as fiercely as he had ever, this world and Lilith forgotten at first. He ripped the bodies open, drained the blood, the juice, the symbolism of life and creation that his kind so much craved for, and wished to exterminate. As his dream body was filled with glacial energy, alive in pure ruse, he couldn't deny his thoughts, the thoughts of an artist or a soldier, so loud Byron thought they rose above the frenzy of his meal; he was almost worried The MoonQueen might hear him.

It doesn't matter, Lilith. It just doesn't matter. They might as well have their heads on their mortal shoulders. Just like in Xanadu and the rest of your empire, hiding something, brushing it away with consoling lies doesn't change the tragedy of truth. The truth is always there, vicious and unforgiving, ready to swallow you when you just about have found a comfort zone in creation. I am still stealing from life, turning it into destruction, gorging myself with hatred and the yearning for more destruction. And if I have to analyze this forever, dissect it until I think I know all the answers and crumble because of my passion, so be it, Lilith, so be it!

But Byron couldn't turn his gaze towards the cracks of the flanking fence, knowing that the heads of these bodies probably formed mounds festooned with clouds of flies and rats for suitors, all with lost gazes. And those gazes would probably never soften at his noble thoughts while he fed, while Byron Solsbury teetered between the factions like the buffoon of time, a marionette trapped in a dream, in between ages.

He kept on feeding.

3

Byron didn't know what time it was in this land. It was night, *Luna* and the world rotated in flirtation between one another, and his body was sated. They reached the circus on the southern part of the city called Paris, viewing more pandemonium. Fires and fighting and fury were contaminating the streets. Orators and orders marked street corners. The desperate gallop of horses and carriages interrupted the stony roads. The pair ignored everything and everything ignored the pair. Lilith had continued chatting, speaking about how a Robespierre and a Napoleon had attended a few nights ago, how other nations had reacted to their endless shows. Byron could only agree silently, feeling the ardent nervousness pulsing through Paris, as if the flesh of security was slowly being torn from the bones of flat and secure identity. Part of him could only admire The Queen of Darkness for her tenacity. The other cursed himself for feeling more than comfortable with this deity. She had cursed the world with ash and fire, she doomed all he knew as a Warm One, made him slay his family, and then tied puppet strings on him in Xanadu. But every time he peered into the glazed looks of these French folk, ready to implode on themselves, Byron wondered if what she wrought was worse than if she had left it untouched. Lilith had brought out the worst in them, but hadn't it been there the whole time?

The circus was tended in a wide zone between a wooded area and a bridged river. There were few campfires before the realm of tents, while cages and wagons littered the posterior sections. As soon as the pair neared it, the air hummed with coolness, warped almost by some force. "No curious mortal ever comes here unless I will it," Lilith told him, her feet barely touching the crumbly ground. "And those here must leave as vapor and travel to the other side of the city in order to feed."

Byron didn't have time to ask anything else, seeing that the entertainers had quickly formed a circle around them when the pair came before some of the fires. Many bowed, some just ogled, most appeared less than content to be presently here. Byron suppressed any reaction, recognizing many who were here, from the loathed Elders to The Forgotten of New Atlantis. Yet even if he had time to dodge the intent gazes of Shibboleth, Black Gomez, Feltch, Quidam, and Marcion, he couldn't have avoided the heat of their curiosity. It was almost as if they recognized him.

Great, Centurion, Byron thought, wishing cigarettes had been invented in this era. Bring me back again to my victories and defeats. Show me they're all the same in your grayness, your damn shadows.

Lilith took a step forward and spoke directly and loudly, like an unquestionable ruler, like a child issuing orders to a group of playmates. Her voice sounded clear, both in the enchanted air and his mind.

"There will be no performance tonight," she said. "We are done here, my apostles. There are other places and the pulse of my yearning will take us there."

As Byron would have assumed, they didn't show any disappointment. They probably never had wanted to debase themselves by pleasing Warm Ones, many surely would have rather existed in solitude, wrestling with their hunger, their plights, and the residue of the memories of what they once were. Some, of course, wanted to serve her plan; others would have loved to be continents away from her, perhaps finding ways to banish The God-Soul. But none had a choice.

The crowd of Stargazers didn't disperse, but closed in, the important ones breaking away to look beyond The Queen of Darkness to Byron. Lilith turned her head, almost annoyed she wasn't the center of attention.

"What is wrong?" she asked. "Am I not allowed to bring guests?"

It was Yammamoto, personally slain by Medea in Byron's reality, who pointed at him and said with a shaky voice, "Mistress, he—"

"It is *mademoiselle*," Lilith corrected. "Speak correctly, Mongol."

"*Mademoiselle*," he said, eyesight darting to his colleagues. "This person...is he Lucius? Has he woken from his sooty slumber?"

Others nodded, eyes wide and burning with myriad colors. Lilith simply raised her head and laughed.

"Of course not," she said, and Byron caught a glint of sadness in her sugary voice. "The Centurion is far away in a guarded vault that is no concern of yours. As I said, he is a guest and naught else." She looked Byron. "Do you agree?"

"I agree," Byron responded, seeing little belief in their eyes, especially in the light of Marcion.

"*C'est bon?*" Lilith said. "Then get to work, little purrs. We will leave tomorrow at sunset. I must get changed. Paris is as smoky as the latrine of a salamander."

The Stargazers began to scatter. Byron assumed to follow The Queen of Darkness, avoiding the remaining inspections with a lowered head, somehow disappointed he wouldn't have a chance this or the next evening to see the spectacle. Someone close to him had enjoyed it from the stands.

He bumped into one of the performers, quickly raising his head for an apology. It never came, surprise widening his eyes at the shorter figure that had engaged him in the hurried dispersion.

"Proxos," Byron said, unable to prohibit the smile following the surprise. "Proxos! It's you!"

"Yes?" There was no recognition behind his eyes, only a polite bow.

"Proxos, my…" Byron shook his head and pursed his lips briefly. "You're here and you're okay!"

"Have we met before, sir?" he questioned. "*Mademoiselle* did not give us your name."

Byron knew other Stargazers with their honed ears were waiting for a name, interested to know if Byron was his ancestor, the one who shared in both The Light and The Dark Instinct. Byron simply magnified his smile, tweaked it into a grin, so happy to see his old friend, part of him recalling their adventures. There was another one in memory, one who threatened that joy, that had seen the circus and wasn't here…wasn't anywhere any longer…

We'll never be apart.

"No," he said in mild tone. "We haven't met…before. But you're here and you're okay."

"It seems so, sir," he said with his perpetual dryness. "And your name?"

Come, he heard Lilith's voice. She was nearing a lavender tent towards the area of cages, where the grotesque Stargazers like The Kappa and other beings still played their part.

Byron patted him on the shoulder and said, "I really don't know at this stage of my career, but as usual, you'll always call me the same thing."

He left the puzzled Elder standing in his tracks and entered the tent, again trying not to massage sights with the caged beings, many of whom he'd seen in The City of The Unsane. For a second time, surprise made a visit to his senses, this time many pulses stronger and sans the throb of joy.

The contours of the tent appeared bigger inside. A kind amber light emanated from several candles in different holders that were scattered on a large carpet of gold and dark brown trim, etching a vision of angels and devils battling. Towards the back, there was a large coffin of sandalwood and mother of pearl, nothing protective except for a scaly creature that was coiled around it. It moved a slightly smoking head towards Byron, eyes shimmering in saffron.

"It is a dragon," Lilith explained, standing before a mirror that was created from rippling water that rose from a basin. Next to it was a plain opened wardrobe that, like this tent, defied its physics, stretching back through racks of dresses until it ended with the glow of something akin to daylight. "One of the last of its kind, Byron. But do not worry, *Andalucia*. The saints and wisemen and holy dreamers will slowly vanish in the ensuing centuries."

The creature coiled around her body in an adoring fashion, giving Byron a warning hiss. It returned to the floor, seemed to smile, lowered its head on the floor again, and closed its moody eyes. Lilith began undressing, and all Byron could do was stand at the entranceway trying to appear as casual as possible. For the first time in his existence as a Stargazer, Byron felt a steely lust, a sweeping appetite that scorched his mind. It was a very mortal sensation, a craving for the physical. But it was more, as if the passion towed with it his soul and reason at this banquet of the vision of flawlessness. Every gentle curve, every feature patted by the candlelight was drawn, designed in taintless beauty. Lilith was slim and chalky, yet with a striking geometry Byron had never truly given much thought to as a Stargazer. It wouldn't have mattered who or what beheld the goddess, for she was the epitome of fevered desire.

"What should I wear tonight?" she mused, fondling through the clothes in the wardrobe. The MoonQueen's breasts bounced in such slow, rippling way it fascinated Byron to the point that focus was lost on her words. "Then we can discuss what to do, *Mon Cheri.*"

He couldn't speak, couldn't dare to move. His gaze was assigned to the slopes of her buttocks and their soft sheen, on the way the muscles of her thighs tightened as she leaned forward, on the flow of her hair down her slim back. It was almost as if he were holding a breath he didn't need.

You're so lovely. I've never seen anything like you. You're sweet and intelligent and make me want to change in any way. You are...

Lilith pivoted, holding up two gowns. One was of pastel turquoise, laced in the pattern of flowers. The other was simple dark blue, low cut in front in a way that would avert any gaze towards her chest.

"Which one do you like, Byron? I suppose it depends where we go. We can go anywhere we want in the world tonight. Even beyond, if you wish."

You're so lovely. Someone else was lovely.

I know your face.

You're so lovely.

"You are not speaking, my sweet."

You're so...

The Queen of Darkness!

"Can you ask your eyes to rise from in between my legs and grant me an opinion?"

I hate you.

It was like pulling a pasted square of paper from a wall, Byron the paper, her visage the wall. He practically stumbled out of the tent while a fierce sickness gurgled in his stomach. Before he could reach the cages, Byron was taking for the air, flying as hard and as fast as he could.

What am I doing? She's The Queen of Darkness, my enemy! It's just another one of her seductions. Why did you bring me here, Centurion or Arden or whoever you are? To show me that besides a failure I still can yearn for love. I had love with someone I can't place. But she? She is evil and horrible, a damn demon queen!

His thoughts were devoured by the rushing of the wind.

Byron navigated high, uncaring of the mantle of stars and the dark, uneven silhouette of the land. He looked back once, seeing Paris vanish under the horizon, still blazing with its enlightened fury. He flew into a different wilderness, but a wilderness nonetheless, where he truly belonged, in dreams or reality, for there he couldn't harm anyone, debase himself further. That's where he belonged.

After a while, his shameful anger coagulating into shameful sadness, he lost altitude and zoomed over the treetops, sometimes shaving the tips. Wood crackled and leaves, which he'd never seen before, gave way against his body. Byron had never experienced many things before this dream, which brought back the shameful anger, for one individual had stolen this from him when he was born between the ages.

He growled and plummeted into the forest, smashing bark and branches and rubbery twigs. He destroyed, for that is all he was ever good at in this incarnation, in any incarnation. Odd creatures with fur or feather complained at intervals, but he didn't care.

Damn you, damn you all! Damn the world and damn the dream! Most of all, damn myself for all that I have done!

The vegetation gave way into an opening where an oval lake greeted him quiet and unmoving. Byron descended upon a solitary log by its shores and sat down. Much of his clothing was torn, but he didn't care, concentrating of the shameful anger that was burning itself out, that hopefully would leave an orphaned numbness like respite, enough for him to reflect since the gray storm was nowhere to be seen now that the circus had been experienced.

That wouldn't happen, for she was already waiting for him a few paces away. She had chosen neither dress, keeping the one worn during the evening. Her face was serious, concerned perhaps, arms limp to her sides betraying no mood or feeling. She then sat down next to him and followed his gaze into the expanse of the lake.

"That was not very gentlemanly," Lilith simply said.

Chapter 15

"I don't care," Byron said, not wanting to look at The Queen of Darkness. "You're bad, lady. You're not good."

Lilith crossed her legs and tapped her long nails on her knees.

"You're being rude, Byron," she said after a few seconds.

"I don't care. You're evil."

"There is nothing truly evil, Byron, it—"

He raised his hands. "Yeah, yeah, I've heard it before. Nothing is evil if it follows its nature or something like that. You are who you are. I am who I am. Great!" He extended that word to make sure no sarcasm was missed. Byron truly didn't care anymore, in this dream or the other place. He knew now he was doomed outside the gray storm, for he could see the vision of a crucifixion that was not the progeny of The Mad God. It had been him. He had been doomed from the beginning but needed to have people continuously shove his face in that shit.

"So what is the problem?" The Queen of Darkness asked. "Do you have to be complicated even in the middle of what was an enjoyable evening?"

"Yes," he said with a few, slow nods. "Because, Lilith, maybe you're not evil, but you're worse. You're not good and you're a hypocrite."

Byron noticed her hands move from her knee and up to her face. Glancing briefly, he saw her touch her lips.

"Shit," she said. "I mean *merde*. That is the first time I have ever been called that, little purr. Why would you say such a thing?"

"Because you are," he said with irritation. "I've recently had the pleasure to witness history, much of your history. You run around like some drama queen, almost feeling sorry for yourself and the cards you were dealt, but you spend your time destroying these 'creatures of wonder' you profess to relate to, you know." He sent her a hard glare, trying not to soften at her comely features, at the ember of pain sparked in her eyes. "You turned them into vampires for your own needs, so you can continue your little war against creation."

She emitted a brief, incredulous laugh.

"Byron, Byron, you are an amusing fellow. If you have seen my history, then you did it with your eyes closed."

"They were open," he said firmly. Even though I didn't have them, he added in thought.

Lilith shook her head. "No, they were not. Why did you think I did such things, will do such things?"

"Out of spite?"

"No," Lilith said. "Out of caring."

It was his turn to laugh with disbelief.

"Gimme a break. So the Kappa, the fairies, and all the others were devolved into monsters because of your concern?"

"Yes, Byron," she said with a sliver of sadness. "As I said, you are not seeing. Did you think they would have existed in these times? Do you think that He would allow them to thrive after his finest creation in the universe was shat on? No, their time was over, sooner or later. The wavelets of the new ages, the human ages, were ending all of them. His new offspring, before and after Christ, were evaporating the old gods, the creatures, like me, from the garden of paradise, and everything else from The Unimaginable, Byron. It is not bad or evil, but it is the way it is. I chose not to accept this, to fight back, you see. Making them part of my God-Soul was a way to preserve them, perhaps to recruit them before they left to oblivion or the pages of some snot-filled child's storybook. These beings serve me, the heroic Warm Ones, many of the dreamers, also serve me."

Byron hadn't thought of it this way, feeling a hard jolt of realization.

"So the circus," he said. "Simply used these creatures to further bring this barren era of W...humans."

"Yes," she said softly. "No dreams, no magic, no faith. I will hand it to Him and his favorite creation like the feast they crave. Perhaps I have not been subtle, careful, or merciful enough, but that occurs when you fight alone, Byron. I am sure you have been in that predicament before."

"The bloodshed you have caused...will cause...is beyond." He paused to search for the words. He chuckled. "Beyond imagination, Lilith. Beyond imagination."

She sighed while toying with one of her golden strands. "Oh, Byron. You are still thinking like a mortal. If life is truly life then there is no death." She edged closer to him. "And I did not write suffering into the fabric of reality—our creator did. There is a Zen saying that goes 'suffering there is, but none who suffer.' We chose to write ourselves in the story, though, and thus we fell in suffering. I am trying to change that."

"You're so esoteric, yet so sane for a change you almost sound believable."

The MoonQueen elbowed him playfully. "Everything will work out. One of these nights you're actually going to trust me. Have you ever?"

"No since the first moment I met you," he answered, remembering when she appeared before his family after he had all but destroyed the first Stargazer city, Utopia. Byron killed his daughter and wife, but Lilith cursed him with the Dark Instinct before he could put a bullet in his own head.

"Perhaps you should. You have nothing to lose here."

This time he had to fully behold her. The desire returned, this time gentler, as if a hope of friendship had latched on to the lust. Was this what courtship was about, complicating the obvious, playing a game of layers and discovery?

"But what happens, Lilith?" he asked. "What happens if you fall into what you are doing to creation, this 'trying to stop suffering?' What happens if you eventually become no better than these humans—without faith or wisdom or even hope, rigid and out of touch with, with…" He glanced up at the sky and recalled his thoughts the first time he saw a naked sky in the wilderness.

Stars reminded us of what we were, what we might be, all in a brief twinkle. Then I wondered if anything would be the same if we could all gaze at stars, for Our Mistress had lost that joy a long time ago.

"The stars," Byron finished.

She also raised her head. "Could that happen? Perhaps. When you lead a war, seek a goal with determination, sometimes you forget why you started it in the first place."

"So what would you do?" he asked quickly.

"I do not know," she said. "Perhaps I would have to reflect for a while, find a way to touch that innocence, that faith. Perhaps I would just become a mortal and wonder what was so horrible about them in the first place, for I had lost all perspective."

"I can only hope," Byron said.

"Or perhaps I would ask you for your trust to lean against as I prop myself up."

"That would take a lot on my part...but I guess nothing new, eh?"

"But what about you, *Mon Sheri*? What will you do? You are wonderful, but you are burdened, I can sense. There are shadows over your face, and you will not exorcise them."

"Why should I? I failed, you see. I tried hard and failed."

She smiled tenderly at him. "You have not failed yet. If you are reflecting, as I might fail to do in the future, then you have not failed."

"I have failed others," he said, finding the words dense in his throat, leaving him. "I have failed so many, so many." He clenched his fists, thinking of cities and friends, bartenders and Heretics, prophecies and those damn hopes. All those images were filling him, slamming into the rims of his mind.

"Have you?" She placed a hand on one of his fists. "Did you ever force those others into anything?"

"No, but they depended on me."

"Perhaps, but did you open their eyes, give them something to look forward to?"

"Yes," he hissed. "And sometimes they opened my eyes."

"Good. Did you ever stop believing, ever stop fighting?"

"I'm still trying," Byron admitted. "But is that good? Is it worth it?"

"I do not know," Lilith said. "But sometimes that is all we have. You said that quaint expression of the cards being dealt. You are a true hero, Byron, or I would not have allowed your company, never would have endured your rudeness. You are a brave knight. You remind me of someone."

He engaged her look, feeling at peace in his mind but with another storm rising from his stomach.

"And so do you," he said, not knowing why. His fist had opened. Fingers caressed fingers, tightened, and shared in bonding.

Lilith only giggled at his seriousness. She moved her hand to pat the side of his face.

"You must relax at times, Byron," she said. "And do not listen to Marcion so much. He is the real 'drama queen', as you said."

The Queen of Darkness stood up and walked to the lip of the watery body. She removed her shoes and touched the surface with one foot. Immediately, it glossed over in a carapace of ice. The whole lake was frozen in a matter of seconds, gleaming with its own spectral blue light. Lilith strolled to the middle and began to dance. It was an elegant dance of gentle pirouettes and serpentine arm movements. There was no music, but there didn't need to be for the sound was the rhythm, the joy was the free, ginger motion of her dance. A wind blew from all directions, bringing with it distant voices, sensations, making the circling trees bow to her performance. At the same time, her eyes glowed with a searing red that was as dangerous as it was sensual, touched with a smile that showed those pulsing fangs that had created armies from the heroes and doomed races of the universe.

Byron could only smile widely. He wouldn't see the circus in its full bloom, but would watch the yearning performance that ended it every evening. Her features were as free as her dance, so amazingly blithe and devoid of burden. That Lilith was, Byron suddenly realized, a being that had been expunged from a garden into another one, perhaps for no reason other than she was too independent, too enigmatic and unpredictable. Although her might was breathtaking, she was still and truly only a child that had never been tutored, really cared for or had boundaries set. She was a fugitive who had tried to make the best of a situation, but that couldn't deny her childish hatred for this universe and its creator. Yes, she was destruction incarnate, but perhaps hadn't been allowed to take her place in the turning of the wheel, never learned or accepted the rules, simply dealing it out in her own way. Perhaps she truly wasn't destruction incarnate, becoming the hunger of The Dark Instinct in order to lash out at her uncaring parent, maybe just for attention, while the others of The Unimaginable flickered away, gave way to science and reason and mortality. How could he have forgotten what she said the first time they met in Xanadu, he rabid with anger at being framed, she so shrill with joy.

"Call it survival, Byron," Lilith had told him. *"Call it something I've had to do for a long time, a demon in a universe of beauty and grace, much like you, with no choice of who I was. The joke was also played on me."*

But that was who she was, how the cards were dealt, and Lilith didn't realize that she would turn stagnant and a user of science and reason, becoming so much worse than the mortals she annihilated, fled from, and manipulated for many, many years. If The Queen of Darkness, who now danced for him and made him wanting, only knew how the future would untangle…

Byron stood up with a wild look. The future, where he was from yet was a part of his memory. She had mentioned something that stung him right then. He ran towards her, having to use flight to keep upright after slipping twice on the ice. Once Byron Solsbury had slipped on ice within her chambers right before his first battle against The MoonQueen, one that he lost, for vengeance of the child Clannad and his search for Medea. But that wasn't it. That wasn't it! She had mentioned something. His mind raced like his legs, a shard of what she's said piercing his consciousness like a stern blade. The Queen of Darkness kept dancing.

"Lilith!" Byron shouted through the orchestra of wind. "Lilith! You said not to listen to Marcion!"

After all, as he had just recalled, The Pharisee had broken him down slowly through his stay in New Atlantis. Byron had been trying to find something—cure for a sickness—for that someone, while The Pharisee made him see the futility of his deeds, the self-betrayal that was his actions to end the Stargazer civilization.

She stopped, smiling rather timidly, as if enjoying that notion that Byron had noticed she somehow had seen into the future. The wind wrestled curls of her locks over her face, her smile, only making her lovelier.

"Are you a ghost?" she asked when Byron halted his motion. The outdoors had become oddly silent, the wind had departed, and *Luna* seemed to oscillate above them, gain roundness and illumination. "Sometimes ghosts come to me, angry spirits who pester me like toothless hags."

"I don't know," he said honestly. "I really don't know, Lilith. I'm wondering if I've really traveled in time or I'm part of a memory."

She raised her arms and swayed dreamily. "It is the same thing, dearest. Time is memory. Time is not my keeper. And—"

"Neither should it be mine," Byron said sadly. "You told me that once, or you're going to tell me this."

"Who sent you, sad little ghost?" She kept swaying in a slow dance.

"I think you know who did, Lilith."

She bowed before him, spreading her skirt at the same time.

"Then you should ask a lady for a dance. It is the only honorable thing, Byron."

"I..." He started, shaking his head with a half-smile. "I...I've never danced before."

She grabbed his arms and positioned one behind her waist and held on to the other in an outstretched manner. Byron had to tilt his head in order not to stare right into her bust.

"Then I shall lead," Lilith declared.

"You're good at it," he said with a grin. She grinned back before happily hugging him.

And the two enemies danced, not upon the rigid, static surface of the lake, but in the air, in a clean atmosphere and the vibration of freedom. Byron and The Queen of Darkness rose above the tree lines and higher, passing the dark horizon, their silhouettes crossing the shape of *Luna*. Byron thought he heard music, perhaps a melancholic harp somewhere on this world, in this time. He didn't care about music but about the dance, the sense of feeling so close to this being he thought he understood, who somehow, once in a while, possessed the power to love, to be delicate and vulnerable. Perhaps more than once in a while.

Was that why The Prince of Shadows had broken open his

domain and brought him here? To show that his mistress was more than a beast, the antichrist? To counter The Forgotten's wilted attitude on the one who had really saved them from extinction? If this was an illusion, a hoax, Byron couldn't help enjoy how he was being edified while it lasted.

Lilith pulled away from his shoulder, her hair a sinuous current behind her. Her eyes glittered with strong silver, her fanged smile was full of hopeful joy, all heightened by a *Luna* that seemed large enough to engulf them. He knew his features reflected the same, knew that harmony and something else was silently shared between them.

But Byron Solsbury also felt that her face was familiar somehow, that he had seen it this close.

"That is how you dance," she whispered. "Have you ever kissed before, Byron?"

He nodded, the familiarity sending raw pangs, images with it. "I'm afraid I have."

"Will you again?" she asked.

"Yes," he barely said, feeling like everything in the world, in the cosmos, in this moment of time had suddenly come to a sensitive halt. "But I don't..."

"It's just a kiss...that's all."

"That's all," he echoed dumbly.

"One last and deadly kiss, Byron," she mouthed.

And then he kissed The Queen of Darkness.

Byron also knew immediately who that someone not recalled was at the moment their lips sparked together with cold fire. He knew who that person was, that memory of his prior identity which was not allowed to enter this place for obvious reasons. The person had a name, and he yelled it out while pulling away from Lilith.

"MEDEA!"

In the other place, where he had been sacrificed, where New Atlantis had surely been pulverized by an atomic tsunami, where the Stargazer civilization and any civilization was finished, a friend of his had probably vanished from existence, as Marcion had told him, as it should have been while The Killer of Giants took another piece in the game of chess between The Mad God and his most obstinate daughter.

"MEDEA, NO!" Byron cried, pulling at his own hair, reaching out to *Luna* and the cold sky, thought and sensations burning away against his grief, with the balmy aching that sizzled in his chest. All he could do, as he had before when they were separated by destiny, was reach out for his dear friend, for the one he hated, for the love of his existence.

"Byron," was all Lilith said. He barely listened.

"Medea," he said in a lower tone, placing a hand over his eyes and hovering away from The MoonQueen. There it was, far away beyond this memory, this illusion of history. There was a connection! Part of her still existed.

We'll never be apart.

"Medea," Byron said one more time, unaware that something changed the world, blurred it from above, covered the stars and *Luna*.

"Byron," Lilith said, arms outspread to him. "We only had one evening. We never had enough time."

He had no time to reply at his outburst, at anything. The gray storm had decided this act was over. As if he had invisible puppet strings, which he'd likely always had, Byron was wrenched upward into the shadows that was the gray dusk. Lilith, the night-land of France, and everything else was obfuscated as he rippled away, moving faster, falling faster than ever before.

Byron knew he probably wasn't going to any other points in history, that there could be no more lessons to be taught by The Centurion. He was going to the final destination, the one intended by The Pharisees, by The Prince of Shadows himself, or Arden, or Lucius, or whatever name legend chose to baptize him in.

Byron Solsbury, with full body and identity, was finally going to meet The Centurion. And he heard his plea once again.

Help me.

2

Help me.

Marcion stopped his speech, blinking away high on a podium before a slice of the population of The Egg. He had heard those words. He recognized who spoke those words. More than that, he sensed it was going to pass, that The Centurion was soon to leave his cocoon, become whole for the first time since drinking the juice of The Mad God's progeny.

Many of The Forgotten glanced at each other, wondering why The Pharisee had interrupted a lovely speech during such a tense time. No longer did they wear the clothing of a unified theme. They were garbed in different outfits, from periodic dresses to uniforms creating a motley crowd before The Pharisee. Fights and arguments had spread like daylight across the city. Many still were in conflict in other sections. Marcion was here to pacify these Stargazers, nurture their souls, bring them together now that there was no privacy.

He tried to open his mouth, but used all of his concentration to hide agitation. The Prince of Shadows was awakening! He would have identity and body one more time, ready to serve The Forgotten. No, not all of these fools. It had all gone wrong. Lhiannon-Shee had always been correct in saying they could never exist in the same domain as the rest. The Centurion would need his counsel only, his intelligence and gifts. After all, he called out for help to one who could see beyond the material, beyond the gluttony of the Stargazer.

"Please forgive me," The Good Neighbor said, taking a backward step. "I have the sudden need to meditate. There is another shift in time and space…and it is important that I deal with it." There was no need for the truth anymore.

"Marcion," Revenant whined from the front row in male American revolutionary apparel, waiving a stack of papers at him. "We must come to an agreement. We're only a night away from the island. I have drafted a constitution and—"

"Not right now," Marcion said with a raised hand, walking away from the podium. "It will take me less than half of the night. I will call another assembly."

He ignored the violent shouts from The Forgotten, who surely would retreat into conflict now that he wasn't orating. As soon as he reached the hallway, he shifted into fog in order to increase speed and avoid any followers. The Centurion was awakening. All he had to do was reach his chambers, retrieve his harp, don some suitable clothes, and he would make a final pilgrimage to The Yolk. Perfect timing, he mused. We are almost in the land once called Australia, where the Warm Ones have thrived underground and in space ports that almost reach the heavens, who are very different from the ones we knew before The Holocaust or in the other city-states. It didn't matter who they were or what the rest of the population did. It was time to get reacquainted with The Prince of Shadows and then truly take over the world. Marcion had never been one for conquest or silly campaigns, but this was the last one this planet would see, and it would bring true harmony, and it would never be like all the past ones.

That was true duty in a world in need of true stewardship. No stewardship from the dead, but from the living. Duty. Completion. As Quidam had once told him.

The mist that was The Good Neighbor increased its current, closing in on his chambers.

3

Feltch growled, puking viscous, hairy saliva all over the floor. The other citizens had left, leaving all The Kappa to surround him.

"If there is one thing I know," he said, "It's when Mac is lying. He's never done that before, stop himself from one of his speeches."

His subjects growled, exuding fluids from different parts of their bodies, their purple liquids on the basin of their heads pulsing erratically.

"I know what you're thinking," Feltch hissed. "And that's what I'm thinking. He's going to meet The Centurion. Bastard wants all the glory for himself. But he's not going to get it."

Some started tearing pieces of the steel floor apart, others bounced off the walls, denting them. The rest howled in frustration.

"Don't worry, people," Feltch said with a nasty smile. "He's gonna get primped up. That'll take a while. Most of the computers in this city ain't working, so getting through doors and shit will take him a while. We can rip them apart."

Heads nodded, eyes glowed with yellowish hope.

The Kappa raised a finger. "So this is what we're going to do. First, like I promised, we're going to take care of Proxos right now. We don't need no wild cards. Then." He grinned with exploding eyes. "Then, people, we're going to make sure Mac never gets to meet The Centurion."

His kind began jeering and clapping furiously, while all he did was raise his gnarly hands as if victory had already been attained. Before long, a herd of Kappa was smashing through New Atlantis, going directly toward the cell of Proxos Commodore.

4

Perhaps it was the last lesson of history, but there was one more lesson in the potential of the future or perhaps the future of potential. A frightening image appeared before Byron's senses. It was his world, his reality of caustic weather and impotent land, devoid of real beauty or the touch of the day. Yet it was much worse.

So much worse.

The Stargazer cities still glistened in the foggy radiation, caused by factories that made sure the world held on to its gloomy cosmetics. But there weren't just a handful of cities, lonely and almost vulnerable in their newness, but thousands of Stargazer cities—more than that—stretching, covering the planet and connected like a golden spider web. Their innumerable lights glowed together so strongly the low clouds were kindled at their bellies.

It was a true empire of complete domination, Byron knew with dread, many centuries more advanced reflected by the mammoth tanks patrolling what was left of the land; the keen noise of sound waves only a Stargazer could hear; and the speedy ships soaring through the sky and beyond...into space. Deafening information entered his senses, stunning him with such news as mighty Stargazers that were half flesh and half machinery, many times more powerful than The Centurion or him, advanced science that scoffed at all the old theories of physics, mighty sorcery that shook the foundations of reality. It was the kingdom Lilith and The Elders had lusted for after The Holocaust, a dead domain except for the billions of Warm Ones that toiled underground in blindness and true despair, considered worse than animals, more like insects. It was a reality where Byron had been slain as a Warm One during the fall of Utopia, or been defeated by Dante at The Farm, or was destroyed by Lilith in their first encounter, or left in disgust in the wilderness with Proxos, or so many other possibilities. It was an experiment that had worked from its beginning as the circus, a dark dream that could only darken the rest of the universe.

And why not? Byron thought, seeing rockets leaving the atmosphere, plunging into the cosmos. Stargazers, The Dark Instinct, cared little for time and the taste of achievement. It had eternity to claw at any souls or reflexes of The Mad God beyond this planet, if there were any. It would force science and magic to grow, to snuff out light and gasses and anything hovering in creation. It would never be sated.

Feed me.

Its heart was obvious by the massive blue cupola that throbbed somewhere in the North Pole. Within it, Lilith still churned in her cold tempest, colder with each passing cycle, so far away from the bold, if foolish, creature that had tried to save The Unimaginable. And her laughter grew and so did her power, as the globe truly perished and the Stargazer vessels flew into the dark galaxy.

So perhaps I didn't do too badly, Byron thought in his perfect view of this possible history. Perhaps I stopped something that during the eras would have never stopped growing. Maybe there wasn't hope for Lilith, maybe there wasn't hope for this world except for a merciful extinction and a chance to begin again. Maybe...

Help me.

The vision heaved away from him, and now he knew he

was truly at the end of this voyage that had dimmed him as much as enlightened him.

Maybe…

Help me.

Byron still had his body and identity. He wasn't falling anymore, but hovering at the apex of the gray storm. It was as if he'd been in The Yolk the entire lesson. But when, where, and how were irrelevant to the being that waited to give him other answers. Before him, The Centurion waited for him. He wasn't a murky shape anymore, a splotch of human characteristics like some impressionistic apparition, but looked exactly the way he looked when he became The Prince of Shadows: dressed in that Roman armor, as proud as he always would and should be. He also smiled at Byron.

Help me.

To his left, the personified shape of The Dark Instinct was also present; Byron couldn't help but silently be thankful that it hadn't joined him in his tour. Then again, looking at how feminine it made itself in the gray storm, Lilith and The Centurion were aspects of it as it was aspects of them. It also smiled at him, with little rancor or mocking this time.

To the right of Arden, something else was forming, a canyon of vast white light, a tunnel to an unfathomable place. Byron knew what this was, for he had glimpsed part of it when he spoke with his mortal father in Xanadu. It was The Light, the primal source of creation and The Mad God. It also was a major ingredient of the duality that was The Prince of Shadows. The sheer joy and awe of seeing such a shred of The Light made it hard for Byron to concentrate on the other two.

Help me.

Byron nodded, knowing he would aid this kinsman of sorts, knowing that the lesson through time and memory were as much to help him learn about himself, as it was of the Stargazer's and Warm One's intertwined stories. After all, Marcion hadn't been totally right when he was breaking him down. Yes, maybe Byron was a puppet, but he was also a hero. Most beings were puppets, manipulated or shaped like small rivers, from gods to mortals, from the inside or externally, but few were a hero, a champion of eternity.

He now understood that he really had never betrayed anyone or anything, never sold out to outer agendas in his heart. Yes,
he had left the Warm Ones to battle alone in the ruins of Xanadu,
but what choice did Byron Solsbury have? Even if he were The
Liberator of their myth, many didn't know this important morsel
of information, and eventually the faith-magic would have probably scoured him. He was after all a Stargazer, a vampire. A monster. He could have never been their leader, their moral expectan-
cy.

Before that, in Utopia, Byron also knew that part of him
just wanted to follow through with their revolution against the
vampire horde. Perhaps he should have waited until daylight to
evacuate the Warm Ones, but it wouldn't have mattered. Lilith
would have destroyed them, sooner or later. The odds of surviving
in the wilderness without the vampire's corralling protection were
slim to naught, no matter what Wendy and the others thought.
Better to watch the monster burn in a suicidal plan than remain in
desperation on the other side of the river.

Even with the other actions, from the failed battle in the
canyon to his behavior in New Atlantis, Byron knew he was just
being himself and couldn't be anyone else. Like a maiden had
said, he had never forced anyone into his actions, his decisions. A
hero must fail, learn, and try yet another night, regret only to be
slightly sipped in the thirst for learning, even if he is cursed with
the Dark Instinct, even if he is the pawn of destruction. Those
were the cards dealt to him.

And if he hadn't acted, there might have been that dead
world where Stargazers did more than seek the stars. They also
devoured them.

Help me.

Byron also knew how to help The Centurion. After all, the
knight he was had already awoken part of Arden's consciousness,
part of what made him human. They were connected through
DNA and fate, and thus The Prince of Shadows might finally do
what he'd never done before—pass his power down and release
himself from this dimension, go into The Light, for that is all his
tired, worn soul craved. When this happened, in the personified

shrine of the wheel, Byron would truly be reborn, with an unparalleled might, balanced with Dark Instinct and The Light, and truly be unstoppable as the champion of eternity.

Are you sure, Byron asked in thought.

Arden looked towards the light with a weary expression. He nodded. It was his time, it had been another time, another time when it was his duty to be the hero.

Help me.

All Byron had to do was accept, which would have never happened after the quests in Utopia, Xanadu, or New Atlantis. But he had dissected the storm and found perspective. And he had hope—hope to find Medea, hope to fulfill his quest and wipe the world of his kind, begin something new with the power of The Light, and hope to, as usual, take it all the way.

Byron accepted, reaching for The Prince of Shadows. Arden also reached for him, while The Dark Instinct and The Light chaperoned with their soundless blessing in the gray storm. The two closed in, ready to touch each other, two similar beings that were really the same, with the same flaws, manipulations, and victories. Byron felt a little nervous, but he had gone through so much, what else would surprise him?

Their fingers almost joined, each slowing a bit as what was about to transpire weighed on both of their states.

But suddenly, there was neither Dark Instinct nor The Light. Suddenly, The Centurion was pulled away into a massive sound that was nothing more than an evil cackle. And suddenly Byron Solsbury was falling, not into the gray storm, but into another form of oblivion.

Help m...

Chapter 16

Proxos Commodore awoke from *Moratoria*. In the last few nights, he had hoped with severity that he might return to the past world back in his caverns, as a Heretic, with his little hobbies and promenades in the wilderness. Perhaps he might return as an Elder in Utopia, trying to nurture the new society, materially and philosophically. Even returning during the circus, as the one who took coins at the entrance (that's all he got) would have been more bearable, or back in Leros as a slave to a king he couldn't place in memory any longer.

Anything was better than what he faced for the last week: a bare room of black metal, no fire, and the corpse of the person called Medea. That was it, and the simple scenario was wounding his sanity to the point he was having trouble recognizing himself after each *Moratoria*. He was still fed by the Warm One servants, but that wasn't enough respite from his tormented thoughts. The obvious realization he still existed, coupled by that massive shaking nights ago, told that the nuclear missile had failed at frying The Egg and its Prince. That had even gone wrong, everything had gone wrong. Proxos Commodore didn't want to exist; he should have never followed Byron on his mission. Now there was no hope, no answers, and New Atlantis ruled over the sterile world. He could have sworn movement was felt, but it had to be his eroding rationality.

On this particular night, Proxos would show some outward emotion since weeping at the passing of Medea. It wasn't because of the distant shouts of The Kappa nearing his location, full of angry elation, the curses meant for him very distinct. That didn't bother the elderly Stargazer, for eventually a verdict had to be sanctioned against him in this prison, whether it be by Quidam or The Pharisees. Then again, it would have been twistedly appropriate for The City of The Unsane that they would leave him languishing for eternity with his still companion.

That is not what soaked him with a terror never experienced, though, for it would have given him satisfaction to be torn apart by bestial Kappa. No, it was the fact that when Proxos awoke he couldn't move any longer, for something had grown over his legs, his abdomen. The same substance, seen by his eyes in only places after The Holocaust, matted the floor, the walls, hid the door in a glazed luster.

Worst of all, the substance completely covered the body of Medea. An answer to something he had worried about since Byron entered The Egg alone finally disembarked to his senses. Proxos Commodore didn't want that answer. He screamed as loud as possible, bloody tears sprinkling from shut eyes that never wanted to witness the miracle of light again.

2

The Kappa heard the scream, racking and horrible, but cared very little. They were busy in a large chamber down the hall, beating their wrinkled chests, hooting loudly, prancing around in the opened area in order to enjoy a small celebration before they said goodbye to Proxos. Feltch stood in the center, watching his subjects brim with fighting lust. Once the Kappa had been gentle creatures, refined and eloquent, but now with The Dark Instinct they couldn't wait to terminate all that opposed them with brutish impunity. King Feltch was the epitome of this; it almost made him angrier that they had been placed in New Atlantis, where they couldn't freely flex their ire towards the world.

Now they would because there were scores to settle, a world to splinter apart, and many asses to suck dry. Not kiss anymore, but suck, baby, suck.

"Alright," he bellowed. "Let's get going. We tore half of this city to get here, let's make him suffer for a few minutes and then make Mac suffer even longer."

Feltch pointed at the hallway, but none of The Kappa's eyesight followed there. He turned his spacious frame to see what took their attention away from his grandiose leadership. From the other doors of the chamber, Warm One soldiers exited, armed with Radiovaks, plasma-acid rifles, electrical nets, and explosive harpoons. Feltch watched incredulously as the flow of militia wouldn't stop, as dozens, soon hundreds formed a wall between The Kappa and the hallway.

"What the crap?" he said with a blend of anger and astonishment, clenching his large teeth. By their stances, he knew the Warm Ones were ready for the obvious—by their positioning it was clear what they came here to stop them from, and it wasn't destroying the city. Who had sent them? The bastard Quidam was finished. The population had assumed that now they would exist to plainly defend The Egg until The Centurion came around. Had Marcion found a way to tap into their collective mind?

"Impossible!" Feltch snarled. "But it don't matter, does it? These armored clowns aren't going to let us through, and we ain't backing down."

To prove he was the one and only King, the paladin for their vulgar causes, Feltch charged the Warm One barricade. The others followed as soon as several types of weaponry aborted his assault.

3

He wasn't falling. He had been rudely thrown, propelled somewhere like a piece of debris caught in the backdraft. What had happened? The gray was congealing, tanning into somber colors. He fought the insubstantial current with all of his will, twirling around to even shift the direction of his violent motion, understanding that he would be swept away, absorbed into this new spectrum of the storm.

The one thing that stood out like the truth was the burning anger, a polluted rage that absorbed everything in the storm with insolent confidence.

Byron wanted to scream in frustration but was too busy clenching his jaw, clamping his eyes to find the resolution to stop the teetering in this furious hurricane. After a while, feeling as if his body and identity were dissolving once again, he managed to shout at the new storm.

Something reached out for him. He wasn't afraid, but worried about the presence that closed on him in an attempt to stop is flinging into oblivion

4

Marcion neared The Yolk. His airy footsteps were confident, his head was tilted upward, his smile tiny but with potential. His right hand clutched the harp, the rest of his body was dressed in long robes the pallor of dark rose. His golden mane was unbound except for two hair clips over each temple, the same color of his garments.

The Pharisee ignored most of the wreckage through his final pilgrimage to The Centurion. The Forgotten fought amongst themselves, pillaged entertainment zones out of spite for their captivity, and tried to mold the city to their true tastes. If that wasn't the case, they made new entrances and hallways because New Atlantis wasn't working as before. Automatic functions worked sporadically, the Warm One vassals acted erratically, and most computers and screens showed a porridge of inane hues. Already, Marcion sensed with his gifts that a few of The Forgotten had perished in fiery or chemical accidents, while a few others had fallen in battle, sundering large sections of The Egg. No Warm One drones came to repair this time.

Marcion cared little for this. The Prince of Shadows was almost alert, his awakening consciousness creating earthquakes in the hallways. Heat hemorrhaged from the walls, decorative light fixtures quivered and threatened to blink out of functioning. The Good Neighbor also sensed The Egg was commencing its descent, plunging into the alkaline clouds. They would arrive at the last Warm One kingdom when they next retreat from *Moratoria*. Then the potential was staggering…

Revenant was waiting for him in one of the corridors before The Yolk. Along with three other ghouls, they floated patiently and without their bodies. Their throbbing organs almost trailed on the floor, their spines gyrated in anticipation. It was obvious that they were expecting nothing amicable.

"You are not the only one who has the power of true sight," Revenant said, while the others gnashed their notched teeth. "Now that we are free, my kind is getting reacquainted with their gifts."

Marcion said nothing, but simply handed them a fastidious smile, small and pressed. The walls clattered each time with more vigor. He still had a few minutes, though.

"Your reasoning for power and rulership are as transparent as morning glaze," she continued. "But morning glaze is something you miss, something you might want to behold in the future."

The Good Neighbor nodded, the smile condensing.

"You know The Centurion's power, Marcion. You think he is the only hope for you to return to your former state. You believe he could burn away The Dark Instinct in you, make you a full Sidhe once again."

There was no nod, no words, and no smile this time. But his bright expression told the ghouls that Revenant was correct.

"And would you include us in your supplication, Marcion?"

"If we are to be responsible stewards of a new world, unlike Her, being on the side of goodness is imperative."

"We do not think it would work," she said, floating closer to him. "We think it would only destroy our physical beings."

"Very little is beyond The Centurion," Marcion said. "The forces of Light are within him as well."

"It does not matter!" she said with a screeching edge. "We will not allow you to play with these powers, to use the one boon to reverse the kiss of The Queen of Darkness. After all, not all Stargazers despise their hunger, their frigid immortality, Marcion. Some of us asked for it, called it from the expanse of oblivion. But now that we are free, we want more, and we certainly wish to retain our immortality, our power."

"Freedom is wanting more," he agreed with a look of sorrow. "Freedom is always wanting more, never being satisfied."

"Yes," Revenant hissed and the corridor shook so hard metal dimpled. "Now, Good Neighbor, will you turn back or at least promise not to meddle with our prior intention with The Prince of Shadows?"

"No," he answered.

"Yes, you will." Her spine pointed at him with threat. "Or we will skewer you into extinction, Sidhe."

The smile returned to his features. "All I have to do is become vapor, and your spears will not harm me. You disappoint me in your simpleness."

The ghouls looked at one another in waxing confusion. That was all the time he needed. With his long fingers, The Good Neighbor strummed the right cords of his harp. Before the ghouls had time to lunge at him, Marcion spoke the right words, projected the subtle emotions. Yes, he thought, they are re-learning their prior gifts, but that makes them malleable, slightly vulnerable.

The Pharisee continued his march towards The Yolk. To his back, the ghouls writhed on the floor, screaming in terror, their organs sprawled and wetting the floor, their spines banging on the same wet floor. Their minds were inundated by the feeling, the visions of the time when they were punished by the same beings they once were. Images of roastings at the stake or drownings in black iron vats or torture sessions within spiked boxes mushroomed into their brains, with the added visions of screaming crowds, the foreboding of death, and the cry of despair each one of them had at the unfairness of their fates. And all they had done, these witches and warlocks and wights, was call upon the Dark Instinct, dooming them even more. Now they understood, Marcion knew, sending them back to that despair. Eventually, they would compromise, deny, and strangle these distant recollections.

But then it would be too late, for before him The Yolk appeared, in one of the chambers, glass and metal smashing away.

And there he was, The Prince of Shadows.

5

The door opened briefly, the substance covering it falling to the floor in a loud raspy thud. The din of battle echoed lightly down the corridor. Screams of pain and victory were mingled with each other, light broke into the darkness of the chamber. Proxos was still screaming. Through the roar of anguish, he heard one of the Warm One soldiers speak to him briefly. Despite the ragged voice, garnished with electronic timbers, Proxos thought he recognized the intonation.

"You were the only one who was ever kind," the soldier said. "You were the only one who cared at all. We are now even, Elder."

The door closed, and Proxos Commodore kept screaming, more and more of him swallowed by the substance that would soon devour him.

6

The Egg was descending. It increased its sluggish fifty mile per hour movement and dipped into the clouds. The clouds were not as caustic as the others that covered the rest of the planet. Below them, an entire civilization anticipated its coming with reverent dread, seeing their own prophecies coming to potential.

Feltch had once called it a Pandora's Box. He was right. From this civilization, numerous assaults arrived from the land and the sky, but were shrugged off by a force that protected its husk. It kept descending and would only stop when it touched somewhere in one of the deserts of the land once called Australia. There was nothing these forgotten Warm Ones could do to stop if from crashing, bursting open once it fell. They knew it; they had hoped this for generations.

It was the ending of one age, the beginning of a new one. And in between, The Egg, Pandora's Box, would open and send out its monsters yet one more time.

7

There was no more gray. The shadows were gone. Replacing it was a choleric vermilion that expanded, constricted, and revolved around the figure of The Centurion. Marcion waited patiently, playing a comforting song in the crumbling chamber. He tried not to think of his people, Byron, the servitude to Lhiannon-Shee, the imprisonment in this lair, but of what lay ahead. It had all come to pass; and Marcion might be whole again, as well as the other Unimaginable, and finish the Dark Instinct once and for all since it would have no vessels for its hunger. That was noble, good, and worth all the pain he and the rest had caused. That would make a better universe, vanquish The Queen of Darkness' anger and its remnants. If The Mad God decided to create another avatar of destruction, then so be it, but Marcion, The Good Neighbor, would be out of the wheel, the rotation, and he would teach others how to avoid it. He had played his part, keeping his true intentions hidden in the vaults of his heart for so many centuries. So many centuries.

Marcion had to close his eyes for a few seconds when he noticed The Centurion extending his arms as if stretching after a long, serious nap. When he opened them, the arms were before his face, as if recognizing that he had now a genuine body. Details were very blurry in the red light storm, but Marcion knew that he had seen The Pharisee. The former Prince of Shadows began to drift towards his chamber. Marcion placed the harp on the floor and stood up from the chair. The walls and glass dissolved, tendrils of heat wriggled past him to further nullify The Yolk. Why had he chosen this furious aspect? Was his soul angered at the several millennia of sleep, of hovering between The Dark Instinct and The Light, prostrate to Lhiannon-Shee, which he loved so much?

It didn't matter. The Centurion still owed The Forgotten a boon, for The Queen of Darkness had pledged this. While the rest of the citizens of The City of The Unsane faltered against the searing weight of freedom, Marcion would ask for this boon. He proudly straightened his posture, noticing now detailed features on The Centurion. Arden was nude, his skin wasn't pale but the opposite-- a polished ebony like obsidian. No matter, he was still Arden, The Centurion.

"You are no longer The Prince of Shadows," Marcion shouted as the figure neared, less than twenty feet away. "For your kingdom is sundered and you no longer dwell in the safe cradle of neutrality, in a nook that helps you negotiate the light and darkness that surround you."

The Centurion stopped at ten feet. The features seemed different than Marcion recalled, but the crimson haze still surrounded him.

"But you must follow old commands and old rules," he continued. "Just as we all do in the time when Giants walked this earth. Thus, you must remember that you, in your almost infinite power, must grant us, me, The Forgotten, one favor as The Queen of Darkness, The MoonQueen, Our Mistress, and all her names asked of you more than two hundred years ago."

Marcion couldn't help but flinch with widening eyes when The Centurion slowly shook his head. He also noticed a large smile from a fanged mouth. The heat around him grew.

"Arden, Lucius, and all the names you have worn, I implore you to recall in your new state of existence. I granted you this, and you cannot deny the command of Lhiannon-Shee. You must—"

One of the tendrils of unknown heat slapped him in the chest. Marcion flopped in midair and violently met the part of the back wall. Already worn, it gave way to his thin frame, his trajectory continuing until he landed at the end of one of the hallways.

The Pharisee didn't know how long he sat against one of the doorways that no longer opened at their mental command. Quick blinking brought him back to some of his senses. The first thing he did was lower his head to watch fumes drifting from a ruined chest. The ghostly pain made him cringe and gag with hard shaking. But he couldn't move his legs or arms anymore, the damage total enough to inform him existence was escaping along with the smoke from the large hole in his chest.

That was soon forgotten, for before him the hallway was melting away against a cyclone of redness. In the center, The Centurion roared towards him. The features became apparent again. The smile—no, the leer—was still present.

Marcion tried to speak, but his vocal cords would not respond. All he could do was widen his eyes one last time as the fury and its source stood right in front of him and everything else was destroyed in their path. He finally recognized the face that wasn't Arden.

"We..." The Centurion started with the voice like the rumble of an oven. "No...not **'We'** anymore. There is no duality." His gaze was steady, the tics were forever gone. He stared right into The Pharisee with gleeful victory. "It is **'I'**, now..."

No, Marcion mouthed, feeling now a different cold taking him away from the furious heat.

"Yes," he said. "It is only **I, Me**. It is..."

No!

His eyes burst like twin *Sol's*, which Marcion knew he would never see in a thousand changes of the ages.

"BALKROS!" he roared and everything was swallowed within that roar.

Epilogue

Now, that would have been a good ending. But not good enough.

I still don't know what happened, but I survived and was born again. Somehow, that rage that had interrupted the ritual between my ancestor and me never reached me. It was as if something aided me, placed me in a protective container somewhere through and beyond the gray storm. It was like *Moratoria* for a while, in the solitude of dreams and orphaned emotions. There, I organized all that had happened to me since just wanting a drink at a bar and the beginning of this quest. *All I wanted was a drink!* I was born in between the ages, seemed like a good start in this mental diary. Again, I should have told Crow 'no' but would that have mattered? A hero is a pawn of destiny, an enemy of all that is, because he only accepts all that might be, all that once was, and is only truly victorious, truly growing when he fails and returns home.

I still don't know if I failed or not, appearing in the middle of a great devastation— twisted metal, rubble, charred equipment, fractured floors—are what spreads around me, all the way to the edges of my sight. My booted feet, for oddly I still wear the same outfit I had during my evening with Lilith, touch hard ground with a few tufts of grass. It's real, too, not a dream, not a tour through history and memory. Vegetation also grows in between the mess and above me. Beyond the remains of a dome that looks like the curling teeth from some behemoth's jaw, I can see a cloudy night, with ponds of stars breaking in patches. Where am I? Is the first thing I wonder, for it's not like any part of the world I knew for too long. Two things are very obvious, though.

One is that this is the cadaver of New Atlantis. I once had a dream of a floating, metallic Egg and now understand that it ends with it being flattened against the ground, broken open in another part of the world. I also recall what Marcion had said about seeking other parts of the planet. For the first time in a refreshed state of mind and body, I gulp on some flowing anger that comes from the rivers of remembrance.

The other thing is that time has passed. The unknown vegetation, the rust and old burnt residue on the remnants inform me silently that nights, perhaps months have crawled by in the place where I was protected. I don't know why, but standing here isn't going to help me. Action, Byron. Take it all the way.

I fly about thirty feet high and notice that the horizon isn't as quiet as the sky. There are flashes in the distance, the faint roaring of machinery. Eyes narrowing, I sense the pulse of battle, the scent of warfare. I don't know who or why, but the emptiness of this place gives me some clues. Damn Marcion and his Forgotten! But I'm back again, revitalized and with a sense of peace. They broke me down, but I put myself together with the help of an ancestor and I'm purer than before. They can't stop Byron Solsbury.

Looking at my hands, I realize that this ancestor didn't give me his power while showing me perspective. What had happened? This rage had appeared and almost sent me to nothingness. But I was still a Stargazer, still a living corpse in the twilight. I feel no appetite yet, but that will change very soon.

"Medea," I say with emotion and my hands turn to tight fists. She and what she meant to me has kept me going from the beginning, even unconsciously in the gray storm. Yet I had kissed Lilith and recalled her, finishing The Centurion's tour through history. Now the anger fully rushes from the rivers of remembrance as I finally grasp what had happened in the end. The Killer had taken her, Marcion told me before I was nailed to the cross. I had sensed her slipping, then gone, but in the gray storm I had felt her again.

Closing my eyes, I attempt to find the right cord to the path to her being. Part of me cringes with dread, for if she is gone then part of me will be gone, lost without her stability and kind heart, half a hero in a whole world of shit.

Medea, where are you?

We'll never be apart.

Medea!

Medea?

I gasp, feeling something akin to her. It's very close! Had she been left behind or had she been trapped here? I stop asking myself stupid things and run towards the direction of the connection. I ignore what were once the wonderful sights of this city: the museums, auditoriums, and re-built snapshots of pre-Holocaust times, all gone forever in the ambition of The Forgotten. It's all a waste, but everything is a waste since The Holocaust. The only thing not wasted is all that is good, that still struggles to escape the ash, and Medea is part of that, has always been part of that. I transverse most of the city and never look back. My time to look back is over, regret and 'what if's' lost in the haze of the gray storm and my long sleep. I am Byron Solsbury, champion of eternity, hero and monster, and here or anywhere I'll play with the cards dealt to me, play my part but won't leave the stage, and, of course, take it all the way, my friends.

At this point, I only want to reach Medea. Her sensation is stronger but different, as if corrupted. It had to be the time apart, the changes we surely had gone though. After all, I'm wearing a new body although I should have The Light tattooed to my soul along with The Dark Instinct. But I'll worry about that later.

The one thing I do look at, though, coming towards what once was the lower part of The Egg, is a substance that becomes more predominant as I get closer. It mats bent metal and snake-like wiring; it covers the ground and half-intact objects with no discernibility. And then it starts to dominate the temperature.

Ice.

Before I can ask myself anything else, I fatten my speed, taking to the air in order not to slip. Probably some cooling system that had finally ruptured. It doesn't matter, for I'm very close.

I come into an opened area that is covered in small glaciers. Whiteness and soft blues steal away the harshness of the destruction. I glance around, a sense of familiarity and excitement impeding my search for Medea. I find myself pacing the frozen area, my godly sight pricking every corner. Where are you? Where are you, damn it?

I lurch at one of the small glaciers. My hands break apart several feet of ice, while I grunt with determination. I stop immediately, coming into another opening. Stepping into this enclave, my eyes notice a silhouette behind a wall of ice. Crouching, I recognize him, unmoving, almost unrecognizable. His mouth is open, his eyes are wide, like I've never seen before. It also appears he's missing an arm, like when he fought Arden in Greece.

"Proxos," I whisper, wiping away some of the residue from his covering. "Proxos Commodore, my friend...what happened?"

He won't answer, for some reason completely sealed, perhaps not existing anymore. I want to smash through, get him out of there in any condition but now another presence makes itself clear behind my back.

Medea?

Something azure glows behind a mound I hadn't seen at first. The ice quivers, then starts to crackle. An acute joy bursts within me as the ice is also bursting. It has been so long, Medea, it seems as if we never had enough time! I turn quickly and stand before it, all thought and emotion pushed away against pure emotions I don't understand.

Medea?

Medea, it's you!

But there is a light seeping through the cracks, there is more of that cold chaperoning the light.

No, it's different.

"Medea?" I ask, suddenly wanting to take a step backward but unable to. The mound loses all of its contours while a pillar of that blue light rises, lighting this whole section, lighting the whole night sky for many miles upward.

"Medea," I croak, a well of terror threatening to swallow me entirely, shaking my head in realization, knowing it was her, knowing it wasn't her all the time.

It was always you.

And a tall figure stands in the middle of that pillar, freezing the world, freezing my emotions, smiling at me as she had that evening when we danced upon a lake that, like everything in creation, is frozen by her rage. She reveals herself to me as she did in Xanadu, still beautiful and ancient, wearing gowns of light, jewels of liquid energy. She is towering above me, surrounded by clouds of dusty ice, a morning star of forbidden desires....

"I told you once to always remember me in your dreams," Medea says, reaching for me. "And you always did, *Mon Cheri.* In one dream, by a lake, I told you everything would work out."

I think I fall to my knees, I think I cry out some pitiful sound. It doesn't matter. Nothing ever really mattered, I finally learn. It's a waste, from the beginning, in the end. The hero is not going home.

"But remember this, too, my sweet," she says, hands on the sides of my face, which, of course, begin to freeze-over. "I was always a thousand times more evil than thou."

And she brings me towards her own smiling face, gleaming with those translucent fangs, in order to give me one last and deadly kiss.

THE END

About the Author,

Miguel Conner is the author of the critically acclaimed *Voices of Gnosticism*. His fantasy novel, *The Executioner's Daughter*, will be released late in 2012 by Solstice Publishing. His articles, fiction, and reviews have appeared in such publications as *Mindscape Magazine*, *The Gnostic Journal*, *Reality Sandwich*, *Houston Public News*, *The Vortex*, *The Cimmerian Journal*, *Examiner* and many others. He is the host of *Aeon Byte Gnostic Radio*, a popular webcast dealing with the ancient mysteries, heretical faiths, and occult ideologies. He is a sought after public lecturer, radio and print guest, as well as a ghostwriter and researcher for various novelists, scholars, screenwriters, and secret society leaders. For more information visit: *http://www.thegodabovegod.com*

He currently lives in the lawful dystopia of Chicago with his family, patiently waiting for the beginning of the world.